FIMA

£3.95

u

To Veronica
With much love
Simon & Penelope
Christmas 1993.

FIMA

Amos Oz

Translated from the Hebrew by
Nicholas de Lange

Chatto & Windus
LONDON

This edition first published 1993
3 5 7 9 10 8 6 4 2

Published in Hebrew as *Ha-matsav Ha-shelishi* in 1991
by Keter Publishing House Limited

First published in the United Kingdom in 1993 by
Chatto & Windus Limited
Random House, 20 Vauxhall Bridge Road, London SW1V 2SA

Random House UK Limited Reg. No. 954009

A CIP catalogue record for this book
is available from the British Library

ISBN 07011 40046

Typeset by Pure Tech Corporation, Pondicherry, India
Printed in Great Britain by
Clays Ltd, St Ives, PLC

Contents

I

Promise and grace

FIVE nights before the sad event, Fima had a dream which he recorded at half past five in the morning in his dream book, a brown notebook that always lay beneath an untidy heap of old newspapers and magazines on the floor at the foot of his bed. In this book Fima had made it his habit to write down, in bed, as the first pale lines of dawn began to appear between the slats of his blinds, whatever he had seen in the night. Even if he had seen nothing, or if he had forgotten what he had seen, he still switched on the light, squinted, sat up in bed, and, propping a thick magazine on his knees to serve as a writing desk, wrote something like this:

'Twentieth of December – blank night.'

Or:

'Fourth of January – something about a fox and a ladder, but the details have gone.'

He always wrote the date out in words. Then he would get up to relieve himself and lie down in bed again until the cooing of the doves came into the room, with a dog barking and a bird nearby that sounded surprised, as though it could not believe its eyes. Fima promised himself he would get up at once, in a few minutes, a quarter of an hour at most, but sometimes he dropped off again and did not wake till eight or nine, because his shift at the clinic only started at one o'clock. He found less falsehood in sleeping than in waking. Even though he had long ago come to understand that truth was beyond his reach, he wanted to distance himself as much as possible from the petty lies that filled his everyday life like a fine dust that penetrated even to the most intimate crannies.

On Monday morning early, as a murky orange glimmer began to filter through the blind, he sat up in bed and entered the following in his book:

'A woman, attractive rather than beautiful, came up to me; she didn't approach the reception desk but appeared from behind me, despite the notice saying STAFF ONLY. I said, "Sorry, all inquiries must be made from the front of the desk." She laughed and said, "All right, Efraim, we heard you the first time." I said, "If you don't get out of here, ma'am, I'll have to ring my bell" (although I haven't got a bell). At these words the woman laughed again, a pleasant, graceful laugh, like a limpid brook. She was slim-shouldered and had a slightly wrinkled neck, but her bosom and stomach were well rounded and her calves covered by silk stockings with curving seams. The combination of curvaceousness and vulnerability was both sexy and touching. Or maybe it was the contrast between the shapely body and the face of an overworked teacher that was touching. I had a little girl by you, she said, and now it's time for our daughter to meet her father. Although I knew I wasn't supposed to leave the clinic, that it would be dangerous to follow her, especially barefoot, which I suddenly was, a sort of inner signal formed itself: If she draws her hair over her left shoulder with her left hand, then I'll have to go. She knew; with a light movement she brought her hair forward until it spread over her dress and covered her left breast, and she said: Come. I followed her through several streets and alleys, several flights of steps and gates, and more stone-paved courtyards in Valladolid in Spain, though it was really more or less the Bukharian Quarter here in Jerusalem. Even though this woman in the girlish cotton dress and sexy stockings was a stranger and I had never set eyes on her before, I still wanted to see the little girl. So we walked through entrances to buildings that led to back yards full of loaded clotheslines, which led us to new alleyways and an ancient square lit by a street lamp in the rain. Because it had started to rain, not hard, not pouring, very few drops in fact, just a thick mist in the darkening air. We didn't meet a living soul on the way. Not even a cat. Suddenly the woman stopped in a passageway that had vestiges of decaying

2

grandeur, like an entrance to an Oriental palace, but probably it was just a tunnel joining two sodden courtyards, with battered letter boxes and flaking ceramic tiles, and removing my wrist-watch, she pointed to a tattered army blanket in an alcove under the steps, as though removing my watch was the prelude to some kind of nakedness, and now I had to give her a baby daughter and I asked where we were and where the children were, because somehow along the way the daughter had turned into children. The woman said, *Chili.* I couldn't tell whether this was the little girl's name or the name of the woman herself, who was clasping my hand to her breast, or if she was cold because of the naked-ness of the skinny daughters, or if it was an invitation to hug her and warm her up. When I hugged her, her whole body shook, not with desire but with despair, and she whispered, Don't be afraid, Efraim, I know a way and I'll get you across safely to the Aryan side. In the dream this whispered phrase was full of promise and grace, and I continued to trust her and follow her ecstatically, and was not at all surprised when in the dream she turned into my mother, nor did I ask where the Aryan side was. Until we reached the water. At the water's edge, with a blond military moustache and legs spread wide, stood a man in a dark uniform who said: Have to separate.

'So it became clear that she was chilly because of the water, and that I would not see her again. I woke with sadness and even now as I conclude these notes the sadness has not left me.'

2

Fima gets up for work

EFRAIM got out of bed in his sweaty underwear, opened his shutters a crack, and looked out at the beginning of a winter day in Jerusalem. The nearby buildings did not look near: they seemed far from him and from each other, with wisps of low cloud drifting among them. There was no sign of life outside. As though the dream were continuing. Except that there was no stone-paved alley now, but a shabby road at the southwest edge of Kiryat Yovel, a row of squat blocks of flats jerry-built in the late 1950s. The balconies had been mostly closed in with breeze-block, plasterboard, aluminium, and glass. Here and there an empty window box or a neglected flowerpot stood on a rusting balustrade. Away to the south the Bethlehem hills merged with the grey clouds, looking unattractive and grubby this morning, more like slag heaps than hills. A neighbour was having difficulty starting his car because of the cold and the damp. The starter wheezed repeatedly, like a terminally ill lung case who still insisted on chain-smoking. Again Fima was overcome by the feeling that he was here by mistake, that he ought to be somewhere completely different.

But what the mistake was, or where he ought to be, he did not know this morning. In fact he never did.

The car's wheezing brought on his own morning cough, and he moved away from the window. He did not want to start his day in such a pointless and pathetic way. He said to himself, Lazy bastard! and began to do some simple exercises, bends and stretches, in front of the mirror that was dappled with dark islands and continents. The mirror was fixed to the front of the old brown wardrobe his father had bought for him thirty years ago. He should have asked the woman what it

4

was he was supposed to separate. But he had missed his chance.

As a general rule Fima loathed people standing at windows. He especially loathed the sight of a woman looking out of a window with her back to the room. Before his divorce he had often irritated Yael by grumbling when she stood like that, looking out at the street or the hills.

'What's wrong? Am I breaking the rules again?'

'You know it annoys me.'

'That's your problem, Effy.'

This morning, even his exercises in front of the mirror annoyed and tired him. After a minute or two he stopped. Calling himself lazy bastard again. He panted and added mockingly:

'That's your problem, pal.'

He was fifty-four, and during his years of living alone he had fallen into the habit of talking to himself. He reckoned this among his old bachelor's foibles, along with losing the lid of the jam, trimming the hair in one of his nostrils and forgetting to do the other, unzipping his fly on the way to the bathroom to save time but missing the bowl when he started to piss, or flushing in the middle in the hope that the sound of rushing water would help him overcome his stuttering bladder. He would try to finish while the water was still running; so there was always a race between his own water and that from the cistern. It was a race he always lost, and he would be faced with the infuriating alternative of standing there, tool in hand, until the cistern refilled and he could have another go, or admitting defeat and leaving his urine in the bowl till next time. He did not like to admit defeat or to waste his time waiting, so he would impatiently pull the handle before the cistern was full again. This would provoke a premature eruption which was insufficient to flush the bowl but was enough to confront him yet again with the abhorrent choice between waiting longer or giving up and going away.

In the course of his life he had had several love affairs, several ideas, a book of poems that aroused some expectations, thought about the purpose of the universe and clear insights into where the country had lost its way, a detailed fantasy about founding a new political movement, longings of one sort or another, and the constant desire to open a new chapter. And here he was now in this shabby flat on a gloomy wet morning, engaged in a humiliating struggle to release the corner of his shirt from the zip of his fly. While outside some soggy bird kept repeating the same three-note phrase over and over again, as though it had come to the conclusion that he was so dimwitted he would never understand.

In this way, by painstakingly identifying and classifying his middle-aged bachelor habits, Fima hoped to distance himself from himself, to open up a space for mockery and defend his longings and his self-respect. But there were times when this obsessive quest for the ridiculous or compulsive habits appeared to him in a revelation not as a line of defence between himself and the middle-aged bachelor but in fact as a stratagem employed by that bachelor to get rid of him and usurp his place.

He decided to return to the wardrobe and take a look at himself in the mirror. And to view his body not with disgust, despair, or self-pity, but with resignation. In the mirror he beheld a pale, rather overweight clerk with folds of flesh at the waist, whose underwear was none too fresh, who had sparse black hair on white legs that were too skinny in relation to the belly, and greying hair, weak shoulders, and flabby male breasts growing on the untanned plot of his chest, dotted with pimples, one of which was surrounded by a livid redness. He squeezed the pimples between his forefinger and thumb, watching in the mirror. The bursting of the pimples and the squirting of the yellowish pus afforded a vague, irritable pleasure. For fifty years, like the gestation of an elephant, this faceless clerk had been swelling inside the womb of child and youth and grown man, and now the fifty years were up, the gestation was complete, the womb had burst open, the butterfly had begotten a chrysalis. In this chrysalis Fima recognised himself.

He also saw that now the roles were reversed, that from here on, in the depth of the cocoonlike womb, the wide-eyed child with the gawky limbs would be forever hiding.

Resignation accompanied by faint mockery sometimes contains its opposite: an inner craving for the child, the youth, the grown man out of whose womb the chrysalis emerged. And so sometimes he experienced, for an instant, the restoration of that which could never be restored, in a pure refined state, immune to decay, proof against longing and sorrow. As though trapped inside a glass bubble for an instant Yael's love was restored to him, with the touch of her lips and tongue behind his ear and her whispered, 'Here, touch me here.'

In the bathroom Fima was put in a quandary when he discovered that his shaving foam had run out, but he had the bright idea of trying to shave with a thick layer of ordinary toilet soap. Except that the soap turned out to have a rancid smell, like armpits in a heat wave. He scraped his jaws till they were raw but forgot to shave the bristles under his chin. Then he took a hot shower and found the courage to end with thirty seconds of cold water, and for a moment he felt fresh and vigorous and ready to open a new chapter in his life, until the towel, which was damp from the day before and the day before that and more, wrapped him again in his own stale night smell, as though he had been forced to put on a dirty shirt.

From the shower he made for the kitchen and put on the water for coffee; he washed a dirty cup from the sink, put two saccharin tablets and two spoonfuls of instant coffee in it, and went to make his bed. His struggle with the bedspread lasted several minutes. When he returned to the kitchen, he saw that he had left the refrigerator door open overnight. He took out the margarine and the jam and a yogurt he had started the day before, but it turned out that some feeble-minded insect had for some reason selected the yogurt to commit suicide in. He attempted to fish the cadaver out with a teaspoon, but succeeded only in drowning it. He dropped the yogurt pot in the bin and made do with black coffee, having decided without checking that the milk must have turned sour because the fridge door had been left open. He intended to turn on the radio and listen to the news. The cabinet had been sitting late into the night. Had the special airborne commando been parachuted into Damascus and captured President Assad? Or did Yasser Arafat want to come to Jerusalem and address the Knesset? Fima preferred to suppose that at most the news would be a devaluation of the shekel or some case of corruption. He visualised himself convening his cabinet for a midnight sitting. An old revolutionary sentiment from his days in the youth movement made him hold this meeting in a classroom in a run-down school in Katamon, with peeling benches and sums chalked on the blackboard. He himself, wearing a workman's jacket and threadbare trousers, would sit not at the teacher's desk but on the windowsill. He would paint a pitiless picture of the realities, startling the ministers with his portrayal of the impending disaster. Towards dawn he would secure a majority for a decision to withdraw all our armed forces, as a first step, from the Gaza Strip, even without an agreement. 'If they fire on our settlements, I'll bomb them from the air. But if they keep quiet, if they demonstrate that they are serious about peace, then we'll wait a year or two and open negotiations with them about the future of the West Bank.'

After his coffee he put on a worn brown sweater, the chunky one Yael had left behind for him, looked at his watch, and saw he had missed the seven o'clock news. So he went downstairs to collect the morning paper from the letter box. But he had forgotten the key and had to tug the paper through the slit, tearing the front page in the process. On his way upstairs, reading the headlines as he climbed, he concluded that the country had fallen into the hands of a bunch of lunatics, who went on and on about Hitler and the Holocaust and always rushed to stamp out any glimmer of peace, seeing it as a Nazi ploy aimed at their destruction. By the time he reached his front door, he realised that he had contradicted himself again, and he warned himself against the hysteria and whingeing that were so typical of the Israeli intelligentsia: We must beware of the foolish temptation to assume that history will eventually punish the guilty. As he made himself a second cup of coffee, he mentally deployed, against his previous thoughts, the argument he tended to use in his political discussions with Uri Gefen and Tsvika and the rest of the gang: We've got to learn at long last how to exist and operate in interim situations that can drag on for years, instead of reacting to reality by sulking. Our lack of mental readiness to live in an open-ended situation, our desire to reach the bottom line immediately and decide at once what the ending will be, surely these are the real causes of our political impotence.

By the time he had finished reading what the television critic had to say about a programme he had forgotten he had meant to watch the previous evening, it was past eight o'clock and he had missed the news again. Angrily he decided that he ought to sit down to work right away. He repeated to himself the words from the dream, Have to separate. Separate what from what? A warm, tender voice that was neither male nor female but held a deep compassion said to him, And where are you, Efraim? A very good question, Fima replied.

He sat at his desk and saw the unanswered letters and the shopping list he had written out on Saturday evening, and remembered he was supposed to phone someone this morning about something that could not wait, but he could not for the life of him recall who it was. So he dialled Tsvika Kropotkin's number, woke him up, and stammered a long embarrassed apology, but still kept Tsvi on the line for a good twenty minutes about the tactics of the left and the changes that were appearing in the US position and the time bomb of Islamic fundamentalism that was ticking away all around us, until Tsvi interrupted: 'Fima, I'm sorry, don't be mad, but I simply have to get dressed. I'm late for a class.' Fima concluded the conversation as he had begun it, with an excessively long apology, and he still could not remember if he was supposed to call somebody this morning or instead wait for an urgent phonecall, which he might have missed now because of his chat with Tsvi. Which on second thoughts had been less a chat than a monologue. So he dropped his idea of calling Uri Gefen as well, and checked over his computerised bank statement, but he couldn't work out if six hundred and fifty shekels had been credited to his account and four hundred and fifty debited or the other way around. His head sank on his chest, and inside his closed eyes passed crowds of Muslim fanatics excitedly chanting suras and shouting slogans, smashing and burning everything that stood in their way. Then the square was empty, with only tatters of yellowed paper fluttering in the breeze and

9

blending with the pattering rain that fell all the way from here to the Bethlehem hills swathed in grey mist. Where are you, Efraim? Where is the Aryan side? And if she is chilly, why is she?

Fima woke to the touch of a heavy warm hand. He opened his eyes and saw his father's brown hand resting like a tortoise on his thigh. It was an old, thick hand with yellowing nails, pitted with hills and valleys, crisscrossed with dark blue blood vessels, dotted with patches of pigment and sparse tufts of hair. For a moment he panicked. Then he realised that the hand was his own. He woke and read over, three times, the headings he had written down on Saturday for an article he had promised to deliver by today's deadline. But what he had intended to write, what had excited him yesterday to polemical impishness, today seemed totally flat. The very urge to write had been dulled.

A little reflection revealed that all was not lost: it was nothing more than a technical difficulty. Because of the overcast sky and the damp mist there was not enough light in the room. He needed light. That was all. He switched on his desk lamp, hoping by so doing to make a fresh start on his article, his morning, his life. But the lamp was broken. Or perhaps it needed a new light bulb. Angry, he hurried to the cupboard in the hall, where, contrary to his expectation, he actually did find a bulb, and he managed to replace the old one without any setback. But the new bulb must have been a dud, or perhaps it had fallen under its predecessor's influence. He went back to look for a third one, and on the way it occurred to him to try the light in the hall, and then he had to exonerate both bulbs, because it turned out there was a power cut. To save himself from idleness he decided to call Yael. If her husband answered, he would hang up. If she was there, no doubt the inspiration of the moment would tell him what to say. Like that time, after a flaming row, when he had mollified her with the words: If only we weren't married, I'd ask you to be my wife. And she, smiling, had answered through her tears, If you weren't already my husband, I think I might say yes. After ten or twenty hollow rings Fima understood that Yael did not want to speak to him, unless Ted was leaning on the phone to prevent her picking up the receiver.

In any case he felt weary. His long nocturnal prowl through the alleys of Valladolid had ruined his whole morning. At one o'clock he had to be at his post behind the reception desk of the private clinic where he worked in Kiryat Shmuel, and already it was twenty past nine. Fima crumpled up the headings for his article and his electricity bill and his shopping list and his computerised bank statement and tossed them all in the bin, leaving his desk cleared for action at last. He went to the kitchen to make himself a fresh cup of coffee, and while he was waiting for the water to boil he stood in the half-darkness remembering the evening light in Jerusalem some thirty years before, in Agrippa Street outside the Eden cinema a few weeks after his trip to Greece. Yael had said then, Yes, Effy, I do quite love you and I like loving you and I like it when you talk, but what makes you think that if you stop talking for a few minutes you'll stop existing? And he had shut up like a child scolded by its mother. When after a quarter of an hour the kettle was still not boiling, even though he had remembered twice to plug it in, he finally realised that without electricity he would never have his coffee. So he lay down again fully dressed under the heavy winter blanket, set the alarm for quarter to twelve, hid his dream book under the pile of newspapers and magazines at the foot of his bed, covered himself up to his chin, and concentrated his thoughts on women until he managed to arouse himself. He clasped his erection with all ten fingers, like a burglar climbing a drainpipe or, rather – he chuckled – like a drowning man clutching at a straw. But fatigue was much stronger than desire, and he let go and dropped off. Outside, the rain grew heavier.

3

A can of worms

O N the midday news he heard that an Arab youth had been
hit and killed that morning by a plastic bullet fired presumably from a soldier's rifle in the Jebeliyeh refugee camp in the
course of a stone-throwing incident, and that the corpse had been
snatched from the hospital in Gaza by masked youths. The circumstances were being investigated. Fima pondered the wording
of the announcement. He particularly disliked the expression
'killed by a plastic bullet'. And the word 'presumably' made him
seethe. He was angry, too, in a more general way, about the
passive verbs that were beginning to take over official statements
and seemed to be infecting the language as a whole.

Although in fact it might be a healthy and wholly laudable
sense of shame that prevented us from announcing simply: a Jewish soldier has shot and killed an Arab teenager. On the other
hand, this polluted language was constantly teaching us that the
fault lay with the rifle, with the circumstances that were being
investigated, with the plastic bullet, as if all evil was the fault of
Heaven and everything was predestined.

And in fact, he said to himself, who knows?

After all, there is a sort of secret charm in the words 'the fault
of Heaven'.

But then he was angry with himself. There was no charm and
it was not secret. Leave Heaven out of it.

Fima aimed a fork at his forehead, at his temple, at the back of
his head, and tried to guess or sense what it must feel like the
instant the bullet pierces the skull and explodes: no pain, no
noise, perhaps, so he imagined, perhaps just a searing flash of
incredulity, like a child preparing himself for a slap on the face
from his father and receiving instead a white-hot poker in his

eyeball. Is there a fraction, an atom of time in which, who knows, illumination arrives? The light of the seven heavens? When what has been dim and vague all your life is momentarily opened up before darkness falls? As though all those years you have been looking for a complicated solution to a complicated problem, and in the final moment a simple solution flashes out?

At this point Fima croaked angrily to himself, Just stop fucking up your mind. The words 'dim and vague' filled him with disgust. He got up and went out, locking the door of his flat behind him and taking particular note of which pocket he put the key in. In the entrance hall of the block of flats he spotted the white of a letter through the slit of his letter box. But the only key in his pocket was his front-door key. The key to the letter box was presumably still lying on his desk. Unless it was in the pocket of another pair of trousers. Or on the corner of the kitchen counter. After a moment's hesitation he shrugged; the letter was probably nothing but the water bill or the phone bill, or else just a handbill. While he lunched on a salami omelette, a salad, and a fruit compote in the café across the road, he was startled to see, through the window, that the light was on in his flat. He thought about this for a while, weighing up the faint possibility that he was in both places at once, but preferred to assume that the fault had been repaired and the current had been restored. Glancing at his watch, he decided that if he went up to the flat, switched off the light, found the key to the letter box, and retrieved the letter, he would be late for work, so he paid for his meal, saying, 'Thank you, Mrs Schoenberg.' As usual, she corrected him:

'It's Scheinmann, Dr Nisan.'

'Of course,' Fima replied. 'I'm sorry. How much do I owe you? I've already paid? Well, all I can say is it can't have been an accident. I must have wanted to pay twice, because your schnitzel – it was schnitzel, wasn't it? – was especially tasty. I'm sorry. Thank you. Good-bye. I must run now. Just look at this rain. Aren't you looking a little tired? Or unhappy? It's probably just the weather. It'll brighten up soon. See you tomorrow.'

Twenty minutes later, when the bus stopped at the National Auditorium, it occurred to Fima how ridiculous it had been to come out on a day like this without an umbrella. Or to promise the proprietress of the café that the weather would brighten up. On what grounds? Suddenly a fine, burnished sliver of reddish light piercing through the clouds dazzled him by setting fire to a window high up in the Hilton tower. Though dazzled, he could see a towel waving on the railing of a balcony on the tenth or twentieth floor, and he sensed in his nostrils the precise scent of the woman who had just dried herself on it. Look, he said to himself, nothing is ever really wasted, nothing gets written off, and there is scarcely a moment without some minor miracle. Maybe everything is for the best after all.

The two-room flat on the edge of Kiryat Yovel had been bought for Fima when he remarried in 1961, less than a year after receiving his BA in history with distinction at the university in Jerusalem. In those days his father pinned high hopes on him. Others too believed in Fima's future. He was awarded a scholarship, and almost went on to do a master's degree; there were even thoughts of a doctorate and an academic career. But in the summer of 1960 Fima's life underwent a series of mishaps or complications. To this day his friends chuckled with amused affection whenever, in his absence, the conversation turned to 'Fima's billy-goat year'. The story ran that in the middle of July, straight after the end of his finals, in the garden of the Ratisbonne Convent he fell in love with the French guide of a party of Catholic tourists. He was sitting on a bench waiting for a girl-friend, a student at the nursing college named Shula, who married his friend Tsvi Kropotkin a couple of years later. A sprig of oleander was flowering between his fingers and the birds were arguing overhead. Nicole addressed him from the next bench: Was there any water here? Did he speak French? Fima replied in the affirmative to both questions, even though he did not have the faintest idea where there was any water, and he knew only a smattering of French. From that moment on he dogged her footsteps wherever she went in Jerusalem; he would not leave her alone despite her polite requests; he did not even give her up when her group leader warned him that he would be obliged to lodge a complaint about him. When she went to Mass at the

Dormition Abbey, he waited for her outside like a dog for an hour and a half. Every time she came out of the Kings' Hotel, opposite the Terra Sancta Building, she encountered Fima standing in front of the revolving door, his eyes blazing. When she went to the museum, he was lurking in every room. When she flew back to France, he followed her to Paris and even to her home in Lyons. Late one moonlit night, so the story goes in Jerusalem, her father came out of the house and fired a double-barrelled shotgun at him, grazing his leg. During the three days he spent in a Franciscan hospital he made inquiries about what one had to do to become a Christian. Nicole's father, visiting him in the hospital to ask his forgiveness, offered to help him convert. Meanwhile Nicole had had enough of her father too and ran away from both of them, first to her sister in Madrid and then to her sister-in-law in Málaga. Dirty, desperate, and unkempt, he pursued her on dusty buses and trains until his money ran out in Gibraltar and, with the help of the Red Cross, he was returned almost forcibly to Israel on board a Panamanian cargo vessel. On arrival at Haifa he was arrested, and he spent six weeks in a military prison because he had tampered with the date on the form authorising a soldier on the reserve list to leave the country. They say that at the beginning of this passion Fima weighed seventy-two kilogrammes and that in September, in the prison hospital, he weighed less than sixty. He was released from prison after his father interceded for him with a senior official, whose wife, a well-known woman-about-town with a famous collection of etchings, subsequently fell outrageously in love with him; she was ten years younger than her husband and at least eight years older than Fima. In the autumn she became pregnant by him and moved into his lodgings in Musrara. They were the talk of the whole city. In December Fima boarded another cargo boat, a Yugoslav one this time, and turned up in Malta, where he spent three months working on a tropical-fish farm and writing his cycle of poems, *The Death of Augustine and His Resurrection in the Arms of Dulcinea*. In January the woman who owned the cheap hotel where he was staying in Valletta fell for him and moved his luggage into her own apartment. Afraid she might get pregnant too, he decided to marry her in a civil ceremony. This marriage lasted less than two months, because meanwhile his father, with the help of friends in Rome, had managed to discover his whereabouts; he informed Fima that his Jerusalem lover had lost the baby, succumbed to depression, and returned to her husband and her etchings. Fima decided that there was no forgiveness for him and made up his mind to leave his landlady at once and give women a wide berth forever. He decided that love leads inexorably to disaster, whereas relations without love cause only humiliation and hurt. He left Malta without a penny, on the deck of a Turkish fishing boat. His plan was to hole up for at least a year in a certain monastery on the island of Samos. On the way he was smitten with panic at the thought that his ex-wife might also be pregnant and wondered if he ought to go back to her, but at the same time he felt he had acted wisely in leaving her his money but no address that she could trace him by. He disembarked at Thessaloniki and spent a night in a youth hostel, where with sweetness and pain he dreamed of his first love, Nicole, whom he had lost track of in Gibraltar. In the dream her name had changed to Thérèse, and Fima saw his father with a loaded shotgun holding her and the baby prisoner in the cellar of the YMCA in Jerusalem, except that by the end of the dream he himself had become the captive child. The next morning he set off to look for a synagogue, even though he had never been a practising Jew and was certain that God was not in the least religious and had no use for religion. But, having no other address, Fima decided to try and see. Outside the synagogue he came across three Israeli girls who were backpacking around Greece and were about to head north, into the mountains, because by now spring had arrived. Fima joined them, and on the way, so they say, fell head over heels for one of them, Ilia Abravanel, from Haifa, who to him was the image of Mary Magdalene in a painting he had seen somewhere, he could not remember where or who the artist was. And as Ilia did not yield to his advances, he slept a few times with her friend Liat Sirkin, who invited him to share her sleeping bag as they spent the night in some highland valley or sacred grove. Liat Sirkin taught Fima one or two unusual, exquisite pleasures, but he felt, beyond the carnal thrills, faint hints of spiritual elation: almost day by day he fell under the spell of a secret mountain joy mingled with a sense of exaltation which endowed him with heightened powers of vision such as he had never experienced before or since. During these days in the mountains of northern Greece he was able, looking at the sunrise over a clump of olive trees, to see the creation of the world. And to know with absolute certainty, as he passed a flock of sheep in the midday heat, that this was not the first time he had lived. And actually to hear, sitting on the vine-shaded terrace of a village tavern, over wine and cheese and salad, the roar of a snowstorm in the polar wastes. He played tunes to the girls on a pipe he had fashioned from a reed, and was not ashamed to leap and whirl in front of them like a crazy child until he brought them to peals of childlike laughter and simple happiness. All that time he could see no contradiction between pining for Ilia and sleeping with Liat, but he barely noticed the third girl, who mostly chose to stay silent. Though she was the one who dressed his foot when he cut it on a piece of broken glass. These three girls, with the previous women in his life, including his mother, who had died when he was ten, almost merged into a single woman in his mind. Not because he thought that a woman is only a woman, but because with his inner illumination he sometimes felt that the differences between people, any people – men, women, or children – were of no consequence except perhaps for the outermost layer, the ephemeral surface. Just as water took the form of snow or mist or steam or a lump of ice or clouds or hailstones. Or just as the bells of the monasteries and village churches differed only in their pitch and rhythm, all having the same meaning. He shared these thoughts with the girls, two of whom believed, whereas the third called him a simpleton and contented herself with patching his shirt; in this too Fima saw only different expressions of a single statement. This third girl, Yael Levin from Yavne'el, did not refrain from joining in their nude swimming on warm moonlit nights if they found a spring or stream. Once, they watched stealthily, from a distance, a fifteen-year-old shepherd boy satisfying his urges on a nanny goat. And once, they saw a pair of pious old women in widow's weeds with large wooden crosses on their chests sitting silently on a rock in the middle of a field in the noonday heat, motionless, their fingers interlaced. One night they heard sounds of music coming from an empty ruin. And one day a wizened old man walked past them, going the other way, playing on a broken accordion that made no sound. The next morning there was a brief cloudburst, and the air became so clear that they could see the shadows of trees shifting on the red-tiled roofs of little villages in distant valleys, and almost make out the individual needles of the cypress and pine trees on the flanks of the mountains. One of the peaks still wore a cap of snow, which looked silver rather than white against the deep blue of the sky. Flocks of birds were performing a sort of scarf dance overhead. Fima, for no particular reason, suddenly said something that made all the girls laugh:

'This,' he said, 'is where the dog is buried.'

Ilia said: 'I feel dreamier than in a dream and more awake than waking. I can't explain it.'

Liat said: 'It's the light. That's all.'

And Yael: 'Who's thirsty? Let's go down to the water.'

Less than a month after the conclusion of this trip Fima went to Yavne'el to look for the third girl. He discovered that Yael Levin was a graduate of the aeronautical engineering department of the Haifa Technion and worked in a top-secret air force installation in the hills west of Jerusalem. After a few meetings he found that her presence made him feel restful, while his presence amused her in her placid way. When he asked her, hesitantly, whether she thought they were suited to each other, she replied, 'I quite like the way you talk.' He thought this indicated a hint of affection. Which he treasured. Next he sought out Liat Sirkin and sat with her for half an hour in a little seaside café, simply to make certain he had not made her pregnant. But afterwards he allowed himself to sleep with her again in a cheap hotel in Bat Yam, so he wasn't certain any more. In May he invited all three girls to Jerusalem to meet his father. The old man charmed Ilia with his old-style courtesy, entertained Liat with anecdotes and fables with morals, but he preferred Yael, who showed, he thought, 'signs of depth'. Fima agreed with him, although he was not entirely sure he understood what the signs were. He continued to go out with her, until one day she said to him: 'Look at your shirt, half inside your trousers and half outside. Wait. I'll sort it out for you.'

And in August 1961 Yael and Efraim Nisan were married in the small flat his father had bought him on the edge of Kiryat Yovel, on the edge of Jerusalem, after Fima had given in and signed, in the presence of a notary, an agreement drawn up by his father, containing a solemn undertaking to refrain henceforth from any act that his father might define as an 'adventure'. He also undertook to begin, at the end of the wasted year, studying for a master's degree. The father, for his part, agreed to finance his son's studies as well as the final stage of Yael's training, and even granted them a modest monthly allowance for the first five years of their marriage. From then on Fima's name was no longer mentioned in Jerusalem gossip. The adventures had come to an end. The billy-goat year had finished, and the tortoise years began. But he did not go back to the university, except perhaps with one or two ideas that he gave to his friend Tsvi Kropotkin, who had meanwhile proceeded without a pause from MA to doctorate and was already laying the foundation for a great tower of historical articles and books.

In 1962, at the urging of his friends and thanks to special efforts on the part of Tsvika, Fima published the cycle of poems he had written during his short-lived marriage in Malta: *The Death of Augustine and His Resurrection in the Arms of Dulcinea*. For a year or two there were some critics and readers who saw in Efraim Nisan a promise waiting to be fulfilled. But after a time even the promise faded, because Fima's muse fell silent. He wrote no more poems. Every morning Yael was picked up by a military vehicle and taken to work at a base whose location Fima did not know, where she was engaged in some technological development that he neither understood nor wanted to. He would spend the entire morning prowling around the flat, listening to every news broadcast, raiding the fridge and eating standing up, arguing aloud with himself and with the newsreaders, furiously making the bed that Yael had not managed to make before she went out, in fact couldn't, because he was still asleep in it. Then he would finish reading the morning paper, go out to buy one or two things at the grocer's, come back with two afternoon papers, immerse himself in them until the evening and leave their pages scattered all over the flat. Between reading the papers and listening to the news, he made himself sit down at his desk. For a while he was occupied by a Christian book, the *Pugio Fidei* of Father Raymond Martini, published in Paris in 1651 to refute once and for all the faith of the 'Moors and the Jews'. Fima was contemplating a fresh study of the Christian origins of antisemitism. But his work was interrupted by a vague interest in the idea of the Hidden God. He plunged himself into the biography of the hermit Eusebius Sophronius Hieronymus, who learned Hebrew from a Jewish teacher, settled in Bethlehem in 386, translated both Testaments into Latin, and may have deliberately deepened the rift between Jews and Christians. But this study did not quench Fima's thirst. Lassitude got the better of him, and he sank into idleness. He would leaf through the encyclopedia, forget what he was looking for, and waste a couple of hours reading through the entries in alphabetical order. Almost every evening he would pull on his battered cap and go out to visit his friends, chatting till the early hours about the Lavon affair, the Eichmann trial, the Cuban missile crisis, the German scientists in Egypt, the significance of the Pope's visit to the Holy Land. When Yael got home from work in the evening and asked if he had eaten, Fima would reply irritably, Why? Where does it say I've got to eat? And then, while she was in the shower, he would explain to her through the closed door who was really behind the assassination of President Kennedy. Later, when she asked if he was going out to have another row with Uri or Tsvika, he would answer, No, I'm going to an orgy. And he would ask himself how he had allowed his father to attach him to this woman. But there were other times when he suddenly fell in love all over again with her strong fingers as they rubbed her little ankles at the end of the day, or with her habit of stroking her eyelashes, lost in thought, and he would court her like a shy, passionate youth until she allowed him to give pleasure to her body, and then he would thrill her eagerly and precisely, with a sort of profound attentiveness. Sometimes he would say to her, as some petty quarrel brewed, Just wait, Yael, it'll pass. It won't be long before our proper life starts. Sometimes they would go for a walk together in the deserted lanes of north Jerusalem on a Friday evening, and he would talk to her with barely suppressed excitement about the union of body and light according to the ancient mystics. This made her feel so joyful and tender that she snuggled against him and forgave him for putting on weight, for forgetting to change his shirt again for the weekend, for his habit of correcting her Hebrew. Then they would go home and make love as if they were beyond despair.

In 1965 Yael went to work, on special contract, at the Boeing research centre in Seattle. Fima declined to join her, arguing that a period of separation might do them both good. He stayed behind in the two-room flat in Kiryat Yovel. He had a modest post as receptionist in a private gynaecological clinic in Kiryat Shmuel. He kept his distance from academic life, unless Tsvi Kropotkin dragged him to a one-day conference on the importance of personality in history, or on the notion of the historian as eyewitness. At weekends he would turn up at Nina and Uri Gefen's or at other friends', and was easily caught up in their political discussions; he would occasionally astound all those present with some mordant summing-up or paradoxical prediction, but he never knew how to stop when he was winning, he would persist like a compulsive gambler, arguing volubly on subjects he knew nothing about, even over trivial details, until he wore out even his most loyal friends. Sometimes he would arrive with a few books and keep an eye on his friends' children while they went out for the evening. Or cheerfully offer to help them with an article, by proofreading, copyediting, or preparing an abstract. Sometimes he would undertake shuttle diplomacy on a mission of mediation for a feuding couple. Every now and again he would publish a short trenchant article in *Ha'arets* on some aspect of the current political scene. Once in a while he would take a few days' holiday alone in a private guesthouse in one of the older settlements in the northern Sharon. Every summer he attempted with renewed enthusiasm to learn to drive, and every autumn he failed the driving test. Now and again a woman he had met at the clinic or through friends found her way to his untidy bachelor flat and into his bed, whose sheets needed changing. She would soon discover that Fima was more interested in her pleasure than his own. Some women found this wonderful and moving; others found it unsettling and hastened to disengage themselves. He could spend an hour or two inflicting endless varied exquisite sensations full of playful inventiveness and physical humour, before casually snatching his own satisfaction, and then, almost before his partner noticed that he had exacted his modest commission, he would be devoting himself to her again. Any woman who tried to obtain a measure of continuity or permanence in her relationship with Fima, who succeeded in extracting a key from him, caused him to take refuge after a week or two in a run-down guesthouse in Pardés Hanna or Magdiel and not come home until she had given him up. But even these episodes had become rare in the past five or six years.

When Yael wrote to him from Seattle early in 1966 to say there was another man in her life, Fima laughed at the trite expression. The love affairs of his billy-goat year, his marriage to Yael, Yael herself, now seemed as trite, as overacted, as childish as the underground revolutionary cell he had tried to set up when he was in high school. He decided to write her a line or two simply to send his best wishes to her and the other man in her life. He sat down at his desk that afternoon, and did not stop writing until midday the following day: in a feverish missive of thirty-four pages he confessed the depth of his love for her. After reading it through, he rejected it, tore it up, and flushed it down the lavatory. You cannot describe love in words, and if you can, that's a sign the love no longer exists. Or is on the way out. Finally he tore a page of graph paper from a notebook and scrawled on it: 'I can't stop loving you because it's not up to me, but of course you're a free agent. How blind I've been. If there's anything you need from the flat, let me know and I'll send it. Meanwhile I'm sending you a parcel with three of your nighties and your furry slippers and the photos. But if you don't mind, I'd like to keep

the picture of the two of us at Bethlehem in Galilee.' Yael took
this letter to mean that Fima would not place any obstacles in
the way of a divorce. But when she came back to Jerusalem and
introduced a colourless, inexpressive man with a jaw that was
too broad and thick eyebrows like a pair of bushy moustaches,
saying, Efraim Nisan, Ted Tobias, let's all be friends, Fima
changed his mind and adamantly refused to grant a divorce. So
Ted and Yael flew back to Seattle. They lost contact, apart from
a few aerogrammes and postcards about practical matters.

Several years later, early in 1982 Ted and Yael turned up at
Fima's flat one winter afternoon with their three-year-old son, a
slightly cross-eyed albino child-philosopher with thick glasses,
dressed in an American astronaut's space suit bearing a shiny
metal badge inscribed with the word CHALLENGER. The little fellow soon revealed an ability to compose complicated conditional
sentences and to duck awkward questions. Fima instantly fell for
little Dimi Tobias. Regretting his earlier opposition, he offered
Yael and Ted a divorce, his assistance, and his friendship. Yael,
however, no longer attached any importance to the religious
divorce and saw no point in friendship. In the intervening years
she had managed to leave Ted twice and have affairs with other
men before making up her mind to go back to him and to have
Dimi at what was almost the last moment as far as she was concerned. Fima won the heart of the thoughtful little Challenger
with a story about a wild wolf who decided to give up being wild
and tried to join a colony of rabbits. When the story was over,
Dimi offered his own ending, which Fima found logical, sensitive,
and not unfunny.

Thanks to the intervention of Fima's father, the divorce was
arranged discreetly. Ted and Yael settled in the suburb of
Beit Hakerem, found jobs together in a research institute, and
divided their year into three: the summer in Seattle, the fall in
Pasadena, the winter and spring in Jerusalem. Sometimes they
invited Fima round on Friday evening, when the Kropotkins and
the Gefens and the rest of the group were there. Sometimes they
left Dimi with Fima in Kiryat Yovel and went off to Elat or
Upper Galilee for a couple of days. Fima became their unpaid

baby sitter, because he was available and because a friendship had grown up between him and Dimi. By some odd logic Dimi called him Granpa. He called Fima's father Granpa too. Fima taught himself to make houses, palaces, and castles with loopholes out of matchsticks, matchboxes, and glue. This was totally at odds with the image of Fima shared by his friends, by Yael, and by Fima himself, namely, a clumsy oaf who was born with two left hands and could never get the hang of replacing the washer on a tap or sewing on a button.

Apart from Dimi and his parents, there was the gang: pleasant, respectable people, some of whom had known Fima from student days and had been indirectly involved in the ordeals of the billy-goat year, and some of whom still hoped that one day the lad would wake up, get his act together, and one way or another take Jerusalem by the ears. True, they said, he sometimes gets on your nerves, he overdoes it, he has no sense of proportion, but on the other hand when he's brilliant he's really brilliant. One day he's really going to get somewhere. He's worth investing in. Last Friday, for example, early in the evening, before he started making a fool of himself with his imitations of politicians, the way he snatched the word 'ritual' out of Tsvi's mouth and held us all spellbound like little kids when he suddenly said, 'Everything is ritual,' and fired his theory at us straight from the hip. We haven't stopped talking about it all week. Or that amazing comparison he threw out, of Kafka and Gogol, and of the two of them with Hasidic folk tales.

Over the years some of them grew fond of Fima's unique combination of wit and absent-mindedness, of melancholy and enthusiasm, of sensitivity and helplessness, of profundity and buffoonery. Moreover, he was always available to be roped in to do some proofreading or to discuss a draft of an article. Behind his back they said, not unkindly, True, he's a – how to put it? – he's an original, and he's goodhearted. The trouble is, he's bone idle. He has no ambition. He simply doesn't think about tomorrow. And he's not getting any younger.

Despite which, there was something in his podgy form, his shuffling, abstracted way of walking, his fine, high brow, his weary shoulders, his thinning fair hair, and in his kindly eyes that always seemed lost and looking either inward or out beyond the mountains and the desert, something in his appearance that filled them with affection and joy and made them smile broadly even when they caught sight of him from a distance, on the other side of the street, wandering around the city centre as though he did not know who had brought him there or how he was going to get out again. And they said: Look, there's Fima over there, waving his arms. He must be having an argument with himself, and presumably he's winning it.

In the course of time a certain uneasy friendliness, filled with anger and contradictions, developed between Fima and his father, the well-known cosmetics manufacturer Baruch Nomberg, who was a veteran member of the right-wing Herut party. Even now, when Fima was fifty-four and his father eighty-two, the father would slip a couple of ten-shekel notes, or a single twenty-shekel note, into his son's pocket at the end of every visit. Meanwhile Fima's little secret was that he deposited eighty shekels each month in a savings account in the name of Ted and Yael's son, who was ten now but still looked like a seven-year-old, dreamy and trustful. Strangers on buses sometimes noticed a vague resemblance between Fima and the child, in the shape of the chin or the forehead, or in the walk. The previous spring Dimi had asked to keep a pair of tortoises and some silkworms in a little storage space that Fima and Ted cleared for him on the balcony of the messy kitchen of the flat in Kiryat Yovel. And even though Fima was considered by others and even by himself as incorrigibly idle and absent-minded, all through the summer there was not a single day when he forgot to attend to what he took to calling 'our can of worms'. Now, in the winter, the silkworms were dead, and the tortoises had been set free in the wadi, at the point where Jerusalem abruptly ends and a rocky wilderness begins.

4

Hopes of opening a new chapter

THE private clinic in Kiryat Shmuel was approached through the garden behind the building, along a pathway paved with Jerusalem stone. Now that it was winter, the path was covered with slippery rain-soaked pine needles. Fima was totally absorbed in considering whether a frozen bird he had just spotted on a low branch could hear the thunder that was rolling from west to east; the bird's head and beak were buried deep in the plumage of its wing. Struck by a sudden doubt, he turned back to see if it really was a bird or if it was just a wet pine cone. That was how he came to slip and fall to his knees. He stayed crouching, not because he was in pain, but because of self-mocking pleasure at his own predicament. Softly he said, Well done, pal.

For some reason he felt he had deserved this fall as a sort of logical sequel to the minor miracle he had experienced outside the Hilton Hotel on his way here.

When he eventually managed to get to his feet, he stood absent-mindedly in the rain, looking like someone who does not know where he has come from or where he must go. Raising his head towards the upper floors, he saw nothing but closed shutters or blank curtained windows. Here and there on a balcony was a geranium in a pot. The rain had given them a sensual sparkle that brought to his mind the painted lips of a vulgar woman.

Beside the entrance to the clinic there was an elegantly restrained plate of black glass inscribed in silver lettering: DR WAHRHAFTIG DR EITAN CONSULTANT GYNAECOLOGISTS. For the thousandth time Fima asked himself why there were not specialists for male disorders too. He also objected to the Hebrew phrase in question, which contained a construction that the language does not tolerate. Then he found himself ridiculous for using such an absurd expression. And felt shame and confusion as he recalled how indignantly he had reacted to the news, not because of the death of an Arab boy in the Jebeliyeh refugee camp but because of the phrase 'killed by a plastic bullet'.

As if it's the bullets that do the killing.

And was he getting soft in the head himself?

He summoned his cabinet for another meeting in the dilapidated classroom. At the door he posted a burly sentry in khaki shorts, Arab headdress, and knitted cap. Some of his ministers sat on the bare floor at his feet, others leaned against the wall, which was covered with educational diagrams. In a few well-chosen words Fima presented them with the need to choose between the territories conquered in '67 and our very identity. Then, while they were still buzzing excitedly, he called for a vote, which he won, and immediately gave them his detailed instructions.

Before we won the Six Days' War, he mused, the state of the nation was less dangerous and destructive than it is now. Or perhaps it wasn't really less dangerous, just less demoralising and less depressing. Was it really easier for us to face up to the danger of annihilation than to sit in the dock facing the accusations of international public opinion? The danger of annihilation gave us pride and a sense of unity, whereas sitting in the dock now is gradually breaking our spirit. But that's not the right way to state the alternatives. In fact, sitting in the dock may be breaking the spirit only of the secular intelligentsia of Russian or Western origin, whereas the ordinary masses are not in the least nostalgic for the pride of David standing up to Goliath. Anyway, the expression 'ordinary masses' is a hollow cliché. Meanwhile, because you fell, your trousers are covered with mud and the hands that are wiping them clean are also muddy and the rain is pouring down on your head. It is already five past one. However hard you try, you'll never get to work on time.

The clinic was two ground-floor flats joined together. The windows, guarded by arabesque grilles, looked out on a typical back garden, damp and deserted, shaded by dense pine trees around whose bases a few grey boulders sprouted. A rustle of treetops started at the slightest breeze. Now, with a strong wind blowing,

Fima had a fleeting image of a remote village in Poland or one of the Baltic States, with storms shrieking through the surrounding forest, whipping across snowbound fields, assailing thatched cottage roofs, and making the church bells ring out. And wolves howling not far away. In his head Fima already had a little story about this village, about Nazis, Jews, and partisans, which he might tell to Dimi this evening, in exchange for a ladybird in a jam jar or a spaceship cut out of orange peel.

From the first floor came the sounds of piano, violin, and cello being played by the three elderly women who lived there and gave private music lessons. They also probably gave recitals and played at memorial meetings, at the presentation of a prize for Yiddish literature, at the inauguration of a community centre or a day-centre for the elderly. Although Fima had worked at the clinic for several years now, their playing still wrung his heart, as though a cello deep inside him responded with its own mute sounds of longing to the one upstairs. As though a mystic bond was growing stronger with the passing years, between what was being done down here to women's bodies with stainless-steel forceps and the melancholy of the cello upstairs.

The sight of Fima, podgy and dishevelled, smiling sheepishly, with his hands and knees covered with mud, filled Dr Wahrhaftig as usual with good humour mingled with affection and a strong urge to reprimand him. Wahrhaftig was a gentle, rather shy man, so emotional that he had difficulty holding back his tears at times, especially when anybody apologised to him and asked to be forgiven. Maybe that was why he cultivated a severe manner, and always tried to terrorise those around him by shouting rebukes at them. Rebukes that turned out to be mild and inoffensive.

'Hah! Your Excellency! Herr Major General von Nisan! Straight from the trenches, I see! We should pin a medal on you!'

'I'm a little late,' Fima replied bashfully. 'I'm sorry. I slipped on the path. It's so wet outside.'

'Ach so!' roared Wahrhaftig. 'Once more this fatal lateness! Once again force majeure!' And he recounted for the nth time the joke about the dead man who was late for his own funeral.

He was a stocky man with the build of a basso profundo, and his face had the florid, flabby look of an alcoholic, crisscrossed with an unhealthy network of blood vessels that were so near the surface, you could almost take his pulse by their throbbing. He had a joke for every occasion, invariably introduced with the phrase 'There is a well-known story about.' And he always burst out laughing when he got close to the punch line. Fima, who had already heard ad nauseam why the dead man was late for his own funeral, nevertheless let out a faint laugh, because he was fond of this tender-hearted tyrant. Wahrhaftig was constantly delivering long lectures in his stentorian voice about such subjects as the connection between your eating habits and your world-view, or about the 'socialistic' economy and how it encouraged idleness and fraud and was therefore unsuited to a civilised country. Wahrhaftig would utter these last words in a tone of mystical pathos, like a true believer praising the works of the Almighty.

'It's quiet here today', Fima remarked.

Wahrhaftig replied that they were expecting a famous artist any minute now with a minor obstruction of the tubes. The word 'tubes', in its medical usage, reminded him of a well-known story, which he did not spare Fima.

Meanwhile, stealthily as a cat, Dr Gad Eitan emerged from his office. He was followed by the nurse, Tamar Greenwich, who looked like an early pioneer, a woman of forty-five or so in a light-blue cotton dress with her hair pinned neatly back into what looked like a small ball of wool at the base of her skull. As a result of a pigment peculiarity one of her eyes was green and the other brown. She crossed the reception hall supporting a pale patient, whom she escorted to the recovery room.

Dr Eitan, lithe and muscular, leaned on the desk, chewing gum with a leisurely motion of his jaws. He replied with a movement of the chin to Fima's greeting or to a question from Wahrhaftig, or perhaps to both at once. His watery blue eyes were fixed on a spot high above the reproduction Modigliani on the wall. With his self-satisfied expression and his thin blond moustache, he looked to Fima like an arrogant Prussian diplomat who has been posted against his will to Outer Mongolia. He allowed Wahrhaftig to finish another well-known story. Then there was a silence, after which, like a lethargic leopard, almost without moving his lips, he said quietly:

'Let's cut the chatter and get on with it.'

Wahrhaftig obeyed at once and followed him to the treatment room. The door closed behind them. A sharp, antiseptic whiff escaped between its opening and closing.

Fima washed his hands and made a cup of coffee for the patient in the recovery room. Then he made another cup for Tamar and one for himself, donned a short white coat, sat down behind his desk, and began to look through the ledger in which he kept track of patients' visits. Here too he wrote the numbers out in words, not figures. He noted down accounts that were settled or deferred, dates for laboratory tests and their results, and any alterations to appointments. He also managed the filing cabinet that contained patients' medical records and details of prescriptions, ultrasound tests, and x-rays. This, with answering the telephone, was the sum total of his job. Apart from making coffee every couple of hours for the two doctors and the nurse, and occasionally also for a patient if her treatment had been painful.

Across the hall from his desk there was a small coffee table, two armchairs, a rug, a reproduction Degas and Modigliani on the walls: the waiting area. Sometimes Fima would help a patient through the difficult period of waiting by engaging her in light conversation about some neutral subject such as the rising cost of living or a TV programme that had been shown the previous evening. Most of the visitors, however, preferred to wait in silence, leafing through magazines, in which case Fima would bury his eyes in his papers and minimise his presence so as not to cause embarrassment. What went on behind the closed doors of the treatment rooms? What caused the groans that Fima sometimes heard or thought he heard? What did the various women's faces express when they arrived and when they left? What was the story that ended in this clinic? And the new story that was just beginning here? What was the male shadow behind this or that woman? And the child that would not be born, what was it?

What would it have turned out to be? These things Fima tried at times to decipher, or to invent, with guesswork linked to a struggle between revulsion and the feeling that he ought to participate, at least in his imagination, in every form of suffering. Sometimes womanhood itself struck him as being a crying injustice, almost a cruel illness that afflicted half the human race and exposed it to degradations and humiliations that the other half was spared. But sometimes a vague jealousy stirred inside him, a sense of deprivation or loss, as though he had been cheated of some secret gift that enabled *them* to relate to the world in a way that was barred to him forever. The more he thought about it, the less he was able to distinguish between his pity and his envy. The womb, conception, pregnancy, childbirth, motherhood, breast feeding, even menstruation, even miscarriage and abortion – he tried to imagine them all, struggling over and over again to feel what he was not meant to feel. Sometimes, while he was thinking, he absently fingered his own nipples. They seemed a hollow joke, a sad relic. Then he was swept by a wave of profound pity for all men and women, as though the separation of the sexes was nothing but a cruel prank. He felt that the time had come to rise up and with sympathy and reason do something to put an end to it. Or at least minimise the suffering that resulted from it. Without being asked, he would get up, fetch a glass of cold water from the refrigerator, and with a faint smile hand it to a woman waiting her turn, and murmur, It'll be all right. Or, Have a drink, you'll feel better. Usually this only provoked mild surprise, but occasionally he generated a grateful smile, to which he replied with a nod, as if to say, It's the least I can do.

When he had free time between answering the telephone and keeping his records up to date, Fima would read a novel in English or a biography of a statesman. Generally, though, he did not read books, but devoured the two evening papers he had bought on the way, taking care not to miss even the short news items, the commentary, the gossip: embezzlement in the co-op in Safed, a case of bigamy in Ashkelon, a story of unrequited love in Kfar Saba. Everything concerned him. After scouring the papers, he would sit back and remember. Or convene cabinet meetings, dressing his ministers up as revolutionary guerrillas, lecturing them, prophesying rage and consolation, saving the children of Israel whether they wanted it or not, and bringing peace to the land.

Between treatments, when the doctors and the nurse emerged for their coffee break, Fima would sometimes suddenly lose his ability to listen. He would wonder what he was doing here, what he had in common with these strangers. And where he ought to be if not here. But he could find no answer to that question. Even though he felt, painfully, that somewhere someone was waiting for him, surprised he was so late. Then, after scrabbling for a long time in his pockets, he would find a heartburn tablet, swallow it, and continue scanning the newspapers in case he had missed what really mattered.

Gad Eitan was Alfred Wahrhaftig's ex-son-in-law: he had been married to Wahrhaftig's only daughter, who ran away to Mexico with a visiting poet she had fallen for while working at the Jerusalem Book Fair. Wahrhaftig, the founder of the clinic and the senior partner, held Gad Eitan in strange awe: he would lavish on him little gestures of submission and deference which he camouflaged with explosions of polite rage. Dr Eitan, who although his particular speciality was infertility also served whenever necessary as the anaesthetist, was an icy, taciturn man. He had a habit of staring long and hard at his fingers. As if he was afraid of losing them, or as if their very existence never ceased to amaze him. The fingers in question were well shaped and long, and wonderfully musical. He also moved like a drowsy wild beast, or one that was just waking up. At times a thin, chilly smile spread over his face: his watery eyes took no part in it. Evidently his coolness aroused in women a certain confidence and excitement, and an urge to shake him out of his indifference or to melt his cruelty. Eitan would ignore any hint of an overture, and respond to confessions on the part of a patient with a dry phrase such as 'Well, yes, but there's no alternative' or 'What can one do: these things happen.'

In the middle of Wahrhaftig's stories Eitan would sometimes turn quickly through 180 degrees, like the turret of a tank, and vanish on cat's paws through the door of his consulting room. It seemed as though all people, men and women alike, caused a faint revulsion in him. And because he had known for several years that Tamar was in love with him, he enjoyed occasionally firing an acerbic remark at her:

'What do you smell of today?'

Or:

'Straighten your skirt, will you, and stop wasting your knees on us. We have to watch that kind of view at least twenty times a day.'

This time he said:

'Would you kindly put that artist's vagina and cervix on my desk. Yes, the famous lady. Yes, the results of her tests. What did you think I meant? Yes, hers, I've no use for yours.'

Tamar's eyes, the green left one and the brown right one, filled with tears. And Fima, with an air of someone rescuing a princess from the dragon's jaws, got up and placed the file in question on the doctor's desk. Eitan shot a vacant glance at him and then turned his icy eyes to his own fingers. Under the powerful theatre lights his womanly fingers took on an unnatural pink glow: they almost looked transparent. He saw fit to aim a lethal salvo at Fima too:

'Do you happen to know what menstruation means? Then please tell Mrs Licht, today – yes, on the phone – that I need to have her here exactly two days after she next menstruates. And if that doesn't sound nice on the phone, you can say two days after her next period. I don't care what you say. You can say after her festival, for all I care. The main thing is to fix an appointment for her accordingly. Thank you.'

Wahrhaftig, like a man catching sight of a fire and hurrying over to throw the contents of the nearest bucket on it without stopping to check whether the bucket contains water or petrol, intervened at this point:

'Festivals – that reminds me of a well-known story about Begin and Yasser Arafat.'

And he embarked for the nth time on the story of how Begin's shrewdness once got the better of Arafat's villainy.

Eitan replied:
'I'd hang the pair of them.'
'Gad's had a hard day,' said Tamar.
And Fima added his own contribution:
'These are hard times all round. We spend all our time trying to repress what we're doing in the Territories, and the consequence is that the air's full of anger and aggression, and everybody's at everybody else's throat.'

At this point Wahrhaftig asked what the difference was between Ramallah and Monte Carlo, and then launched into another anecdote. He started laughing heartily halfway between Monte Carlo and Ramallah. Then, remembering his position, he suddenly puffed himself up, flushed deep red with the network of veins throbbing in his cheeks, and thundered carefully:

'Please! The break is finished. Sorry. Fima! Tamar! Please close this beer garden right away! This whole country of ours is more Asian than Asia! Not even Asia! Africa! But at least in my clinic we are still working as in a civilised country.' A superfluous exhortation, since by then Eitan had shrunk back to his room, Tamar had gone to wash her face, and Fima had in any case not left his desk.

At half past five a tall, golden-haired woman in a beautiful black dress came out. She stopped at Fima's desk and asked, almost in a whisper, whether it showed. Whether she looked a fright. Fima, who had not heard the question, replied mistakenly to another one:

'Naturally, Mrs Tadmor. Of course nobody will find out. You can rest assured. We are totally discreet here.' Although he tactfully refrained from looking at her, he sensed her tears and added:

'There are some tissues in the box.'
'Are you a doctor too?'
'No, ma'am. I'm only the receptionist.'
'Have you been here long?'
'Right from the start. Ever since the clinic opened.'
'You must have witnessed all sorts of scenes.'
'We do have our awkward moments.'

'And you're not a doctor?'

'No, ma'am.'

'How many abortions do you do a day?'

'I'm afraid I can't answer that question.'

'I'm sorry for asking. Life has suddenly dealt me a cruel blow.'

'I understand. I'm sorry.'

'No, you don't understand. I didn't have an abortion. Just a little treatment. But it was humiliating.'

'I'm very sorry. Let's hope you'll feel better now.'

'You've probably got it on record, exactly what they did to me.'

'I never look into the medical notes, if that's what you mean.'

'You're lucky you weren't born a woman. You can't even begin to guess what you were spared.'

'I'm sorry. Can I get you some coffee, or tea?'

'You're always sorry. Why are you so sorry? You haven't even looked at me. You keep looking away.'

'Sorry. I didn't notice. Instant or Turkish?'

'Strange, isn't it? I could have sworn you were a doctor too. It's not the white coat. Are you a student? Doing your practical stint?'

'No, ma'am. I'm just a clerk. Would you rather have a glass of water? There's some mineral water in the fridge.'

'What's it like, working in a place like this for such a long time? What sort of a job is it for a man? Don't you develop an aversion to women? A physical aversion even?'

'I don't think so. Anyway, I can only speak for myself.'

'So what about you? You don't have an aversion to women?'

'No, Mrs Tadmor. If anything, the opposite.'

'Oh! What's the opposite of an aversion?'

'Sympathy, perhaps? Curiosity? It's hard to explain.'

'Why aren't you looking at me?'

'I don't like to cause embarrassment. There, the water's boiling. What's it to be, then? Coffee?'

'Embarrassment to yourself or to me?'

'Hard to say exactly. Maybe both. I'm not sure.'

'Do you happen to have a name?'

'My name is Fima. Efraim.'

'I'm Annette. Are you married?'

'I have been married, ma'am. Twice. Nearly three times.'

'And I'm just getting divorced. To be more accurate, I am being divorced. Are you too shy to look at me? Afraid of being disappointed? Or maybe you just want to make sure you never have to hesitate whether to say hello to me if we meet in the street?'

'Sugar and milk, Mrs Tadmor? Annette?'

'It would actually suit you, to be a gynaecologist. Better than it suits that ridiculous old man who can't stick a rubber-gloved finger into me without trying to distract my attention with some joke about the Emperor Franz Joseph deciding to punish God. May I use the phone?'

'Of course. I'll be back there, in the records room. When you've finished, just call me so we can make you another appointment. Do you need one?'

'Fima Efraim. Please. Look at me. Don't be afraid. I'm not going to cast a spell on you. Once, when I was beautiful, men used to fall for me like flies; now, even the assistant in the clinic won't look at me.'

Fima looked up. And at once recoiled, because the combination of anguish and sarcasm he saw on her face made him throb with desire. He lowered his eyes to his papers and said carefully:

'But you are still a very beautiful woman. At least, to me you are. You don't want to make a phone call?'

'Not any more. I've changed my mind. I'm changing my mind about lots of things at the moment. So I'm not ugly?'

'On the contrary.'

'You're not too good-looking yourself. Pity you've made the coffee. I didn't ask for anything. Never mind. You can drink it. And thank you.'

She stopped at the door and added:

'You have my phone number. It's in your files.'

Fima pondered this. The words 'a new chapter' seemed rather cheap, yet he knew that in other times he might well have fallen

36

for this Annette. But why only in other times? Finally, in Yael's old words, he said to himself:

'Your problem, pal.'

And, after filing the papers away, he locked the records room and washed the cups, ready to shut up shop.

5

Fima gets soaked in the dark in the pouring rain

AFTER locking up the clinic, he took a bus into the center of town and found a cheap eating place in a side street not far from Zion Square, where he had a mushroom pizza washed down with Coca-Cola and chewed a heartburn tablet. Because he did not have enough cash with him, he asked if he could pay by cheque, but was told he could not. He offered to leave his identity card and come back the next morning to pay. However, he could not find the document in question in any of his pockets: he had bought a new electric kettle on Sunday, or before the weekend, to replace the one he had burned out, and, not having enough cash, had left his identity card in the shop as security. Or was it at Steimatsky's Bookshop? Finally, when he was beyond hope, a crumpled fifty-shekel note dropped out of his back pocket: his father must have put it there a couple of weeks ago.

During this search a telephone token came to light in one of his pockets, and Fima located a public call box outside the Sansur Building in Zion Square and phoned Nina Gefen; he vaguely remembered that her husband, Uri, was leaving or had already left for Rome. Maybe he could inveigle her into going to the Orion with him to see the French comedy with Jean Gabin that Tamar had told him about during the coffee break. He couldn't remember the name of the film.

But the voice that came on the line was the wooden voice of Ted Tobias, who asked drily, with a heavy American accent, 'What's up this time, Fima?' Fima mumbled, 'Nothing. It's the rain,' because he couldn't make out what Ted was doing at Nina Gefen's. Then he realised he had absent-mindedly dialled Yael's number instead of Nina's. Why had he lied and said it was raining? It hadn't rained a drop since the afternoon. Eventually he recovered his presence of mind and asked Ted how Dimi was and how they were getting on with enclosing their balcony. Ted reminded him that they had finished that job by the beginning of the winter. Yael had taken Dimi to a children's play and wouldn't be back much before ten. Did he want to leave a message? Fima peered at his watch, guessed that it was not yet eight, and suddenly, without meaning to, asked Ted if he could invade him, in quotation marks, of course; there was something he wanted to discuss with him. He hurriedly said that he had already eaten, and that whatever happened he wouldn't stay more than half an hour.

'OK,' said Ted. 'Fine. Come right on up. Just bear in mind that we're a bit busy this evening.'

Fima took this as a hint that he shouldn't come, and that whatever happened he shouldn't stay till past midnight as he usually did. He was not offended; he even gallantly offered to come some other time. But Ted firmly and politely stood his ground.

'Half an hour will be fine.'

Fima was particularly glad it was not raining, since he had no umbrella, and he did not want to visit the woman he loved looking like a drowned dog. He also noticed that it was getting colder, and decided that it might snow. This made him even happier. Through the window of the bus, somewhere near Mahane Yehuda Market, by the light of a street lamp, he saw a black slogan scrawled on a wall: ARABS OUT! Translating into German and substituting Jews for Arabs, he felt an upsurge of rage. On the spot, he appointed himself president and decided on a dramatic step. He would make an official visit to the Arab village of Deir Yassin on the anniversary of the massacre there and deliver a simple, trenchant statement amid the ruins of the village: Without going into the details of which side is more to blame, we Israeli Jews understand the depth of the suffering that the Palestinian Arabs have undergone during these past forty years, and to put an end to it we are willing to do anything that is reasonable, short of committing suicide. Such a speech would immediately echo through every Arab hovel; it would fire the imagination and might help to start the emotional ball rolling. For a moment Fima hesitated between 'start the emotional ball rolling' and 'achieve an emotional breakthrough'. Which would make a better heading for the short article he intended to write next morning for the weekend paper? Then he rejected them both and dropped the idea of the article.

In the lift, on the way up to the sixth-floor flat in Beit Hakerem, he made up his mind to be calm and cordial this time, to try to talk to Ted as equal to equal, even on political topics, though normally he was very quickly irritated by the other's way of talking, his slow, balanced speech, his American accent and sort of desiccated logicality, his way of buttoning and unbuttoning his expensive cardigan, like an official spokesman from the State Department.

Fima stood at the door for a couple of minutes without pressing the bell. He rubbed his soles on the doormat so he wouldn't bring any mud into the flat. While he was in the middle of this ball-less game of football the door opened, and Ted helped him out of his overcoat, which had been turned into a snare by the rip in the lining.

'What foul weather,' Fima said.

Ted asked if it was raining outside.

Even though it had stopped before he left the clinic, Fima replied pathetically: 'Raining? A deluge, more like.'

Without waiting to be asked, he advanced straight into Ted's study, leaving a trail of damp footprints across the hall. He proceeded steadily between piles of books, diagrams, sketches, and printouts on the floor until his progress was blocked by the massive desk on which stood Ted's word processor. He peered without permission at a mysterious green-and-black graph that was flickering on the screen. Joking about his hopelessness with computers, he began to urge Ted politely, as if he himself were the host and the other the guest: 'Sit down, Teddy, sit down; make yourself at home.' And without hesitating he grabbed the office chair in front of the computer screen.

Ted asked what he would like to drink. Fima answered:

'Anything. A glass of water. Don't waste any time. Or some brandy. Or else something hot. It really doesn't matter. I've only dropped in for a moment anyway.'

With his broad, slow accent, with the dryness of a telephone operator, without a question mark at the end of any of his sentences, Ted stated:

'OK. I'll get you a brandy. And you're sure, positive, you've had some supper.'

Fima had a sudden urge to lie, to say no, though actually he was dying of hunger. But he chose to restrain himself.

Ted, in the rocking chair, swathed himself in silence and tobacco smoke. Despite himself, Fima enjoyed the smell of the fine pipe tobacco. And he noticed that Ted was observing him calmly, with a faintly anthropological curiosity. He looked as though he would not raise an eyebrow if his guest suddenly burst out singing. Or crying. Instead of doing either, Fima remarked:

'So Yael's out and so is Dimi. I forgot to bring some chocolate for him.'

'Right,' said Ted, stifling a yawn. And he exhaled another cloud of pleasant blue smoke.

Fima fixed his eyes on the pile of computerised plans, flicked through them as though they were his own, and made a special point of comparing pages six and nine, as though he had just made the decision to qualify, instantly, as an aeronautical engineer himself.

'And what are you concocting for us here? A spacecraft that fires rubber bullets? Or a flying gravel gun?'

'It's a paper we're writing for a British journal. Something quite experimental, actually: jet-propelled vehicles. As you probably know, Yael and I have been working on that for quite a few years now. You've asked me several times to explain it to you, but after a couple of minutes you always beg me to stop. I'm committed to finishing this paper by the weekend. There's a deadline. Can't you teach me the Hebrew for "committed" and "deadline", by the way? You must know, being a poet. Don't you?'

Fima, straining his brain, almost managed to remember the Hebrew equivalents of the two English words Ted had used.

They seemed to be sniggering at him from the threshold of his memory, slipping between his fingers like playful kittens just when he had almost caught them. Then he remembered, and opened his mouth to reply, but they escaped from under his tongue and vanished again into the darkness. Embarrassed, he said:

'Can I do anything to help?'

'Thanks, Fima,' Ted replied. 'I don't think there's any need. But surely you'd be more comfortable waiting in the living room till they get back? You can watch the news.'

'Let me have Dimi's Lego,' said Fima. 'I'll make him David's Tower. Or Rachel's Tomb. Or whatever. I won't disturb you while you do your work.'

'No problem,' said Ted.

'What do you mean, no problem! I came here to see you!'

'So, talk,' said Ted. 'Has anything happened?'

'It's like this,' Fima began, without the faintest idea how he was going to continue. To his astonishment he heard himself saying: 'You know that the situation in the Territories is intolerable.'

'That's the way it looks,' Ted said calmly, and at that moment Fima had a devastatingly vivid and precise mental image of this colourless bushy-eyebrowed jackass stroking Yael's naked body with his heavy hands, crouching on top of her, rubbing his penis between her small, firm breasts with a laborious, unvarying rhythm, like someone sawing a plank. Until Yael's eyes filled with tears and suddenly Fima's did too, and he hastily buried his nose in a grubby handkerchief, which, as he extracted it from his pocket, dislodged yet another note, a twenty-shekel one this time, presumably either the change from the restaurant near Zion Square or a previous offering from his father.

Ted picked up the note and handed it to Fima. Then he tamped down his pipe and relit it, spreading a fine screen that Fima wanted to hate but found himself enjoying.

'So,' said Ted, 'you were talking about the situation in the Territories. It sure is complicated.'

'What the hell do you mean, the situation in the Territories,' Fima exploded. 'That's just another brand of self-delusion. I

42

wasn't talking about the situation in the Territories; I was talking about the situation right here in Israel. Inside the Green Line. Inside Israeli society. The Territories are nothing but the dark side of ourselves. What happens there every day is just a concretisation of the process of degeneration we have been undergoing since the Six Days' War. If not before. If not from the beginning. Yes, every morning we read our papers, all day long we listen to the news, every evening we watch *What's New*, we sigh, we tell each other it simply can't go on, we sign petitions now and then, but in fact we do nothing. Zero. Zilch.'

'Right,' said Ted, and after consideration, after tamping and relighting again, slowly and intently, he added mildly: 'Yael does voluntary work twice a week at the Council for the Advancement of Tolerance. But they say there's going to be a split in the Council.' And he added, uncertain of the meaning of the Hebrew word, 'What do you mean by "petition"?'

'Petition?' Fima replied. 'A scrap of paper. Masturbation.' He was so enraged that he thumped the keyboard of the word processor accidentally with his fist.

'Hey, watch out,' Ted said. 'If you break my computer, that won't help the Arabs.'

'Who the hell's talking about helping the Arabs?' Fima erupted in an injured roar. 'I'm talking about helping ourselves. . . . It's just them, the nuts, the right, who say we're helping the Arabs!'

'I don't get it,' said Ted, scratching his tousled hair in a kind of overacted portrayal of someone who is slow on the uptake. 'Do you mean that we're not trying to improve the Arabs' living conditions?'

So Fima started from square one, suppressing his anger with difficulty. He explained in simple Hebrew his view of the tactical and psychological factors that made the moderate left appear to the masses to be identifying itself with the enemy. He fumed at himself again for using that wretched expression 'the masses'. In the course of his lecture he noticed that Ted was stealing sideways glances at the diagrams scattered on the rug, while his hairy finger kept tamping down the tobacco in his pipe. His wedding ring glinted on his finger.

Fima strove in vain to dispel the mental picture of that same finger prodding with the selfsame motion at Yael's labia. He instantly fell prey to a suspicion that he was being lied to and deceived, that Yael was hiding from him in the bedroom, weeping silently, with shaking shoulders, stifling her tears in the pillow, as she sometimes wept in the middle of sex and as Dimi sometimes wept soundlessly when he became aware of injustice perpetrated against him or against one of his parents or Fima.

'In any civilised country,' Fima continued, unconsciously borrowing Dr Wahrhaftig's pet phrase, 'there would be a campaign of civil disobedience by now. A common front of workers and students would have forced the government to end the horror at once.'

'Let me get you another brandy, Fima. It'll calm you down.'

Fima feverishly downed the brandy in one gulp, tipping his head back the way Russians drink vodka in films. He could see a detailed image of this log with steel-wool eyebrows bringing Yael a glass of orange juice in bed on Saturday morning, and of her, drowsily, luxuriantly, with her eyes still half-closed, reaching out and stroking the opening of his pyjamas, which were doubtless made of real silk. The image aroused in Fima not jealousy or rage or fury but, to his astonishment, profound pity for this diligent, upright man, who made one think of a beast of burden, working day and night at his computer, searching for a way to perfect the jet propulsion of vehicles, and with barely a single friend in the whole of Jerusalem.

'The saddest thing,' Fima said, 'is the way the left is paralysed.'

Ted said: 'True. You're quite right. It was much the same with us at the time of Vietnam. Coffee?'

Fima followed him to the kitchen and continued heatedly:

'The comparison with Vietnam, that's our biggest mistake, Teddy. This is not Vietnam and we're not the flower people. The second mistake is to expect the Americans to do the job for us and get us out of the Territories. What do they care if we're going to the devil?'

'True,' said Ted, in the tone he used for praising Dimi for getting his sums right. 'Too right. Nobody does anybody else any favours. Everyone looks after himself. And they don't always even have enough sense for that.' He put the kettle on and started emptying the dishwasher.

Fima excitedly pushed Ted out of the way and started to help him unbidden, as though bent on proving him wrong. He pulled a large handful of knives, forks, and spoons out of the dishwasher and ran around the kitchen with them, flinging doors open, pulling out drawers, looking for somewhere to unload his booty, and not interrupting for a moment his lecture on the difference between Vietnam and Gaza and between the Nixon syndrome and the Shamir syndrome. A few stray items of cutlery slipped through his fingers and lay scattered on the kitchen floor. Ted bent down to pick them up, and expressed his unfamiliarity with the Hebrew word for 'syndrome': was it a newly invented word?

'Syndrome: like the Vietnam syndrome that you went through in the States.'

'Didn't you say a moment ago that the comparison with Vietnam was a mistake?'

'Yes. No. In a certain sense yes. That is, perhaps we need to distinguish between a syndrome and a symptom.'

'Here,' said Ted, 'just put them here in the middle drawer.'

But Fima had already abandoned the struggle, and left his bundle of cutlery on top of the microwave. Pulling his handkerchief out of his pocket, he wiped his nose again and then absent-mindedly set about wiping the kitchen table too, while Ted was still sorting plates according to type and size and putting each pile away in its proper place in the cupboard over the sink.

'Fima, why don't you give that to the newspapers. You should publish it so that more people can read it. Your language is so rich. And it'll do your soul good too: anyone can see you're suffering. You take politics so personally. You take the situation too much to heart. Yael will be back with Dimi in another three-quarters of an hour. Now I've got to do some work. How do you say "deadline" in Hebrew again? Maybe the best thing would be if you took your coffee with you into the living room and I'll put the TV on for you; you can still catch about half the news. OK?'

Fima immediately assented: he had never intended to intrude for the whole evening. But instead of picking up his coffee and heading for the living room, he forgot the mug on the draining board in the kitchen and insisted on pursuing Ted all the way down the hallway until Ted excused himself and locked himself in the lavatory. Fima concluded his sentence through the locked door:

'It's all right for you; you've got American passports, you can always get out of here by jet propulsion. But what'll happen to the rest of us? OK. I'll go and watch the news. I won't pester you any more. The only trouble is, I don't know how to switch your television on.'

Instead of going to the living room, he turned into the boy's bedroom. Instantly he was overcome by great tiredness. Unable to find the light switch, he lay down in the dark on the little bed surrounded by shadows of robots and aeroplanes and time machines, while overhead a gigantic phosphorescent spaceship hovered, suspended from the ceiling by an invisible thread, its nose pointing straight at him, revolving slowly, menacingly at the slightest draught like an accusing finger. Until Fima closed his eyes and said to himself suddenly:

'What's the point of all this talking? The die is cast, and what is done cannot be undone.'

Then sleep overtook him. Just as he was dropping off, he was vaguely aware of Ted covering him with a soft woollen blanket. Indistinctly he mumbled:

'The truth, Teddy? Just between the two of us? The Arabs have evidently realised that they can't throw us in the sea. The sad thing is, it's hard for Jews to live without someone wanting to throw them in the sea.'

Ted whispered:

'No. The situation really isn't looking too good.' And he went out.

Fima curled up inside the blanket. He meant to ask to be woken up the moment Yael got home. He was so tired that what came out was:

'Don't wake Yael.'

He slept for about twenty minutes, and when the phone rang in the next room, he reached out and knocked over one of Dimi's Lego towers. He tried to fold the blanket, but gave up because he was in a hurry to find Ted. He still had to explain what it was that had brought him here this evening. Instead of going to the study, he strayed into the bedroom, which was lit by a warm red night-light. He saw that the wide bed was ready for the night: two identical pillows, two dark-blue blankets encased in silky sheets, two bedside tables, each with an open book lying face down on it, and he buried his face and his whole head in Yael's nightdress. At once he pulled himself together and rushed out to look for his coat. He searched every room in the flat with a sleepwalker's thoroughness, but he found neither Ted nor his coat, even though he doggedly checked every lighted place. Finally he sank down onto a stool in the kitchen and looked around for the knives that he hadn't been able to find a place for earlier.

Ted Tobias emerged from the darkness with a slide rule in his hand, and announced slowly and emphatically, like a soldier transmitting a message by shortwave radio:

'You fell asleep for a while. Shows you were tired. I can warm your coffee in the microwave.'

'No need, thanks,' said Fima. 'I've got to run; I'm late.'

'Oh. Late. What for?'

'A date,' said Fima, to his own surprise, in a man-to-man voice. 'I completely forgot I have a date tonight.' And he went to the front door and started wrestling with the latch until Ted took pity on him and handed him his overcoat, opened the door, and said softly and, Fima thought, rather wistfully:

'Look, Fima, it's none of my business, but I think you could do with a break. You're looking a little run down. What'll I tell Yael?'

Fima inserted his left arm into the torn lining of his coat sleeve and wondered why the sleeve had turned into a cul-de-sac. He lost his temper, as though Ted was responsible for upsetting the insides of his coat.

'Don't say anything to Yael,' he hissed. 'There's nothing to say. I didn't come to see her, anyway. I came to talk to you, Teddy, but you're such a numbskull.'

47

Ted Tobias did not take offence. It is likely he didn't understand the last word. He answered carefully, in English:

'Wouldn't it be better if I called you a taxi?'

Fima immediately felt profound shame and regret.

'Thanks, Teddy,' he said. 'No. I'm sorry I flew off the handle. I had a bad dream last night, and today just hasn't been my day. All I've done is kept you from working. Tell Yael I'm free to look after the kid any evening you need me. I can tell you the Hebrew word for "commitment" but I can't think of the one for "deadline". Maybe you can translate it literally, a dead line. By the way, what do we need jet-propelled vehicles for? Don't we rush around enough as it is? Why don't you invent something that'll make us just sit quietly? Sorry. Bye, Teddy. You shouldn't have given me that brandy. I talk enough nonsense as it is.'

As he stepped out of the lift he bumped into Yael in the dark. She was carrying Dimi, fast asleep, wrapped in her bomber jacket. Yael let out a little cry of alarm, and almost dropped the child. Then, recognising Fima, she said in a tired voice: 'What an ass you are.'

Instead of apologising, Fima embraced them roughly with his free arm and his crippled sleeve, and covered the drowsy Challenger's head with frantic pecks, like a starving chicken. He kissed Yael too, whatever he could lay hold of in the dark: not finding her face, he bent over and kissed her wet back, wildly, from shoulder to shoulder. Then he rushed outside to look for the bus stop in the dark in the pouring rain. Because in the meantime his prophecy had come true, when he said to Ted, 'Raining? A deluge, more like.' And at once he was soaked to the skin.

6

As if she were his sister

AND in fact he did end up having a kind of date that evening. Soon after half past ten, frozen and drenched, with his shoes oozing water, he rang the bell at the Gefens' garden gate. They lived in a secretive, thick-walled stone house in the German Colony, surrounded by old pines, set deep inside a large plot protected by a stone wall.

'I was just passing and I saw a light on,' he explained hesitantly to Nina, 'so I decided to bother you for a minute or two. Just long enough to collect that book about Leibowitz from Uri and to tell him that on second thoughts we were both right about the Iran-Iraq War. Should I come back another time?'

Nina chuckled, grabbed his arm, and tugged him indoors.

'But Uri's in Rome,' she said. 'You phoned yourself on Saturday night to say good-bye to him, and you gave him a whole lecture on the telephone about why it would be better for us if Iraq defeated Iran. Just look at you: what a sight! And am I really supposed to believe that you just happened to be strolling down our road at eleven o'clock at night? Whatever will become of you, Fima?'

'I had a date,' he muttered, struggling to disentangle himself from his dripping overcoat. He explained:

'The sleeve's stuck.'

Nina said:

'Sit yourself down here by the heater. You've got to get dry. I don't suppose you've eaten anything either. I was thinking about you today.'

'I was thinking about you too. I wanted to try to tempt you into coming to a film with me, to see a comedy with Jean Gabin at the Orion. I called you but there was no answer.'

'I thought you had a date. I got held up at the office till nine. An importer of sex aids has gone broke and I'm liquidating him. The creditors are a pair of ultra-pious brothers-in-law. You can imagine how funny that is. I hardly need Jean Gabin. Never mind. Come on, get those clothes off; you look like a drowned cat. Wait! Have a shot of Scotch first. It's a pity you can't see yourself. Then I'll get you something to eat.'

'What was it that made you think of me today?'

'Your article in Friday's paper. It was OK. Possibly a touch too hysterical. I don't know if I'm supposed to tell you this, but Tsvi Kropotkin is secretly scheming to get a search party to break into your flat, ransack your drawers, and publish the poems he's convinced you're still writing. So you won't be completely forgotten. Who did you have a date with, a mermaid? Even your underwear's soaked.'

Fima, who had stripped down to his long johns and a yellowing winter undershirt, laughed.

'As far as I'm concerned, they can forget me. I've already forgotten myself. What, take the underwear off too? Why, are you still liquidating your sex boutique? Are you planning to hand me over to your ultra creditors?'

Nina was a lawyer, a friend and contemporary of Yael, a chain-smoker of Nelson cigarettes, and her glasses gave her a bitter look. Her thin, greying hair was severely cropped. She was small and skinny, like an underfed vixen. And her triangular face reminded Fima of a cornered vixen. But her breasts were full and appealing, and she had beautifully shaped hands, like those of a young girl from the Far East. She handed him a bundle of Uri's clothes, freshly ironed and clean-smelling.

'Put these on,' she ordered. 'And drink this. And come and sit by the fire. Try not to talk for a few minutes. Iraq is winning the war without your help. I'll make you an omelette and a salad. Or shall I warm you some soup?'

'Don't make me anything,' Fima said, 'I'm leaving in five minutes.'

'Got another date, have you?'

'I left the lights on in my flat this morning. And anyway . . .'

'I'll run you home,' Nina said. 'After you've dried out and warmed up and had something to eat.'

'Yael called,' she added. 'She told me you haven't eaten. She said you've been pestering Teddy. You're the Eugene Onegin of Kiryat Yovel. Quiet now. Don't say anything.'

Uri Gefen, Nina's husband, was once a famous combat pilot, and later became a pilot with El Al. In 1971 he went into private business, starting a complex network of importers. He had a reputation in Jerusalem as a hunter of married women. The whole city knew that Nina had reconciled herself to his adventures, and that for several years their marriage had been purely platonic. Sometimes Uri's lovers ended up as Nina's friends. Uri and Nina had no children, but their charming home had become the regular Friday-evening rendezvous of a group of lawyers, army officers, civil servants, artists, and university lecturers. Fima was fond of them both, because both of them, in their different ways, had taken him under their wings. He was indiscriminately fond of anyone who could put up with him, and he had an unbounded affection for that circle of dear friends who still continued to have faith in him and endeavoured to spur him on, lamenting how he frittered away his talents.

On the sideboard, the mantelpiece, and the bookshelves stood photographs of Uri in or out of uniform. He was a large, stocky, rumbustious man, who exuded a rough physical affection that gave women and children and even men a cuddly feeling about him. Facially he bore a faint resemblance to Anthony Quinn. His manner was always coarsely hearty. He had a habit of touching people he was talking to, men and women alike, prodding you in the stomach, putting an arm around your shoulder, or resting a large freckled hand on your knee. When the spirit moved him, he could reduce a roomful of people to tears of laughter by mimicking the intonation of a stallholder in the central market, impersonating Abba Eban addressing an audience of immigrants in a transit camp, or casually analysing the impact of an article of Fima's about Albert Camus. Sometimes he would offer frank revelations, in the company of friends and in his wife's presence, about his own conquests. He spoke cheerfully, tastefully, without making fun of his lovers or revealing their identities, never boasting, recounting the progress of a romance with wistful good humour, like someone who has long since learned how intimately love and ridicule are interwoven; how both seducer and his victim are guided by fixed rituals; how absurdly childlike was his own indefatigable urge to conquer, in which carnal needs played only a minute part; how lies, mannerisms, and pretences are woven into the very fabric even of true love; and how the passing years deprive us all of the power of thrilling and the power of longing alike, as everything wears out and fades. He himself figured in this Friday-night Decameron in a faintly ludicrous light, as though Uri Gefen the narrator were examining Uri Gefen the lover under a microscope, dispassionately isolating the comic element. Sometimes he would say, By the time you begin to make sense of something, your term of office is over. Or, There's a Bulgarian proverb: The main thing an old cat remembers is how to meow.

It was in Uri's presence, rather than in Nina's arms, that Fima always felt a dizzying sensual exhilaration. Uri aroused in him an overwhelming urge to impress or even shock this magnificent male. To get the better of him in an argument. To experience that powerful hand grasping his elbow. But Fima did not always manage to get the better of him, because Uri too was endowed with a penetrating intellect, no less penetrating than Fima's own. And they had in common the tendency to switch easily, almost offhand, from ridicule to tragic empathy and back again, and to demolish with a couple of sentences an argument they had taken a quarter of an hour to build up.

During those Friday nights at Uri and Nina's, Fima was at his best. Whenever he got going, he could enthrall and entertain into the early hours of the morning with a series of motley paradoxes, amaze with his political analysis, and produce laughter or excitement.

'There's only one Fima,' Uri would say with paternal affection.

And Fima for his part would finish the sentence for him.

'. . . and that's one too many.'

Nina would say:

'Just look at the pair of them. Romeo and Julius. Or, rather, Laurel and Hardy.'

Fima didn't doubt that Uri had known for a long time about his occasional sex with Nina. Perhaps he found it entertaining. Or touching. Perhaps right from the word go he had been the author, director, and producer of that little comedy. Sometimes Fima imagined Uri Gefen getting up in the morning, shaving with a classy razor, sitting down to breakfast with a clean white napkin on his lap, glancing at his pocket diary, noticing the little twice-monthly cross, and remarking to Nina as he drank his coffee, hidden behind his newspaper, that it was time to give Fima his regular service, to make sure he didn't dry up completely. This suspicion did not detract from his affection for Uri or from the physical pleasure and euphoria he always experienced in the company of his charismatic friend.

Every few weeks Nina would appear without warning at ten or eleven in the morning, having parked her dusty Fiat in front of the squat block of flats in Kiryat Yovel. She would be carrying two baskets full of food and cleaning materials bought on her way from the office. She would look like a social worker boldly taking her life in her hands as she entered the front lines of deprivation. After coffee she would stand up and remove her clothes purposefully, almost without a word. They would have sex hurriedly and get up the moment it was finished, like a couple of soldiers in a trench hastily consuming food between bouts of shelling.

Immediately after the lovemaking Nina would shut herself in the bathroom. After scrubbing her skinny body, she would proceed, as a sort of followthrough, to scrub the lavatory and the wash basin. Only then would they sit down to have another cup of coffee and chat about poetry engagé or the coalition of national unity, with Nina chain-smoking and Fima gulping down one slice of black bread and jam after another. He could never resist the strong warm black bread she brought him from a Georgian bakery.

Fima's kitchen always looked as though it had been abandoned in haste. Empty bottles and eggshells under the sink, open jars on

the worktop, blotches of congealed jam, half-eaten yogurts, cur-
dled milk, crumbs, and sticky stains on the table. Sometimes
Nina, smitten with missionary fervour, rolled up one sleeve, put
on rubber gloves, and with a lighted cigarette protruding from
the corner of her mouth and seemingly glued to her lower lip,
would set upon cupboards, fridge surfaces, and tiles. In half an
hour she could transform Calcutta into Zurich. During this combat, Fima would lounge in the doorway, redundant yet willing,
debating with Nina and himself the collapse of Communism or
the school of thought that rejects Chomsky's linguistic theories.
When she went on her way, he would be overcome with a mixture of shame, affection, longing, and gratitude; he wanted to
run after her with tears in his eyes, to say Thank you, my
beloved, to say I am not worthy of these favours, but then he
would pull himself together and hurriedly throw open the windows to expel the cigarette smoke that polluted his kitchen. He
had a vague fantasy of lying ill in bed while Nina tended him, or
else of Nina on her deathbed and himself wetting her lips and
wiping the perspiration from her brow.

Within ten minutes of coming in out of the rain, Fima was sitting in Uri's ingenious armchair, which Fima described as 'a
cross between a hammock and a lullaby'. Nina served him a
bowl of steaming, well-seasoned pea soup, refilled his whisky
glass, and gave him a shirt, trousers and red sweater of Uri's that
were too big for him but felt good nevertheless. She encased his
feet in a pair of furry slippers that Uri had brought back from
Portugal. His own clothes she hung up to dry on a chair in front
of the fire. They talked about recent Latin-American literature,
about magical realism, which Nina saw as a continuation of the
tradition of Kafka, whereas Fima tended to attribute it to a vul-
garisation of the heritage of Cervantes and Lope de Vega, and he
managed to annoy Nina by stating that, for his money, he would
give the whole of this South American circus, with all its fireworks and candy floss for a single page of Chekhov. *A Hundred
Years of Solitude* for just one *Lady with the Little Dog*.

Nina lit another cigarette and said:

'Paradoxes. OK. But what's going to become of you?'

And she added:

'When are you going to take yourself in hand? When are you going to stop running away?'

Fima said:

'I've noticed at least two signs lately that Shamir is beginning to realise that without the PLO it won't work.'

And Nina, through her thick lenses and the cigarette haze:

'Sometimes I think you're a lost cause.'

To which Fima riposted:

'Aren't we all, Nina?'

At that moment he felt as affectionate and tender towards the person sitting opposite him, dressed in a well-worn pair of men's jeans with a zip fly and a wide-cut man's shirt, as if she were his sister, his own flesh and blood. Her lack of prettiness and femininity suddenly struck him as painfully feminine and attractive. Her large soft breasts cried out to him to lay his head between them. Her short grey hair drew his fingertips. And he knew precisely how to wipe that hunted vixen look off her face and replace it with the her pampered little girl expression. At this his organ began to stir deep down inside Uri's trousers. With Fima, kindness, generosity, compassion for a woman always heralded the stirrings of lust. His loins were on fire with a desire that was close to pain: it was two months since he had slept with a woman. The smell of damp wool that he had sniffed on Yael when he kissed her back in the dark entrance to her building was blended now with the smell of his clothes drying in front of the fire. His breathing quickened, and his lips parted and quivered. Like a child's. Nina noticed, and said:

'Just a minute, Fima. Let me finish my cigarette. Give me another moment or two.'

But Fima, bashful yet burning with lust and pity, ignored this, knelt in front of her, and tugged at her leg until he succeeded in dragging her down to join him on the rug. A clumsy tussle with his clothes and hers ensued by the table legs. With some difficulty he disposed of her lighted cigarette and spectacles, while he rubbed uninterruptedly against her thigh and smothered her face with kisses as if to distract her attention from the ever more furious friction. Until she managed to push him away and release both of them from their clothes, whispering, 'Gently, Fima: you're eating me alive.' But, heedless, he lay on top of her with all his weight, still kissing her face, still whispering entreaties and stammering excuses. When she finally relented and said, 'All right, come on then,' his organ suddenly shrivelled. It withdrew into the recesses of its lair like a startled tortoise.

Even so, he did not stop kissing and hugging and apologising for his tiredness; he had had a bad dream last night, and this evening Ted had thrown him out after making him drink brandy, and now the Scotch. It seemed as though today really wasn't his day.

Two tears appeared in the corners of Nina's short-sighted eyes. Without her glasses, she looked frail and dreamy, as though her face were much more naked than her body. They lay for a long while, holding each other tight. Humiliated, and bound together by their humiliation. Until she broke loose, groped for a cigarette, lit it, and tried to say 'Never mind, child,' and tried to make him understand that at this moment he was reaching deeper inside her than he could by screwing. Again she called him 'child', and said, Come and have a wash, and let's put you to bed.

Fima, consoled and elegiac, laid his head in the hollow of her shoulder but pushed her glasses away, because he was ashamed of their naked bodies, ashamed of his shrunken member, wanting only to cuddle up to her, not to see and not to be seen. Close and silent, they lay sprawled on the rug in the dying firelight, listening to the raging wind and the rain beating against the windows and the gurgling of the water in the drainpipe, both of them soft and satisfied, as though they had made love tenderly and given each other pleasure. Suddenly Fima saw fit to ask:

'What do you think, Nina: have Yael and Uri had it off?'

The spell was broken. Nina pulled sharply away from his embrace, grabbed her spectacles, wrapped the tablecloth around herself, abruptly lit another Nelson, and said:

'Tell me, why is it you can never keep your mouth shut for five minutes on end?'

Then he asked her what it was exactly she had liked about his article in Friday's paper.

Nina said:

'Wait.'

He heard a door slam. A moment later came the sound of rushing water as the bath filled. He rummaged in his heap of clothes, searching all the pockets for his heartburn tablets. Self-mockingly he repeated Ted's words:

'You're looking a bit run down.'

And Yael's:

'What an ass you are.'

When Nina emerged twenty minutes later, scrubbed and scented, in a brown bathrobe, eager to make up, she found her husband's clothes scattered on the floor, the fire dying, and the furry slippers Uri bought in Portugal lying like dead kittens by the door. Fima had vanished. But she noticed he had finished his drink and forgotten the book about Leibowitz and also one of his socks, hanging on the back of a chair in front of the fire, which flickered for a moment with its last remaining strength then expired. Nina picked up the clothes and slippers, cleared away the glass, soup bowl, and sock, and straightened a corner of the rug. Her thin, well-shaped fingers, like those of a pretty Chinese child, groped for a cigarette. She was smiling through her tears.

7

With thin fists

A T A quarter past six in the morning he wrote down in his brown dream book what he had seen in the night. A coffee-table book about Jerusalem in Hebrew poetry resting slantwise on his raised knees served as a writing desk. He wrote the date, as always, in words, not in figures.

In the dream, war had broken out. The setting resembled the Golan Heights, only more barren. Like a moonscape. Dressed in military uniform but without belt or gun, he was walking along a deserted dirt track, both sides of which, he knew, were lined with minefields. He particularly remembered that the air was very close and grey, as though a storm were approaching. Far in the distance a bell tolled slowly, with long pauses between strokes, the sound echoing through invisible valleys. There was no other soul. Not so much as a bird. And no sign of human habitation. We had been caught off guard again. An enemy armoured column was steadily approaching a narrow mountain pass, a sort of ravine that Fima could make out farther up the road, where the rugged heights began. He realised that the greyness in the air was the dust rising from their tracks. He also began to hear dimly, behind the clanging of the bell, a low rumble of engines. Somehow he knew that his appointed task was to wait for them in the ravine at the point where the road crossed the mountains. To delay them by talking to them until reinforcements could be brought up to block the canyon. He started to run as hard as he could. He was panting heavily. The blood throbbed in his temples. His lungs ached. He had a stitch in his side. Although he was exerting his muscles to the utmost, he was hardly moving at all, he was almost running on the spot, and all the while he was frantically searching for words he could use to delay the enemy. He simply had to find something, a phrase, an idea, a message, perhaps even something funny, words that would make the armoured column that was advancing towards him stop, make heads emerge from turrets to listen to him. If he could not change their hearts, at least he must gain time. Without which there was no hope. But his strength was failing and his feet were stumbling and his head was empty of ideas. Not a word passed through his mind. The rumble of engines was getting closer, louder; he could already hear the thunder of guns and the barking of machine guns behind a bend in the road. And he could see flashes inside the cloud of smoke or dust that filled the ravine and filled his eyes and made his throat burn. He was too late. He would never make it in time. There were no words in the world that could hold back the mad bull charging towards him. In a moment or two he would be flattened. And the most terrible thing was not the fear; it was the shame of failure, of being at a loss for words. His crazed running slowed and turned to a shambling gait, because a heavy weight had settled on his shoulders. When he managed to turn his head, he discovered that there was a child riding him, pommelling his head with vicious thin fists, and forcing his head between his knees. Until he began to choke.

Fima also noted in his book:

'My bedclothes smell. I ought to take a bundle of washing to the laundry today. Yet there was something: I was left with a longing for those barren mountains and the weird light, and especially for the tolling of the bell that echoed in the deserted valleys with very long pauses between the strokes, and seemed to be coming to me from an unimaginable distance.'

8

A disagreement on the question of who the Indians really are

AT TEN o'clock in the morning, as he was standing at the window counting the raindrops, he saw Baruch Nomberg taking his leave of the taxi driver. Fima's father was a dapper old man in a suit and bow tie, with a pointed white beard that curved upward like a Saracen scimitar. At the age of eighty-two he still kept a firm hold of the reins of the cosmetics factory he had set up in the thirties.

His father was bending over the window of the taxi, apparently lecturing the driver, with his white hair waving in the breeze, his hat in his left hand and his carved stick with the silver band in the other. Fima knew that the old man was not haggling about the fare or waiting for his change; he was finishing an anecdote he had started telling on the way. For fifty years now he had been conducting an extended seminar with Jerusalem taxi drivers on Hasidic tales and pious stories. He was a dedicated storyteller. And he had a fixed habit of commenting on every anecdote and pointing up the moral lesson. Whenever he told a joke, he would follow it by explaining what the point was. Sometimes he would carry on and explain both the apparent point and the real point. His commentaries always made his listeners laugh, which encouraged the old man to tell more stories and explain them too. He was convinced that the point of the stories had escaped everybody, and that it was his duty to open their eyes.

As a young man Baruch Nomberg had fled from the Bolsheviks in Kharkov and studied chemistry in Prague, then he had come to Jerusalem and started producing lipsticks and face powders in a small domestic laboratory. From these small beginnings a

60

successful cosmetics factory had developed. He was a flirtatious, garrulous old man. A widower for several decades now, he was always surrounded by female friends and companions. Jerusalem gossip had it that they were attracted to him only for his money. Fima thought otherwise: he considered his father, for all his bluster, a good and generous man. All these years it had been his habit to lend his financial support to any cause he found deserving or moving. He was a member of endless committees, councils, societies, associations, and groups. He was a regular participant in fundraising campaigns for the homeless, for the absorption of immigrants, for people in need of complex surgical operations abroad, for land purchase in the Occupied Territories, for the production of commemorative volumes, for the restoration of historic ruins, for the creation of homes for abandoned children and shelters for battered wives. He volunteered his support for needy artists, for the ending of experiments on laboratory animals, for the purchase of wheelchairs, and for the prevention of pollution. He saw no contradiction in backing traditional values in education while also funding a campaign for the prevention of religious coercion. He dispensed grants to students from minority groups, to victims of violent crime, and also for the rehabilitation of the violent criminals. In each of these initiatives the old man committed modest sums, but together they apparently consumed about half of the total income yielded by the cosmetics factory, as well as the greater part of his time. In addition, he had a passion verging on addiction for anything to do with contracts and small print. Whenever he had to purchase new chemicals or dispose of used equipment, he would engage a veritable battery of lawyers, consultants, and accountants in order to block every conceivable loophole. Legal agreements, notarial ultimatums, copies of initialled memorandums would excite in him a thrill of the game that almost bordered on artistic fulfilment.

He spent his spare time in the company of women. Even now that he was over eighty, he still loved sitting in cafés. Summer and winter alike he wore a formal suit and bow tie, with a triangle of gleaming white silk protruding from his breast pocket like a snowflake in a heat wave, with silver cuff links, a jewelled ring flashing on his little finger, his white beard sticking out in front like a wagging finger, his carved stick with the silver band parked between his knees, and his hat on the table in front of him. A pink old man, scrubbed and polished, he was invariably accompanied by an elegant divorcée or a well-preserved widow, always cultured European women with refined manners in their late fifties or early sixties. He would sometimes sit at his usual table in the café with two or three of them. He would order them espresso and strudel, while he normally had a liqueur and a dish of fresh fruit in front of him.

As the taxi drove off, the old man waved it good-bye with his hat, following his invariable habit. Being a sentimental person, he treated every farewell as final. Fima went out to meet him. He could almost hear him humming a Hasidic folk tune to himself as he climbed the stairs. Whenever he was alone, and even sometimes when he was being spoken to, the old man would be constantly intoning the characteristic ya-ba-bam. Fima sometimes wondered whether he did it in his sleep too: like a musical liquid welling up from some invisible hot spring, overflowing his father's shrunken body, or seeping out through the tiny cracks caused by old age. Fima could also almost sniff his father's special smell wafting up the stairs, that smell that he remembered from his infancy and could identify even in a roomful of strangers: the scent of airless rooms, old furniture, steaming fish stew and boiled carrots, feather beds, and sticky liqueur.

As father and son exchanged a perfunctory embrace, this Eastern European aroma aroused in Fima a revulsion mixed with shame at the revulsion, together with the long-standing urge to pick a quarrel with his father, to trample on some sacrosanct principle of his, to disclose the irritating contradictions in his views, to exasperate him a little.

'Nu,' the old man began, panting and wheezing from the exertion of his climb, 'so what does my esteemed professor have to report to me today? Has the Redeemer come unto Zion? Have the Arabs had a change of heart and made up their minds to love us?'

'Hello, Baruch.' Fima contained himself.

'Right. Hello, my dear.'

'What's new? Is your back still bothering you?'

'My back?' said the old man. 'Fortunately my back is doomed to be forever behind me. I am here, it is there; it will never overtake me. And if, God forbid, it ever does, why, I'll simply turn my back on it. But my breath is getting shorter. Like my temper. And here the roles are reversed: It is not chasing me; I am chasing it. So, what is Herr Efraim busying himself with in these awesome days? Still bent upon setting the world to rights in readiness for the Kingdom of God?'

'There's nothing new,' said Fima, and, taking his father's stick and hat, he saw fit to add:

'Except that the country's going to the dogs.'

The old man shrugged. 'I've been hearing such obituaries for fifty years already – the country this, the country that – and in the meantime the obituarists are all six feet underground and the country is improving every day. For all your protestations: The more they afflict it, the more it flourishes. Don't interrupt me, Efraim. Let me tell you a charming little story. Once in Kharkov, before Lenin's revolution, a silly anarchist daubed a slogan on the wall of a church in the middle of the night: GOD IS DEAD SIGNED FRIEDRICH NIETZSCHE. He was alluding to the late demented philosopher. *Nu*. So, the next night someone more clever comes along and writes: FRIEDRICH NIETZSCHE IS DEAD SIGNED GOD. Wait a minute – I haven't finished yet. Kindly permit me to explain to you the point of this little story, and in the meantime why don't you put on the kettle and pour me a minuscule drop of that Cointreau I gave you last week. By the way, it's time you had this old ruin of yours redecorated, Fimuchka. Before the evil spirits take it over. Just call in a decorator and send me the bill. Where were we? Yes, tea. Your beloved Nietzsche is a noxious contagion. I wouldn't touch him with a barge pole. Here, I'll tell you a true story about Nietzsche and Nachman Krochmal when they met once on the train to Vienna.'

As usual, his father insisted on adding an explanation of the point of the story. Fima laughed: unlike the story, the explanation was amusing. His father, delighted by Fima's reaction, was encouraged to offer him a further anecdote concerning a train journey, this time about a honeymoon couple who found themselves compelled to seek the assistance of the guard. 'And you do see, don't you, Efraim, that the real point is not the bride's behaviour, but the bridegroom's gormlessness. He was a real *shlemazel*.'

Fima recited to himself the words he had heard Dr Eitan say the day before: 'I'd hang the pair of them.'

'Do you know the difference between a *shlemiel* and a *shlemazel*, Efraim? The *shlemiel* spills his tea and it always lands on the *shlemazel*. That's what they say. But in reality, behind this joke there is something mysterious and quite profound. The *shlemiel* and the *shlemazel* are both immortal. Hand in hand they wander from country to country, from century to century, from story to story. Like Cain and Abel. Like Jacob and Esau. Like Raskolnikov and Svidrigailov. Or like Rabin and Peres. Or perhaps even, who knows, like God and Nietzsche. And while we're on the subject of trains, I'll tell you a true story. Once upon a time the director of our state railways went to take part in an international meeting of railway chiefs. A kind of *Konferenz*. Now the Lord opened the mouth of the ass, and our buffoon talked and talked; he simply wouldn't stop. He wouldn't get down from the podium. Until the American train chief had had enough. He raised his hand and asked our man, "With all due respect, excuse me, Mr Cohen, but just how many miles of track do you have in your country that you talk so much?" *Nu*, so our delegate doesn't lose his presence of mind; with the assistance of the Almighty, Who grants discernment even to the simple rooster, he says: "The length I don't rightly remember, Mr Smith, but the width is exactly the same as yours." By the way, I heard this story once told by a foolish fellow who got it wrong and said Russia instead of America. He spoiled the whole point of the story, because the Russian railways have a different gauge from ours; in fact, it's different from the whole of the rest of the world. No reason; just to be different. Or else so that if Napoleon Bonaparte comes back and tries to invade them again, he won't be able to take his wagons to Moscow. Where were we? Yes, the honeymoon couple. In fact, there's no reason why you shouldn't bestir yourself and wed some lovely lady. If you wish, I'll be delighted to help by finding the lady et cetera. But do get moving, my dear: after all, you're not a stripling any more, and as for me, *nu*, any day now the fateful tocsin will sound and I shall be no more. Baruch Nomberg is dead, signed God. The amusing thing in the story of the honeymoon couple is not the bridegroom having to ask the guard for instructions on how to handle a bride. No, sir. It's the association with punching tickets. Although, on second thoughts, tell me yourself; what's so funny about it? Is there really anything to laugh at? Aren't you ashamed of yourself for chuckling? It is really sad, even heartbreaking. Most jokes are actually based on the improper pleasure that we derive from the misfortunes of others. Now why is that, Fimuchka? Perhaps you can kindly explain to me, since you yourself are a historian, a poet, a thinker, why is it that other people's misfortunes make us feel good? Make us guffaw? Afford us this curious satisfaction? Man is a paradox, my dear. A very curious creature indeed. Exotic. He laughs when he ought to weep. He weeps when he ought to laugh. He lives without sense and he dies without desire. Frail man, his days are as the grass. Tell me, have you seen anything of Yael lately? No? And your little boy? You must remind me later on to tell you a marvellous story from Rabbi Elimelech of Lizensk, a parable of divorce and longing. He intended it to be a parable about the relationship between the community of Israel and the Divine Presence, but I have my own personal interpretation of it. But first of all tell me about your own life and doings. This is all wrong, Efraim: Here am I prattling on just like our dear railway chief, and you're saying nothing. Like the story about the cantor on the desert island. I'll tell you later. Don't let me forget. There was this cantor who found himself cast away on a desert island during the High Holy Days; it shouldn't happen to us! But there I go again, chatting away while you are silent. Say something. Tell me about Yael and that melancholy child. Just remind me to tell you afterwards about the cantor: after all, in a way we're all like cantors on a desert island, and in a sense all days are High Holy Days.'

Fima registered a faint, low, wheezing sound, almost like a cat's purring, coming from his father's chest with every breath. As though the old man had put a whistle in his throat as a joke.

'Drink your tea, Baruch. It's getting cold.'

The old man said:

'Did I ask you for tea, Efraim? I asked you to talk. I asked you to tell me about that forlorn child that you insist on pretending to everybody is the son of that American dummkopf. And I asked that you should put a little order in your life. That you should be a *mensh*. That you should worry about the future for a change instead of worrying night and day about your beloved Arabs.'

'I'm not,' Fima corrected him, 'worried about the Arabs. I've explained to you a thousand times. I'm worried about us.'

'Of course, Efraim, of course. Nobody can impugn the integrity of your motives. The sad thing is, the only people you manage to take in are yourselves. As though your Arabs are just asking nicely and politely if they can have Nablus and Hebron back, and then they'll go home happily ever after, peace be upon Israel and upon Ishmael. But that's not what they want from us. It's Jerusalem they want, Fimuchka, and Jaffa, and Haifa, and Ramla. To slit our throats a little bit, that's all they want. To wipe us out. If you only took the trouble to listen a little to what they say among themselves. The sad thing is, all you ever listen to is yourselves, yourselves, yourselves.' Another low, drawn-out whistle escaped from his father's chest, as though he were bewildered by his son's naïveté.

'Actually, they've been saying rather different things recently, Dad.'

'Saying. How very nice. Let them say to their heart's content. Saying is easy. They've simply learned from you the rules of how to speak nicely. Eloquence. Winning words. Superciliousness. It's not important what they say. What counts is what they really want. As that roughneck Ben Gurion used to say about Jews and gentiles.' Apparently the old man was about to expatiate on this theme, but he was overcome by breathlessness and let out a

66

wheeze that ended in a cough. As though inside him a loose door on squeaky hinges were being blown by the breeze.

'They want to find a compromise now, Baruch. And now we're the intransigent side that refuses to make concessions and won't even talk to them.'

'Compromise. Of course. Well spoken. There's nothing as fine as compromise. All life depends on it. Apropos, there's a wonderful story they tell about Rabbi Mendel of Kotsk. But who will you compromise with? With our sworn killers who long to destroy us? Now just you call me a taxi, so I won't be late, and while we're waiting for it, I'll tell you a true story about how Jabotinsky once met the antisemitic interior minister of tsarist Russia, Plehve. And d'ye know what Jabotinsky said to him?'

'It was Herzl, Dad. Not Jabotinsky.'

'It would be better for you, Mister Wise Guy, if you didn't take the names of Herzl and Jabotinsky in vain. Take your shoes off when you approach their hallowed ground. They must turn in their graves every time you and your friends open your mouths to pour scorn on Zionism.'

Fima, suddenly beside himself with fury, forgot his vow of self-restraint and almost gave in to the dark urge to pull his father's goatee or smash his untouched teacup. He exploded in a wounded roar:

'Baruch, you are blind and deaf. Open your eyes. We're the Cossacks now, and the Arabs are the victims of the pogroms, yes, every day, every hour.'

'The Cossacks,' his father remarked with amused indifference. 'Nu? What of it? So what's wrong with us being the Cossacks for a change? Where does it say in Holy Scripture that Jew and gentile are forbidden to swap jobs for a little while? Just once in a millennium or so? If only you yourself, my dear, were more of a Cossack and less of a shlemazel. Your child takes after you: a sheep in sheep's clothing.'

Having forgotten the beginning of their conversation, he explained all over again, while Fima furiously crushed matchsticks one after another, the difference between a *shlemiel* and a *shlemazel* and how they constituted an immortal pair, wandering hand in hand through the world. Then he reminded Fima that the Arabs have forty huge countries, from India to Abyssinia, whereas we have only one tiny country no bigger than a man's hand. He began telling off the names of the Arab states on his bony fingers. When he enumerated Iran and India among them, Fima could no longer endure in silence. He interrupted his father with a plaintive, self-righteous howl, stamped his foot, and exclaimed petulantly that Iran and India are not Arab states.

'Nu, so what? What difference does it make to you?' the old man intoned in a ritualistic singsong, with a sly, good-natured chortle. 'Have we managed at last to find a satisfactory solution to the tragic question of who is a Jew, that we need to start breaking our heads over the question of who is an Arab?'

Fima, in despair, leaped from his chair and rushed to the bookcase to fetch the encyclopaedia, hoping at last to silence his father forever with a crushing defeat. However, as in a nightmare, he could not for the life of him imagine in which article to start looking for a list of the Arab states. Or even which volume. He was still fuming and frantically pulling out one volume after another, when he suddenly noticed that his father had got to his feet, quietly humming a Hasidic melody, mingled with a slight dry cough, had picked up his hat and stick, and in the midst of taking his leave was furtively slipping a folded banknote into his son's trouser pocket.

'It's just not possible,' Fima muttered. 'I simply can't believe it. This isn't happening. It's crazy.'

But he did not attempt to explain what exactly was not happening, because his father, standing in the doorway, added:

'Nu, never mind. I give up. So forget about the Indians. Let's call it thirty-nine states and have done with it. Even that is more than enough and far more than they deserve. We must never let the Arabs come between us, Fimuchka. We won't give them that satisfaction. Love, so to speak, always overcomes discord. My taxi is probably waiting outside, and we mustn't stand between a man and his work. And we never got onto the real subject. Which is that my heart is weary. Soon, Fimuchka, I shall be going on my way, signed God Almighty. And then what will become of you, my dear? What will become of your tender son? Just think, Efraim. Apply your mind to it. After all, you are a thinker and a poet. Think carefully and tell me, please: Where are we all going? For my sins I have no other children. And you and yours, it seems, have nobody apart from me. The days go by with no purpose, no joy, and no profit. In fifty or a hundred years' time, there will doubtless be people still unborn in this room, a generation of mighty heroes, and the question of whether you and I once lived here or not, and if we did, what we lived for, and what we did with our lives, whether we were worthy or wicked, happy or miserable, and whether we did any good, will matter to them less than a grain of salt. They won't spare us a thought. They will simply be here, living their own lives, as if you and I and all the rest of us were no more than last year's snow. A handful of dust. You haven't got enough air to breathe here, either. And the air is stale. You don't just need a decorator, you need a whole army of workmen. Send me the bill. As for the Cossacks, Efraim, leave them be. What does a young man like you know about Cossacks? Instead of worrying your head about Cossacks, better you should stop squandering the rich treasure of life. Like a tamarisk in the wilderness. Farewell.'

Without waiting for Fima, who had intended to see him out, the old man waved his hat as though departing forever, and began to descend the stairs, hitting the banister railings rhythmically with his stick and humming a Hasidic melody under his breath.

9

'There are so many things we could talk about, compare . . .'

Fima still had a couple of hours left before he had to be at
work. He thought he would change the sheets, and while he
was at it his shirt and underwear and the teatowels and the bathroom towels, and drop the whole lot off at the laundry on his
way to the clinic. When he went into the kitchen to take the
towel off its hook, he saw that the sink was full of dirty dishes
and that there was a frying pan on the draining board with the
remains of a fry-up in it, while on the table the jam had congealed in a jar that had lost its lid. A rotting apple was attracting
swarms of flies on the windowsill. Fima gingerly picked it up between forefinger and thumb, as though it might be contagious,
and threw it in the bin under the overfull sink. But the bin was
overfull too. The infected apple rolled off the top of the heap and
managed to find itself a hiding place among the old canisters and
bottles of cleaning fluid. It could only be reached by getting
down on all fours. Fima made up his mind that this time there
would be no compromise, he would not give up as usual, he
would recapture the fugitive at all costs. If he succeeded,
he would take it as a green light, and he would maintain the
momentum by taking the bin downstairs to empty it. On the way
back he would remember to fish the newspaper and his post out
of the letter box at last. He would continue by washing up and
tidying the refrigerator, and at the risk of making himself late he
would even change the sheets.

But when he prostrated himself and started searching behind the
dustbin for the lost apple, he discovered half a roll, a greasy margarine wrapper, and the burned-out light bulb from yesterday's

power cut, which it suddenly dawned on him was probably not burned out after all. Suddenly a cockroach came strolling towards him, looking weary and indifferent. It did not try to escape. At once Fima was fired with the thrill of the chase. Still on his knees, he slipped off a shoe and brandished it, then repented as he recalled that it was just like this, with a hammer blow to the head, that Stalin's agents murdered the exiled Trotsky. And he was startled to discover the resemblance between Trotsky in his last pictures and his father, who had been here a moment before, begging him to marry. The shoe froze in his hand. He observed with astonishment the creature's feelers, which were describing slow semicircles. He saw masses of tiny stiff bristles, like a moustache. He studied the spindly legs seemingly full of joints. The delicate formation of the elongated wings. He was filled with awe at the precise, minute artistry of this creature, which no longer seemed abhorrent but wonderfully perfect: a representative of a hated race, persecuted and confined to the drains, excelling in the art of stubborn survival, agile and cunning in the dark; a race that had fallen victim to primeval loathing born of fear, of simple cruelty, of inherited prejudices. Could it be that it was precisely the evasiveness of this race, its humility and plainness, its powerful vitality, that aroused horror in us? Horror at the murderous instinct that its very presence excited in us? Horror because of the mysterious longevity of a creature that could neither sting nor bite and always kept its distance? Fima therefore retreated in respectful silence. He replaced his shoe on his foot, ignoring the rank smell of his sock. And he closed the door of the cupboard under the sink gently, so as not to alarm the creature. Then he straightened up with a grunt and decided to put off the household chores to another morning, because there were so many of them and they seemed unfairly burdensome.

He switched the electric kettle on to make himself a cup of coffee, turned the radio to the music programme, and managed to catch the beginning of Fauré's Requiem, whose tragic opening notes made him stare out of the window for a while in the direction of the Bethlehem hills. Those still unborn people his father had

71

mentioned, who a hundred years from now would live in this very flat without knowing anything about him or his life, would they really never feel any curiosity about who had lived here at the beginning of 1989? But why should they? Was there anything in his life that might be of use to people whose parents had not even been born yet? Something that might at least provide them with food for thought as they stood at this window on a winter's morning in the year 2089? No doubt in a hundred years' time jet-propelled vehicles would have become so commonplace that the people living here would have no special reason to remember Yael and Teddy, or Nina and Uri and their crowd, or Tamar and the two gynaecologists. Even Tsvi Kropotkin's historical research would probably be out of date by then. At most all that would remain of it would be a footnote in some obsolete tome. His envy of Tsvi seemed pointless, vain, and ridiculous. That envy that he obstinately denied, even to himself, and whose insidious nibbling he silenced with endless arguments, calling Tsvi up on the phone and slipping in a question, out of the blue, about the exiled king of Albania, entangling them in a bad-tempered argument about Albanian Islam or Balkan history. After all, in the BA exams Fima had had slightly better marks than his friend. And he was the one who had had certain brilliant insights that Tsvi had made use of, insisting despite Fima's protestations on acknowledging him in footnotes. If only he could overcome his tiredness. He still had it in him to leap ahead, make up the time lost in the billy-goat year, and in a couple of years overtake that spoiled, conventional professor, clad in his sporty blazer and whining out his bland truisms. Not a stone would be left standing of all Kropotkin's edifices. Fima would smash and flatten the lot like a hurricane. He would cause an earthquake and establish new foundations. But what was the point? At the very most some student at the end of the next century would refer in passing, in a parenthesis, to the outmoded approach of the Nisan-Kropotkin school which enjoyed a short-lived vogue in Jerusalem in the late twentieth century, in the declining phase of the socio-empiric period, which was marred by hyper-emotionalism and the use of clumsy intellectual tools. The student would not even take the trouble to distinguish between them. He would link them together with a hyphen before closing the brackets on the two of them.

The student, who would live in this flat a century from now, suddenly took on in Fima's mind the name Yoezer. He could see him in his mind's eye standing at this same window and staring out at those same hills. And he said to him: Don't you mock. It's thanks to us that you're here. Once there was a tree-planting ceremony in the city of Ramat Gan. The first mayor, the old man, Avraham Krinitzi, stood up in front of a thousand youngsters, from all the nursery schools, each one holding a sapling. The mayor too held a sapling. His task was to make a speech to the children, and he did not know what to say. Suddenly, out of the turmoil of his mind, a one-sentence speech burst forth, delivered with a heavy Russian accent: 'Moy dzear cheeldren, you are the trees, and we are the manure.' Would there be any point in carving that sentence here, on the wall, like a prisoner on the wall of his cell, for that arrogant Yoezer to read? To force him to think about us? But by then surely the walls will have been repainted, replastered, perhaps even rebuilt. In a hundred years life will be more vital, more vigorous, more reasonable, and more joyful. The wars with the Arabs will be remembered with a shrug, as a sort of absurd cycle of obscure tribal skirmishes. Like the history of the Balkans. I don't suppose Yoezer will waste his mornings hunting cockroaches or his evenings in grubby eating places behind Zion Square. Which will probably have been completely flattened and rebuilt in an energetic, optimistic style. Instead of eating greasy fried eggs, jam, and yogurt, they'll probably just swallow a couple of capsules every few hours. No more filthy kitchens, no more ants and cockroaches. People will be busy all day with useful, exciting things, and their evenings will be devoted to learning and beauty. They will live their lives in the bright light of reason, and if ever there are any stirrings of love, there will probably be some way of exchanging minute electromagnetic pulses from a distance to find out in advance whether there is any point trying to translate this love into physical intimacy. The winter rain will have been swept away from Jerusalem forever. It will be diverted to the agricultural regions. Everyone will be taken across safely to the Aryan side, as it were.

Nobody, nothing will smell bad. The word 'suffering' may sound to them the way the word 'alchemy' does to us.

We've had another power cut. The lights came on again after a couple of minutes. It's probably a hint to me that I ought to pop into the bank to pay my bill, otherwise they'll cut me off and leave me sitting in the dark. I owe the grocer a lot of money too. And did I pay Mrs Schneider across the road for her schnitzel yesterday, or did I sign for it again? I forgot to get that book for Dimi. What's holding us up? Why are we still here? Why aren't we getting up and clearing out, and leaving Jerusalem to those who will come after us? A very good question, he said under his breath.

This time he convened his cabinet in the old Sha'arei Zedek hospital on the Jaffa Road, a splendid abandoned building that had fallen into decay since the hospital was moved to a new site. By lamplight, among remnants of broken benches and pieces of rusting bedsteads, he arranged his ministers in a semicircle. He asked each of them in turn for a briefing on the situation in their various departments. Then he stunned them all by announcing that he intended to fly to Tunis at dawn to address the Palestine National Council. He would place the main burden of historic responsibility for the plight of the Palestinian Arabs fairly and squarely on the shoulders of their extremist leadership since the 1920s. He would not spare them our anger. However, he would offer to break out of the vicious circle of bloodshed and start building together a reasonable future based on compromise and conciliation. The only condition for starting to negotiate would be the total cessation of violence on both sides. At the close of the session, in the early hours, he appointed Uri Gefen minister of defence. Gad Eitan received the foreign-affairs portfolio. Tsvi would be responsible for education, Nina for finance, Wahrhaftig was put in charge of social welfare, and Ted and Yael would look after science, technology, and energy. Information and internal security he was retaining himself for the time being. And from now on the cabinet would be renamed the Revolutionary Council. The revolutionary process would be completed within six months. By then peace would be established. And immediately thereafter we can all return to our occupations and no longer interfere in the work of the elected government. I myself shall withdraw into total anonymity. I shall change my name and disappear. Now let us disperse separately by side entrances.

What about involving Dimi?

During the winter holidays the child spent a morning in the laboratory at the cosmetics factory in Romema. When Fima arrived to take him to the Biblical Zoo, he found that the old man had shut himself up in the lab with the child and taught him how to use acetone to manufacture explosives. Fima was furious with his father for corrupting the child: Haven't we got enough murderers already? Why poison his soul? But Dimi interrupted the argument by observing gently, like a mediator:

'Granpa's explosives are only for painting fingernails.'

And they all burst out laughing.

On the wall to the left of the window, about four feet away, in a corner of a patch of peeling plaster, Fima saw a grey lizard, immobile, staring like himself, longingly, towards the Bethlehem hills. Or watching a fly that was invisible to Fima. Once upon a time, on those hills and in their winding valleys, there wandered judges and kings, conquerors, prophets of consolation and wrath, world-reforming saviours, impostors, dreamers, priests and hearers of voices, traitors, messiahs, Roman prefects, Byzantine governors, Muslim generals, and crusader princes, and ascetics, hermits, wonderworkers, and sufferers. To this day Jerusalem still resounds with their memory in the ringing of its church bells, sobs out their names from the tops of its minarets, and conjures them back with cabbalistic incantations. And now, at this moment, there was, it seemed, not a living soul left in the city, bar himself and the lizard and the light.

When he was younger he too used to fancy he could hear a voice as he walked among Jerusalem's alleys and boulder-strewn waste plots. He even tried to record in words what he fancied he had heard. In those days he might still have been able to stir some hearts. Even now he could sometimes fascinate a few souls, particularly women, in those Friday-night get-togethers at the Tobiases' or the Gefens'. Sometimes he would throw out a dazzling idea, and for an instant the whole room would hold its breath. His ideas would then make their way around by word of mouth, and occasionally they even reached the columns of the newspapers. Sometimes, when the spirit moved him, he managed to coin a new phrase, to formulate a perception of the situation in words that had not previously been used, to utter some penetrating aperçu which made the rounds of the city until he came across it a few days later on the radio, severed from him and his name, and often distorted. His friends enjoyed reminding him, as a sort of mild rebuke, how once or twice he had shown real foresight, as for example in '73, when he had gone around lamenting to the point of ridicule the blindness that was afflicting Israel, the impending catastrophe. Or on the eve of the invasion of Lebanon. Or before the wave of Islamic fundamentalism. Whenever his friends reminded him of these prophecies, Fima would recoil and reply with a rueful grin that it was nothing, the writing was already on the wall and any child could read it.

Tsvi Kropotkin sometimes copied pieces for him from a literary supplement or a periodical with some allusion to the *Death of Augustine*, when some critics bothered to drag those poems out of oblivion to use them as auxiliary ammunition in a campaign for or against current trends in poetry. Fima would shrug and mutter, That's enough, Tsvika, just drop it. His poems, like his prophecies, seemed to him remote and irrelevant. Why does the soul pine when it has no idea what it is pining for? What really exists and what only seems to exist? Where can you look for something lost when you have forgotten what it is you lost? Once, in his billy-goat year, during his brief marriage to the hotel owner in Valletta, he was sitting in a waterfront café on the harbour watching a couple of fisherman play backgammon. In point of fact it was not so much the fishermen he was watching as an alsatian dog that sat, panting, on a chair between them. The dog's ears were pricked forward earnestly, as though it were listening for the next move, and it kept following the players' fingers and the rolls of the dice and the moving counters with eyes that seemed to Fima full of fascination and humble wonderment. Fima had never, before or since, seen such a concentrated effort to understand the unintelligible, as if in its longing to decipher the game the dog had achieved a degree of disembodiment. Surely that is precisely the way we ought to look at what is beyond us. To grasp as much as we can, or at least to grasp our inability to grasp. Fima sometimes pictured the creator of the universe, in whom he did not entirely believe, in the form of a Jerusalem tradesman of Middle Eastern origin, aged about sixty, lean and tanned and wrinkled, eaten away by cigarettes and arak, in threadbare brown trousers and a not very clean white shirt buttoned right up to the skinny neck but without a tie, and with worn-out brown shoes and a shabby old-fashioned jacket a little too small for him. This creator sat drowsily on a wicker stool, facing the sun, his eyes half-closed, his head sunk on his chest, in the doorway of his haberdashery shop in Zichron Moshe. A dead cigarette end hung from his lower lip and a string of amber beads was frozen between his fingers, where a broad ring flashed from time to time. Fima stopped and dared to address him, with exaggerated politeness, in the third person, hesitantly: Might I be permitted to disturb Your Worship with just one question? A twitch of irony flitted across the wrinkled, leathery face. Perhaps just a fly buzzing? Would Your Worship deign to consider the Brothers Karamazov? The argument between Ivan and the Devil? Mitya's dream? Or the episode of the Grand Inquisitor? No? And what would Your Worship deign to reply to that question? *Vanity of vanities?* Would Your Worship resort yet again to the old arguments: *Where wast thou when I laid the foundation of the world? I am that I am.* The old man released a kind of belch reeking of tobacco and arak, turned up his two palms, which were as pitted as a plasterer's, and spread them empty on his knees. Only the ring on his finger glimmered for a moment and then faded. Was he chewing something? Smiling? Dozing? Fima abandoned his quest. Apologising, he went on his way. Not running, not hurrying, yet nevertheless like one who is running away and knows he is, and also knows that running away is useless.

From his window Fima watched the sun straining to free itself from the clouds. An elusive change was coming over the streets and the hills. Not so much a brightening as a slight quivering of hues, as though the air itself were smitten with hesitations or doubts. All the things that filled the lives of the gang – Uri, Tsvi, Teddy, and the rest of them – the things that stirred them to longing or enthusiasm, seemed to Fima as forlorn as the dead leaves rotting under the bare mulberry tree in the garden. There is a forgotten promised land somewhere here – no, not a land, not promised, not even really forgotten, but something calling to you. He asked himself whether he would care if he died today. The question did not arouse anything in him: neither apprehension nor desire. Death seemed as boring as one of Wahrhaftig's stories. Whereas his daily life was as predictable and weary as his father's moralising. In his head he suddenly agreed with the old man, not about the identity of the Indians, but when he said that the days go by without joy or purpose. The shlemiel and his friend did indeed deserve pity rather than ridicule. But what were they to him? Surely he, Fima, was full of unbelievable powers, and it was only tiredness that made him put off exercising them. Like someone waiting for the precise timing. Or for a blow to smash the inner crust. He could, for example, drop his job at the clinic, extract a thousand dollars from the old man, and sail away on a cargo boat to start a new life. In Iceland. In Crete. In Safed. He could shut himself up in that guesthouse in Magdiel and write a play. Or a confession. He could devise a political programme, pick up some followers, and start a new movement that would shatter the mood of indifference and sweep through the public like wildfire. Or he could join one of the existing parties, apply himself to public activities for five or six years, moving from branch to branch, casting new light on the national situation until even the most stolid hearts were jolted, and eventually he would get his hands on the tiller and bring peace to the land. In 1977 a private citizen named Lange or Longe had managed to get himself elected to the New Zealand parliament, and by 1982 he held the reins of power. Or else Fima could fall in love, or get involved in his father's business and turn the cosmetics factory into the nucleus of an industrial conglomerate. Or he could scoot up the academic ladder, overtake Tsvi and his gang, get a chair, and start a new school. He could take Jerusalem by storm with a new book of poems. What a ridiculous expression, 'take Jerusalem by storm'. Or win back Yael. And Dimi. Or he could sell this ruin and use the money to restore an abandoned house on the outskirts of a remote village in the hills of Upper Galilee. Or do the opposite: bring in builders, carpenters, decorators, renovate the whole flat, send the bill to his father, and open a new chapter.

The sun suddenly came out of the fleeting clouds above Gilo and cast a tender, precious light on one of the hills. This time Fima did not find any exaggeration in the expression 'precious light', but he chose to discard it. Not before saying the words aloud and feeling a flush of inner response and pleasure. He went on to say the words 'sharp and smooth', and again he experienced enjoyment mixed with mockery.

A sliver of glass caught fire below him in the garden, as though it had found the way and was signalling to him to follow. In his mind Fima repeated his father's words. Snows of yesteryear. A handful of dust. Somehow instead of saying 'snows of yesteryear', he said 'bones of yesteryear'.

What did the lizard, immobile on the wall, and the cockroach under the kitchen sink have in common, and how did they differ? Seemingly, neither of them wasted the treasure of life. Even if they too were subject to Baruch Nomberg's iron rule about living without sense and dying without desire. But at least without fantasising about seizing power or bringing peace to the land.

Stealthily, Fima opened his window, taking great care not to startle the meditative reptile. Even though his friends, and he himself, considered him to be a clumsy oaf, he managed to open it without a squeak. He was certain now that the creature was focusing on some point in space that he too ought to be looking at. From what remote province of evolution's realm, from what dim, primeval landscape replete with volcanoes gushing clouds of smoke and jungles and misty vapours rising from the ground long before the word and knowledge came into being, whole aeons before all those kings and prophets and saviours who once roamed these hills, came this creature that now stared at Fima from a distance of not more than three feet with a kind of anxious affection? Like a distant relation concerned about your health. Yes, a perfect little dinosaur, shrunk to the size of a yard lizard. Fima seemed to intrigue the creature, otherwise why was it moving its head to left and right, slowly, as if to say: I'm really surprised at you. Or as if regretting the fact that Fima was acting unwisely but that there was no way of helping him.

And truly it is a distant relation: there is no doubting that it belongs to a remote branch of the family. Between you and me, pal, and between both of us and Trotsky, there is much more in common than divides us: head neck spine curiosity appetite limbs sexual desire the ability to tell light from darkness and cold from warmth, ribs lungs old age digestive and secretory systems nerves to perceive pain metabolism memory sense of danger a ramifying maze of blood vessels a reproductive mechanism and a mechanism for limited regeneration programmed ultimately for self-destruction. Also a heart functioning as a complex pump and a sense of smell and an instinct for self-preservation and a talent for escape and concealment and camouflage and also direction-finding systems and a brain, and apparently also loneliness. There are so many things we could talk about, compare, learn from each other, and teach each other. Perhaps we should also take into account an even more remote kinship that links the three of us to the vegetable kingdom. Lay your hand on a fig leaf, for instance, or a vine leaf: only a blind person would deny the similarity of form, the spread of the fingers, the branching vessels and sinews, whose function it is to distribute nourishment and eliminate waste matter. And who can say whether behind this kinship there does not lurk an even subtler one between all of us and the minerals in particular or the inanimate world in general. Every living cell is made up of a mass of inanimate substances which are not really inanimate at all but are constantly pulsing with infinitesimal electrical charges. Electrons. Neutrons. Perhaps there too there is a pattern of male and female that can neither merge nor separate? Fima smiled. It would be best, he decided, to come to terms with young Yoezer, standing at this window in a hundred years' time, staring at his own lizard. I shall matter to him less than a grain of salt. Perhaps something of me, a molecule, an atom, a neutron, will actually be present in this room, possibly indeed in a grain of salt. Assuming people still use salt a hundred years from now.

And why shouldn't they?

Dimi is the only person I might be able to talk to about these fantasies.

At any rate, better to fill his head with prophets and lizards and vine leaves than bombs made out of nail varnish.

In an instant the lizard had wriggled away and hidden itself inside or behind the gutter. It had disappeared, sharp and smooth. Fauré's Requiem ended and was followed by Borodin's Polovtsian Dances, which Fima did not like. And the brightening light was beginning to hurt his eyes. He closed the window and began to look for a sweater, but he was too late to save the electric kettle, which had boiled dry some time before and now smelt of smoke and burnt rubber. Fima would have to choose between taking it to be mended on his way to work and buying a new one.

'Your problem, pal,' he said to himself.

He chewed a heartburn tablet and opted for freedom. He called the clinic and told Tamar he would not be coming in today. No, he wasn't ill. Yes, he was sure. Everything was perfectly OK. Yes, a personal matter. No, there was nothing wrong and he didn't need any help. Thanks anyway, and please say I'm sorry. He looked in the phone book, and, lo and behold, under T he found Tadmor, Annette and Yeroham, in one of the suburbs, Mevaseret.

It was Annette herself who answered. Fima said:

'I'm sorry to bother you. It's the reception clerk from yesterday. Efraim. Fima. Do you remember? We chatted at the clinic. I thought . . .'

Annette remembered it well. She said she was delighted. And suggested meeting in town. 'Shall we say in an hour? An hour and a half? If that suits you, Efraim? I knew you'd call today. Don't ask me how. I just had a feeling. There was something, well, unfinished between us yesterday. So, shall we say an hour then? At the Savyon? If I'm a bit late, don't give me up.'

Fima forgives and forgets

H E waited for a quarter of an hour at a table to one side
of the café, then ordered coffee and a cake. At a nearby
table sat a right-wing member of the Knesset with a slim, good-
looking, bearded youth who looked to Fima like an activist
for the Jewish settlements in the Territories. The youth was
saying:

'You are eunuchs too. You've forgotten where you came from
and who put you where you are.'

They lowered their voices.

Fima remembered how he had left Nina's house the previous
night, how he had disgraced himself with her, how he had disgraced himself in Ted's study, how he had shamed himself and
Yael in the hall in the dark. In fact, it would be quite nice to pick
an argument with these two conspirators now. He could easily
tear them to shreds. He guessed that Annette Tadmor had
changed her mind, thought better of it, would not keep their
date. Why should she? Her full, rounded form, her misery, her
plain cotton frock like a schoolgirl's uniform, all stirred in him a
hint of desire mingled with self-mockery: Just as well she
changed her mind; she spared you another disgrace.

The young settler stood up and in two long strides he was at
Fima's table. Fima was startled to see that the youngster had a
gun in his belt.

'Excuse me, are you by any chance Mr Prag, the lawyer?'

Fima considered the question, and for a moment he was
tempted to answer in the affirmative. He'd always had a soft spot
for Prag.

'I don't think so,' he said.

The settler said:

'We've arranged to meet someone we've never seen. I thought perhaps it was you. I'm sorry.'

'I'm not,' Fima declared forcefully, as though firing the first shot in a civil war, 'one of you. I think you're all a plague.'

The young man, with an innocent, sweet smile and a look suggesting Jewish solidarity, said:

'Why not save expressions like that for the enemy? It was groundless hatred that brought down the Temple. It wouldn't hurt all of us to try a little groundless love for a change.'

A delicious argumentative thrill went through Fima like wine, and he had a devastating reply poised on his tongue, when he caught sight of Annette in the doorway, looking around vaguely, and he was almost disappointed. But he was obliged to wave to her and drop the settler. She apologised for being late. As soon as she was sitting opposite him, he said that she had arrived just in time to rescue him from the Hezbollah. Or, rather, to rescue the Hezbollah from him. He went on to unburden himself of the essence of his views. Only then did he remember to apologise for ordering without waiting for her. He asked what she would like to drink. To his surprise she said a vodka, and then began to tell him all about her divorce, after twenty-six years of what she had considered to be an ideal marriage. At least on the surface. Fima ordered her vodka, and another coffee for himself. He also ordered some bread and cheese and an egg sandwich, because he still felt hungry. He continued to listen to her story, but with divided attention, because in the meantime a bald man in a grey raincoat had joined the next table. Presumably their Mr Prag. Fima had the impression that the three of them were scheming to drive a wedge into the state prosecutor's department, and he tried to intercept their conversation. Hardly aware of what he was saying, he remarked to Annette that he could scarcely believe what she had said about being married for twenty-six years, because she didn't look a day over forty.

'That's sweet of you,' Annette answered. 'There's something about you that radiates kindness. I believe that if only I can tell the whole story from beginning to end to someone who's a good listener, it may help me to sort out my ideas. To grasp what's happened to me. Even though I know that once I've told the story, I'll understand even less. Have you got the patience?'

The politician said:

'Let's try to play for time at least: it can't do any harm.'

And the man in the raincoat, presumably the lawyer Prag:

'It may look very easy to you. In fact, it isn't.'

'As if Yeri and I had been standing quietly for a long time on a balcony,' Annette said, 'leaning on the railing, looking down on the garden and the woods, shoulder to shoulder, and suddenly, without any warning, he grabs me and throws me off. Like an old crate.'

Fima said:

'How sad.'

Then he said:

'Terrible.'

He laid his hand on hers, which lay clenched on the edge of the table, because there were tears in her eyes again.

'So we're agreed, then,' the settler said. 'Let's keep in touch. Just be careful of using the phone.'

'Look,' said Annette. 'In novels, in plays, in films, there are always these mysterious women. Capricious, unpredictable. They fall in love like sleepwalkers and fly away like birds. Greta Garbo. Marlene Dietrich. Liv Ullmann. All sorts of femmes fatales. The secrets of the female heart. Don't make fun of me for drinking vodka in the middle of the day. After all, you don't look too happy yourself. Am I boring you?'

Fima called the waiter and ordered her another vodka. He ordered a bottle of mineral water and some more bread and cheese for himself. The three conspirators got up to leave. As they passed his table, the settler gave him a sweet, saintly smile, as though he could see into his heart and forgave him. He said:

'Bye now, and all the best. Don't forget, when it comes to the crunch, we're all in the same boat.'

In his mind Fima relocated this moment to a coffeehouse in Berlin in the last days of the Weimar Republic, putting himself in the role of martyr: Carl von Ossietzky, Kurt Tucholsky. Immediately he cancelled the whole picture because the comparison was ridiculous, almost hysterical. To Annette he said:

'Take a good look at them. Those are the creatures that are dragging us all down.'

Annette said:

'I'm already as low as I can go.'

And Fima:

'Go on. You were talking about fatal women.'

Annette emptied her second glass. Her eyes were gleaming, and a hint of coquetry slipped into her words:

'The nice thing about you, Efraim, is that I really don't mind what sort of impression I make on you. I'm not used to that. Generally, when I'm talking to a man the most important thing for me is what impression he has of me. It's never happened to me before to sit like this with a strange man and talk so freely about myself without getting all sorts of signals, if you know what I mean. Just one person talking to another. You're not offended?'

Fima unconsciously smiled when she used the expression 'a strange man'. She noticed his smile and beamed at him like a child consoled after tears. She said:

'What I meant was, not that you're not masculine, just that I can talk to you like a brother. We've had to put up with so much bullshit from the poets, with their Beatrices, their earth mothers, their gazelles, their tigresses, their seagulls, their swans, and all that nonsense. Let me tell you, being a man strikes me as a thousand times more complicated than that. Or maybe it's not complicated at all, all that lousy bargaining. You give me sex, I'll give you a bit of tenderness. Or an impression of tenderness. Be a whore and a mother. A puppy by day and a kitten by night. Sometimes I have the feeling that men like sex but hate women. Don't be offended, Efraim. I'm just generalising. There must be exceptions. Like you, for instance. I feel good now, the way you're listening to me quietly.'

Fima bent forward to light the cigarette she had taken out of her handbag. He was thinking: In the middle of the day, in broad daylight, in the middle of Jerusalem, they're already walking

85

around with guns in their belts. Was the sickness implicit in the Zionist idea from the outset? Is there no way for the Jews to get back onto the stage of history except by becoming scum? Does every battered child have to grow up into a violent adult? And weren't we already scum before we got back onto the stage of history? Do we have to be either cripples or thugs? Is there no third alternative?

'At the age of twenty-five,' Annette continued, 'after a couple of love affairs and one abortion and a BA in art history, I meet this young orthopaedic surgeon. A quiet, shy man, not at all like an Israeli, if you know what I mean. A gentle person who courts me with sensitivity and even sends me a love letter every day but never tries to touch me. A hard-working, honest man. He likes to stir my coffee for me. He thinks of himself as an average, middle-of-the-road sort of fellow. As a junior doctor, he works like a madman, long hours on duty, on call, night duty. With a small group of close friends who are all very much like him, with refugee parents who are cultured and good-mannered like him. And after less than a year we get married. Without any upheavals, without any ups and downs. He handles me as though I'm made of glass, if you know what I mean.'

Fima almost interrupted her to say: But we're all like that; that's why we've lost the state. But he restrained himself and said nothing. He merely made a point of carefully putting out the cigarette stub that Annette had left smouldering on the edge of the ashtray. He finished off his sandwich and still felt hungry.

'We put together our savings, our allowances from our parents, and we buy a small flat in Givat Shaul; we buy furniture, a fridge, a cooker, we choose curtains together. We never disagree. All respectful and friendly. He simply enjoys giving way to me, at least that's what I think at the time. Friendly is the right word: we both try our best to be good the whole time. To be fair. We compete with each other at being considerate. Then our daughter is born, and, two years later, our son. Yeri, naturally, is a reasonable, devoted parent. Consistent. Stable. The correct word is reliable. He's happy washing nappies, he knows how to clean the mosquito nets, learns from books how to cook a meal and look after plants. He takes the children into town whenever the burdens of work allow. In time he even improves in bed. Gradually he realises I'm not made of glass, if you know what I mean. Occasionally he can tell a funny story over a meal. Still, he also starts to develop one or two habits I find quite irritating. Little inoffensive habits that won't go away. Tapping on things with his finger, for instance. Not like a doctor tapping on a patient's chest. More like tapping on a door. He's sitting reading the paper, and all the time he's unconsciously tapping on the arm of his chair. As if he's trying to get in. He locks himself in the bathroom, splashes around in the bath for half an hour, and all the time he's tapping on the tiles as if he's searching for a secret compartment. Or his habit of saying in Yiddish, *Azoy* instead of replying to what you're saying to him. I tell him I've found a mistake in the electricity bill, and he says, *Azoy*. Our little girl tells him her doll is angry with her, and he smiles, *Azoy*. I intervene, and say, Why don't you listen to what your children are saying once in a while? And all he can say is, *Azoy*. Or the sarcastic whistle he lets out through the gap in his front teeth: it's probably not a whistle, not sarcastic at all, just letting the air out through his pursed lips. No matter how often I tell him it's driving me insane, he can't stop it. He doesn't even seem to notice he's done it again. But when all's said and done, these are minor irritants; you can learn to live with them. There are drunken husbands, lazy husbands, adulterous brutes, perverts, lunatics. In any case, I may well have developed some habits myself that he doesn't like but says nothing about. There's no point in making a big fuss about his tapping and whistling, which he can't even control. So the years go by. We close in the balcony to make an extra room; we take a trip to Europe, buy a small car, replace our first furniture. We even get an alsatian. We get all four of our parents into a private old people's home. Yeri does his bit; he tries to make me happy, he's pleased with everything we've achieved together. Or so I think. And he goes on whistling and tapping and occasionally muttering *Azoy*.'

Fima was thinking: The parliament building surrounded by tanks, paratroopers seizing the broadcasting station, a colonels' putsch – that's not what will happen here. Here we'll just have creeping deterioration. An inch a day. People won't even notice the lights going out. Because they won't go out: they'll fade out. Either we'll finally get our act together and deliberately precipitate a serious national crisis, or else there just won't be a definite moment of crisis. And he said:

'You describe it so vividly, I can see it.'

'I'm not boring you? Don't be angry with me for smoking again. It's hard for me to talk about all this. I must look a real sight; I've been crying. Be nice and don't look at me.'

'On the contrary,' Fima said, and after a moment's hesitation he added:

'Your earrings look nice too. Special. Like a pair of glow-worms. Not that I have the slightest idea what glow-worms look like.'

'It's nice being with you,' said Annette. 'First time in ages I've felt so good. Even though you hardly say anything, just listen and understand. Yeri encourages me to take a part-time job with the Jerusalem City Council when the children are a bit older. We start saving. We buy a new car. We dream of building ourselves a red-tiled house, with a real garden, outside the city, in Mevaseret. Sometimes in the evenings, when the children are in bed, we sit and look at American homemaking magazines, drawing up all sorts of plans. Sometimes he taps on our sketches with his finger, as though to test how solid they are. Both our children reveal a talent for music, and we decide to invest in music lessons, private teachers, the conservatory. We take summer holidays by the seaside, the four of us, at Nahariya. In December we leave the children behind and rent a bungalow in Eilat. Ten years ago we sold his parents' flat and bought the bungalow. On Saturday nights we generally have a few couples round. Don't be shy about stopping me, Efraim, if you're tired of listening. Maybe I'm going into too much detail? Then this reliable man is appointed deputy head of his department. He starts seeing private patients at home. So the dream of the house with a garden in Mevaseret starts to become a reality. Both of us become experts on marble and ceramics and roof tiles, if you know what I mean. All these years, aside from superficial rows, not a shadow falls between us. Or so I think. Every row ends with apologies on both sides. He says he's sorry, I say I'm sorry, and he mutters *Azoy*. And then we change the sheets or start making supper together.'

Five thousand men, Fima thought, five thousand of us simply refusing to do our reserve service in the Territories – that's all it would take. The whole occupation would collapse. But it's just those five thousand who have turned into experts on roof tiles. Those bastards are right when they say that all they need to do is play for time. At the end of her story she'll go to bed with me. She's working herself up to it.

'For a few winters,' Annette continued, a sly, bitter line appearing at the corner of her mouth, as though she could read his mind, 'he spends one night a week in Beer Sheva, because he's been asked to teach some course or other at the medical school there. Thoughts of other women in his life never crossed my mind. I just didn't think it was in him. Especially since even his domestic consumption had dwindled over the years, if you know what I mean. What would he do with a mistress? Just as it would never have occurred to me to imagine that he was, let's say, a Syrian spy. It was simply impossible. I knew everything about him. At least, that's what I thought. And I accepted him as he was, including that sarcastic whistle that I was convinced by now wasn't really a whistle and definitely wasn't sarcastic. On the other hand – I'm embarrassed to tell you this, but I really feel like telling everything – eight years ago, in the summer, I went to stay with a cousin of mine in Amsterdam for three weeks and I had a whirlwind romance with a stupid blond security officer from the embassy, twenty years younger than me. A real animal in bed, if you know what I mean, but the guy soon showed himself to be a narcissistic half-wit. It might make you laugh to know that someone thinks women get a kick out of having their stomachs smeared with honey. Just imagine! In a word, he was just a disturbed child. Not worth my good husband's little finger.'

Fima ordered her another vodka without her asking, and, yielding to his hunger pangs, another plate of bread and cheese for himself. The last. In his mind he resolved to be patient and gentle. Not to pounce on her. To drop politics. To talk only about poetry and loneliness in a general sort of way. Above all, to be patient.

'I got back from Amsterdam riddled with guilt. It was hard for me to resist the urge to confess to him. But he suspected nothing. On the contrary. Over the years we have got into the habit of lying in bed sometimes, once the children are asleep, reading magazines together. We learn how to do all sorts of things from them that we didn't know before. Compromise, consideration and concession paint our lives a dull shade of brown. True, we don't have a lot of subjects for conversation. After all, I'm not that interested in orthopaedics. But the silences never get us down. We can sit for a whole evening reading, listening to music, watching television. Sometimes we even have a drink before bedtime. Sometimes I wake up when I've been asleep only an hour, because he has trouble dozing off and is tapping absent-mindedly on the shelf at the head of our bed. I ask him to stop. He apologises and stops and I go back to sleep and he falls asleep too. Or so I think. We remind each other to stick to our diet, because we both have a tendency to put on weight. Am I a bit fat, Efraim? Are you sure? Meanwhile we purchase all sorts of electrical appliances for the home. We engage a help three mornings a week. We visit his parents and mine – we've put all four of them in the same old people's home. He goes to a medical congress in Canada without me, but invites me to join him for an orthopaedic conference in Frankfurt. While we're there, we even go out one evening to see what a striptease joint is like. I was quite disgusted, but today I think I made a mistake in saying so to him. I should have kept my mouth shut. The fact is, Efraim, I'm afraid to imagine what you'll think of me if I ask you to order me another vodka. Just one more and that's it. It's so hard. And you're such a good listener. An angel. Well then, six years ago we finally moved into the house in Mevaseret. We had it built ourselves, and it turned out almost exactly like our dream, with a separate wing for the children, and a gabled attic bedroom like an Alpine chalet.'

An angel with an erection like a rhinoceros, Fima thought and chuckled to himself, and once more he felt how along with the compassion there welled up inside him desire, and with the desire shame, anger, and self-mockery. And while he was thinking of rhinos, he remembered the motionlessness of the prehistoric lizard that had nodded to him that morning. And he thought about Ionesco's *Rhinoceros*, and, while bewaring of superficial comparisons, he had to smile, because the lawyer Prag had looked more like a buffalo than a rhinoceros.

'Tell me, Annette, aren't you hungry at all? Here am I gulping down bread and cheese nonstop, and you haven't even touched your cake. Shall we take a look at the menu?'

But Annette, showing no sign of having heard, lit a fresh cigarette, and Fima passed her the ashtray, which the waiter had emptied, and the vodka he had brought her. 'Coffee, perhaps?'

'No, really,' said Annette. 'You make me feel good. We only met yesterday, and it's as if I've found a brother.'

Fima inwardly almost used her husband's favourite expression, *Azoy*. But he refrained and, reaching across almost unconsciously, stroked her cheek.

'Carry on, Annette,' he said. 'You were talking about the Alps.'

'I was a fool. Blind. I thought the new house was the embodiment of happiness. How excited we were to be living out of town! With the view, the peace and quiet. At the end of the day we would go out in the garden to measure how much the saplings had grown. Then in the last light we would sit on the veranda to watch the hills go dark. Almost without talking and yet as friends. Or so I thought. Like a pair of comrades-in-arms who no longer need to exchange words, if you can understand that. Now I think even that was a mistake. That by tapping on the railing of the veranda he was trying to express something in a kind of Morse code, and waiting for my reply. Sometimes he would look at me over the top of his glasses, with his chin dropped on his chest, with a slightly surprised expression, as though I was new to him, as though I had changed completely, and he would let out a low whistle. If I hadn't known him so many years, I might have imagined he had taken up wolf-whistling. Today I think I didn't begin to understand that look of his. Then our daughter is called up to the army, and a year ago our son is called up too; he was accepted for the army orchestra. The house seems empty. We generally go to bed at ten-thirty. We leave a light on so the garden won't be pitch-black at night. The two cars stand outside, silent under the carport. Except twice a week, when he does a night shift at the hospital and I sit in front of the TV until close-down. Recently I've taken up painting. Just for myself. Without any pretensions. Even though Yeri suggested showing my pictures to an expert in case they're worth anything. I said, whether they're worth anything or not, that's not what interests me. Yeri said, *Azoy*. And then it hit me. One day, it was a Saturday morning six weeks ago – if only I'd bitten my tongue and said nothing – I said to him: Yeri, if growing old is like this, then why should we worry about it? What's wrong with it? He suddenly stands up, facing Yossel Bregner's "Butterfly Eaters" on the wall – do you know it? – he gave me the print once as a birthday present. Any-way, he stands there all tense and strained, lets out a low whistle between his teeth, as if he's just noticed a line in the picture that wasn't there before, or that he's never spotted, and he says: Speak for yourself. I'm not even thinking about growing old just yet. And there's something in his voice, in the angle of his back, which seems to have stiffened and hunched, like a hyena's, and the redness of the back of his neck – I'd never noticed before how red it is – which makes me shrink into my armchair with fear. Has something happened, Yeri? It's like this, he says, I'm very sorry, but I've got to get out. I can't take any more. I've just got to. You must understand. Twenty-six years now I've been danc-ing to your tune like a tame bear; now I feel like dancing to my own tune for a change. I've already rented a small flat. It's all fixed up. Apart from my clothes and books, and the dog, I won't take anything with me. You must understand: I've got no choice. I've had it up to here with lying. Then he turns and goes into his study, and he comes back carrying two suitcases – he must have packed them in the night – and he heads for the front door. But what have I done, Yeri? You must understand, he says, it's not you, it's her. She can't stand the lies any more. She can't stand seeing me being used as your doormat. And I can't live without her. I would suggest, he says from the doorway, that you try not to be difficult, Annette. Don't make any scenes. It'll be easier for the children that way. Just imagine I've been killed. You must understand, I'm suffocating. With that, he taps lightly on the doorpost, whistles to the dog, starts the Peugeot, and disappears. The whole thing has taken maybe a quarter of an hour. Next day when he called, I hung up. Two days after that he called again; I wanted to hang up again but I didn't have the strength. Instead I pleaded with him, Come back and I promise to be better. Just tell me what I did wrong, and I won't do it again. And he kept repeating, in his doctor's voice, as though I were a hysterical woman patient, You must understand, it's all over. I'm not crying because I'm angry, Efraim. I'm crying because I feel insulted, humiliated. Two weeks ago he sends me this little lawyer, incredibly polite; apparently he's of Persian origin. He sits bolt upright in Yeri's chair, and I'm almost surprised he doesn't tap on the arm or whistle at me through his teeth, and he starts to explain: Look here, madam, you will get at least twice as much from him as any rabbinic or civil court would dream of giving you. If I were you, I'd jump at our offer, because the plain truth, madam, is that in my whole professional life I've never before encountered someone who is prepared to offer the entirety of the joint possessions right away, as an opening position. Excluding the Peugeot and the bungalow in Eilat, of course. But all the rest is yours, despite all that he's had to put up with from you. If he went to court, he could claim mental cruelty and get the lot. I hardly heard what he was saying; I begged that ape just to tell me where my husband was, just to let me see him, at least to let me have his phone number. But he started explaining to me why at the present juncture it would be preferable not to, for the benefit of all the parties concerned, and that in any case my husband and his friend were leaving for Italy the same evening and they'd be away for two months. Just one more vodka, Efraim. I won't drink any more. Promise. I'm even out of cigarettes. I'm crying about you now, not him, because I'm remembering how wonderful you were to me at the clinic yesterday. Now just tell me to calm down, please, explain to me that things like this must happen in Israel at the rate of one every nine minutes or something like that. Don't take any notice of my crying. I actually feel better. Ever since I got home from the clinic yesterday, I haven't stopped asking myself the same question: Will he phone or won't he? I had a feeling you would, but I was afraid to hope. Aren't you divorced too? Didn't you tell me you'd been married twice? Why did you give them the push? D'you want to tell me?'

Fima said:

'I didn't give them the push. It was the other way round.'

Annette said:

'Tell me anyway. Some other time. Not today. Today I can't take it in. I just need you to tell me the whole truth. Am I boring? Selfish? Self-centred? Repulsive? Do you find my body repulsive?'

Fima said:

'On the contrary. I don't think I'm good enough for you. And yet I can't help feeling we're in the same boat. But look, Annette, the weather's cleared. These beautiful winter days in Jerusalem, the sunshine between the showers, as though the sky is singing. Shall we go for a walk? Nowhere in particular, just a stroll? It's half past four now: it'll be dark soon. If I were bold enough, I'd tell you that you're a beautiful, attractive woman. Don't get me wrong. Shall we go? Just for a stroll, to look at the evening light? Will you be cold?'

'No, thanks. I've already taken hours of your time. Actually, yes. Let's have a stroll. If you're not too busy. That's beautiful, what you said, that the sky is singing. Everything you say comes out so beautiful. Just promise me you're not expecting anything from me, so you won't be disappointed. You see, I just can't. Never mind. I shouldn't have said that. Sorry. Let's go on talking while we walk.'

Later that evening, full of shame and regret that he had not changed his sweaty sheets, embarrassed that apart from an omelette and a single soft tomato and the liqueur his father had brought him he had nothing to offer her, Fima carefully, deferentially removed her outer garments, like a father getting his daughter ready for bed. He handed her a pair of worn flannel pyjamas: he sniffed them as he took them out of the wardrobe, and hesitated, but he had no others. He draped his blanket over her and went down on his knees next to her on the cold floor, apologising on behalf of the radiator, which did not give out enough heat, and the mattress, with its hills and valleys. She drew his palm towards her face and for an instant her lips touched the back of his hand. He rewarded her generously, kissing her on the forehead, the eyebrows, the chin, not daring to approach her lips, while he kneaded and stroked her long hair. As he stroked her, he whispered, Cry. Never mind, it's all right. When she sobbed so much that the crying made her face ugly and puffy like a beetroot, Fima turned out the light. Very carefully he touched her shoulders, her neck, lingering for a quarter of an hour before he proceeded down the slope of her breasts, restraining himself from touching the peaks. All the while he continued his fatherly kisses, which he hoped would distract her attention from his fingers slipping between her knees. I feel bad, Efraim, I feel bad and worthless. Fima whispered, You're wonderful, Annette, you thrill me, and as he spoke his finger crept closer to her sex and stopped, ready to be repulsed. When it was clear to him that she was totally absorbed in her predicament, repeatedly describing in broken whispers the injustice she had suffered, as though she did not notice what he was up to, he began to play with her gently, struggling to dismiss from his mind her husband's habit of tapping, until she sighed and laid her hand on the back of his neck, and said, You're so good. From this whisper he drew the courage to touch her breasts and to lodge his lust against the side of her body, still not daring to rub himself against her. He simply went on stroking her here and there, learning the strings, uttering whispers of reassurance and consolation that he himself did not listen to. Until at last he sensed that his patience was beginning to pay off: he felt a responsive ripple, a slight arching, a tremor, even though she still went on talking, grieving, explaining to herself and to him where she went wrong, how she may have made Yeri hate her, how she wronged her husband and her children, and confessing in the dark that besides the Amsterdam episode there had been two other affairs, with a couple of his friends, frivolous, foolish affairs admittedly, but possibly that meant she deserved what had happened to her. Meanwhile his finger found the right rhythm and her sighs were interspersed with groans, and she did not protest when he began rubbing his erection against her thigh. Fima therefore went along with her pretence of being overwhelmed with sorrow, so that she did not even notice her underwear being removed, her body still responding and her thighs gripping his musician's fingers as her own fingers stroked his neck. But at the very moment he decided that his own moment was ripe, and he was on the point of substituting his body for his finger, her body arched like a bow and she released a soft, childlike cry of surprised delight. And the next instant she relaxed. And burst into tears again. Feebly she pummelled his chest, wailing, Why did you do that to me? Why have you humiliated me? I was a wreck even without you. Then she turned her back on him and cried to herself like a baby. Fima knew he was too late. He had missed. For an instant there welled up inside him a mixture of laughter and anger and frustration and self-mockery: at that instant he could have shot the sweet-smiling settler dead with his lawyer and his member of parliament, while he called himself an idiot. Then he collected himself, and reconciled himself to the need to forgive and forget.

He got up, covered Annette, and asked her gently if he should pour her another drop of liqueur. Or should he make some tea?

She sat up violently, clutching the grubby sheet to her chest, groped for a cigarette, lit it furiously, and said:

'What a bastard you are.'

Fima, who was struggling to dress while covering himself to hide his shameful rhino horn, muttered like a punished child:

'But what have I done? I didn't do anything to you.'

And he knew that these words were both true and false, and he almost burst into grim laughter, almost mumbled, *Azoy*. But he controlled himself, apologised, blamed himself, he couldn't understand what had come over him, it was being with her that put him in a spin and made him forget himself, could she find it in her to forgive him?

She dressed hurriedly, roughly, like an angry old woman, with her back to him; she combed her hair violently, her tears dried, she lit a fresh cigarette and told Fima to call her a taxi and never to phone her again. When he asked if he could see her downstairs, she replied in a flat, icy voice:

'That will not be necessary. Good-bye.'

Fima got under the shower. Even though the water was tepid, almost cold, he steeled himself, lathered himself thoroughly, and stayed under for a long time. The real villain of the three, he mused, was the lawyer. Then he put on clean underwear, and furiously gathering the dirty sheets and towels as well as the tea-towel and his shirt, he packed them all into a plastic bag and put it near the front door so that he would not forget to take it to the laundry the next morning. While he made the bed with clean sheets, he tried whistling between his two front teeth, but he couldn't do it. We're all in the same boat, that was what the pretty settler had said, and Fima discovered, much to his surprise, that in a certain sense he was right.

As far as the last lamppost

WHEN he had finished preparing his laundry, he went to the kitchen to get rid of Annette's cigarette ends. Opening the door of the compartment under the sink, he found the cockroach, Trotsky, lying dead on his back beside the overfull bin. What had killed him? There were no signs of violence. And there's no question of a cockroach dying of hunger in my kitchen. Thinking about it, Fima concluded that the difference between a cockroach and a butterfly was only a matter of variation on a theme, certainly not enough of a difference to justify the fact that butterflies symbolised to us freedom, beauty, purity, whereas the cockroach was perceived as the embodiment of everything disgusting. So what was the cause of death? Fima recalled that in the morning, when he brandished his shoe over Trotsky's head and changed his mind, the creature had made no effort to escape its fate. Perhaps it was already sick then, and he did nothing to help.

Bending down, Fima gently picked up the cockroach in a piece of newspaper folded into a funnel. Instead of disposing of it in the bin, he dug it a grave in the flowerpot that stood on the windowsill with nothing growing in it. After the funeral he attacked the pile of dishes in the sink. He washed the plates and mugs. When he reached the frying pan, which was thick with congealed fat, he got tired of scouring it and decided that the pan would have to wait patiently with the rest of the washing up until the next day. He could not make tea, because the electric kettle had boiled itself dry while he was peering into the abyss of evolution and searching for a common denominator. He went to piss, but his patience ran out and he pulled the lever in the middle to encourage his stuttering bladder. He lost the race again, but instead of waiting for the cistern to refill, he retreated, turning the light off behind him. Must try to play for time, he said to himself. And he added, If you know what I mean.

Shortly before midnight he put on the flannel pyjamas that Annette had thrown down on the rug, got into bed, and enjoyed the clean sheets as he began reading Tsvi Kropotkin's article in *Ha'arets*. He found it academic and bland, like Tsvika himself, but he hoped it would help him get to sleep. When he turned the light out, he remembered the soft cry of pleasure full of childlike excitement that had suddenly burst from Annette's throat as her thighs tightened around his finger. Desire surged again, together with resentment and a sense of grievance. Almost two months had gone by since he had last slept with a woman, and now he had missed two on successive nights, even though he had actually had both of them in his arms. Because of their selfishness he would not be able to get to sleep now. For an instant he thought Yeri, Dr Tadmor, was right to leave Annette, because he was suffocated by the lies. And almost at once he said to himself: You bastard. Unconsciously his hand began slowly comforting his penis. Suddenly a stranger, a moderate, reasonable man whose parents were not even born yet, the man who would be in this room on a winter's night a hundred years from now, was watching him out of the darkness with eyes that seemed sceptical, only half-curious, almost amused. Fima let go of himself and complained aloud:

'Don't you go judging me.'

Then he added sardonically:

'Anyway, in a hundred years there won't be anything here. Everything will have been destroyed.'

And he added:

'Shut up, you. Who was talking to you?'

At this they both fell silent, Yoezer and he, and his desire also subsided. In its stead came a burst of nocturnal energy, a sharp wide-awake lucidity, a rush of inner force and mental clarity. At this moment he was capable of taking on those three conspirators from the Café Savyon and defeating them with ease; he could write an epic poem, found a political party, or draw up a peace treaty. Words and snippets of sentences formed themselves in his mind, gleaming with cleanness and precision. He threw off his blanket, rushed to his desk, and, instead of convening the Revolutionary Council for a midnight sitting, he wrote in half an hour, without crossing out or changing anything, an article for the weekend paper: a reply to Tsvi Kropotkin on the question of the price of morality versus the price of immorality in times of everyday violence. These days all sorts of wolves and would-be wolves are preaching a primitive Darwinism, howling that in time of war morality, like women and children, should stay at home, and that if only we could shrug off the burden of morality we would be able blithely to smash whoever stood in our way. Tsvi gets bogged down in his effort to counter this with pragmatic arguments: The enlightened world, he says, will punish us if we go on behaving like wolves. But surely the fact is that ultimately all oppressive regimes collapse and vanish, while the societies and nations that survive are precisely those that foster the values of humane morality. From a historical viewpoint, Fima wrote, rather than you defending morality, morality defends you, and without it even the fangs of the most ferocious wolves are doomed to rot and decay.

Then he put on a clean shirt and trousers, the chunky sweater he inherited from Yael, and his overcoat, this time being agile enough to avoid the trap of the sleeve. He chewed a heartburn tablet and went down into the street, bubbling with a happy feeling of responsibility, taking the steps two at a time.

Jauntily wide awake, oblivious to the chill of the night air, intoxicated with the silence and emptiness, Fima marched down the road as though to the sound of a military band. There was not a soul in the sodden streets. Jerusalem had been handed over to him, to protect it from itself. The blocks of flats stood heavy and massive in the darkness. The streetlamps were shrouded in a pale yellow haze. At the entrance to each staircase the numbers glimmered with a dim electric glow, which was reflected here and there off the windscreen of a parked car. Automatic living, he thought, a life of comfort and achievement, accumulating possessions, honours, and the routine eating, mating, and financial habits of prosperous people, the soul sinking under folds of flesh, the rituals of social position; that was what the author of the

Psalms meant when he wrote, 'Their heart is gross like fat.' This was the contented mind that had no dealings with death and whose sole concern was to remain contented. Herein lay the tragedy of Annette and Yeri. It was the crushed spirit that knocked in vain, year after year, tapping on inanimate objects, pleading for the locked door to be reopened. Whistling sarcastically through the gap between its front teeth. Snows of yesteryear. Bones of yesteryear. What have we to do with the Aryan side?

And how about you, my dear Prime Minister? What have you ever done? What did you do today? Or yesterday?

Half-unconsciously Fima kicked at a tin can, which went rolling down the street and startled a cat in a dustbin. You made fun of poor Tamar Greenwich simply because, on account of a fluke of pigmentation, she was born with one brown eye and one green one. You detested Eitan and Wahrhaftig, but how exactly are you better than they? You were gratuitously rude to Ted Tobias, an honest, hard-working man who has never harmed you. Another man in his place would not have allowed you so much as to set foot in his home. Not to mention the fact that thanks to him and Yael we may soon have jet-propelled vehicles.

What have you done with life's treasure? What good have you done? Apart from signing petitions.

And as if that were not enough, you needlessly distressed your father, who feeds you and whose generosity benefits dozens of people every day. When you heard on the radio about the death of the Arab boy from Gaza whom we shot in the head, what exactly did you do? You got worked up about the style of the announcement. And the way you humiliated Nina, after she took you in off the street all wet and filthy in the middle of the night and gave you light and warmth and even offered you her body. And how you hated that young settler, who, after all, even when you make allowances for the stupidity of the government and the blindness of the masses, has no choice but to carry a gun, because he really does risk his life driving at night between Hebron and Bethlehem. What do you want him to do – stick his neck out to be slaughtered? And what about Annette, you guardian of morality? What did you do today to Annette? Who trusted you from the first glance. Who had faith in your healing powers, like a simple peasant woman prostrating herself at the feet of a holy man in some Orthodox monastery and pouring her heart out to him. The only woman in your whole life ever to call you brother. You will never receive such a gift again, to be called brother by a strange woman. She trusted you without knowing you, so much so that she let you undress her and put her in your bed, and called you an angel, and you cunningly dressed yourself up as a saint to conceal your lust. Not to mention the cat you startled just a moment ago. And that is, more or less, the sum total of your latest exploits, you chief of the Revolutionary Council, you peacemaker, you comforter of deserted wives. To which we might add taking time off from work on false pretences, and an unconsummated act of self-abuse. Plus the piss that's still floating in the lavatory bowl and the funeral you gave to the first insect in history to have died of filth.

With this, Fima reached the last lamppost and the end of the street, which was also the end of the housing development and the end of Jerusalem. Beyond stretched a muddy wasteland. He felt the urge to keep on walking into the darkness, to cross the wadi, climb the hill, press on as long as his strength endured, fulfilling his allotted task as the night watchman of Jerusalem. But out of the dark came a sound of distant barking and two stray shots separated by an interval of silence. After the second shot a westerly breeze stirred, bringing a strange rustling and a smell of wet earth. Behind him in the narrow street there was an indistinct tapping, as though a blind man were groping his way with a stick. A fine drizzle filled the empty air.

Fima trembled and turned for home. As though by way of self-mortification he finished washing the dishes, including the greasy frying pan; he wiped the surfaces in the kitchen; he flushed the lavatory. The only thing he did not do was take the rubbish downstairs – because it was already a quarter to two in the morning, because he was frightened of the blind man tapping his way through the darkness outside. And why not leave something for tomorrow?

12

The fixed distance between him and her

I N his dream he saw his mother. The place was a grey, neglected garden that extended over several low hills. There were
parched lawns overgrown with thistles. And there were a few
bare trees and traces of flower beds. Below him on the hillside
was a broken bench, and next to it he saw his mother. Death had
transformed her into a schoolgirl from a religious boarding
school. From behind she looked very young, a pious girl in a
modest long-sleeved dress that came down over her ankles. She
was walking alongside a rusty irrigation pipe. At fixed intervals
she stopped and bent down to turn on a tap. The sprinklers did
not revolve, but merely released a thin spray of brownish water.
Fima's task was to follow her down the hill and turn off each tap
she'd turned on. So he saw her only from behind. Death had
made her light and lovely. It had endowed her movements with
grace but also with a certain childlike awkwardness. The sort of
mixture of agility and clumsiness that is seen in newborn kittens.
He called after her, using her Russian name, Lizaveta, her nick-
name, Liza, and her Hebrew name, Elisheva. To no avail. His
mother did not turn around or react. So he began to run. After
every seven or eight strides he had to stop, crouch down, and
turn off a tap. The taps were made of something soft and slimy
to the touch, like a jellyfish, and it was not water that dripped
from them but a sticky liquid that felt like jellied fish stock. For
all his running, breathlessly, like an overweight child, for all his
shouts that echoed dimly in the grey distance, mingled at times
with a sharp sound reminiscent of a snapping cord, it was impossible to reduce the fixed distance between him and her. He
was overcome by the desperate fear that the pipe would never
end. But at the edge of the wood she stopped and turned towards

him. Her lovely face was the face of a slain angel. Her forehead glowed in the moonlight. A skeletal pallor covered her sunken cheeks. Her lipless teeth gleamed. Her flaxen plait was made of dry straw. Her eyes were hidden by the dark glasses of the blind. On her religious schoolgirl's uniform he could see dried blood where the wires had pierced her: her knees, her belly, her throat. As though she had been made into a stuffed hedgehog. She shook her head sadly at Fima and said, Look what they've done to you, stupid. She reached up with her dry fingers to remove the dark glasses. Terrified, Fima turned away. And woke up.

13

The root of all evil

W HEN he had finished writing in his notebook, he got up
and stood by the window. He saw a bright, shiny morning. On a bare branch crouched a cat that had climbed closer to
hear what the birds were singing. Don't fall, chum, Fima said
affectionately. Even the Bethlehem hills looked as though they
were within reach. The nearby buildings and gardens were
drenched with cold, clear light. Balconies, garden walls, cars,
everything was sparkling clean after the rain that had fallen in
the night. Even though he had slept less than five hours, he felt
fresh and full of energy. He did his exercises in front of the mirror, arguing all the time with the arrogant woman reading the
seven o'clock news on the radio and who was able to declare
without hesitation what the Syrians were planning to do and
could even suggest a simple countermove. More contemptuous
than angry, Fima replied: You can't be very bright, lady. And he
saw fit to add, But look how lovely it is outside. The sky is singing a song. How would you like to take a little walk with me?
We'll stroll down the street, we'll wander through the woods and
wadis, and as we go, I'll explain to you the policy we really ought
to be adopting towards the Syrians, and where their Achilles heel
is, and where our own blind spot is.
   He went on thinking about the life of this newsreader, who had
to leave her warm bed at five-thirty on a cruel winter morning to
get to the studio in time to read the news at seven. Suppose one
morning her alarm failed to ring? Or suppose it rang on time but
she gave in to the temptation to snuggle up in bed for another
couple of minutes and then fell asleep again? Or suppose her car
wouldn't start because of the cold, as happened every morning to
the neighbour with the barking starter motor? Or perhaps this

girl – Fima pictured her: shortish, freckled, with bright laughing eyes and curly fair hair – slept at night on a camp bed at the studio. Like the doctors on night duty at the hospital. How did her husband, the insurance salesman, cope with that? Did he spend his lonely nights imagining all kinds of wild scenes between her and the technicians? There's no one worth envying, Fima decided. Except perhaps Yoezer.

It was because of Yoezer that Fima cut himself shaving. He tried without success to stanch the flow of blood with a piece of toilet paper, with cotton wool, finally with a damp handkerchief. Consequently he forgot to shave the folds of skin under his chin. Which he hated shaving anyway, because they put him in mind of the crop of a plump chicken. Pressing the handkerchief against his face as though he were suffering from toothache, he went to get dressed. And came to the conclusion that the positive side of last night's disgrace was that at least there was no fear that he had made Annette pregnant.

While he was looking for the chunky sweater he had inherited from Yael, his eye suddenly caught a glimpse of a small insect gleaming on the seat of the armchair. Was it really possible that some foolish glow-worm had forgotten to switch itself off at the end of the night? Actually, he had not seen a glow-worm for forty years at least and had no idea what they looked like. With the cunning of a seasoned hunter Fima leaned over and with a lightning movement of the right hand that began like a slap and ended with a clenched fist he managed to capture the creature without hurting it. The rapidity and accuracy of the movement belied his reputation of a clumsy oaf. Opening his fingers to examine what it was he had caught, he wondered whether it was one of Annette's earrings, a buckle of Nina's, a piece of one of Dimi's toys, or one of his father's silver cuff links. After a careful inspection he chose the last of these possibilities. Although some doubt remained.

Going to the kitchen, he opened the fridge and stood pensively holding the door open, fascinated by the mystic light shining behind the milk and the cheeses, re-examining in his mind the expression 'the price of morality' in the title of the article he had written in the night. He found no reason to revise or alter it. There was a price of morality and a price of immorality, and the real question was: What is the price of this price, i.e., what is the point and purpose of life? Everything else derived from that question. Or ought to. Including our behaviour in the Occupied Territories.

Closing the fridge, Fima decided to go out for breakfast this morning, to Mrs Scheinbaum's little café across the road, partly because he did not want to spoil the impeccable tidiness of his newly cleaned kitchen, partly because the bread was stale and the margarine reminded him of the horrible jellylike taps in his dream, and above all because the electric kettle had burned itself out the previous day, and without a kettle there would be no coffee.

At a quarter past eight he left the flat without noticing the bloodstained wad of cotton wool clinging to the cut on his cheek. But he did remember to take the rubbish down, and he also remembered to slip the envelope containing the article he had written in the night into his pocket, and he did not even forget the key of the letter box. At the shopping centre three blocks away he bought fresh bread, cheese, tomatoes, jam, eggs, some yogurt, coffee, three light bulbs, so as to have a reserve, and also a new electric kettle. He instantly regretted not having checked to see if it was made in Germany: he did his best to avoid buying German products. To his relief he discovered that it came from South Korea. Unpacking the shopping, he changed his mind and decided to skip the café and have his breakfast at home after all. Although, on second thoughts, South Korea was also a notoriously repressive country, famous for smashing the skulls of demonstrating students. While he waited for the water to boil, he reconstructed the Korean War, the era of Truman, MacArthur, and McCarthy, and ended with the destruction of Hiroshima and Nagasaki. The next nuclear holocaust won't start with the superpowers, it'll start with us here, he thought. With our regional conflict. The Syrians will invade the Golan Heights with a thousand tanks, we'll bomb Damascus, they'll fire a salvo of missiles at the coastal towns, and then we'll set off the doomsday mushroom. In a hundred years there won't be a living soul here. No Yoezer, no lizard, no cockroach.

But Fima rejected the word 'holocaust' because it could also be associated with natural disasters such as floods, epidemics, and earthquakes. What the Nazis did, by contrast, was an organised, premeditated crime that ought to be called by its proper name: murder. And nuclear war will also be a criminal act. Neither 'holocaust' nor 'doomsday'. Fima also ruled out the word 'conflict', which might describe the business of Annette and her husband, or Tsvi Kropotkin and his teaching assistant, but not the bloody war between us and the Arabs. In fact, even the sad case of Annette and Yeri could hardly be categorised with such a sterile term as 'conflict'. As for the expression 'bloody war', it was a tired cliché. Even 'tired cliché' was a tired cliché. You've got yourself into a muddle, pal.

Suddenly he felt disgusted with his linguistic niceties. Gulping down thick slices of bread and jam, sipping his second coffee, he said to himself: When the whole planet has been destroyed by atom bombs or hydrogen bombs, what difference will it make whether we describe it as a conflict, holocaust, doomsday, or a bloody war? And who will be left to decide which is the most appropriate description? So Baruch was right when he used the expressions 'a handful of dust', 'a putrid drop', 'a fleeting shadow'. And the Likud member of parliament was right to recommend playing for time. Even the orgiastic radio announcer was right when she said that there were lessons to be drawn.

But what lessons? What precious light, for heaven's sake?

Snows of yesteryear. Bones of yesteryear.

I'd hang the pair of them.

Look what they've done to you, stupid.

Your problem, pal.

So surely that is the root of all evil, Fima suddenly shouted, alone in his kitchen, as though he had received a dazzling revelation, as though a simple solution to the problem of jet propulsion on land had flashed into his head. That is the original sin. The Other Side is the source of all our misfortunes. Because there is no such thing as your problem, my problem, her problem, his problem, their problem. It's all *our* problem. There, the Korean kettle's boiling again, and if you don't switch it off, it'll go exactly the way of its predecessor. Who asked for coffee anyway? I've had two cups already. Instead of drinking coffee you'd better go back to the shopping centre, because although you remembered to put a stamp on the envelope with the article in it and to put it in your pocket, you forgot to take it out of your pocket and post it when you bought the kettle. What's going to become of you, mister? When are you going to be a *mensh*?

14

Discovering the identity of a famous Finnish general

O NE Friday evening the muse descended on Fima, and he entertained the company with the story of how he was called up for reserve duty during the Six Days' War and dumped on a barren hilltop just outside Arnona with a painter and a couple of university professors. They were given a pair of binoculars and a field telephone and told not to fall asleep. On the next hill some Jordanian soliders were setting up mortars and a machine gun; they were going about it calmly, like boy scouts at a camp. When they had finished all their preparations, they lay down and started firing at Fima and his pals. 'Can you guess,' Fima asked, 'what my first impulse was? No, it wasn't to run away. It wasn't to fire back, either. No. It was simply to phone the police and complain that there were some madmen shooting at us. Even though they could see perfectly well that there were people here on this hill. What did they take me for, a friend or acquaintance? Had I seduced their wives? What did they know about me anyway? I had to get the police to come right away and take care of them. That was how I felt.'

There was a news item in *Ha'arets* that seemed to hint at a slight softening in the government's position. A kind of sign of readiness to rethink at least one element in the official line. Fima saw in this a confirmation of his theory about tiny movements. He therefore convened the Revolutionary Council for a short morning meeting in Tsvika's seminar room at the Mount Scopus campus. He announced that he had changed his mind and decided to put off flying to Tunis. This time the peace process must begin not with an operatic overture, in the style of Begin and

Sadat, but with an exchange of small gestures that might gradually break down the barriers of hatred and anger. Or set in motion the first stirrings of an emotional détente. Joycean ripples rather than Shakespearean breakers. Tropisms rather than cataclysms. The proposal on the agenda is the following: The PLO agrees to assist in the rescue of the remaining Jews of Ethiopia. Or Yemen. We send a letter of thanks to their Tunis headquarters, thus opening up a chink in the deadlock. Tsvi is wrong to hope for US pressure. And Uri Gefen is definitely wrong in maintaining that the situation has to get much worse before there can be any change for the better. Both attitudes express the tacit inclination of the doveish left to wait resignedly for a change in reality instead of getting up and doing something. Even if it is something limited.

He suddenly felt a longing for Uri's presence: his broad shoulders, his jokes, his deep warm laughter, his youth leader's manner, his peasantlike habit of hugging your shoulders, punching you in the stomach, and saying, for instance, Come here, you Salman Rushdie; where have you been hiding yourself? And after a furtive sniff and an ostentatious wrinkling of the nose, When did you last change your shirt? For Ben Gurion's funeral? And then again: All right, get on with it, if there's no alternative: give us your lecture on Christian ascetic sects. But first help yourself to a slice of this smoked ham. Or have you turned Muslim on us?

The longing for Uri's warm voice and body brought with it a desire to rest his own pale fingers on his friend's huge freckled hand, gnarled like a stoneworker's, and to generate flashing sparks of wit that would cause the discussion to take amazing turns at every point. Like three weeks ago, at the Kropotkins', when Shula was voicing her fear of Islamic fundamentalism, and Fima interrupted her and dazzled everyone by arguing that our feud with the Arabs is merely a hundred-year-old episode, a mere dispute over land, whereas the real danger always was and still is the bottomless chasm between the Jews and the Cross. Despite his longing, Fima hoped that Uri was still in Rome. He dialled Nina's office, and hung on patiently until the secretary passed him Nina's tobacco-charred voice saying, Yes, Fima, but make it short; I'm in a meeting. He tried to tempt her into going out with him that evening, to see the late showing of the film with Jean Gabin at the Orion. I made a real ass of myself two nights ago, he said, but tonight I'll be on my best behaviour. You'll see. Promise.

Nina said:

'As it happens, I've got rather a long day today. But why not call me here at the office between seven-thirty and eight and we'll see how things look. Meanwhile, Fima, just count how many socks you have on.'

Fima did not take offence, but started to tell her the main points of his new article about the price of morality and the price of abandoning morality, and the different meanings of the term 'price' for people with different value systems. Nina interrupted him: Right now we happen to be having a meeting here, the room's full of people, we'll talk some other time. He began to ask whether the meeting was about her ultra-pious sex shop, but he thought better of it and said good-bye, and he held off for nearly a quarter of an hour before calling Tsvi Kropotkin and telling him about the article he had written in the night in reply to his. He was secretly hoping to score a pleasant telephonic victory: checkmate in four or five moves. But Tsvi was on his way to a class, he was late already: Why don't we talk about it later, Fima, when we've had a chance to read your new gospel in the paper?

It occurred to him to ring his father, to read him the facts about India, force him to admit his mistake, and tell him he'd left one of his cuff links behind. Unless the glow-worm really was one of Annette's earrings. He decided it was best to drop the idea of ringing Baruch, so as not to get involved.

Since he had no one left to call, Fima stayed in the kitchen for a few minutes longer, picking up the crumbs from his breakfast to preserve the new clean look and admiring the gleaming new kettle. A little willpower, he thought, a little energy, a little elbow grease: it's not that difficult to start a new chapter. Having arrived at this conclusion, he phoned Yael. He hoped that it would not be Ted who answered. And trusted to the inspiration of the moment to put words in his mouth and tell him what to say to her.

'It must be telepathy,' Yael exclaimed. 'I was just telling Teddy to give you a ring. You're barely half a minute ahead of us. It's like this. Teddy and I are going to a conference at the Aircraft Industry. We can't be back till this evening. I don't know what time. Our neighbour is collecting Dimi from school and looking after him for the rest of the day. Could you be a dear and pick him up from her after work? Put him to bed and keep an eye on him till we get home? He'll have had his supper, and he's got the key in his pocket? What would we do without you? Sorry, I've got to hang up now. Teddy's calling me from downstairs that they've come to pick us up. You're wonderful. I'm off now. Thanks a million and see you late tonight. He can have half a Valium tablet if he can't get to sleep. Help yourself to anything you fancy in the fridge.'

Fima cherished the words 'see you late tonight', as though they contained a secret promise. After a moment he laughed at himself for being so pleased, and set to work tidying the heap of newspapers and dusty magazines at the foot of his bed. But his glance fell on an old article by Yehoshaphat Harkabi and he started reading it and thinking about the failure of the Jewish revolt against the Romans. He thought the analogy with our own times was brilliant and original, if in some respects simplistic.

In the bus on his way to work he saw a woman, an immigrant from an Arab country, sobbing on the back seat, while a little girl, probably her daughter, aged seven or eight, comforted her by repeating over and over again, 'He didn't do it on purpose.' At that instant the word 'purpose', good purpose, bad purpose, not on purpose, suddenly seemed to contain one of the secrets of existence: love and death, loneliness, desire, and jealousy, and the wonders of light and forest, mountains, plains, and water – is there or is there not a purpose in these things? Is there or is there not a purpose in the basic similarity between you and the lizard, between a vine leaf and your hand? Is there or is there not a purpose in the fact that your life is trickling away day by day between burned-out kettles and dead cockroaches and the lessons of the Great Revolt? The word 'trickling', which he had stumbled across many years before in Pascal's *Pensées*, struck him as cruelly apposite, as though Pascal had selected it after delving into his, Fima's, life, just as he himself studied the life of Yoezer even though Yoezer's parents were not yet born. And what might the wizened Sephardic señor dozing on a wicker stool in front of the haberdashery shop think of Pascal's gamble, in which, according to its author, the gambler cannot lose? And can a wager which one can only win properly be called a gamble? And by the way, would His Worship please explain Hiroshima or Auschwitz? Or the death of the Arab child? Or the sacrifice of Ishmael and Isaac? Or the fate of Trotsky? I am that I am? Where wast thou when I laid the foundations of the earth? His Worship is silent. His Worship is dozing. His Worship is smiling. His Worship is amused. Amen. Meanwhile, Fima missed his stop and had to get off at the next one. Despite which, he did not forget to thank the driver and say good-bye. As he always did.

At the clinic he found Tamar Greenwich alone. The two doctors had gone to sort something out at the tax office and would not be back till four o'clock or so. 'Yesterday, when you didn't come to work,' Tamar said, 'it was a really crazy day. And today it's completely quiet. There's nothing to do except answer the phone. We could have an orgy. Only your shirt's buttoned up wrong. You've missed a button. Tell me, Fima, can you think of a river in Eastern Europe, three letters beginning with B?'

She was sitting on his chair at the reception desk, bent over a crossword magazine. She had stern square shoulders like an elderly sergeant major, a stout body, and a kindly, open face, and her splendid silky hair was soft and gleaming. Every visible patch of her skin was covered with freckles. Presumably they also covered the parts that were concealed. The unusual trick of pigmentation that gave her one green eye and one brown one made him feel not amusement at her expense but wonder and even a certain awe. He himself might have been born with one of his father's ears and one of his mother's. He might have inherited out of the evolutionary abyss the lizard's tail or the cockroach's feelers. Kafka's story about Gregor Samsa, who woke up one morning to find he had turned into a giant cockroach, seemed to Fima to be neither a parable nor an allegory, but a realistic possibility. Tamar did not know the story, but vaguely recalled that Kafka was a poor Yugoslav who was killed fighting against the bureaucrats. Fima could not contain himself: he told her all about Kafka and his various love affairs. Once he was certain he had whetted her appetite, he went on to give her a summary of the plot of *Metamorphosis*. He told her that the Hebrew title of the story was not an accurate translation, but he failed in his effort to explain what was wrong with it and how the title ought to be translated.

Without looking up from her crossword Tamar said:

'But what was he trying to say? That the father was a bit of a murderer? Maybe he was trying to be funny, but it doesn't amuse me at all. I'm in exactly the same situation myself. Not a day goes by without him poking fun at me. He never misses an opportunity to humiliate me. Actually, yesterday, when you weren't here, he hardly insulted me at all. He treated me almost like a human being. He even offered me a throat pastille. Can you think of a bird in seven letters ending with L?'

Fima peeled an old orange he found under the counter: he managed to avoid cutting his fingers though he did rather massacre the orange. Handing a few segments to Tamar, he replied:

'Maybe he wasn't feeling well yesterday, or something.'

'Do you have to joke about it too? Can't you see it's painful. Why don't you talk to him about it? Can't you ask him why he's always so cruel to me?'

'It must be seagull,' said Fima. 'But why did you get involved with that monster in the first place? He hates the human race in general and women in particular.'

Tamar said:

'You must understand, Fima. It's not up to me.'

'Disentangle yourself,' Fima said. 'What is there to love in him anyway? Or maybe it's not him you're in love with but your own unrequited affection?'

'Philosophising,' said Tamar. 'When you try to be clever, you're a real idiot, Fima.'

'Yes, an idiot,' Fima said, and a shy smile spread on his lips. 'I know. And yet I think I've found the answer for you. Bug.'

'I don't get it,' said Tamar. 'Why don't you just keep quiet for a while and let me finish this crossword?'

'Bug, sweetheart. The Eastern European river in three letters. Incidentally, historically speaking, the river Bug . . .'

'Stop it, Fima. Once in a blue moon I say two words about myself; why do you have to go changing the subject and speaking historically? Why can't you listen for a moment? I can never get a word in. With anyone.'

Fima apologised. He hadn't meant any harm. He'd make her a glass of tea and get himself coffee, and then he'd shut up like a clam. He'd help her do her crossword and not philosophise at all.

But once they were sitting down together drinking, Fima could not restrain himself. He started outlining his peace plan to Tamar. This very night he would call a meeting of the cabinet and describe ruthlessly to the ministers the surgery they must apply at once to rescue the state. When he said 'surgery', he suddenly had a vivid image of the expression of Prussian arrogance on Gad Eitan's face. Perhaps it was due to the fact that Dr Eitan was not only an excellent gynaecologist but also the clinic's anaesthetist. As the need arose, he anaesthetised his own patients and Wahrhaftig's.

Tamar said:

'My misfortune, Fima, is that I can't stop loving him. Even though I haven't got one chance in a million with him, even though I've known for a long time that he's a cruel man and that he loathes me. What can I do when all the time, for years now, I feel that underneath his cruelty there's a hurt little boy hiding, a lonely little boy who doesn't hate women, he's frightened of them, he's afraid that he just won't be able to stand another blow? It may be just cheap psychology. Or maybe he's still in love with his wife who left him? Maybe he's waiting for her to come back to him? Maybe the reason he's so poisonous is because inside he's full of tears. Or do you think I've just seen too many romantic films? Often, when he torments me, I feel he's really calling out to me like a little boy lost. Try arguing with your feelings. What's a country in Africa, eleven letters, third letter E, eighth letter also E?'

Fima's eyes explored the recovery room through the open door, the reception area, the desk, as though he was looking for an answer to her question. An air conditioner. Reproductions of a Degas and a Modigliani. Two unpretentious plants in hydroponic gravel. A white fluorescent tube. Pale green wall-to-wall carpet. A clock with Roman numerals. A telephone. A combined coat and umbrella stand. A basket full of magazines. A few magazines lying on the table. A blue leaflet: 'Osteoporosis – Accelerated Deterioration of the Bones: A Guide for Women. Which women are especially vulnerable? High-risk groups: Underweight women. Women with fine bone structure. Women who have had their ovaries removed. Women who have undergone radiation therapy and ceased to produce oestrogen. Women who have never been pregnant. Women with a family history of the condition. Women who have been on a low-calcium diet. Women who smoke. Women who do not take sufficient physical exercise, or whose consumption of alcohol is excessive, or who suffer from hyperthyroidism.'

He peered at another explanatory leaflet, in purple this time, on the table in front of him. 'My Little Secret . . . the Menopause: Hormone-Replacement Therapy. What is the menopause? What are female hormones and how are they produced? What are the characteristic signs of the onset of the menopause? What are the changes resulting from decreased production of female hormones? Comparative graph of oestrogen and progesterone. What are hot flushes and when can you expect them? What is the connection between oestrogen, high blood-fat levels, and heart disease? Is it possible to improve your ability to cope emotionally with the changes in your body at this time of life?'

Fima contented himself with reading the main headings. Tears of compassion suddenly flooded his eyes, not for a specific woman, Nina, Yael, Annette, Tamar, but for womanhood in general. The separation of humankind into two sexes struck him as an act of cruelty and an irreparable injustice. He felt that he had a share in this injustice and was therefore partly to blame, because he had sometimes unintentionally benefited from its consequences. Then he thought for a while about the punctuation of the leaflet and how it could be improved. Whoever left these leaflets here foolishly forgot that men sometimes come to the clinic, including religious men: problems of infertility and so forth. Pamphlets like these might embarrass them. Women might even be embarrassed, waiting and watching a man reading this kind of literature. Then he recalled that it was he himself who put the pamphlets out: he had never looked at them before. Also, despite the risk of embarrassment or tactlessness, various pictures, ornaments, and souvenirs were displayed on the walls and shelves bearing messages of thanks from grateful patients. They signed their dedications only with their initials or with their first name and the first letter of the surname, like that brass dish from Carmela L, 'in eternal gratitude to the dedicated and wonderful staff'. Fima had not forgotten this Carmela, because one day he heard that she had killed herself. Even though she always struck him as somebody outstandingly courageous and cheerful. The mayor of Jerusalem ought to ban the use of the word 'eternal', at least within the city limits.

He began to comb the map of Africa in his mind from north to south, from Egypt to Namibia, and then again from east to west, from Madagascar to Mauretania, looking for the country that was holding up Tamar's crossword puzzle. While he did so, he conjured up a vision of Gad Eitan, the arrogant catlike Viking, as a miserable unloved child wandering forlornly through the jungles and deserts of Africa. He could not find the answer. But he asked himself whether those who come after us, Yoezer and his contemporaries, living here in Jerusalem a hundred years from now, would also be solving crossword puzzles. Would they too suffer the humiliation of unrequited love? Would they button their shirts up wrong? Would they be condemned to a lack of oestrogen? Would abandoned children in a hundred years continue to roam forlornly around the Equator? Fima could feel sadness gripping him. In his sadness he was ready to lean over and hug Tamar. To press her wide face to his chest. To stroke her beautiful hair, which was gathered in a chaste bun at the back, like a pioneer's in the previous generation. If he were to suggest that she sleep with him here and now, on the sofa in the recovery room, she would no doubt turn red and white in alarm, but in the end she would not refuse him. After all, they would be alone till four o'clock at least. He could give her pleasure such as she had never known in her life, and draw forth laughter, pleas, sobs, whispered requests, low groans of surprise, sounds that would produce in him too the sweetest thrill he knew: the joy of altruism. So what if she was not pretty? Good-looking women only made him feel humble and submissive. Only the unwanted and rejected were capable of igniting in him that spark of generosity that always fuelled his desire. But what if she wasn't protected? What if she got pregnant here, of all places, in this abortion inferno?

Instead of love he offered her an orange, though he omitted to check first that there was another one left in the drawer under his desk. He startled her by adding that her light-blue skirt flattered her figure and she should wear it more often. And he thought her hair was lovely.

Tamar said:

'Stop it, Fima. It's not funny.'

Fima said:

'I suppose it's like a fish: it's only when it's lifted out of the water for the first time that it realises it needs to be in the water to live. Never mind. I just want to tell you I wasn't joking. I meant exactly what I said about the light blue and your hair.'

'You're rather a darling yourself,' Tamar said timidly. 'You're very knowledgeable, you're a poet and all that. A good man. The trouble is, you're a child. It's just incredible how childish you are. Sometimes I feel like coming around in the morning and shaving you myself so you don't cut yourself, your cheeks and your chin. Look, you've done it again today. You're nothing but a baby.'

After that they sat facing each other and hardly spoke. She concentrated on her crossword while he looked at an old copy of *Woman* that he picked out of the basket. He found an article about an ex-call girl who had married a handsome Canadian millionaire and then left him for a group of Bratslav Hasidim in Safed.

After a silence Tamar said:

'I've just remembered. Gad asked us to clean and tidy his room. And Wahrhaftig said to sterilise the forceps and speculums and boil the towels and gowns. Only I don't feel like moving. I'll just finish this crossword first.'

'Forget it,' Fima said enthusiastically. 'Just you sit there quietly like a queen, and I'll do it all. It'll be all right, you'll see.'

At that he stood up and went into Dr Eitan's room, holding the duster. First he changed the roll of paper sheets, which felt pleasantly rough to his fingertips. Then he tidied the drugs cupboard, pondering on his father's anecdote about the length and width of railway tracks. He discovered he had a soft spot for the Israeli representative: in refusing to give way to his US counterpart, he had delivered a devastating reply. It was only on the surface that it appeared funny: in fact, it was the American's position that was ridiculous. As if there was any sense in his implied claim that in an international gathering of railway chiefs each delegate's speech should be in direct ratio to the length of track in his country. Such a crude approach was both morally untenable and logically absurd. While he was pursuing this line of thought further, he absent-mindedly attempted to take his own blood pressure with the device he found on Eitan's desk. Perhaps it was because he had remarked jokingly to Tamar that Gad Eitan may not have been feeling well the day before, since he had failed to tyrannise her. But Fima's efforts to bind the rubber tube, phylactery-like, around his arm with his free hand were unsuccessful, and he abandoned the attempt. He contemplated a coloured poster on the wall: a humorous picture of a good-looking young man with a pregnant tummy holding a plump baby in his arms, the two of them beaming with joy. The wording read: 'Materna 160 – *your* vitamin supplement. Easy to take. Odourless. Tasteless. The leading product in the field. Massively endorsed by expectant mothers in the USA. Available strictly on medical prescription only.' One of the two words, 'strictly' and 'only', was redundant, Fima mused, but for some reason he could not decide which to delete. The expression 'leading product' struck him as crude, while 'massively endorsed by expectant mothers' was positively offensive.

Moving on, he flicked an imaginary speck of dust from the examination couch. He struggled against the sudden urge to lie down with his legs apart for a minute or two, just to experience the sensation. He was certain there must be a mistake in Tamar's crossword: the only country he could think of in Africa with eleven letters was South Africa, but that didn't fit because it didn't have two Es. As though if it did have two Es, everything there would be perfect!

Fima eyed the stainless-steel speculums intended for taking cervical smears. When he imagined to himself the mysterious entrance exposed and dilated by means of the metal jaws, he felt a dull pang of revulsion in his stomach. He made a sound like an intake of breath through clenched teeth, as though he had been scalded but was determined not to shriek. Laid out with obsessive precision beside the speculums were long-bladed scissors, forceps, IUDs hermetically sealed in sterile plastic. To the left behind the doctor's desk, on a small trolley, stood the suction pump that was used, Fima knew, to terminate pregnancy by means of suction. He shuddered at the grim thought that this was a kind of enema in reverse, and that womanhood was an irreparable injustice.

And what did they do with the foetuses? Put them in a plastic bag and drop them into the rubbish bins that he or Tamar emptied at the end of the day? Food for alley cats? Or did they flush them down the lavatory and rinse with disinfectant? Snows of yesteryear. If the light within you darkens, it is written, how great is the darkness.

On a little stand was the resuscitation equipment, an oxygen bottle and an oxygen mask. Nearby was the anaesthetic equipment. Fima switched on the electric radiator and waited for the elements to glow red. He counted the drip bags, trying to understand the formula printed on them, glucose and sodium chloride. With his duster poised in his hand he reflected on how anaesthesia and resuscitation, fertility and death, rubbed shoulders with each other within this little room. There was something absurd, something unbearable about it, but what it was he could not say.

After a moment he pulled himself together and caressed the

screen of the ultrasound machine with his duster. It did not seem much different from the screen of Ted's computer. When Ted had asked him how to say 'deadline' in Hebrew, he had not been able to think of the answer. The only equivalent he could think of sounded artificial and anaemic. 'Tasteless and odourless', like the leading product that was massively endorsed by expectant mothers in the USA. Meanwhile he upset a neat pile of transparent plastic gloves made by a firm called Pollack, each encased in a sterile wrapping that was similarly transparent. As he carefully remade the pile, he asked himself what it meant, this transparency that was so prevalent here, as if it were an aquarium.

Eventually he made his way to the utility room, a kind of open cubicle formed by closing in a balcony with opaque glass. He fed a heap of towels into the washing machine, pushed his duster in too, read and reread the instructions, and surprised himself by getting the machine to work. To the left of the washing machine stood the steriliser, with the instructions printed on a panel in English: 200° centigrade, 110 minutes. Fima decided not to put this machine on yet, even though it contained a couple of pairs of scissors and several forceps, as well as some stainless steel bowls. Perhaps it was because the temperatures struck him as lethal. Going into the lavatory, he inhaled with a strange pleasure the pungent cocktail of disinfectant smells. He tried to empty his bladder but failed, perhaps because of his thoughts about drowned infants. Angrily he gave up, cursed his penis, zipped up, returned to Tamar, and, resuming their earlier conversation, said: 'Why don't you try breaking off contact? Just ignore his rudeness? Signal nothing from now on except utter indifference? I dusted and tidied everything and put the washing machine on. As if he was thin air, that's the way to treat him.'

'How can I, Fima? I'm in love with him. Why can't you understand? But there is one thing I ought to do, really: instead of looking glum, I ought to slap him round the face. Sometimes I have a feeling he's just waiting for me to do it. I think it might do him good.'

'The truth is' – Fima grinned – 'he's earned himself an honest slap from you. What is it Wahrhaftig says: "like in a civilised country." I'd really enjoy seeing that. Even if in principle I'm not keen on violence. There, I've found it for you.'

'Found what for me?'

'Your African country. Try Sierra Leone. I didn't put the steriliser on because it was almost empty. A waste of electricity.'

Tamar said:

'Stop loving him. That's the only thing that would save me. Stop just like that. But how do you do it? You know everything, Fima. Do you know that too?'

He laughed, shrugged his shoulders, muttered something, regretted it, finally pulled himself together and said:

'What do I understand of love? Once I used to think that love is the point where cruelty and compassion meet. Now I think that's idle chatter. Seems to me now I never understood anything. I comfort myself by reflecting that apparently other people understand even less than I do. It's all right, Tamar, just cry, don't hold back, it'll make you feel better. I'll make you a glass of tea. Never mind. In a hundred years love and suffering will go the way of the dinosaurs, along with blood feuds, crinolines, and whalebone corsets. Men and women will mate by exchanging tiny electrochemical impulses. There will be no mistakes. Do you want a biscuit with it?'

After making the tea, and after some hesitation, he told her the story about the conference of railway chiefs, and he explained why in his opinion Mr Cohen was right and Mr Smith was wrong, until she smiled faintly through her tears. In the drawer of his desk he found a pencil sharpener, a pencil, some paper clips, a ruler and a paperknife, but there were no more oranges, and no biscuits. Tamar said it didn't matter, thanks. She was feeling better already. He was always so goodhearted. Her projecting Adam's apple seemed not so much funny as tragic. Because of this tragic feeling he began to doubt whether those to come, Yoezer and his friends, would really manage to live more rational lives than ours. At most, cruelty and stupidity would adopt subtler and more sophisticated forms. What use are jet-propelled vehicles to someone who is aware that his place does not know him?

This biblical phrase, 'his place does not know him', so moved and fascinated him that he had to whisper it to himself. Suddenly, illuminated, he could see a whole sublime, beguiling Utopia enfolded in that everyday phrase. He made up his mind not to talk to Tamar about it, so as not to add insult to injury.

Tamar said:

'Look: the paraffin heater is almost empty. Why are you talking to yourself?'

Fima said:

'I put the electric one on in Gad's room. I didn't go into Alfred's room at all. I'll do it in a minute.'

Then he grasped what he was being asked, and went outside to refill the container. When he came back in, there was an urgent roll of thunder, as though a desperate tank battle had begun. Fima suddenly remembered the text 'He toucheth the hills and they smoke,' and he could almost visualise it. He trembled. From the flat upstairs came the sound of the cello, slow, solemn, soft, the same two heavy phrases repeated over and over again. Even though it was only half past three, the room was growing so dark that Tamar had to switch the light on to see her crossword puzzle. As she stood there with her back to him, Fima made up his mind to stand behind her and hug her, to bury her weary head in the hollow of his neck and switch off their thoughts, to sprinkle kisses on the nape of her neck and the roots of her lovely hair gathered up into such a neat little bun, which could be undone for once and set free. But he thought better of this, and they spent a little while together trying to discover the identity of a famous Finnish general, ten letters. At that moment Fima resigned himself to the realisation that, when all was said and done, he was not made of the stuff of great leaders who have the power to make history, to end wars, to heal the hearts of the masses consumed by suspicion and despair. He derived some comfort from the thought that the present political leaders were not made of this stuff either. Less so, if anything.

15

Bedtime stories

DIMI Tobias, an albino child with thick glasses and small red eyes, was ten years old but looked younger. He said little and spoke politely, in well-balanced sentences, sometimes surprising grown-ups with his striking phraseology and his cultivated ingenuousness, in which Fima imagined he could detect a trace of irony. His father sometimes called him a Levantine Einstein, but Yael complained that she was bringing up a devious, manipulative child.

He was sitting in the living room, huddled silently in a corner of his father's wide armchair, looking like an elongated parcel that had been abandoned on a park bench. In vain did Fima attempt to get him to say what the trouble was. All through the evening Dimi sat motionless, apart from his rabbit's eyes that blinked nonstop behind the thick lenses. Was he thirsty? Did he want a glass of milk? Juice? Fima had made up his mind that the child was dehydrating and needed fluids. Some iced water, perhaps? Some whisky?

Dimi said:

'Stop it.'

Fima, who was certain he was not doing the right thing but was damned if he could think what he ought to be doing or saying, opened a window to let in some cool air. Then it struck him that the child might be nursing the flu, so he hurriedly closed it. He poured himself a glass of mineral water in the kitchen and came back to the living room to drink it, perhaps in the hope that Dimi would follow his example and drink something too.

'Sure you're not thirsty?'

Dimi raised his pale face slightly and looked at Fima with consternation, as one looks at a grown-up who is getting

into difficulties but who cannot be helped. Fima attempted
another line:

'Well, let's play cards then. Or how about a game of Mono-
poly? Or would you like to watch the news with me? Just show
me how to switch on this TV of yours.'

'You press the button. The top one,' Dimi said. And he added:
'You don't offer spirits to a child.'

Fima said:

'Course you don't. I was just trying to make you laugh. Tell me
what you feel like doing. Shall I do an impersonation of Shamir
and Peres?'

'Nothing. I've told you three times already.'

In vain Fima suggested an adventure story, a computer game,
jokes, a pillow fight, a game of dominoes. Something was weighing on the child, and though Fima quizzed him about school,
about the afternoon at the neighbour's, tiredness, tummy aches,
the US space programme, all he could get out of him was 'stop
it'. Could it be the beginning of tonsillitis? Pneumonia? Menin-
gitis? Fima squeezed himself into the armchair, forcing the
skinny Challenger to huddle even further into his corner. He put
an arm around the limp shoulders, and insisted:

'Tell me what's happened.'

'Nothing,' said Dimi.

'Where does it hurt?'

'Nothing.'

'Shall we be a little wild together? Or would you like to go to
sleep? Your mother said to give you half a Valium. Do you want
a story?'

'You already asked.'

Fima was uneasy. Something nasty, something serious and
possibly even dangerous was happening in front of his eyes and
he could not think what to do. What would Teddy do now if he
were here? He ran his fingers through the albino hair and muttered:

'But you're obviously not well. Where do they keep that Valium? Tell me.'

Dimi recoiled from the caress and slipped away like a cat

whose rest is disturbed. He tottered to the other armchair, and buried himself under a heap of cushions so that only his head and shoes were visible. His eyes blinked behind his thick lenses.

Fima, whose anxiety had turned into panic mixed with mounting anger, said:

'I'm going to call a doctor. But first we'll take your temperature. Where do they keep the thermometer?'

'Stop clowning,' said Dimi. 'Why don't you watch the news?'

As though he had been hit in the face, Fima sprang to his feet in a muddled frenzy and tried to switch on the television, but he pushed the wrong button. Instantly, realising that he was being made a fool of, he regretted coddling the child and shouted at him:

'I'll give you sixty seconds to tell me what's wrong, and if you don't, I'm going to leave you here by yourself.'

'Go on then,' said Dimi.

'Very well then,' Fima snapped, attempting to imitate Ted's strictness and even his accent. 'I'm going. OK. But before I go, you've got exactly four minutes on the clock to get ready and into bed. And no fuss. Teeth, glass of milk, pyjamas, Valium, the lot. And no more ridiculous scenes.'

'You're the one who's making ridiculous scenes,' said Dimi.

Fima walked out of the room and made his way to Ted's study. He had no intention of leaving the sick child alone. On the other hand, he had no idea how to retract his ultimatum, so he sat down on Teddy's padded chair in front of the computer, without turning the light on, and urged himself to think rationally. There were only two possibilities: either the child was developing some illness and needed immediate treatment, or he was tormenting him on purpose, and he, Fima, was behaving like a clown. Suddenly he felt full of pity for the pale, tortured Challenger. And for himself too: 'They hadn't even bothered to leave a phone number. They're probably having a night out in Tel Aviv, living it up in some exotic restaurant or nightclub, without so much as a thought for us. What if something terrible is happening? How can I get hold of them? What if he's swallowed something? Caught a lethal virus? Appendicitis? Polio? Or perhaps it's his parents who are in trouble? A car crash on the way back to Jerusalem? Or a terrorist attack?'

Fima made up his mind to ask the downstairs neighbour. On second thoughts he did not know what he could say to her, and was afraid of again making a fool of himself.

So he walked back sheepishly to the living room and wheedled:

'Are you angry with me, Dimi? Why are you doing this to me?'

A ghost of a tired old man's smile flitted across the child's mouth. In a factual tone he remarked:

'You're bugging me.'

'In that case,' Fima said, fighting back a fresh wave of fury, a mighty urge to give this devious, impertinent creature a small slap across the face, 'you can be bored all by yourself. Good night. I've gone off you.'

But instead of leaving he feverishly pulled down from the shelf the first book his fingers encountered. It turned out to be an orange-bound tome in English on the history of Alaska in the eighteenth or nineteenth century. Collapsing onto the sofa, he began to leaf through it, straining to take in the pictures at least. He made up his mind to pay no attention to the little enemy. But he had trouble concentrating. Every now and then he peeped at his watch. Whenever he looked, it was always twenty-five past nine, and he was furious not only because time seemed to be standing still but also because he had missed the news. A sense of disaster weighed on his chest like a stone. Something really bad is happening. Something you are going to regret bitterly. Something that will eat away at you for days and years, while you wish in vain that you could turn back the clock to this moment and correct the terrible error. To do the simple, obvious thing that only a blind man or an idiot would not be doing now. But what is that thing? Time and again he stole a glance at Dimi, who was lying inside his den of cushions in the armchair, blinking. Eventually he managed to latch onto the story of the early whale hunters who reached Alaska from New England and set up beach stations that were often attacked by savage nomads who had crossed the Bering Straits from Siberia. And suddenly Dimi said:

'Tell me something. What's oedema?'

'I don't know exactly,' said Fima. 'It's the name of an illness. Why?'

'What kind of illness?'

'Show me where it hurts. Fetch the thermometer. I'll call a doctor.'

'Not me,' said Dimi. 'Winston.'

'Who's Winston?' It occurred to Fima that the child might be delirious. To his surprise this discovery made him feel easier. Now, how could he get hold of a doctor? Call Tamar and ask her advice. Not *our* doctors, that's for sure. Not Annette's husband, either. And anyway, what *was* oedema?

'Winston's a dog. Tslil Weintraub's dog.'

'Is the dog ill?'

'He was.'

'And you're afraid you may have caught it?'

'No. We killed him.'

'Killed him? Why did you do that?'

'They said he had oedema.'

'Who killed him?'

'Only he isn't dead.'

'He's not alive and he's not dead.'

'He's alive and he's also dead.'

'Will you explain that to me?'

'I can't explain.'

Fima stood up and put one hand on Dimi's forehead and the other on his own. He couldn't feel any difference. Maybe they were both ill?

'It was murder,' said Dimi. And suddenly, horrified by what had come out of his mouth, he snatched another cushion and, hiding his face behind it, began to sob. Broken, strangled gasps that sounded like hiccups. Fima tried to pull the cushion away, but Dimi held fast to it and would not let go, so he gave up. And he realised that there was no illness, no fever, but suffering that required patience and silence. He sat down on the rug in front of the armchair and took Dimi's hand, feeling that he too was close to tears and that he loved this weird child with his thick glasses and paper-white hair, his stubbornness, his knowingness, his perpetual air of solitary, premature old age. Fima's body ached with the desire to snatch the sobbing creature up from the armchair and squeeze him to his chest with all his strength. A desire to hold him stronger than any he had ever felt for a woman's body in his life . But he controlled himself and did not stir so long as the gasps continued. Until Dimi stopped. And, oddly, it was just when he fell silent that Fima said gently:

'That's enough now, Dimi.'

Suddenly the child slid out of the chair and into his arms. He huddled against Fima so hard, he seemed to be burrowing inside him. And he said:

'I will tell.'

And he began to talk, clearly, in a soft, steady voice, without any more sobs and without halting for a moment to search for a word, even blinking less than before, about how they had found the dog crouching in the filth among the dustbins. A repulsive sort of dog, with a mangy back, with open wounds and flies on one of his hind legs. Once he had belonged to a friend of theirs, Tslil Weintraub, but ever since the Weintraubs went abroad he belonged to nobody. He just lived on scraps. The dog was lying on his side behind the bins, coughing like someone who smokes too much. They gave him a medical examination, and Yaniv said, 'He's going to die soon, he's got oedema.' Then they forced his mouth open and made him swallow a spoonful of a medicine invented by Ninja Marmelstein: muddy water from the pond mixed with a little sand and leaves and a little cement powder and some aspirin from Yaniv's mother. Then they decided to carry him down to the wadi in a blanket and do the sacrifice of Isaac with him like they learned in Bible. It was Ronen's idea, and he even ran home and got a bread knife. All the way to the wadi this Winston lay quietly in the blanket. Actually he seemed happy, wagging his tail gratefully. Maybe he thought they were taking him to the vet. Anyone who came close to him got a lick on his face or his hands. In the wadi they collected stones and built an altar, and they put the unresisting dog on it. He looked at them all with a kind of curiosity, like a baby, trustingly, as though he was sure he was among loving friends, or as if he understood the game and was glad to be playing. His wounds were revolting, but his face was cute, with brown eyes that showed sense and feeling. There's this thing sometimes – isn't that right, Fima? – when you look at an animal and you think it can remember things that human beings have forgotten. Or at least it looks like it. Anyway, he was a dirty, rather irritating dog, covered with fleas and ticks, always fawning on everyone; he loved to put his head on your knees and drool on you.

Dimi's idea was to pick some greenery and flowers and decorate the altar. He even arranged a little wreath on Winston's head, like they do in nursery school when it's somebody's birthday. They tied his arms and legs together firmly, and even so he didn't stop fawning and being glad and wagging his tail all the time, as though he was really happy to be the centre of attention. Anyone who wasn't careful got a lick. Then they drew lots: Ninja Marmelstein had to chant the prayers, Ronen had to dig the grave, and he, Dimi, got the job of killing him. At first he tried to get out of it – he had the excuse that his sight wasn't too good – but they made fun of him, and got angry, and said a draw is a draw, stop being such a bleeding heart. So he had no choice. Only it wouldn't work. The knife was shaking in his hand and the dog kept moving all the time. Instead of cutting the throat, he cut off half an ear. The dog went mad and started to cry like a baby and sort of bit the air. Dimi had to cut again, quickly, to stop the howling. But this time instead of the throat the knife went into something soft near the belly, because Winston wriggled and squealed and bled a lot. Yaniv said, So what? It's not so terrible; its only a smelly old Arab dog. And Ninja said, And he's got oedema; he's going to die anyway. The third time Dimi struck with all his might, but he hit a rock and the knife broke in half. He was left holding just the handle. Ninja and Yaniv grabbed Winston's head and said, Come on, hurry up, you dummy. Pick up the blade and cut real fast. But there wasn't enough of the blade left, and it was impossible to saw the throat; it was all slippery with the blood, and each time it cut in the wrong place. In the end everyone was covered with blood, how can it be that a dog has so much blood, maybe it was because of the oedema, and Yaniv and Ninja and Ronen started running away and the dog bit through the rope and got free, but only the front legs, the back ones stayed tied, and with shrieks, not dog shrieks, more like a woman shrieking, he dragged himself away on his belly and disappeared into the bushes, and when Dimi realised the others weren't there, he ran after them in a panic. He found them at last hiding in the garage underneath the block of flats. There was a tap there and they had managed to wash the blood off, but they didn't let him wash and they blamed him. It was all his fault Winston was not alive and not dead, cruelty to dumb animals, his fault Ronen's knife from home got broken, and they blamed him because he would tell on them, they knew him, and they started kicking him and they got some more rope, and Ninja said, Now there's an *intifada* going on here. Let's hang Dimi. Only Ronen was relatively fair and said to them, First just let me put his glasses somewhere so they don't get broken. That was why he didn't see who tied him up and who, after they beat him, stood and peed on him. So they left him tied up down there in the garage and ran away, shouting that he had it coming to him, why did he kill Winston. He didn't tell the neighbour who was supposed to be looking after him. He just said he got dirty from the pond. If his parents found out, it would be the end of him.

'Are you going to tell them, Fima?'

Fima thought about it. All through the confession he had not stopped stroking the albino hair. As in a bad dream he felt that the dog and Dimi and he had become one. In the same psalm where it says, 'Their mind is gross like fat,' it also says, 'My soul droops with sorrow.' He said earnestly:

'No, Dimi, I'm not going to tell.'

The boy peered obliquely up at him. His rabbit's eyes through the thick lenses seemed agonised yet full of trust, as though he was trying to demonstrate what he had described earlier in the eyes of the dog. So this is what love is.

Fima shuddered as though outside, from the depths of the darkness, wind, and rain, his ears had caught an elusive echo of a howl.

He stroked the little Challenger's head and dragged him inside the chunky sweater. As though he were pregnant with him. After a moment Dimi freed himself and asked:

'But why?'

'Why what?'

'Why did you agree not to tell them?'

'Because it wouldn't help Winston, and you've already suffered enough.'

'You're OK, Fima.'

And then:

'Even though you're a rather funny man. Sometimes they call you a clown behind your back. And you really are a bit of a clown.'

'Now, Dimi, you're going to have a glass of milk. And tell me where I can find that Valium your mother said you're to take.'

'I'm a little like a clown too. But I'm not OK. I should have said no. I shouldn't have let myself be carried away by them.'

'But they made you do it.'

'Still, it was murder.'

'You can't tell,' Fima ventured. 'Maybe he was only wounded.'

'He lost a lot of blood. A whole sea of blood.'

'Sometimes you can bleed a lot even from a scratch. Once, when I was little, I was balancing on a wall and fell off, and I bled a huge amount from a tiny little gash on my head. Granpa Baruch nearly fainted.'

'I hate them.'

'They're just children, Dimi. Children sometimes do very cruel things, simply because they don't have enough imagination to know what pain is.'

Dimi said:

'Not the children. Them. If they could have chosen, they wouldn't have had me. And I wouldn't have chosen them either. It's not fair: you can choose who you marry but you can't choose who your parents are. And you can't divorce them either. Fima?'

'Yes.'

'Shall we take a torch and some bandages and iodine and go and look for him down in the wadi?'

'In this darkness and rain there isn't a hope of finding him.'

'True,' said Dimi. 'You're right. We haven't got a hope. But let's go and search anyhow. So at least we'll know we tried and failed.' As he said this, he looked to Fima like a pocket-sized edition of his self-possessed, rational father. Even his intonation was a reflection of Ted's: the quiet voice of a well-balanced, solitary man. Dimi wiped his glasses as he added: 'Tslil's family are also to blame. Why did they go abroad and leave their dog behind when he was sick? They could have taken him. They could have made some arrangements for him at least. Why did they throw him out on the rubbish heap like that? The Cherokees have a law that you mustn't throw anything away. Even a broken pot they keep in the wigwam. Anything you've ever used you mustn't get rid of. It might still need you. They even have a sort of ten commandments, or less than ten, and the first one is, Thou shalt not throw out. I have a chest in the storeroom full of toys from when I was so high. They're always shouting at me to throw them out, who needs them, they just take up space, they're just gathering dust, but I don't agree. "Throwing away is like killing," said Snow Daughter to Whispering Wind Lake, tightening her delicate fingers round the wolfstone.'

'What's that?'

'It's a story about a Cherokee girl. Whispering Wind Lake was the chief of the banished tribe.'

'Tell me.'

'I can't. I can't think about anything else. That dog keeps howling at me, those brown eyes so obedient, so tame, so happy to be the centre of attention, and wagging his tail, and giving a warm lick to anyone who bent over him. Even when Ronen was tying his legs together, he gave Ronen a lick. And his ear came off and fell on the ground like a slice of bread. I keep hearing him crying all the time in my head, and maybe he really is still alive, dying in a puddle among the rocks in the wadi, crying and waiting for the vet. In the night God will come and kill me for it. The best thing for me is not to go to sleep at all. Or he'll kill me because I hate them and it's forbidden to hate your parents. Who told them to have me? I didn't ask for any favours. There's nothing to do around here anyway. Whatever you do turns out badly. It's all just trouble and shouting. Whatever I do, just trouble and shouting. You were married to my mummy once and then you didn't want her. Or she didn't want you. Trouble and shouting. Dad says it happened because you're a bit of a clown. He said it to me in English. They don't have much use for me either. What they need is to always have peace and quiet in the flat and everything to be tidy and in the right place and not to slam the door. Every time a door slams, she yells at me and Dad. Every time some pen isn't where it's supposed to be, he yells at me and Mum. Every time the top of the toothpaste isn't screwed on properly, they both yell at me. No, they don't yell; they just point out. Like this: It would be preferable if, in future . . . Or he says to her in English, Do something so that child doesn't get under my feet. And she says, It's your child, sir. When you were little, Fima, didn't you ever wish deep down that your parents would die? Didn't you want to be an orphan and free like Huckleberry Finn? Weren't you a little clown?'

Fima said:

'Every child seems to have thoughts like that at some time or another. It's natural. But they don't really mean it.'

Dimi said nothing. His albino eyes began to blink again fast, as though the light was hurting them. And he added:

'Say, Fima, you need a child, don't you? How'd you like it if we went away together? We could go to the Galapagos Islands and build ourselves a cabin out of branches. We could catch fish and clams, and grow vegetables. We could track the thousand-year-old tortoises that you told me about once.'

Here we go again, Fima thought: more longing for the Aryan side. For Chili. He picked Dimi up in his arms and carried him to his room. He undressed him and put him into his pyjamas. In the Galapagos Islands there is no winter. It's always springtime. And the thousand-year-old tortoises are nearly as big as this table because they don't hunt and they don't dream and they don't make a sound. As though everything was straightforward and fine. He picked the boy up again and took him to brush his teeth. Then they stood together at the lavatory and Fima said, 'Ready, steady,' and they had a contest to see who would finish first. All the time Fima muttered muddled reassurances, which he hardly heard himself, Never mind little boy the rain will soon stop the winter will soon be over the spring will soon be over we'll sleep like tortoises and then we'll get up and plant vegetables and then we'll be all good and you'll see how great it'll be.

Despite these reassuring words they were both on the verge of tears. They clung to each other as though it was getting colder. Instead of tucking him up in bed, Fima carried the child piggyback in his green flannel pyjamas to his parents' bedroom and lay down beside him on the double bed, carefully removing his thick glasses, and the two of them huddled together under a single blanket while Fima told him one story after another, about lizards, about the evolutionary abyss, about the failure of the unnecessary Jewish revolt against Rome, about the railwaymen's conference and the width of the track, about the forests of Sierra Leone in Africa, about whaling in Alaska, about ruined temples in the mountains of northern Greece, about breeding tropical fish in heated pools in Valletta, the capital of Malta, about St Augustine, about the poor cantor who found himself alone on a desert island at the High Holy Days. At a quarter to one, when Ted and Yael returned from Tel Aviv, they found Fima sleeping fully clothed, curled up like a foetus inside a blanket on their double bed, with his head on Yael's nightie, and Dimi sitting in his green pyjamas at the computer in his father's study, with a very serious look on his owlish face, intent on defeating a whole gang of pirates single-handed, in a complicated game of strategy.

16

Fima comes to the conclusion that there is still a chance

SOME time after one o'clock, on his way home in the taxi Teddy had called for him, Fima remembered his father's last visit. Was it two days ago or the previous morning? How the old man had begun with Nietzsche and ended with the Russian railways, which were constructed in such a way that they could be of no use to invaders. What had his father been trying to say to him? Fima now thought that the old man's conversation had revolved around some point that he could not or dared not express directly. In the midst of all those tales and morals, all those Cossacks and Indians, Fima had failed to notice he had been complaining of a lack of air. Yet his father never talked about ill health, apart from the usual wisecracks about his backache. Now Fima recalled his panting, his coughing, the whistling sound that might have come from his throat or chest. As he was leaving, the old man seemed to be trying to say something, that you didn't want to listen to. Now, he said to himself: You preferred to quibble about Herzl and about India. What was he trying to hint amid all that jocular wordplay? On the other hand, his leave-taking always has an epic quality. If he goes to the café for half an hour, he wishes you a life replete with meaning. If he goes to buy a paper, he warns you not to squander life's rich treasure. What was he trying to say this time? You missed it. You were so intent on the thrills of a victory over the Occupied Territories. As usual. You thought that if you could just get the better of him in an argument, the obstacles to peace would be removed and a new era could begin. Like when you were little: an acerbic child with no keener desire than to catch grown-ups out in a mistake or a slip of the tongue. To win an argument with an adult, force him to hoist the white flag. If some visitor or other used the expression 'most of the majority of people', you chimed in exultantly to the effect that 'most of the majority' actually signified 25.1%, in other words a minority, not a majority. If your father said that Ben Gurion was a blunt speaker, you pointed out that if he was blunt, he could not be very sharp. Yesterday when he was visiting you, there were moments when his cantorial tenor was almost silenced by breathlessness. True, he's an old chatterbox, a dandy and a bore, a philanderer, on top of which he suffers from political blindness of the most self-righteous and infuriating kind. And yet in his own way he is a generous, good-hearted man. He stuffs money into your pocket while he pokes his nose into your love life and tries to run your whole life for you. And just where would you be now without him?

The taxi stopped at the light at the Mount Herzl junction. The driver said:

'It's freezing out there. My heater's broken. The bloody traffic lights aren't working. This whole country's fucked up.'

Fima said:

'Why exaggerate? There may be twenty-five countries in the world that are more decent than ours, but on the other hand there are more than a hundred where you'd be shot for talking like that.'

The driver said:

'The goyim can go burn, the lot of 'em. They're all rotten. They hate us.'

Strange lights flickered on the wet road. Wisps of mist drifted around the darkened buildings. Where the nearest wisps caught the orange glare of the streetlights at the junction, there was a kind of ghostly glow. Fima thought: This must be what the mystical writings call 'the Radiance that is not of this world'. The ancient Aramaic expression suddenly left him feeling dizzy. As if the words themselves came from over there, from other worlds. Not a car went past. There was not a lighted window to be seen. The desolate asphalt, the glare of the streetlights, the shadowy pines that stood shrouded in rain as though all gates had been locked forever, aroused a vague dread in Fima. As if his own life were flickering out, there in the icy mist. As if someone was expiring nearby, behind some damp wall.

The driver said:

'What a rotten fucking night. And these bloody lights won't change.'

Fima reassured him:

'What's the hurry? So we'll wait here another minute or two. Don't worry: I'm paying.'

He was ten years old when his mother died of a cerebral haemorrhage. Baruch Nomberg, in his usual impetuous way, did not wait even a week: the weekend after the funeral he hurled all her belongings into packing cases, all her dresses and shoes and books, and her dressing table with the round Russian mirror, and the bed linen embroidered with her initials, and he hastily donated the lot to the leper hospice in Talbiyeh. He erased every trace of her existence, as though her death had been an act of betrayal. As though she had run away with another man. But he did have her school-leaving photograph enlarged, and hung it over the sideboard, from where she looked down on the two of them all those years with a wistful, sceptical smile and with shyly down-turned eyes, as though she admitted her fault and repented of it. Immediately after the funeral Baruch took his son's education in hand with absent-minded strictness, with unpredictable emotional gestures, with tyrannical good humour. Every morning he checked the exercise books in Fima's satchel one by one. Every evening he stood in the bathroom with his arms crossed while Fima brushed his teeth. He inflicted private tutors in maths, English, and even Jewish tradition on the child. Subtly he would bribe one of Fima's classmates to come home and play with him occasionally so that the child would not be too lonely. Unfortunately he was in the habit of joining in their games himself, and even when for pedagogic reasons he intended to lose, he would be carried away and forget his good intentions, whinnying exultantly when he won. He bought the wide desk that Fima still used. Winter and summer alike he forced the boy into clothes that were too warm. All those years the electric samovar went on steaming till one or two in the morning. Elegant divorcées and cultured widows of a certain age came for visits that lasted five hours. Even in his sleep Fima could hear broad Slavic voices coming from the salon, punctuated occasionally by laughter or weeping or by musical duets. Forcefully, as though tugging him by his hair, his father dragged the idle Fima from one class to the next. He confiscated his reading books in favour of textbooks. He subjected him to early and advanced matriculation exams. He did not hesitate to activate a veritable network of connections to rescue his son from military service in a combat unit and fix him up with a job in charge of cultural activities at the Schneller Barracks in Jerusalem. After his national service Fima became interested in the possibility of joining the merchant navy, at least for a year or two; he was under the spell of the sea. But his father vetoed this and condemned him to study business management, with the aim of involving him in the running of his cosmetics firm. Only after a bitter war of attrition did they compromise on history. As soon as Fima achieved first-class results in his BA, his euphoric father decided to send him to a famous British university to continue his studies. But Fima rebelled, fell in love, fell in love again, the billy-goat year erupted, and the studying was postponed. It was Baruch who rescued him from his successive entanglements, from Gibraltar, from Malta, even from the military prison. He said: 'Women, yes, definitely, but for pleasure, not for selfdestruction. In some ways, Efraim, women are just like us, but in other ways they are totally different. Which ways are which – this is a question I am still working on.'

It was he who bought the flat in Kiryat Yovel and married him to Yael after examining and failing the other two candidates, Ilia Abravanel from Haifa, who looked like Mary Magdalene in an old painting, and the beautiful Liat Sirkin, who had sweetened Fima's nights in her sleeping bag in the mountains of northern Greece. And it was he who, when it was all over, arranged the divorce. Even the overcoat with the booby-trapped sleeve had previously been his.

Fima vaguely remembered one of the old man's favourite anecdotes, about a famous Hasidic saint and a notorious horse thief who exchanged their cloaks and thus in a sense their identities, with tragi-comic consequences. But what was it that his father had seen as the real point of the story, as opposed to the apparent one? As hard as he tried to remember, all he managed was a momentary glimpse of a wayside inn in Ukraine built of rough-hewn wooden beams in the midst of a dark, windswept, snow-covered plain, with wolves howling nearby.

The driver said:

'What the hell! Are we supposed to sit here all night?'

And he put his foot down, crossed on the red, and, as though compensating himself and Fima for the lost time, careered crazily down the empty streets, cutting the corners with a squeal of brakes. Fima said:

'What's this, the Six Minutes' War?'

And the driver:

'So be it, amen.'

Tomorrow, Fima decided, first thing in the morning, I'll take him to the hospital for tests. By force if necessary. This whistling is something new. Unless he's extending his repertoire again, producing comic imitations of trains to accompany his railway stories. Or unless it's just a slight chill and I'm losing my sense of proportion. Though how can I lose something I never had? He never did either, for that matter.

I ought to give Tsvi a call first; his brother is a consultant at Hadassah Hospital on Mount Scopus. Try to fix him up with a private room and all the indispensable little luxuries. That die-hard Revisionist is so stubborn, he won't so much as hear the word 'hospital'. He'll erupt like Vesuvius. In fact, why not ask Yael to soften him up first. He has an old weakness for her. What he calls a soft spot. Maybe it's because he's decided that Dimi is his grandson. Just as he decided that India is an Arab state and that Krochmal met Nietzsche, and that I'm a sort of Toynbee manqué or a Pushkin who's gone off the rails. Typical ridiculous mistakes of someone who refuses to face up to reality and look it straight in the eye.

As the words 'straight in the eye' flashed through his mind, Fima suddenly remembered the dog that was bleeding to death in the pitch-black wadi. He had a vivid mental image of the last blood oozing from the gaping wounds, and the final spasms of the dying creature. In an instant, illuminated, he realised that this horror too was the result of what was happening in the Occupied Territories.

'We've got to make peace,' Fima said to the driver. 'We can't go on like this. Don't you think we ought to make the effort and start talking to them? What's so frightening about talking? You don't get killed by talking. In any case, we're a thousand times better at talking than they are.'

The driver said:

'We ought to kill them while they're young. Not let them raise their heads. Make them curse the day they were crazy enough to start with us. Is this your building?'

Fima suddenly panicked, because he was not certain he had enough money in his pocket for the fare. He decided he would hand his identity card over to the driver and go down to the taxi company next morning to pay. If he could only locate his identity card. But it transpired that Ted Tobias had foreseen this eventuality and paid the fare in advance. Fima thanked the driver, wished him luck, and asked him as he got out:

'So tell me: how long do you think we should go on murdering each other?'

The driver said:

'Another hundred years if necessary. That's how long it was in Bible times. There's no such thing as peace between Jews and goyim. Either they're on top of us and we're underneath, or they're underneath and we're sitting on top of them. Maybe when the Messiah comes, he'll show them their rightful place. Good night, sir. There's no reason to feel sorry for them. It'll be better for this country when Jews start feeling sorry for each other. That's our problem.'

In the entrance hall, near the bottom of the stairs, Fima saw a plump man sitting motionless under the letter boxes, huddled in a heavy cloak. He was so startled that he almost turned tail and ran after the taxi, which was manoeuvring to turn round farther down the street. For a moment he weighed the possibility that this wretched person was none other than himself, sitting and waiting for the dawn to break because he had lost the key to his flat. Then he blamed this thought on his tiredness: it was not a person after all, only a tattered rolled-up mattress that one of his neighbours must have dumped there. Nevertheless he switched the light on and groped frantically in his pockets until he located his key. There was a sheet of paper or a letter showing in his box, but he decided to wait till morning. If he had not been so tired, or so muddled, if it had not been so late, he would not have given up so easily. He should never have let that pass. It was his bounden duty to try to change the driver's mind with calm, cogent arguments, without losing his temper. Deep down under several poisoned layers of cruelty and fear there must lurk some glimmering of reason. We must endeavour to believe that it is possible to dig down and rescue the goodness buried under the rubble. There is still a chance of changing a few minds and opening a chapter here. At any rate, it is our duty to keep on trying. We must not give in.

17

Nightlife

A ND since the taxi driver had used the expression 'kill them while they're young', Fima remembered the mysterious case of the death of Trotsky. Going to the kitchen for a glass of water before retiring to bed, he peered into the rubbish bin under the sink to see if there were any more corpses. Then, noticing the sparkling aluminium of the new Korean kettle, he decided to make some tea. While the water was boiling, he bolted down two or three thick slices of black bread and jam. And immediately had to swallow a heartburn tablet. Standing in front of the open fridge, he brooded on Annette's misfortune. He felt that he could identify with the cruel injustice she had suffered; he could share her humiliation and despair. But at the same time and without contradiction he could understand the husband, the doctor, the dependable, hard-working man who had held back for decades, whistling occasionally between his front teeth, tapping gently on inanimate objects, until he felt the fear of approaching old age and realised that this was his last chance to stop dancing to his wife's tiresome tune and start living his own life. Just now he's sleeping in his young girlfriend's arms in some Italian hotel, his knee between her knees, a man rejuvenated; but some time soon he will no doubt make the discovery that she too wears a sanitary towel inside her knickers, uses a scented deodorant to suppress the smell of her sweat and other secretions, anoints herself with greasy creams in front of her mirror, and perhaps even goes to sleep next to him with curlers in her hair, just like his wife. And hangs her underwear to dry on the rail of the shower curtain so that it drips on his head. And affects migraines and irritating mannerisms just at the moment his desire begins to stir.

'Mannerheim!' Fima suddenly exclaimed aloud with delight:

the girlfriend's mannerisms had reminded him of the name of the Finnish general who stood between Tamar and the solution to her crossword puzzle. He decided to give her a call, even though it was nearly two in the morning. Or should he call Annette? On third thoughts he picked up his by now cold tea, sat down at his desk, and in less than half an hour had written a short piece for the weekend supplement on the close connection between the deteriorating situation in the Territories and the creeping insensitivity that manifested itself, for instance, in the treatment of heart patients, many of whom were condemned to death – literally – on account of the unnecessary queues for operations or because the two sides could not agree on round-the-clock shifts. Or in our indifference to the sufferings of the unemployed, the recent immigrants, the battered wives. Or in the humiliations we inflicted on the homeless elderly, the mentally handicapped, lonely people who had fallen on hard times. But above all our brutalisation manifested itself in the aggressive rudeness that we saw daily in the bureaucracy, in the streets, in bus queues, and most probably also in the privacy of our bedrooms. In Beer Yaakov a man suffering from cancer murdered his wife and children because he could not accept his wife's turning to religion. Four teenagers from good families in Hod Hasharon held a mentally defective cripple captive in a cellar and raped her continually for three days and nights. A furious father ran amok in a school in Afula, injured six teachers and knocked the headmaster unconscious, all because his daughter had failed her Advanced-level English exam. In Holon the police caught a gang of hoodlums who had been terrorising dozens of old age pensioners and robbing them of their pennies. All that was just in yesterday's paper. Fima concluded his article with a harsh prediction: Insensitivity, violence, and cruelty flow backwards and forwards from the state to the Territories and from the Territories to the state, gathering disastrous momentum, redoubling in geometric progression, wreaking havoc on both sides of the Green Line. There is no way out of this vicious circle unless we proceed decisively and without delay to a comprehensive solution of the conflict, along the basic lines that were laid down a hundred and one years ago by Micha Josef Berdyczewski in these simple words: 'Priority to Jews over Judaism, to living people over ancestral heritage.' There is nothing more to add. He had discovered this quotation several years before in an essay entitled 'Demolition and Construction,' in an old journal that he found at Yael's father's, and he had copied it out and stuck it on the front of the radio: he was delighted to be able to make use of it at last. On second thoughts he crossed out 'conflict' and 'vicious circle'. Then he angrily deleted 'geometric progression' and 'disastrous momentum', but he could not decide what to replace them with. He put it off till the next day. Despite the tea and the heartburn tablets, the nausea had not left him. He really ought to do as Dimi had asked, find a powerful torch, go down into the darkness, search for the injured dog, try to save it. If possible.

At half past two he undressed and showered because he felt disgusting. The torrent of water failed to refresh him. The soap and even the water seemed sticky. He stood grumpily in front of the mirror with no clothes on, shivering with cold and recoiling from the unhealthy pallor of his skin with its feeble growth of dark hair and the ring of fat around his waist. Automatically he began squeezing the red pustules on his chest, until he managed to squirt a few white drops out of his flabby breasts. When he was an adolescent, spots like these began to appear on his cheeks and forehead. Baruch forbade him to squeeze them. Once he said to Fima: 'They will vanish overnight when you have a lady friend. If you don't manage to find yourself a lady by your seventeenth birthday, and there are reasons for supposing, my dear, that you will not, then I myself shall fix you up with one.' A rueful sickly grin spread on Fima's lips as he recalled the night before his seventeenth birthday: how he lay awake hoping that his father would forget his promise and praying that he would not. The old man, typically, had only been making a little joke. And you, as usual, failed to grasp the real point.

And what now, dear premier? Is a second adolescence about to begin? Or perhaps the first one is not over yet? In a single day you have had two women in your arms and you managed to lose both of them and inflict embarrassment or, worse, humiliation on them both. Clearly you'll have to go on waiting for your father to remember his promise at long last. Look what they've done to you, stupid, his mother had said to him in the dream. And now, belatedly, standing naked and shivering in front of the bathroom mirror, he answered her peevishly, That's enough. Leave me alone.

As he said this, he had an image of Yael's face twisted with shock and disgust when she turned the light on in her bedroom a couple of hours previously and found him sleeping fully dressed under her blanket, clutching her nightie. She had raised her voice in exasperation, Quick, Teddy, come and see this. As if some insect, some kind of Gregor Samsa, had crept into her bed. He must have looked utterly stupid, if not demented, when he woke in a daze, stretched, and sat up, all rumpled from sleep, and hopelessly tried to explain to them what had happened. As if hoping that if he could explain himself, they would take pity on him and let him curl up and go back to sleep. But he only succeeded in becoming more and more embroiled in his explanation, claiming at first that Dimi had not been feeling very well, then weakening and changing his line of defence, presenting a contrary version of events: Dimi had been fine but he himself had felt unwell.

Tobias, as usual, maintained his self-control. He pronounced a single frosty sentence:

'This time, Fima, I think you've gone a bit too far.'

And while Yael put Dimi to bed, Ted phoned for a taxi and even helped Fima to get his arm into the tricky sleeve, fetched his shabby cap, accompanied him downstairs, and personally gave the driver Fima's address, as though to make certain beyond all doubt that he would not change his mind and come knocking on their door again.

And in fact, why not?

He owed them a full explanation.

At that moment, standing naked and sticky in his bathroom, he made up his mind to get dressed at once, ring for a taxi, march back in there, wake them up, and talk to them earnestly, till dawn if necessary. It was his duty to alert them to the child's misery. To misery in general. To activate them. Confront them with the full urgency of the danger. With all due respect to jet-propelled vehicles, our first responsibility is to the child. This time he would not give in, he would also open the taxi driver's eyes on the way there, shattering all stubbornness and heartlessness: he would counteract all that brainwashing and force everyone to recognise at long last how close disaster was.

But when there was no answer from the taxi company, he changed his mind and called Annette Tadmor. After two rings he gave up. At three o'clock he got into bed with the history of Alaska in English, which he had absent-mindedly carried away with him from Ted and Yael's without asking their permission. He leafed through it until his eyes tracked down a curious section about the sexual habits of the native Eskimos: every spring they took a mature woman who had been widowed during the winter and handed her over to the adolescent boys as part of their initiation rites.

After ten minutes he switched the light off, curled up, and commanded his cock to calm down and himself to go to sleep. But again he had the impression that a blind man was wandering around outside in the empty street, tapping with his stick on the pavement and the low walls. Fima got out of bed, determined to get dressed and go outside to see what really went on in Jerusalem when no one was looking. He sensed with a kind of nocturnal lucidity that he had to render an account of everything that happened in Jerusalem. The hackneyed word 'nightlife' suddenly stepped out of its literal meaning. Severed in Fima's mind from thronged cafés, brightly lit boulevards, theatres, squares, cabarets, 'nightlife' took on a different, sharp, ice-cold meaning that brooked no frivolity. The ancient Aramaic expression *sitra de-itkasia*, the concealed or covered side, passed through Fima's body like a single note on the cello out of the heart of darkness. A shudder of fear ran through him.

So he turned the light on, got out of bed, and sat down in his yellowing long underwear on the floor in front of the brown wardrobe. He had to use force to dislodge the jammed bottom drawer. For twenty minutes or so he rummaged through old notebooks, pamphlets, drafts, photographs, jottings, and newspaper cuttings, until he came upon a shabby cardboard folder with the words 'Ministry of the Interior: Department of Local Government' printed on it.

Fima extracted from this folder a bundle of old letters in their original envelopes. He systematically scrutinised each envelope in turn, determined for once not to be defeated or sidetracked. Eventually he found Yael's farewell letter. The pages were numbered 2, 3, 4. So apparently the first page was lost. Or perhaps it had merely strayed into another envelope. He noticed that the end of the letter was also missing. Lying on the floor in his underwear, he started to read what Yael had written to him when she went off without him to Seattle in 1965. Her handwriting was tiny, pearl-like, neither feminine nor masculine, but rounded and fluent. Perhaps this was the sort of calligraphy that was taught in respectable schools in the last century. In his mind Fima compared this chaste handwriting to his own scrawl, which resembled a mob of panic-stricken soldiers jostling each other out of the way as they fled during a rout.

18

'You've forgotten yourself'

'. . . terrible in you, but I simply didn't understand it. I still don't.
There's no resemblance between the soulful, dreamy young man
who inspired and entertained three girls in the mountains of
northern Greece and the lazy, gossipy receptionist who moons
around at home all morning, arguing with himself, listening to
the news every hour, reading three newspapers and scattering
them all over the flat, opening cupboard doors and forgetting to
shut them, poking around in the fridge and complaining there
isn't any this and there isn't any that. And scurrying off to your
friends every evening, barging in without waiting to be invited,
with a grubby shirt collar, a cap left over from the 1940s, picking
quarrels about politics with everybody into the early hours of the
morning until they are literally praying for you to leave. Even
your outward appearance has a secondhand look. You've put on
weight, Effy. Maybe it wasn't your fault. Those eyes that were
alert and dreamy started to fade and now they've gone dull. In
Greece you could hold Liat, me, and Ilia spellbound from moon-
rise to sunrise with stories about the Eleusinian mysteries, the cult
of Dionysos, the Erinyes, goddesses of fate, and the Moirai, goddesses of furious vengeance, Persephone in the underworld, and
fabled rivers with names like Styx and Lethe. I haven't forgotten
a thing, Effy: I'm a good pupil. Though I sometimes wonder if you
yourself can remember anything. You've forgotten yourself.

'We lay on the ground near a spring and you played on a pipe.
We found you amazing, enchanting, but also a little frightening. I
remember one evening Ilia and Liat made a wreath of oak leaves
and arranged it on your head. At that moment I wouldn't have
minded if you'd slept with one of them in front of my eyes. Or
even with both of them at once. In Greece, in that springtime

four years ago, you were a poet even though you didn't write a single word. Now you sit and cover pages every night, but the poet isn't there any more.

'What charmed us all was your helplessness. On the one hand you were so enigmatic, and on the other hand you were a little clown. A sort of child. One could be a hundred per cent certain that if there was a single sliver of glass in the valley, you would tread on it with your bare foot; that if there was just one loose stone in the whole of Greece, it would fall on your head; that if there was a single wasp in the Balkans, it would sting you. When you played your pipe outside some peasant's hut or at the mouth of a cave, there was sometimes a feeling that your body was not a body but a thought. And vice versa: every time you talked to us at night about thoughts, we felt we could almost touch them. All three of us loved you, but instead of getting jealous, with each day that passed we loved each other more. It was something miraculous. Liat slept with you at night on behalf of all three of us, as it were: through Liat you were sleeping with me and with Ilia too. I can't explain it and I don't need an explanation. You could have had any or all of us. But the moment you made your choice, even though the winner turned out to be me, the spell was broken. When you invited us to Jerusalem to meet your father, the magic was not there any more. Then, when the preparations for the wedding began, you became tired, absent-minded. Once, you forgot me at the bank. Once, you called me Ilia. When you signed that lunatic contract with your father, in the presence of the notary, you suddenly said: 'Goethe ought to be here to see the Devil selling his soul for a mess of pottage.' Your father laughed and I fought back my tears. Your father and I took care of all the arrangements, and you grumbled that your life was foundering in candlesticks and frying pans. Once you lost your temper and shouted at me that you couldn't stand a bedroom without curtains: even in a brothel there were curtains. You stamped your foot like a spoiled brat. Not that I cared: I had no objection to curtains. But that moment was the end of Greece. Your pettiness had begun. One time you made a scene on account of my wasting your father's money, another time on account of your father's money not arriving on time, and several times on account of my over using 'on account of'. You corrected my grammar every other sentence.

'You're not easy to live with. Whenever I pluck my eyebrows or wax my legs, you stare as though you've found a spider in your salad, but if I point out that your socks smell, you start moaning that I've stopped loving you. Every evening you grumble, whose turn is it to take the rubbish down and who washed the dishes yesterday, and whether there were more dirty dishes yesterday or today. And then you ask why it is that the only thing we ever talk about in this house is the washing up and the dustbins. I know, Effy, that these are petty things. We could work on them. We could give up, or get used to them. You don't unpick a family on account of smelly socks. I don't even get worked up any more over your regular wisecracks about aero-dynamics and jet engines, which so far as you're concerned have to do only with war and killing. As though your wife works for a syndicate of murderers. I've managed to get used to your poor jokes. And your grumbling all day long. And your dirty handker-chiefs on the dinner table. And your leaving the door of the re-frigerator open. And your endless theories about who really killed President Kennedy and why. You've developed verbal diarrhoea, Effy. You've even taken to arguing with the radio, correcting the newsreaders' grammar.

'If you ask me exactly when my separation from you began, at what moment in time, or what you did wrong to me, I can't give you an answer. The answer is: I don't know. What I do know is that in Greece you were alive and here in Jerusalem you're not. You merely exist, and you do even that as if existence itself is a bother. You're an infantile thirty-year-old man. Almost a replica of your father, but without his old-world charm, his generosity, his gallantry, and, for the time being, the goatee. Even in bed, you've begun to replace love by submissiveness. You've become a bit of a flatterer. But only with women. With Uri and Micha and Tsvika and the rest of your chums you're in a state of per-petual war in your late-night debates. Every now and again you remember to toss Nina or me or Shula some compliment, the same compliment to any of us indiscriminately, a little flattery by way of payment: the cake was excellent, your new hairstyle is lovely, that's a pretty plant. Even if the cake is a bought one, the hairstyle isn't new, the plant is really a vase of flowers. Just to make us shut up and stop interrupting you and your chums in your endless skirmishes about the Lavon affair, or the fall of Carthage, or the Cuban missile crisis, or the Eichmann trial, or the antisemitism of Pound and Eliot, or who foresaw what in a discussion you had at the beginning of the winter.

'In December, when we went to Uri and Nina's for the surprise party that Shula put on to celebrate Tsvi getting his doctorate, you monopolised the whole evening. You had a fit of spite. I noticed that every time I started to say something, you looked at me like a cat looking at an insect. You simply waited for me to stop for a moment, to draw breath or to look for a word, and then you pounced, snatching my sentence away from me and finishing it yourself. In case I said something silly. Or sided with your opponents. Or wasted your time. Or copied anything from you. Because it was your show, the whole of that evening. It always is. Which did not prevent you cuddling me while you were talking, Nina and Shula too: you joked that I may be the one who keeps the air force in the air, but in this debate you can manage fine without air cover. And you really did. By one in the morning, you had demolished Tsvi's thesis brick by brick, even though he had made a point of thanking you in his acknowledgements and quoting you in his footnotes. And then you dazzled everyone by reconstructing a brand new thesis out of the rubble. A counter-thesis. The more Tsvika tried to defend himself, the more spiteful and ruthless you became. You never let him finish a sentence. Until Uri stood up, blew an imaginary whistle, and declared that you had won by a knockout and that Tsvi could go out and look for a job on the buses. And you said: Why the buses? Maybe Yael could launch him on one of her rockets and send him straight to the court of Ferdinand and Isabella so that he can find out what really happened there and write a new thesis. When at long last Nina managed to change the subject, and we chatted about a Fernandel film, you just went to sleep in your armchair. You even snored. I had difficulty dragging you home. But when we got back at three o'clock, you were suddenly viciously wide awake, you made fun of them all, you gave me a blow-by-blow reconstruction of your victory. You then declared that you deserved a right royal fuck, you had earned it with the sweat of your brow. The sort of fuck that victorious samurai were granted in old Japan. I looked at you, and suddenly it was not a samurai I saw in front of me but a sort of secularised yeshiva student, perverted by sophistry and casuistry, ebullient and none too bright. You had forgotten yourself completely.

'You must understand, Effy: I'm not reminding you of your great night at the Gefens' to explain myself. That's something I haven't even managed to do to myself. At least not in words. After all, it's not your fault you've developed a little paunch. One doesn't wipe out a marriage just because one of the partners snips the hairs in one nostril and forgets to do the other. Or forgets to flush the loo. Especially since I know that despite the pettiness and the vicious remarks you're still fond of me in your own way. Maybe more now than when we came back from Greece and for some reason I was the lucky one, even though you could hardly tell the three of us apart. Maybe it's something like this: You're in love with me, but you don't really love me. No doubt you'll say I'm just playing with words. What I'm saying is that, for you, being in love means wanting to be a baby. You want to be fed and changed and above all adored nonstop, day and night. Admired round the clock.

'I know I'm contradicting myself: it's true that I married you because I was taken by your Grecian childishness, and now that I'm leaving you, I'm complaining that you're childish. OK, you've caught me in a contradiction. Enjoy it. Sometimes I think that if you had to choose between the joy of sex and the joy of catching me in a contradiction, it's the latter you'd find more exciting, more satisfying. Especially as there's no risk of pregnancy. You get so hysterical every month, in case I've fixed you and landed you with a baby on the sly. Which doesn't stop you hinting to your friends that the real reason is that jet engines are Yael's baby.

'A couple of months ago – I expect you've already forgotten – I woke up before dawn and I said, Effy, I've had enough, I'm leaving. You didn't ask why, you didn't ask where I was going, you asked: How? On a jet broomstick? And this brings me to your crude jealousy of my work. Which expresses itself in wisecracks. It's true I'm not allowed to divulge details about the project. But you see this secrecy as a betrayal. As if I've got a lover. And not just any lover, but somebody inferior, somebody despicable. How come the woman who had the rare honour of becoming your wife isn't satisfied with that? How can she have some other interest apart from you? And such a shady business? Not that you'd understand the project even if I were allowed to tell you about it. You wouldn't even show interest. On the contrary, your attention would start wandering after two minutes, or you'd fall asleep, or change the subject. After all, you can't even understand how an electric fan works. Right. Now we're getting to the point.

'Six weeks ago, when I got the invitation from Seattle, and those two air force colonels arrived on Saturday evening to talk to you, to explain that it was actually on their initiative that the invitation had been issued, and that my work with the Americans for the next couple of years was of national importance, you just made fun of them and of me. You started to lecture us about the perpetual lunacy associated with the phrase 'national importance'. You behaved like a Saudi sheik. You ended up more or less telling them to keep their hands off your property and throwing them out of the flat. Up to that evening there was still a part of me at least that wanted to convince you to come along. They say the scenery around Seattle is like a dream. Fjords, snow-covered mountains. You'd be able to attend some lectures at the university. Maybe the change of air and scenery and being cut off from the Israeli papers and news broadcasts would unblock the spring. Maybe away from your father and your friends and Jerusalem you'd be able to get back to some real writing at last. Instead of petty polemics punctuated with jibes and taunts.

'Try to understand, Effy. I know the way you've always thought of me. Yael Levin, the little girl from Yavne'el. A bit foolish, even if she is rather sweet. Nice, but limited. Yet our experts, as well as the Americans, believe that my project may develop into something. I matter to them. That's why I've decided to go. I don't matter to you, even if you are in love with me. Or in love with being in love with me. Or so absorbed in your own things that you can't spare the time or effort to stop loving me.

'If you like, you can come over. I'll send you a ticket. Or your father can pay. And if you don't like, we'll see what time will tell. I deliberately haven't mentioned my deepest pain. The thing that you think can be put right in a moment. I'm not saying anything about that, nor are you. Maybe it's just as well we'll be apart. Sometime I think that only a real blow, a disaster, could bring you back out of your fog: your newspapers, your arguments, your news bulletins. Once you were deep, now you seem to be living superficially most of the time. Don't be offended, Effy. And don't start looking for ways of contradicting everything I've written, of producing counter-claims, of dismantling it brick by brick, of defeating me. I'm not your enemy. Defeating me won't help you. Maybe my trip to America will be the shock that will bring you back to yourself. OK, that's a cliché. I knew you'd say that. Once I've gone, you'll be free to fall in love. Or you can go on being in love with me without having to put up with my washing drying in front of the radiator in the bedroom in the winter. And something else: Try to concentrate. Try not to babble on all day long, fussing and correcting everyone and everything. Don't become just a sore throat. Anyway, there's nobody out there listening. Maybe you should go and look for Liat or Ilia? Go back to Greece? Sometimes when I happen to stay at work for a couple of days, working alone all night, grabbing a snack to save time, suddenly I have . . .'

Fima refolded the truncated letter and replaced it in its envelope, then put the envelope back in the folder from the Ministry of the Interior, Department of Local Government. He replaced the folder in the bottom drawer. It was after half past three. A cock was crowing far away, a dog was barking persistently in the dark, and the blind man was still tapping with his stick in the empty street. For a moment Fima thought he heard the muezzin calling in the village of Beit Safafa. He got back into bed, switched out the light, and started composing in his mind the missing ending. After a moment he fell asleep. He had had a long day.

19

In the monastery

IN his dream Uri appeared in the middle of a snowstorm to
summon him to take his leave of Annette, who was dying of a
complication of childbirth in a British naval hospital. They made
their way on a sledge through a white forest until they reached a
building that vaguely resembled the Monastery of the Cross in
Jerusalem. Wounded and dying people with crushed limbs blocked
their way, rolling on the floor in the corridors, groaning, bleeding. Uri said, They're only Cossacks; you can tread on them.
Eventually behind the monastery they discovered a pleasant little
garden containing a Greek tavern with a vine-shaded terrace and
tables laid for a meal. Among the tables stood a sort of litter.
When Fima parted the velvet curtains, he saw his wife making
love tearfully but eagerly with a dark, shrivelled man who was
lying underneath her uttering feeble moans. Suddenly, in a flash
of horror, it dawned on him that she was copulating with a
corpse. The corpse was the Arab youth from the news bulletin,
the one we murdered in Gaza with a bullet through the head.

20

Fima is lost in the forest

AFTER writing in his notebook he dozed till seven o'clock. Rumpled, dishevelled, hating his body's night smell, he forced himself to get up. He skipped the exercises in front of the mirror. He shaved without cutting himself. He drank two cups of coffee. The very thought of bread and jam or yogurt gave him heartburn. He vaguely remembered that he had to deal this morning with some matter that could not be put off, but for the life of him he could not remember what it was, or why it was so urgent. So he decided to go downstairs to his letter box to fetch the letter he had seen in it last night, and also to bring up the newspaper, but not to spend more than a quarter of an hour on it. Then he would sit down at once to work uncompromisingly on the article he had not managed to finish in the night.

When he turned on the radio, he found that most of the news was over. Some bright spells were expected during the day. Along the coastal plain there was a possibility of scattered showers. Whereas in the northern valleys there was still a serious risk of frost. Drivers were warned of the danger of skidding on wet roads, were asked to reduce their speed and to avoid so far as possible applying their brakes abruptly or turning too sharply.

What's the matter with them, Fima grumbled. Why can't they leave me alone? What do they take me for? A driver? A farmer from the northern valleys? A swimmer from the coastal plain? Why are we asked and warned, when somebody ought to assume the responsibility and say, I ask, I warn. It's sheer madness: everything is falling apart in this country, and they are worried about a risk of frost. In fact, applying the brakes abruptly plus a very sharp turn might just save us from disaster. And even that is highly doubtful.

Fima turned off the radio and called Annette Tadmor: he owed her an apology for his behaviour. At the very least he should show some interest in her welfare. For all he knew, her husband might have had enough of his Italian operetta and returned sheepishly in the middle of the night, lugging a couple of suitcases, falling to the ground and kissing her feet. Was it possible that she had confessed to him about what had happened between them? Was the husband liable to show up here with a loaded pistol? Out of habit or morning vagueness, Fima dialled Tsvi Kropotkin's number by mistake. Tsvi chuckled and said that although he was actually in the middle of shaving he had already asked himself what had become of Fima this morning: had he forgotten us? Tsvi's sarcasm eluded Fima.

'What do you mean, Tsvika? Of course I haven't forgotten you. I never would. I just thought for a change I shouldn't ring you too early. You see, little by little I'm improving. There may be some hope for me yet.'

Kropotkin promised to call back in five minutes, as soon as he had finished shaving.

After half an hour Fima swallowed his pride and rang Tsvi again:

'Well? So who's forgotten who? Can you spare me a couple of minutes?' And without waiting for an answer he said that he needed some advice about an article he'd started writing in the night, and now this morning he wasn't certain he still agreed with himself. The question was this. Two days ago in *Ha'arets* there was a report of a speech by Günter Grass to a student audience in Berlin. It was a courageous, decent speech. Grass had denounced the Nazi period and gone on to denounce all trendy parallels between the atrocities of our own day and Hitler's crimes, including the often-heard comparison with Israel and South Africa. So far so good.

'Fima,' said Tsvi, 'I read it. We talked about it the day before yesterday. Get to the point. Explain your problem.'

'I'm just coming to it,' said Fima. 'But first, just explain one thing to me, Tsvika. Why does this Grass insist on referring to the Nazis as "they", whereas you and I, all these years, whenever we write about the occupation, the corruption of values, the oppression in the Territories, even about the Lebanon War, always and without exception use the pronoun "we"? And Grass was actually a soldier with the Nazi Wehrmacht! The same as the other one, Heinrich Böll. He had to give the Nazi salute every morning and shout "Heil Hitler" with the rest of them. And now he calls them "them". Whereas I, who have never set foot in Lebanon, who have never served in the Territories, so that my hands are definitely cleaner than Günter Grass's, regularly say and write "we". "Our wrongdoings". And even "the innocent blood we have shed". What is it, that "we"? Something left over from the War of Independence: *We are always at the ready, we are here, we're the Palmach?* Who is this "we", anyway? Me and Rabbi Levinger? You and Rabbi Kahane? What does it mean, exactly? Have you ever thought about it, Professor? Perhaps the time has come when you and I and all of us should follow the example of Grass and Böll. Maybe we should all start saying, exclusively, consciously, and emphatically: "they". What do you think?'

'Look,' Tsvi Kropotkin said wearily, 'the thing is with them it's all in the past, whereas with us it's still going on, and that's why.'

'Are you out of your mind?' Fima cut in with an explosion of rage. 'Can you hear what you're saying? What d'you mean, with them it's in the past, whereas with us it's still going on? What the hell do you mean by "it"? What precisely is it according to you that is over and done with in Berlin but still goes on in Jerusalem? Have you gone crazy, Professor? What you're doing is putting them and us on the same level! Worse still, you're implying that the Germans have a moral advantage over us, because they've finished and poor old us, we're still at it. Who do you think you are? George Steiner? Radio Damascus? That's exactly the tainted comparison that even Grass, the graduate of the Wehrmacht, decries and calls demagoguery!'

Fima's passion was spent. In its place came sadness. And he said in the tone one uses to speak to a child who has hurt himself with a screwdriver because he has obstinately refused to take heed of the grown-ups' warnings:

'You can see for yourself, Tsvika, how easy it is to fall into the trap. Look what a fine line we have to tread.'

'Calm down, Fima,' Tsvi Kropotkin pleaded, although Fima was already calm. 'It's just eight o'clock. Why are you leaping on me like this? Come round one evening; we'll sit down and talk it over quietly. I've got some Napoleon brandy from France. Shula's sister brought it back with her. But not this week. It's the end of the semester and I'm up to my ears. They're making me Head of Department. Can you come next week? You don't sound well to me, Fima, and Nina was saying to Shula that you're a bit depressed again.'

'So what, for heaven's sake, if it's not eight o'clock yet. Does our responsibility for the language switch off outside office hours? Does it only operate from eight to four with a break for lunch, weekdays only? I mean it, seriously. Forget Shula and Nina and your brandy for a moment. A fine time for brandy. The only reason I'm depressed is because the rest of you don't seem to be nearly depressed enough, considering what's going on. Have you seen the paper this morning? I'd like you to take what I've said as a proposal for the agenda. Under the heading of the defence of the language against increasing pollution. I'm suggesting that from now on, at least as regards the atrocities in the Territories, we simply stop using the word "we".'

'Fima,' said Tsvi, 'hang on a minute. Just sort yourself out. Which is the first "we" and which is the second one? You've got yourself in a twist, pal. Why don't we just drop it for the time being? We'll talk about it next week. Face to face. We can't settle a subject like this on the phone. And I've got to run along.'

Fima would not give in or let go:

'You remember that famous line in the poem by Amir Gilboa: "Suddenly a man gets up one morning and feels he is a nation and starts walking." That's precisely the absurdity I'm talking about. First of all, Professor, the truth, hand on your heart: Has it ever happened to you that you've got up in the morning and suddenly felt you were a nation? After lunch at the earliest. Who can get up in the morning and feel he's a nation, anyway? And even start walking? Maybe Geula Cohen can. Who gets up in the morning and doesn't just feel lousy?'

Kropotkin laughed. Which encouraged Fima to a new outburst:

'But listen. Seriously. The time has come to stop feeling like a nation. To stop starting to walk. Let's cut that crap. *A voice called to me and I went. Wherever we are sent – we'll go.* These are semi-fascist motifs. You're not a nation. I'm not a nation. Nobody is a nation. Not in the morning and not in the evening. And by the way, we really aren't a nation anyway. At most we're a sort of tribe.'

'There you go again with your "we".' Tsvi chuckled. 'You're a bit over the top, Fima. Just make up your mind: Are we "we" or aren't we? In a hanged man's house you shouldn't throw the rope after the bucket. Never mind. I'm sorry, but now I really must hang up and run along. By the way, I heard that Uri will be back this weekend. Why don't we fix something up for Saturday night? See you.'

'Of course we're not a nation,' Fima insisted, deaf and aflame with self-righteousness. 'We're a primitive tribe. Scum, that's what we are. But those Germans, and the French and the British too, have no right to talk down to us. Compared to them we're saints. Not to mention the rest of them. Have you seen the paper today? The way Shamir went on yesterday in Netanya? And what they did to that old Arab at Ashdod Beach?'

When Tsvi apologetically hung up, Fima continued to harangue the indifferent, bloated gargle emanating from the phone:

'In any case, we've had it.'

He was referring collectively to the state of Israel, the dovish left, himself, and his friend. But after putting the receiver down, he thought it over and changed his mind: we mustn't get hysterical. He nearly called Tsvi again to warn him against the despair and hysteria lurking all around nowadays. He felt ashamed of his rudeness to his long-standing friend, such a learned and intelligent man, and one of the last voices to have stayed sane. Even though he was somewhat saddened by the thought that this mediocre scholar should now be head of the department and sit on the same chair as his illustrious predecessors, compared to whom he was a pygmy. At which point Fima suddenly remembered how, eighteen months ago, when he was admitted to Hadassah Hospital to have his appendix removed, Tsvika had enlisted the help of his brother the doctor. He had also enlisted himself and Shula; in fact the two of them had hardly left Fima's bedside. When he was discharged, Tsvi, with the Gefens and Teddy, had organised round-the-clock shifts to take care of him, and he had run a high fever, behaved like a spoiled child, and pestered them endlessly. And now, here he was not only hurting Tsvi but also interrupting him in the middle of shaving and maybe making him late for his lecture at the university. And just when he was on the point of becoming head of the department too. This very evening, Fima decided, he would ring him again. He would apologise, but he would still try to explain his position all over again. But this time with restraint and cold, sharp logic. And he wouldn't forget to send a kiss to Shula.

Fima hurried to the kitchen, because he had the impression that before his conversation with Tsvika he had put the new electric kettle on to boil, and by now it had probably gone the way of its predecessor. Halfway there he was stopped by the ringing telephone and found himself drawn in two directions. After a moment's hesitation he picked up the phone and said to his father:

'Just a moment, Baruch. There's something burning in the kitchen.'

Rushing in, he found the kettle alive and well, shining happily on the marble worktop. So it was yet another false alarm. But in his haste he knocked the black transistor radio off the shelf and broke it. Returning, panting, to the phone he said:

'Everything's OK. I'm listening.'

It turned out that the old man just wanted to tell him that he had found some workmen, who would be arriving the following week to replaster and paint the flat. 'They're Arabs from Abu Dis village, so from your point of view it's strictly kosher, Efraim.' Which reminded the old man of a charming Hasidic story. Why, according to Jewish tradition, are the righteous in Paradise permitted to choose between feasting on the leviathan or on the wild ox? The answer is that there may always be some ultra-fussy Jew who will insist on eating fish because he can't rely on the kashrut of the Almighty himself.

He went on to explain to Fima the ostensible point and the true point of this joke, until Fima had the impression that his father's distinctive smell had managed to infiltrate the telephone wires: it was an East European cocktail, combining a faint whiff of scent with a lungful of unaired quilts, a smell of boiled fish and carrots, and the fragrance of sticky liqueurs. He was filled with revulsion, which he was ashamed of, and with the ancient urge to provoke his father, to challenge everything that was sacred to him until he lost his temper. And he said:

'Listen, Dad. Listen carefully. First, about the Arabs. I've already explained to you a thousand times that I don't think they're great saints. Can't you understand that the difference between us is not about kosher or non-kosher, or about Hell and Paradise; it's simply a matter of common humanity – theirs and ours.'

Baruch agreed at once:

'Naturally,' he intoned in a Talmudic singsong, 'nobody would deny that the Arab too is created in the divine image. Except the Arabs themselves, Fimuchka: to our regret they do not comport themselves like human beings created in the image of God.'

Fima instantly forgot his solemn vow to refrain at all cost from political arguments with his father. He set out to explain, once and for all, passionately, that we must not become like the drunken Ukrainian carter who beat his horse to death when the beast stopped submissively pulling his cart. Are the Arabs in the Territories our workhorses? What did you imagine, that they would go on hewing our wood and drawing our water for ever and ever, amen? That they would be content to play the part of our domestic servants to all eternity? Are they not human beings too? Every Zambia and Gambia is an independent state nowadays, so why should the Arabs in the Territories continue come hell or high water quietly scrubbing our shit-houses, sweeping our streets, washing dishes in our restaurants, wiping arses in our geriatric wards, and then saying thank you? How would you feel if the meanest Ukrainian antisemite planned a future like that for the Jews?'

The phrase 'domestic servants', or maybe it was 'the meanest Ukrainian antisemite', reminded the old man of a story that was actually set in a small town in the Ukraine. As usual the narration dragged behind it a long train of explanations and morals.

Finally Fima gave up in despair and screamed that he didn't need any decorators anyway and that Baruch should bloody well stop poking his nose into his life all the time, subsidising, plastering, matchmaking. 'You may have forgotten, Dad, but I happen to be fifty-four years old.'

When he had finished, the old man replied placidly:

'Very nice, my dear. Very nice. It seems I was wrong. I sinned, I erred, I transgressed. In that case I shall still try to find you a nice Jewish decorator. Without any taint of colonial exploitation. Assuming that such a paragon still exists in our state.'

'That's just the point,' Fima crowed triumphantly. 'In the whole of this miserable country of ours you can't find a single Jewish builder or male nurse or gardener. That's what your Territories have done to the Zionist dream! The Arabs are building the Land for us while we sit back gorging ourselves on the leviathan and the wild ox. And then we go out and murder them, and their children too, just because they have the gall not to be happy and grateful for the privilege of unblocking drains for the chosen people till the Messiah comes.'

'The Messiah,' Baruch reflected sadly. 'Perhaps he is already among us. Some say he is. And maybe it's just because of fine fellows like you that he hasn't made himself known yet. There's a story about Reb Uri of Strelisk, the Holy Seraph, the grandfather of Uri Tsvi Greenberg the poet, who was once wandering lost in the forest . . . '

'Let him wander!' Fima cut in. 'Let him stay lost forever! And the grandson too. And the Messiah as well, for that matter, to say nothing of his ass.'

The old man coughed and cleared his throat, like an old teacher about to hold forth, but instead of lecturing Fima he asked sadly: 'So that's your humanism? That's the voice of the peace camp? The lover of mankind hopes that his fellow man will be lost in the forest? The defender of Islam prays that saintly Jews will perish?'

Fima was momentarily abashed. He regretted wishing misfortune on the rabbi lost in the forest. But he quickly rallied and counter-attacked with a surprise flanking movement:

'Listen to this, Baruch. Listen carefully. Apropos of Islam. I want to read you word for word what it says here in the encyclopaedia about India.'

'India yourself!' chortled the old man. 'But what's India got to do with it? The demon that's got into you and your friends, Fimuchka, isn't from India; it's all too European. It's a crying shame that precious young people like you have suddenly decided to sell the entire Jewish heritage for a mess of pottage of sham European pacifism. You want to be Jesus of Nazareth. You want to teach the Christians a lesson in turning the other cheek. You love our enemies and you hate Uri Tsvi and even his grandfather the Holy Seraph. But we've had it up to here with the famous European humanism. Our backs still carry the scars of your dear Western civilisation. We've been on the receiving end of it, all the way from Kishinev to Auschwitz. Let me tell you a poignant tale about a cantor who was once marooned – it shouldn't happen to us! – on a desert island, and at the High Holy Days of all times. *There stands a solitary Jew in the midst of the world in the midst of the times and wonders . . .*'

'Hold on a minute,' Fima erupted, 'you with your wondering cantors. Chmielnicki and Hitler equal Western civilisation the way India equals an Arab state. What a ridiculous idea! If it weren't for Western civilisation, for your information, my dear sir, there would not be left of us one that pisseth against the wall. Who do you think sacrificed tens of millions of lives to defeat Hitler? Wasn't it Western civilisation? Including Russia? Including America? Who was it who saved us, your holy rabbi from Strelisk? Was it the Messiah who gave us a state? Is it Uri Tsvi who makes us a present of tanks and jet planes and pours three billion dollars on us every year, as pocket money, so that we can carry on behaving like hooligans? Make a note of this, Dad: Every time in history that the Jews have gone out of their minds and started navigating their way through this world with messianic charts instead of real, universal ones, millions of them have paid with their lives. Apparently we still haven't managed to get it into the famous Jewish head that the Messiah is really our exterminating angel. That's it in a nutshell, Baruch: the Messiah is our angel of death. So it's perfectly OK to disagree about where we want to go; that is a legitimate subject for argument. But on one unshakeable condition: Wherever we decide to go, we must use real, universal charts, not messianic ones.'

The old man suddenly gave a little whistle, as though in amazement at Fima's wisdom or his own foolishness. He coughed, he groaned, he may have intended to interject a few words, but Fima was already carried away: 'Why the hell are we all brainwashed into believing that the concept of human equality is something alien to Judaism, a flawed goyish commodity, tainted Christian pacifism, whereas the muddle-headed mishmash brewed up by some messianic rabbi, the grandfather of Gush Emunim, who has cobbled together a patchwork of scraps from Hegel, Judah Halevi, and Rabbi Loew of Prague, is suddenly considered to be the pure elixir of Judaism, straight from Mount Sinai? What is this? Sheer lunacy! "Thou shalt do no murder" is alien to Judaism, according to you, it's untouchable? Christian pacifism. Whereas Rabbi Georg Wilhelm Friedrich Hegel, that proto-Nazi, is all of a sudden the genuine Jewish heritage! Let me tell you, Dad, Yosef Haim Brenner had more Jewishness in his little finger than all your frock-coated fossils and your psychopaths with their knitted skullcaps. One lot pisses on the state and says it's illegitimate because the Messiah hasn't come yet; the other lot pisses on the state and says it's just a temporary scaffolding that we can dismantle now that the Messiah's standing at the gate. Both groups piss on "Thou shalt do no murder" because they've got more important fish to fry: banning autopsies, or discovering the tomb of our ancestress Jezebel.'

'Fimuchka,' his father sighed, 'have a heart. I'm an old Jew. All these mysteries are beyond me. I may be an anachronism – who knows? My own dear son is like a golem that has turned against its creator. Don't be angry, my dear; I only used the word "golem" because you saw fit to mention Rabbi Loew of Prague. I liked it a lot, as a matter of fact, what you said about the universal charts. Amen, so be it. You scored a bull's-eye there. The only problem is, maybe Your Reverence can tell us which shop you go to to buy such charts. Can you enlighten me? Will you do your father a real favour? No? Never mind. I shall tell you a deep and wonderful thing that Rabbi Loew of Prague once said as he walked past the cathedral. By the way, do you know the original meaning of "real favour"?'

'All right, all right,' Fima conceded. 'So be it, then. Fair exchange You spare me the story of Rabbi Loew and I'll give in over those painters of yours. Send them round on Sunday morning, and that's that.' And to forestall his father's reply, he hurriedly employed the words his friend had uttered earlier: 'We'll talk about the other things when we see each other. I really must run along.'

He intended to chew a heartburn tablet and go down to the shopping centre to have the broken radio mended or to replace it if necessary. But suddenly there appeared before his eyes, so vividly that he could almost touch it, the image of a frail, myopic East European Jew wrapped in a prayer shawl, wandering in a dark forest, muttering biblical verses to himself, hurting his feet on the sharp stones, while softly and silently the snow fell, a night bird gave a sinister shriek, and wolves howled in the darkness.

Fima was gripped by fear.

The moment he put the receiver down, it occurred to him that he had not asked his father how he was. He had forgotten his intention of taking him to hospital for tests. He had even forgotten to notice whether the old man still had a whistle in his chest. He fancied he had heard a little squeak, but on second thoughts he was not certain: it might have been nothing but a slight cold. Or his father might just have been humming a high-pitched Hasidic tune. Or perhaps the noise had come from some fault in the telephone line. All systems were running down in this country and no one cared. This too was a byproduct of our obsession with the Territories. The ironic truth was that, as some future historian would discover, it was really Nasser who won the 1967 war. Our victory condemned us to destruction. The messianic genie that Zionism had managed to seal in the bottle popped out the day the ram's horn was sounded at the Wailing Wall. He laughs longest. Moreover, to pursue this line of reasoning resolutely to its bitter end, without flinching from the most unpalatable truth, perhaps the ultimate conclusion was that it was really Hitler, not Nasser, who had the last laugh. When all's said and done he continues to persecute the Jewish people ruthlessly. Everything that is happening to us now has its origin one way or another with Hitler. Now what was I going to do? Make a phone call. It was something urgent. But who to? What about? What is there left to say? I'm lost in the forest, too. Just like that old saint.

21

But the glow-worm had vanished

A ND because he had forgotten to lock the door when he brought the newspaper up earlier in the morning, and because he was absorbed in a futile attempt to reassemble the radio, he suddenly looked up and saw Annette Tadmor standing in front of him, in a red coat and a navy beret worn at an angle, which made her look like a French village girl. Her eyes were sparkling and her cheeks were glowing from the cold outside. She looked childlike, meek, pure, and painfully pretty. He instantly recalled what he had done to her two days earlier and felt unclean.

The smell of her expensive perfume, tinged perhaps with a faint hint of liquor, aroused in him a mixture of regret and desire.

'I've been trying to ring you all morning,' she said, 'but the phone's always engaged. Sorry to burst in like this. I'll only stay a minute, really. You don't happen to have a drop of vodka, do you? Never mind. Listen. I must have left an earring here. I was in such a muddle. You must think I'm crazy. The nice thing about you, Fima, is that I actually couldn't care less what you think of me. As if we were brother and sister. I can hardly remember a thing of what I burbled on about. And you're so kind, you didn't laugh at me. You haven't found one, have you? Silver, longish, with a little sparkling stone?'

Fima hesitated, made up his mind, tossed aside the newspaper that was occupying the armchair, and seated Annette in its place. At once he stood her up again and worked her arms loose from the sleeves of her red coat. This morning she looked beautiful, thoughtful and very attractive. He hurried to the kitchen to put the kettle on and check if there was any of his father's Cointreau left. On his return he said:

'I dreamed about you last night. You were so lovely and glad because your husband had come back to you and you forgave him for everything. Now you're even lovelier than you were in the dream. Navy really suits you. You ought to wear it more often. What do you say we draw a veil over what happened the day before yesterday? I'm so ashamed of myself. Your presence put me in a spin, and I seem to have behaved like the famous Tearful Rapist. I hadn't been with a woman for over two months. Not that that's any justification for behaving like a swine. Will you teach me how to make amends?'

Annette said:

'That's enough. Stop it. You're making me cry again. You've helped me so much, Fima; you're such a good listener, you've got so much understanding and empathy. I don't think any man in the whole world has ever listened to me the way you did. And I was so weird, so selfish, so absorbed in my own problems. I'm sorry I hurt your feelings.'

She added that she had always been a great believer in dreams. It was a fact that that very night, when Fima was dreaming of her, Yeri had really phoned from Milan. He sounded a bit low. He said he had no idea what would happen, that time would tell, and she should try not to hate him.

'Time . . .' Fima began, but Annette laid her hand over his mouth.

'Let's not talk. We talked enough the other night. Let's just sit quietly for a minute or two, and then I'll be on my way. I've got a million and one things to do in town. But I like being near you.'

They were silent. Fima sat on the arm of her chair, with his own arm barely touching her shoulder, ashamed of the mess, the long-sleeved winter vest thrown over the sofa, the bottom drawer he had not closed last night, the empty coffee cups on the desk, the newspapers everywhere. He mentally cursed the stirrings of desire, and swore to himself that this time his behaviour would be above reproach.

Annette said, thoughtfully, to herself rather than to him:

'I have wronged you.'

These words almost brought tears to his eyes. Ever since he

was a child, he had felt sweetness and joy whenever a grown-up said things like that to him. He had difficulty resisting the urge to go down on his knees before her, exactly like her husband in his dream. Although, to be strictly accurate, it had not been in a dream but in his thoughts this morning. But he saw no difference.

'I've got some good news for you,' he said. 'I've got your earring. I found it on the very armchair you're sitting in. I'm such an idiot: when I opened my eyes this morning, in the first glimmer of dawn, I thought it was a glow-worm that had forgotten to switch itself off.'

Emboldened, he added:

'You know, I'm an extortioner. I won't let you have it back for nothing.'

Annette burst out laughing. She went on laughing while he leaned over her. Pulling him towards her by his hair, she kissed the tip of his nose, as though he were a baby.

'Will that do? Can I have my earring back now?'

Fima said:

'That's more than I deserve. You've got some change coming.'

And to his own astonishment he suddenly clasped her knees and dragged her body down to the floor, desperately dizzy with lust, not stopping for her clothes but forcing his way blindly yet with a sleepwalker's confidence, thrusting into her almost at once, feeling as though it was not his phallus but his whole being that was being enfolded and dissolved inside her womb. He ejaculated instantly with a roar. When he finally surfaced again, feeling drained and as weightless as a sunbeam, as if he had left his bodily mass inside her, he was horror-struck at the realisation of how he had degraded both himself and her yet again. He knew that this time he had shattered it all forever. Then Annette began slowly, tenderly stroking his head and the back of his neck, until he shuddered deliciously and his skin quivered.

'The Tearful Rapist,' she said.

And she whispered to him:

'Hush, child.'

And again she asked if there was any vodka. For some reason

Fima was afraid she might be chilly. Clumsily he attempted to rearrange her clothing. And tried to say. But once again she hastily placed her hand over his mouth, and said:

'Quiet now, little chatterbox.'

As she stood combing her beautiful hair in the mirror, she added:

'I'm off now. I've got a million and one things to do in town. Just let me have my earring back: I've earned it honestly. I'll call you this evening. We'll go and see a film. There's a brilliant French comedy with Jean Gabin at the Orion.'

Fima went to the kitchen and poured what was left of the Cointreau into a glass for her. He rescued the kettle from boiling dry at the very last minute. But try as he might, he could not discover what he had done with the earring. He swore he would turn the flat upside down and return her magic glow-worm safe and sound that evening. As he escorted her to the door, he muttered abjectly that he would never forgive himself.

Annette laughed.

22

'I feel good with you just like this'

THEY passed on the stairs. No sooner had Annette left him than Nina Gefen appeared, with her austerely cropped greying hair, carrying a heavy shopping basket, which she deposited firmly on his desk among the papers and yogurt pots and dirty coffee cups. Roughly she lit a Nelson, not blowing the match out but shaking it. She shot twin lances of smoke from her nostrils. Fima unconsciously grinned. The turnover of his female visitors suddenly made him think of the procession of lady friends who were always trooping in and out of his father's flat. Maybe the time had come for him to sport a cane with a silver band?

Nina asked:

'What's so funny?'

Her nostrils must have picked up a whiff of scent through her cigarette smoke. Without waiting for his reply she added:

'The red lady I bumped into on the stairs was also grinning like a cat that's got the cream. Have you had a visitor by any chance?'

Fima was on the point of denying it. Since when did he have visitors? There were eight flats in the building. But something stopped him from lying to this fragile, embittered woman who looked like a cornered vixen, this woman whom he sometimes called 'my lover' and whose husband he loved. He looked down and said defensively:

'A patient from the clinic. Somehow we've become quite friendly.'

'Are you opening a branch of the clinic at your home?'

'It's like this,' Fima said, while his fingers attempted in vain to rejoin the two parts of the smashed radio. 'Her husband's sort of left her. She came to me for some advice.'

'Broken hearts mended here,' Nina said, meaning to sound witty but sounding close to tears instead. 'Saint Fima, patron saint of grass widows. If it goes on like this, you'll soon be seeing visitors by appointment only.'

She went into the kitchen and took out of her shopping basket a bag full of sprays and cleaning materials, which she placed for the time being on the edge of the worktop. Fima had the impression that her lips, that were closed on her half-smoked cigarette, were trembling. She unpacked various provisions she had brought him, opened the door of the refrigerator, and recoiled in horror.

'What a filthy mess,' she exclaimed.

Fima explained sheepishly that he had actually done a radical cleaning but had not had time to do the fridge.

And when was Uri coming back?

From the bottom of the shopping basket Nina extracted a small plastic bag.

'Late Friday night, i.e., tomorrow. I expect you can both hardly wait. Well, you can have your honeymoon on Saturday night. Here, I've brought you the book about Leibowitz. You ran away and left it on the rug. What's going to become of you, Fima? Just look at yourself.'

And indeed Fima had omitted to tuck his shirt-tail in after Annette, and the bottom of his yellowing flannel vest was showing below the chunky sweater.

Nina emptied the fridge, ruthlessly throwing out ancient vegetables, tuna, mouldy remains of fossilised cheese, an open sardine tin. She attacked the shelves and dividers with a cloth soaked in detergent. Fima meanwhile buttered several thick slices of the fragrant black Georgian bread she had brought with her, spread them generously with jam, and started munching voraciously. All the while he delivered a brief lecture on the lessons to be learned in Israel from the collapse of the left in England, Scandinavia, and in fact all over northern Europe. Suddenly, in the middle of a sentence, he said in a different voice:

'Look, Nina. About the night before last. No, it was the night before that. I burst in looking like a half-drowned dog, I talked nonsense, I jumped on top of you, I upset you, and then I ran away without explaining. Now I'm ashamed. I can't imagine what you must think of me. I just wouldn't like you to think that I don't find you attractive or something. It's not that, Nina. On the contrary. I do, more than ever. I'd simply had a bad day. This just isn't my week. I have this feeling that I'm not really living. Just existing. Creeping from day to day. Without sense and without desire. There's a verse in the Psalms: My soul droops with sorrow. That just about sums it up: drooping. Sometimes I have no idea what I'm doing hanging around here like last year's snow. Coming and going. Writing and crossing out. Filling in forms at the office. Putting my clothes on and taking them off again. Making phone calls. Bothering everybody and driving you all round the bend. Needling my father on purpose. How come there are still people who can stand me? How come you haven't sent me to Hell yet? Will you teach me how to make amends?'

Nina said:

'Be quiet, Fima. Just stop talking.'

Meanwhile she arranged the new provisions on the shelves of the now gleaming refrigerator. Her frail shoulders were trembling. From behind she looked to Fima like a small animal trapped in a cage, and he felt tenderly towards for her. Still with her back towards him, she continued:

'I don't understand it either. Look. An hour and a half ago, at the office, I suddenly had a feeling that you were in trouble. That something bad had happened to you. Maybe you were ill, lying here all alone in a fever. I tried to call, but you were always engaged. I thought perhaps you'd forgotten to put the receiver back, yet again. I dashed out in the middle of quite an important meeting about an insurance company that's gone bust, and came running straight to you. Or, rather, I stopped on the way to do some shopping for you, so you wouldn't starve to death. It's almost as though Uri and I have adopted you as our child. Except that Uri seems to get a kick out of the game, whereas all I get is depressed. The whole time. Time and again I get this feeling that something terrible has happened to you, and I drop everything and come running. Such a frightening, agonising feeling, as though you were calling out to me from far away: Nina, come quick. There's no explanation. Do me a favour, Fima; stop stuffing yourself with bread. Look how podgy you're getting. And anyway, I haven't got the strength or the inclination right now for your earth-shattering theories about Mitterrand and the British Labour Party. Save it for Uri, for Saturday night. All I want you to say is what's wrong. What's happening to you? Something strange is going on that you're keeping from me. Even stranger than usual. As if you were slightly drugged.'

Fima obeyed immediately. He stopped munching the piece of bread he was holding and put it down absent-mindedly in the sink as though it were an empty cup. He began to stammer that the wonderful thing about her was that with her he felt hardly any embarrassment. He wasn't afraid of appearing ridiculous. He didn't even care if he was miserable or stupid in her presence, as happened the other night. As if she was his sister. Now he was going to say something trite, but so what? Trite wasn't necessarily the opposite of true. What he wanted to say was that for him she was a good person. And that she had the loveliest fingers he had ever seen.

Still with her back to him, bending over the sink, picking out the piece of bread Fima had put there, scrubbing the ceramic tiles and the taps, carefully rinsing her hands, Nina Gefen said sadly:

'You left a sock at my place, Fima.'

And then:

'It's ages since we slept together.'

She stubbed out her cigarette, clutched his arm with her hand that was exquisitely shaped, like that of a young girl from the Far East, and whispered:

'Come now. I've got to be back in the office in less than an hour.'

On their way to the bed Fima was glad that Nina was short-sighted, because there was a momentary glimmer in the ashtray she had stubbed her cigarette out in, and Fima deduced it must be Annette's lost earring.

Nina drew the curtains, rolled back the bedspread, straightened the pillows, and removed her glasses. Her movements were plain and sparing, as if she were getting ready to be examined by her doctor. When she began undressing he turned his back to her and hesitated a while before he realised that there was no way out of this, he would have to remove his own clothes too. It never rains but it pours, he said to himself sadistically. And he slipped quickly between the sheets so she wouldn't notice his slackness. Remembering how he had disappointed her last time, on the rug at her house, he was overcome by shame. He pressed himself tightly against her, but his penis was as limp and unfeeling as a crumpled handkerchief. He buried his head between her heavy, warm breasts as if he were trying to hide from her inside her. They lay motionless, clinging to each other like a pair of soldiers huddling together in a trench under shellfire.

And she pleaded in a whisper:

'Don't talk. Don't say anything. I feel good with you just like this.'

He had a vivid mental image of the butchered dog writhing and oozing the last of his blood with a whimper under a low stone wall among wet bushes and rubbish. As though in a profound slumber, he murmured between her breasts words she did not hear, 'Back to Greece, Yael. We'll find love there. And compassion.'

Nina glanced at her watch: half past eleven. She kissed him on the forehead, and shaking his shoulder she said affectionately:

'Wake up, lad. Stir yourself. You fell asleep.'

She dressed jerkily, put on her thick glasses, and lit another cigarette, not blowing the match out but shaking it.

Before she left, she joined the two parts of the broken radio with a faint click. She turned the knob until the voice of Defence Minister Rabin suddenly filled the room:

'The side that displays the most stamina will win.'

'There, that's fixed,' said Nina, 'and I've got to go.'

Fima said:

'Don't be angry with me. I've had a suffocating feeling for days now. As if something awful is going to happen. I hardly sleep at night. I sit writing articles as if there was somebody listening. Nobody's listening and everything seems lost. What's going to become of us all, Nina? Do you know?'

179

Nina, who was already in the doorway, turned her bespectacled, vulpine face towards him and said:

'I have a chance of finishing relatively early this evening. Come straight to my office after the clinic, and we'll go to the concert at the YMCA. Or we'll go and see that Jean Gabin film. Then we'll go back to my place. Don't be gloomy.'

23

Fima forgets what he has forgotten

FIMA returned to the kitchen. He wolfed down another four slices of Nina's fresh black Georgian bread thickly spread with apricot jam. The defence minister said:

'I urge ourselves not to resort to all sorts of dubious shortcuts.'

Slightly mispronouncing the last word. And Fima, with his mouth full of bread and jam, echoed him:

'And ourselves urge you not to report to all sorts of tubeless chalk-huts.'

He immediately recoiled from this petty wordplay. As he turned off the radio, he apologised to Rabin:

'I must run. I'm late for work.' And, chewing a heartburn tablet, for some reason he pocketed Annette's earring, which he found in the ashtray among Nina's cigarette butts. He put on his coat, taking particular care not to trap his arm in the lining of the sleeve. And because the bread had not assuaged his hunger, and because in any case he counted it as breakfast, he went into the café opposite his flat for a bite of lunch. He could not remember if the name of the proprietress was Mrs Schneidmann or simply Mrs Schneider. He decided to put his money on Schneidermann. As usual, she did not take offence. She beamed at him with a cheery sparkle in her childlike eyes, which reminded him of a rustic Russian icon, and said:

'It's Scheinmann, Dr Nisan. Never mind. It's not important at all. The main thing is, God should give good health and prosperity to all Jewish people. And peace should come at last to this dear country of ours. Its hard to take so many deaths all the time. Today the stewed beef for the doctor, or the chicken today?'

Fima thought about it, and ordered the stew and an omelette, and a mixed salad, and a fruit compote. At another table sat a small, wrinkled man who struck Fima as glum and unwell. He was lazily reading *Yediot Aharonot*, turning the pages, staring, picking his teeth, and turning the pages again. His hair seemed to be stuck to his forehead with engine grease. For a moment Fima weighed up the chances that it was just himself, glued to that table since yesterday or the day before, and that all the events of the night and the morning had never taken place. Or that they had happened to somebody else, who resembled him in some ways and differed from him in a few trivial and utterly insignificant details. The very distinction between open possibilities and closed accomplished facts was simplistic. Perhaps his father was right after all: There is no such thing as a universal map of reality; it simply cannot exist. Everyone has to find his own way somehow through the forest with the help of unreliable, inaccurate maps that we are born wrapped in or that we pick up here and there along the way. That is why we are all lost, wandering around in circles, bumping into one another unawares, and losing each other in the dark, without so much as a distant glimmer of the supernal radiance.

Fima was almost tempted to ask the proprietress who the other gentleman was, and how long he had been sitting like that, squandering life's rich treasure, at the green-and-white-oilcloth-covered table. Eventually he decided to make do with asking her what she thought should be done to bring peace nearer.

Mrs Scheinmann reacted with suspicion. She glanced all around apprehensively, before replying shyly:

'What do we understand? Let the high-ups decide. The generals in our government. God should only give them good health. And he should give them also plenty good sense.'

'Should we make some concessions to the Arabs?'

Apparently afraid of spies, or of tripping herself, or simply of words themselves, she glanced towards the door and the curtain to the kitchen before whispering:

'We need to have some pity. That is all we need.'

Fima persisted:

'Pity for the Arabs or pity for ourselves?'

She gave him another timid, coquettish smile, like a peasant girl disconcerted by a sudden question about the colour of her underwear or the distance from here to the moon. She replied with graceful shrewdness:

'Pity is pity.'

The man at the next table, who looked emaciated and tortured, with his greasy hair stuck to his skull, and who Fima imagined to be a petty clerk with haemorrhoids, perhaps a retired sanitation officer, intervened in the conversation with a Romanian accent and a flat intonation, picking his teeth all the time:

'Sir. Excuse. Please. What Arabs? What peace? What state? Who needs it? While we live, we must enjoy. Why you give a damn for the rest of the world? What, the rest of the world give a damn for you? Just enjoy. The most you can do. Just to be fun. All the rest, you waste your time. Excuse for interrupting.'

Fima did not think the speaker looked much like someone who had a good time; more like someone who made a few pounds now and then by informing on his neighbours to the Income Tax Department. The man's hands were shaking.

Fima inquired politely:

'You're saying we should trust to the government in everything? We should look after our own affairs and not meddle in public matters?'

The doleful informer said:

'Best is from the government also they go have a good time. And from the government of the Arabs also. And same thing from the goyim. All heppy all the day. Anyway we all dies.'

Mrs Scheinmann smiled conspiratorially at Fima, ignoring the presence of the sacked clerk. Obsequiously, as though to apologise for what he was obliged to listen to here, she said:

'Pay no attention, Doctor. His little girl is died, his wife is died, his brothers is also died. And also, he has not got a penny. He speaks not from his brains. This is a man which God is forgotten him.'

Fima scrabbled in his pockets but found only loose change, so he asked the proprietress to put it on his account. Next week, when he was paid . . . But she interrupted him blithely:

'Never mind. Don't worry. Everything is fine.'

And without being asked she brought him a glass of sweet lemon tea and added:

'Anyway, everything come from Heaven.'

He did not agree with her on this point, but the music of her words touched him like a caress, and he suddenly placed his fingers on her veined hand and thanked her. He praised the food and expressed enthusiastic agreement with what she had said earlier: 'Pity is pity.'

Once, when Dimi was eight, Ted and Yael had called him in a panic at ten in the morning to ask him to help search for the child, who had apparently run away from school because the other children had been bullying him. Without a moment's hesitation Fima called a taxi and hurried to the cosmetics factory in Romema. And indeed he found Baruch and Dimi shut up together in the small laboratory, bent over a bench, silvery mane touching albino curls; they were distilling a bluish liquid in a test tube over a burner. As he entered, the old man and the child both fell silent, like conspirators caught in the act. In those days Dimi was still in the habit of calling both Baruch and Fima 'Granpa'. The father, with his Trotsky beard curving upwards like a Saracen scimitar, refused to reveal to Fima the nature of their experiment: there was no way of knowing whose side he was on. But Dimi, serious and secretive, said he trusted Fima not to give them away. Granpa and me are developing an antistupidity spray. Wherever stupidity shows up, you can pull out a little canister, give a squirt, and it's gone. Fima said: You'll have to manufacture at least a hundred thousand tons of it in the first batch. Baruch said: Maybe we're wasting our time, Diminka. Clever people don't need the treatment, and as for fools, tell me, my dears, why should we weary ourselves for fools? Why don't we have some fun instead? At once he rang for a tray of sweets, nuts, and fruit. With a sigh he took a bundle of little sticks out of a drawer and told the child to lock the door; the three of them spent the rest of the morning absorbed in a spillikins contest. The memory of that illicit morning's fun shone in Fima's mind as a patch of happiness such as he had never known even in his own childhood. Then, at midday, he had had to stir himself and return Dimi to his parents. Ted sentenced the child to two hours' solitary confinement in the bathroom and a further two days of house arrest. Fima also received a reprimand. He was almost sorry they had abandoned work on the antistupidity spray.

In the bus on the way to work he thought over what Mrs Schoenberg had said about the doleful informer, and said to himself: To be forgotten by God is not necessarily to be doomed. On the contrary, it may mean becoming as light and free as a lizard in the desert. He brooded on the similarity between two Hebrew verbs, the one meaning 'forget' and the other 'dwindle' or 'die away'. The most wretched fate is not to be forgotten but, precisely, to fade away. Will, longings, memories, carnal desires, curiosity, passion, gladness, generosity – everything gradually fades. As the wind dies in the mountains, so the spirit too expires. Indeed, even pain decreases somewhat with the passage of the years, but then, together with pain, other signs of life also decline. The simple, silent, primal things, those things that every child encounters with excitement and wonderment, such as the succession of the seasons, a kitten scampering in the yard, a door swivelling on its hinges, the life cycle of plants, swelling fruit, whispering pines, a column of ants on the veranda, the play of light on the valleys and the hillsides, the pallor of the moon and its halo, spiders' webs laden with dewdrops in the early morning, the miracles of breathing, speech, twilight at sunset, water boiling and freezing, the glitter of the midday sun on a tiny sliver of glass, so many primal things that we once had but have lost. Never to return. Or, worse still, they will return rarely, glimmering in the distance, while the original excitement will have vanished forever. And everything is dimmed and dissolved. Life itself is gradually growing dusty and grubby. Who will win in France? What will the Likud central committee decide? Why was the article rejected? How much does a managing director earn? How will the minister respond to the charges that have been levelled at him? Again and again this morning I was told, and again and again said myself: 'I'm late, I must run along.' But why? Where? For what? Surely even Minister Rabin must have been excited by those primal things once, as he stood a thousand years ago, a withdrawn, ginger-haired child, a thin, freckled child with no shoes on, in a back yard in Tel Aviv, among the clotheslines, at six o'clock on an autumn morning, when suddenly a flock of cranes flew past overhead, white against the dawn clouds, promising him, like me, a pure world, full of silence and blueness, far from words and lies, if only we dare leave everything behind and get up and go. But here we are, this minister of defence just like the rest of us who attack him daily in the newspapers, we've all forgotten and we've all faded. We are all dead souls. Everywhere we go, we leave behind us a trail of lifeless words, from which it is only a short way to the corpses of Arab children killed daily in the Territories. A short way too to the unpalatable fact that a man like me simply erases from the register of the dead, without thinking, the children of the family of settlers burned alive the day before yesterday by a Molotov cocktail on the road to Alfei Menashe. Why did I erase them? Was their death insufficiently innocent? Unworthy to enter the shrine of suffering of which we have, as it were, made ourselves the guardians? Is it just that the settlers frighten and infuriate me, whereas the Arab children weigh on my conscience? Can a worthless man like me have sunk so low as to make a distinction between the intolerable killing of children and the not-so-intolerable killing of children? Justice itself sounded forth from the mouth of Mrs Schoenberg when she said to me simply: 'Pity is pity.' Minister of Defence Rabin is betraying our basic values et cetera, whereas in Rabin's view I and the likes of me are betraying the fundamental principles and so forth. But in relation to the far-away call of the primal splendour of an autumn morning, in relation to that flight of cranes, surely we are all traitors. No difference between the minister and me. We have even poisoned Dimi and his friends. Therefore I ought to write a few lines to Rabin, to apologise, to try to explain that we are both in the same boat after all. Or perhaps to ask for a meeting?

'That's enough.' Fima smiled wryly. 'We have sinned. We have transgressed. That's enough.'

When he got off the bus, he muttered like a captious old man: 'Wordplay. Empty wordplay.' Because suddenly his earlier juggling with the words for 'forget' and 'dwindle' or 'die away' struck him as so cheap that he did not even say thank you or good-bye to the driver as he got off the bus, which he was always very particular about doing, even in moments of absent-mindedness, including yesterday when he inadvertently got off at the wrong stop.

Fima stood in the grey street for a moment or two, among dead leaves and scraps of paper blowing in the wind. He concentrated on the whisper of damp pines behind stone walls and staring at the departing bus. What had he forgotten on board? A book? An umbrella? An envelope? Perhaps a small package? Something belonging to Tamar? Or to Annette Tadmor? 'Cranes wheel and whirl': a forgotten line from an old children's song suddenly came back to him. He consoled himself with the hope that what he had left on the seat was merely the copy of *Ma'ariv* that he had found there. Thanks to the minister and the cranes he could not even remember what was in the main headline.

24

Shame and guilt

IN the garden, as he walked along the paved path that led round the small block of flats to the clinic, he stopped and stood for a moment, because from the first floor, through closed windows, through the wind and the rustling pine trees, there came the sound of a cello. One of the old women, or perhaps a pupil, was practising the same scale over and over again.

Fima tried vainly to identify the tune, standing and listening like a man who does not know where he has come from or where he must go. If only he could change his consistency at this instant, and become air, or stone, or a crane. A cello was being plucked inside him, answering the cello overhead in its own language, a sound of yearning and self-mockery. He could see a vivid mental image of the lives of those three elderly women musicians, rattling along rain-swept winter roads for hours on end in a taxi to give a recital in some remote kibbutz at the far end of Upper Galilee or at the opening ceremony of a war veterans' reunion. How do they spend their free evenings in the winter? After washing up and clearing the kitchen, they probably gather, the three of them, in their communal sitting room. Fima conjured up the image of a severely puritanical room containing a pendulum clock with the hours marked in Roman characters, a sideboard, a heavy, thick-legged round dining table and dark straight-backed chairs. A grey woollen poodle crouches on the carpet in a corner of the room. On the closed grand piano, on the table, on the chest of drawers are spread lace mats, like those that covered every available surface in his father's flat in Rehavia. There is also a heavy, old-fashioned wireless set, and blue dried flowers in a tall vase. The curtains are drawn, the shutters closed tight, and a blue flame glows in the heater, which bubbles faintly from time to time as the paraffin flows from the reservoir to the wick. One of the women, perhaps each in turn, reads softly to the others from an old German novel. *Lotte in Weimar*, for example. There is no sound the whole evening apart from the reader's voice and the ticking of the clock and the bubbling of the paraffin. At eleven o'clock precisely they get up and go to their respective bedrooms. Their three doors close behind them until the morning. And in the sitting room, in the deep silence and the darkness, the clock keeps ticking relentlessly, and chiming softly every hour.

At the entrance to the clinic Fima saw the elegant plate inscribed with the words DR WAHRHAFTIG DR EITAN CONSULTANT GYNAECOLOGISTS. As usual, he was irked by the construction that Hebrew does not tolerate.

'So it doesn't tolerate it. So what?'

And did Nora, Wahrhaftig's only daughter, who had been married to Gad Eitan and ran off ten years ago with a visiting Latin-American poet, ever suffer pangs of nostalgia? Of conscience? Of shame and guilt? Her name was never mentioned here. She was never alluded to, even indirectly. As if she had never existed. Only Tamar occasionally whispered something to Fima about a letter that had been returned to sender, or a telephone hung up without a word. Tamar persisted in trying to persuade him that Gad was not really a bad man but was just frightened and hurt. Except when she occasionally maintained the precise opposite: Any woman would have left such a viper.

Fima put on his short white coat, sat down behind his reception desk, and looked at the appointments book. As though he was unconsciously trying to guess which patient was going to materialise in his life as the next Annette Tadmor.

Tamar said:

'There are two patients inside. The one with Dr Basso Profundo is a bit like Margaret Thatcher; Gad's one looks like a schoolgirl, quite pretty.'

Fima said:

'I nearly phoned you in the middle of the night. I managed to find your Finnish general, the one who begins and ends with M. It's Mannerheim. He was really called von Mannerheim.

A German name. He was the one who amazed the whole world by halting Stalin's invasion in 1938. He led the tiny Finnish army against vastly superior Soviet forces.'

Tamar said:

'You know everything. You could have been a university professor. Or a cabinet minister.'

Fima considered this, agreed with her in his heart, and replied warmly:

'You are the ideal woman, Tamar. It's a disgrace to the male sex that nobody has snatched you away from us yet. Though on second thoughts there isn't a man alive who's worthy of you.'

Her stocky, robust body, her soft, fair hair gathered into a small bun at the back, even her one green eye and one brown one suddenly made her look touchingly childlike, and he asked himself why he shouldn't go up to her, clasp her shoulders, and bury her head in his chest as though she were his daughter. But this urge to console was immediately mixed with another: to boast to her that two women had made the pilgrimage to his flat that morning and offered themselves to him, one after the other. He hesitated, pulled himself together, and said nothing. When had a man's hand last touched that stout body? How would she react if he suddenly reached out and cupped her breasts in his hands? With shock? Outrage? Guilty surrender? You fool, he said to his penis: now you remember. And as though he could feel her nipples nestling in the soft centre of each palm, he clenched his fists and smiled.

Tamar said:

'Can I ask you something else?'

Fima could not remember what the last question was, but he replied cheerily, expansively, as though aping his father's imperious manner:

'Up to half my kingdom.'

'Pacific island, also bathing costume.'

'Pardon?'

'That's what it says here. Do you think it's a misprint? "Pacific island, also bathing costume." Six letters. It's almost the last clue left.'

'I don't know,' said Fima. 'Try Tahiti. I've got a child who keeps asking me to take him away to the Pacific. He wants us to build a cabin out of wattles and live on fish and fruit. I don't mean that he's my child exactly. Well, he is and he isn't. Never mind. Try Hawaii. Would you like to come with us, Tamar? To live in a cabin built of wattles and eat nothing but fish and fruit? Far away from cruelty and stupidity? Far away from this rain?'

'Do you spell Tahiti with an I or a Y? Either way it won't help, because the second letter has got to be an I and the third's a K. Do you mean Yael's little boy, Dimi? Your Challenger? Maybe I shouldn't meddle, Fima, but you ought to think carefully whether you're not complicating that child's life too much by trying to be a spare father to him. I sometimes think . . .'

'Bikini,' said Fima. 'The swimsuit was named after doomsday. Bikini was a tiny island that was evacuated and blown to bits with atom bombs. It was the testing ground for doomsday. In the South Pacific. We'll have to look for some other island. Some other ocean, in fact. Anyway, how can I make a cabin out of wattles: I can't even put up a bookshelf. Uri Gefen assembled my bookcases for me. Please, Tamar, don't stand at the window like that with your back to me and the room. I've told you a thousand times I can't stand it. My problem, I know.'

'What's the matter with you, Fima? You're very funny sometimes. I was only drawing the curtains because I'm fed up with looking at the rain. We don't need to look for any other island: Bikini is just right. What do you think is the name of the ruling party in Nicaragua?'

Fima had the answer to this question on the tip of his tongue, but at that instant the sound of a woman's voice suddenly burst out behind Dr Eitan's closed door. It was a short, piercing scream, full of terror and outrage, the sort of sound that might be wrenched from the throat of a small child who was the victim of searing injustice. Who was being butchered in there? Perhaps someone destined to be Yoezer's father or grandfather. Fima tensed, straining to block his mind, to fortify himself, not to imagine what those plastic-gloved hands were doing in there, on that couch covered in white oilcloth and a disposable sheet of coarse white paper, with a white trolley nearby carrying a set of sterile scalpels, speculums, different-sized scissors, forceps, syringes, a razor, special needle and thread for sewing human flesh, clamps, oxygen masks, and saline drips. And the femininity exposed to its fullest extent, with no hiding place, flooded with bright light from the powerful lamp behind the doctor's head; pink and raw like a wound, looking like a toothless old man's open mouth, oozing dark blood.

While he was still struggling vainly to banish this image, not to see or hear or feel, Tamar said gently:

'You can relax now. It's all over.'

But Fima felt ashamed. Somehow, in a way that was not clear to him, he felt that he himself was not free of guilt. That he too was responsible for the agony going on behind the closed door. That there was a connection between his humiliation of Annette and then Nina this morning and the pain and shame on that spotless couch which now was no doubt far from spotless, full of blood and other secretions. His penis shrank and retreated into hiding like a thief. A vague, repulsive pain suddenly throbbed in his testicles. If Tamar had not been there, he would have reached down to ease the pressure of his trousers. Though actually it was better like this. He must abandon his pathetic attempt to convince Tsvi that we are all entitled to discharge ourselves from responsibility for atrocities committed in our name. We have to admit the guilt. We have to accept that everybody's suffering rests on all our shoulders. The oppression in the Territories, the disgrace of old people poking around in dustbins, the blind man tapping at night in the deserted street, the misery of autistic children in run-down institutions, the killing of the dog with oedema, Dimi's ordeal, Annette's and Nina's humiliation, Teddy's loneliness, Uri's constant wanderings, the surgical procedure that had just taken place on the other side of this wall, stainless-steel forceps deep inside the wounded vulva – everything was on all our shoulders. How useless to dream of running away to Moruroa or the Galapagos Islands. Even Bikini, poisoned by a radioactive cloud, was on all our shoulders. For a moment he pondered the curious fact that in Hebrew the word for 'pity' appears to be related to 'womb', while 'forceps' seems to be derived from 'learning a lesson'. But then he rebuked himself for these verbal games, his poeticisings, which were no less despicable than the Minister of Defence saying 'cost' when he meant 'death'.

'There's a stanza in one of Alterman's poems,' he said to Tamar, 'called 'Songs of the Plagues of Egypt,' that goes like this: *The rabble soon assembled / Bearing the noose of blame, / To hang the King and Council / And free themselves from shame.* That is more or less the bottom line of all history, I think. It's the story of all of us, condensed into a dozen words. Let's make her a cup of coffee. And one for Gad and Alfred too.'

Tamar said:

'That's all right. You're excused. I've put the kettle on. Anyway, it'll take her a while to come around and stand up. You're excused from cleaning up too. I'll do it if you just see to the steriliser and the washing machine. How come you can remember everything by heart? Alterman and Bikini and everything? On the one hand, you're so absent-minded you can't even button your shirt up right or shave without cutting yourself; on the other hand you turn the world upside down for a clue in a crossword puzzle. And you organise everyone's life for them. Just look at your sweater: half in and half out of your trousers. And your shirt collar's half in and half out too. Like a baby.'

At this she fell silent, though her warm smile continued to haunt her broad, open face as though it had been forgotten there. After being absorbed in thought for a while, she added sadly, without explaining the connection:

'My father hanged himself in the Metropole Hotel in Alexandria. It was in '46. They didn't find any letter. I was five and a half. I hardly remember him. I remember that he smoked cigarettes called Simon Arzt. And I remember his wristwatch: yellow, square, with phosphorescent hands that glowed in the dark like a ghost's eyes. I've got a picture of him in British army uniform, but he doesn't look much like a soldier. He looks so sloppy. And tired. In the picture he actually looks fair-haired, smiling, with beautiful white teeth and lots of lovely little lines at the corners of his eyes. Not sad, just tired. And he's holding a cat. I wonder if he suffered from unrequited love too. My mother would never talk to me about him. The only thing she said was: He didn't think about us either. Then she'd change the subject. She had a lover, a tall Australian captain with a wooden arm and a Russian name, Serafim. They explained to me once that it comes from the Hebrew word 'seraphim'. Then she had a weepy banker who took her to Canada and dropped her. In the end she wrote to me from Toronto in Polish. I had to have the letter translated; she never managed to learn to write Hebrew. She said she wanted to come back to Nes Tsiyona to start a new life. But she never made it. She died of cancer of the liver. I was brought up in an institution run by the Working Women's Council. About Alterman: tell me, Fima, is it true what they say – that he has two wives?'

'He died,' Fima replied, 'about twenty years ago.' He was on the point of launching into a crash course on Alterman when Dr Eitan's door opened, a pungent hygienic odour wafted out, and the doctor poked his head out and said to Tamar:

'Hey, Brigitte Bardot. Bring me an ampoule of pethidine chop-chop.'

So Fima was obliged to postpone his lecture. He unplugged the boiling kettle and decided to put a heater on in the recovery room. Then he had two phone calls, one after the other: he booked an appointment for Mrs Bergson for the end of the month and he explained to Gila Maimon that they never gave out the results of tests over the telephone; she'd have to come in and be told the answer by Dr Wahrhaftig. For some reason he addressed them both sheepishly, as though he had done them some wrong. He agreed in his mind with Annette Tadmor when she'd made fun of the clichés of mysterious womanhood, Greta Garbo, Beatrice, Marlene Dietrich, Dulcinea, but she was wrong when she tried to place the cloak of mystery on the shoulders of the male sex. We are all steeped in falsehood. We all pretend. Surely the plain truth is that each and every one of us knows exactly what pity is and when we ought to show it, because each and every one of us aches for a little pity. But come the moment when we should open the gates of compassion, we pretend we know nothing. Or that compassion and mercy are merely a way of patronising others, something too old-fashioned and sentimental. Or that that's the way it is and what can be done about it and why me of all people? That was presumably what Pascal meant by 'the death of the soul' and about human agony being that of a dethroned king. All his own efforts not to imagine what was happening on the other side of the wall struck him as cowardly, ignoble, and ugly. As was his attempt to turn his thoughts from the death of Tamar's father to the gossip about Alterman's life. Surely it was the duty of all of us at least to look suffering in the eye. If he were prime minister, he would make each member of the Cabinet stay for a week with a reserve unit in Gaza or Hebron, spend some time inside the perimeter of one of the detention camps in the Negev, live a couple of days in a run-down psycho-geriatric ward, lie in the mud and rain for a whole winter's night from sundown to dawn by the electronic fence on the Lebanese border, or join Eitan and Wahrhaftig without any intervening barrier in this abortion inferno, which was now once more pervaded with the sounds of piano and cello from upstairs.

A moment later he was disgusted by these reflections, because on second thoughts they struck him as the embodiment of nineteenth-century Russian kitsch. The very term 'abortion inferno' was an injustice: after all, there were times when life was actually created here. Fima recalled a patient by the name of Sarah Matalon who had been advised by leading specialists to give up and adopt a child, and only Gad Eitan persevered single-mindedly for four years, until he finally opened her womb. The whole staff of the clinic was invited to the circumcision of her son. The father suddenly announced that the child would be called Gad, and Fima noticed Dr Eitan biting hard on his leather watch strap; indeed for a moment his own eyes filled too. They had to make do with Dr Wahrhaftig, who held the baby enthusiastically.

Fima leaped forward to assist Tamar, who was helping a dazed girl of about seventeen, pale as a sheet and thin as a matchstick, walk falteringly towards the recovery room. As though to atone for the sins of the whole male sex, Fima bustled hither and thither, hurrying to fetch a soft blanket, a cold glass of mineral water with a slice of lemon in it, paper tissues, aspirins. Later he called a taxi for her.

At four-thirty there was a coffee break. Dr Wahrhaftig came and leaned on the reception desk, wafting a smell of medicine and disinfectant into Fima's face. His massive chest, blown up like that of a tsarist governor-general, and his broad round hips did give his heavy body the look of a basso profundo. His cheeks were crisscrossed by a network of unhealthy bluish, red, and pink blood vessels that were so close to the surface, you could almost take his pulse by their throbbing.

Lithe and silent, with velvety movements like a cat on hot tin, Dr Eitan arrived. He was chewing gum slowly, impassively, with his mouth closed. His lips were thin and pursed. Wahrhaftig said:

'That was a very odd *Schnitz*. Just as well you stitched her up nice and tight.'

Eitan said:

'We pulled her through. It didn't look too good.'

Wahrhaftig said:

'About the transfusion: you were absolutely right.'

Eitan said:

'Big deal. It was obvious from the start.'

And Wahrhaftig said:

'God has given you clever fingers, Gad.'

Fima interrupted gently:

'Drink your coffee. It's getting cold.'

'Herr Exzellenz von Nisan!' roared Wahrhaftig. 'And where has His Highness been hiding all these days? Has he been writing a new *Faust* for us? Or a *Kohlhaas*? We had almost forgotten what your face looks like!' He went on to recount a 'well-known joke' about three layabouts. But he could not restrain himself from bursting into guffaws before he had even reached the third layabout.

Gad Eitan, lost in thought, suddenly remarked:

'Even so, we shouldn't have done it here, under a local. It should have been done in a hospital, with a general anaesthetic. We nearly made a mess of it. We ought to think about it, Alfred.'

Wahrhaftig, in an altered voice, said:

'What? Are you worried?'

Gad Eitan took his time. After a pause he said:

'No. I'm perfectly confident now.'

Tamar hesitated, her mouth opened and closed twice, and finally she said warily:

'You look nice in that white polo neck, Gad. Would you rather have lemon tea instead of coffee?'

Gad Eitan said:

'Yes, but no tail-wagging, please.'

Wahrhaftig, a clumsy peacemaker, hastily turned the conversation to current affairs:

'So, what do you say about that Polish antisemite? They've learned nothing and forgotten nothing. Did you hear on the radio what that cardinal in Warsaw said about the Auschwitz convent? It's a straight replay of their old tunes: Why are the Jews so pushy, why are the Jews making such a fuss, why are the Jews inciting the whole world against poor Poland, why are the Jews trying to make capital out of their dead again? After all, millions of Poles were killed too. And our cute little government, with old-fashioned Jewish obsequiousness, turns a blind eye to the whole thing. In any civilised country we'd have sent their chargé d'affaires home with a good kick up the you-know-where.'

Gad Eitan declared:

'Don't you worry, Alfred. We won't take it lying down. One of these nights we'll drop airborne commandos on them. A lightning raid. An Auschwitz Entebbe. We'll blow that convent sky high, and all our forces will return safely to base. Surprise will be total. The world will hold its breath like the good old days. Then Mister Sharon and Mister Shamir will gabble on about the long arm of the IDF and the renewal of Israel's deterrent force. They can christen it Operation Peace for the Crematoria.'

Fima was instantly ignited. If I were prime minister, he thought, but before he could complete the thought, he had burst out furiously:

'Who the hell needs all this? We've gone out of our minds. We've gone right off our rockers. What are we doing squabbling with the Poles about who owns Auschwitz? It's already beginning to sound like an extension of our usual story about "ancestral rights" and "ancestral heritage" and "we shall never hand back territory that we have liberated". Any moment now our dashing pioneers will be out there planting a new settlement among the gas chambers. Establishing facts in disputed territory. What makes Auschwitz a Jewish site anyway? It's a Nazi site. A German site. As a matter of fact, it really ought to become a Christian site, for Christendom in general and Polish Catholicism in particular. Let them cover the whole death camp with convents and crosses and bells. Wall to wall. With a Jesus on every chimney. There's no more fitting place in the world for Christendom to commune with itself. Them, not us. Let them go on pilgrimages there, whether to beat their breasts or to celebrate the greatest theological victory in their history. For all I care, they can baptise their Auschwitz convent 'The Sweet Revenge of Jesus'. What are we doing scurrying in there with protesters and placards? Are we out of our minds? It's quite right that a Jew who goes there to commune with the memory of the victims should see a forest of crosses all around him and hear nothing but the ringing of church bells. That way he'll understand that he's in the true heart of Poland. The heart of hearts of Christian Europe. As far as I'm concerned, it would be an excellent thing if they'd move the Vatican there. Why not? Let the pope sit there from now to the Resurrection on a golden throne among the chimneys. And for another thing –'

'And for another thing, come out of your trance,' hissed Eitan, holding his elegant fingers up to the light and inspecting them sternly, as though suddenly anxious that they might have undergone some mutation. He did not trouble to specify whether he was of a different opinion.

'In any civilised country,' said Wahrhaftig, trying to get the conversation back on the rails, 'you two would not be permitted to say such macabre things about this tragic subject. There are certain things one must not joke about even in a private conversation behind closed doors. But our Fima is addicted to paradox, while you, Gad, are only happy when you have a chance to poke fun at the government, Auschwitz, the Entebbe raid, the Six Million, anything to be provocative. You're dead inside. You'd hang the lot of them. The Hangman from Alfasi Street. It's because you both hate the state, instead of getting up every morning and thanking God on bended knee for everything we have here, including the Asianness and the Bolshevism. You can't see the cheese for the holes.' And suddenly, swelling with sham fury, as though he had made up his mind to impersonate a fearsome tyrant, the old doctor turned crimson, his toper's face trembled, his crisscrossed blood vessels looked as though they were about to burst, and he roared politely:

'Cut the cackle now! Everyone back to work, quick march! My clinic is not a parliament!'

Barely opening the crack of his lips, Gad Eitan hissed under his blond moustache:

'But that's just what it is. A senile parliament. Alfred, step into my room. And I need you too, you sex-starved Miss World, with Mrs Bergman's notes.'

'What have I done to you?' Tamar whispered tearfully. 'Why do you torment me all the time?' And with a flicker of timorous courage she added:

'One of these days I'll hit you.'

'Great.' Eitan grinned. 'I'm at your service. I'll even turn the other cheek, if that'll help to calm your hormones down a bit. Then Saint Augustine here can comfort you, and me, together with all those who mourn for Zion and Jerusalem, amen.' So saying, he wheeled around with military precision and stalked lithely away, smoothing his white polo neck sweater and leaving silence behind him.

The two doctors disappeared into Dr Eitan's room. Fima rooted in his pocket and managed to produce a crumpled, none too clean handkerchief, which he was about to hand to Tamar, whose eyes were brimming. But, unnoticed by him, a small object fell out of the folds of the handkerchief and landed on the floor. Tamar bent over, picked it up, and returned it to him, smiling through her tears. It was Annette's earring. Then she wiped her eyes, the brown one and the green one, on her sleeve, pulled out the requisite files, and hurried after the doctors. In the doorway she turned her harassed face towards Fima and said with desperate pathos, as though swearing by all that was most dear to her:

'One of these days I'll grab a pair of scissors and murder him. Then I'll kill myself.'

Fima did not believe her, but nevertheless he picked up the paperknife and concealed it in the drawer of the desk. The handkerchief and the earring he tucked carefully back in his pocket. Then he tore off a sheet of paper and placed it in front of him, thinking to jot down his thought about the heart of Christendom. It might develop into an article for the weekend supplement.

But his mind was elsewhere. He had slept for less than three hours, and in the morning he had been worn out by his indefatigable lovers. What did they see in him exactly? A helpless child who stirred their maternal instincts, a child to swaddle and suckle? A brother to wipe away their tears? An eclipsed poet they longed to play muse to? And what got women worked up about a cruel hussar like Gad? Or a garrulous dandy like his father? Fima marvelled, smiling. Perhaps Annette was wrong after all, and there is a mysterious side? The enigma of what women prefer? Or perhaps she didn't make a mistake but was deliberately keeping a secret from the enemy. Cunningly dissimulating its very existence. No doubt she did not really desire me this morning; she was just sorry for me and decided to give herself, so she did. Whereas I, half an hour later, didn't desire Nina but I was sorry for her and tried to give myself to her, but nature itself denied me what it makes possible for them without any difficulty.

And he muttered:

'But that's not fair.'

And then, self-mockingly:

'So, why not sign a petition?'

His tired hand was doodling on the paper in front of him, drawing circles and triangles, crosses, six-pointed stars, missiles, and big breasts. Among these doodles he unconsciously inscribed the line that had come into his head earlier: 'Cranes wheel and whirl.' Underneath he wrote: 'Wains heel and curl.' Then he crossed it all out. Crumpling the page into a ball, he tossed it at the wastepaper basket. And missed.

Then he thought of making use of the spare time by composing two letters, one an open letter, a reply to Günter Grass about guilt and responsibility, and one private, a belated reply to Yael's farewell letter of twenty-four years ago. It was particularly important for him to explain to Yael and to himself why he had been so rude to the two air force colonels who had come to their home that Saturday evening specially to convince him that Yael's going to work in Seattle or Pasadena for a year or two was of national importance. He still remained unshaken in his conviction that the words 'national interest' generally served as a cover for all sorts of monstrosities. But now, half a lifetime later, he no longer saw himself as entitled to preach. By what right? What have you accomplished with your life? Will it be of any use to Yoezer and his friends, living here a hundred years from now, that once in Jerusalem there lived a troublesome layabout who got on everybody's nerves with his petty linguistic corrections? Who fornicated with married women? Who reviled and insulted cabinet ministers? Who argued with lizards and cockroaches? While even vile men like Gad Eitan healed sick women and opened barren wombs?

When the phone rang, instead of his usual greeting, 'Clinic, good evening,' there slipped out of his mouth the words 'Clinic, good dreaming.' He immediately apologised, stammered, tried to cover up his slip with a feeble joke, made a mess of it, corrected himself, tried to explain the correction, and booked an urgent appointment for Rachel Pinto for the following week when she had only asked for a routine checkup.

Who knew? Maybe her husband had also left her. Or found a younger mistress. Or been killed on reserve duty in the Territories, and she had no one to comfort her.

25

Fingers that were no fingers

A T seven o'clock they lowered the blinds and locked the clinic. The rain and the wind had stopped. A clear, glassy cold had descended on Jerusalem. Stars glowed with a sharp wintry radiance. And from the east, Christian bells tolled loudly and forlornly, as though the Crucifixion were happening at Golgotha that very moment.

Dr Wahrhaftig went home in a taxi, taking Tamar with him, since he had offered as usual to drop her off opposite the Rehavia High School. Gad Eitan sneaked through the darkness to the side street where he had parked his sports car. While Fima, in his heavy overcoat, with the collar turned up, with his battered, greasy cloth cap on his head, stood for ten minutes or so at the deserted bus stop waiting for a miracle. He had an urge to go to Tsvi and Shula Kropotkin's flat just down the Gaza Road, accept the Napoleon brandy Tsvi had promised him, put his feet up near the radiator, and expound his theory about the rift between Jews and Christians being all the deeper for being, as it were, in the family. Our quarrel with Islam, by contrast, is merely an ephemeral dispute over land, which will be forgotten within thirty or forty years. But the Christians in a thousand years' time will still see us as deicides and as an accursed elder brother. This last phrase pierced his heart all of a sudden, reminding him of the baby his mother had borne half a century ago, when he was four. Apparently this baby died after only three weeks, of some congenital defect which Fima knew nothing about: it was never discussed in his presence. He had no memory of the baby or of the mourning, but he had a vivid mental image of a tiny light-blue knitted bonnet laid out on his mother's little bedside table. When his father threw out all his wife's belongings at her death, the blue knitted bonnet vanished too. Had Baruch given it to the leper hospital in Talbiyeh along with all her clothes? Fima despaired of the bus and started walking towards Rehavia. Vainly he tried to remember whether he had promised Nina to pick her up from her office after work and take her to see the Jean Gabin film, or whether they had arranged to meet at the cinema. After a while he was not certain that it was not Annette Tadmor that he had arranged to see. Was it possible that in a fit of absent-mindedness he had inadvertently asked them both out? He could not find a telephone token in any of his pockets, so he went on walking the empty streets, which were lit here and there by a yellow streetlight swathed in flickering mist, oblivious to the biting cold, thinking about his mother, who had also been fond of the cold and loathed the summer. And he asked himself what his good friend Uri Gefen was doing at this moment in Rome. He was probably sitting in a crowded café in some piazza surrounded by witty men and pretty, provocative women, roaring in his peasant voice and fascinating his audience with stories of air battles in which he had taken part, or amorous adventures in the Far East, letting fall as usual some wry generalisations about the capriciousness of desire, describing in well-chosen words the inevitable shadow of ridicule that accompanies every action and inevitably conceals one's true motives, and concluding with some indulgent commonplace that would finally spread a sort of veil of conciliatory irony over his whole story, over loves and lies as such and over the generalisation he himself had enunciated only a moment earlier.

Fima ached to feel the touch of Uri's broad, gnarled hand on the back of his neck. He longed for his parodies, his smell, his thick breath, and his warm laughter. At the same time and without any contradiction, he was a little sorry that his friend was returning from abroad in a couple of days' time. He was ashamed of his affair with Nina, even though he suspected that Uri had known for a long time about this sexual welfare work and might even have initiated it himself, out of benevolence and affection for the two of them, Fima and Nina, and perhaps also with a sense of detached amusement or regal irony. Was it possible that he asked for and received from Nina a detailed report after each session? Did they sit and rerun the film in slow motion, chuckling together indulgently? A couple of nights ago he had let Nina down, on the rug at her home, and this morning, thanks to Annette, he had let her down again in his own bed. His heart shrank as he remembered how she had stroked his forehead with her wonderfully shaped fingers and whispered to him that like this, with his limp cock, he was penetrating her more deeply than during intercourse. How rare, almost mystical, those words seemed now; they seemed to glow with a precious radiance as he recalled them, and he craved to mend what he had spoiled, to give her and Annette and also Tamar and Yael and every woman in the world, including the plain and unwanted ones, a proper carnal love, and a fatherly and brotherly love, and a spiritual love too.

From a dark garden an unseen dog barked furiously. Fima, startled, replied:

'What's wrong? What have I done?'

And then he added indignantly:

'I'm sorry: I don't believe we've met.'

He imagined the domestic winter life behind these façades, behind shutters, windows, and curtains. A man is sitting cosily in his armchair, in his slippers, reading a book about the history of dams. There is a small glass of brandy on the arm of his chair. His wife comes out of the shower with wet hair, pink and fragrant, wrapped in a blue flannel dressing gown. On the rug a small child is silently playing dominoes. A delicate flower of flame blossoms in the grate. Soon they will have their supper in front of the television, watching a family comedy. After that they will put the child to bed with a story and a good-night kiss, then sit side by side on the living-room sofa, with their stockinged feet propped up on the coffee table, whispering to each other and gradually settling into silence, perhaps holding hands. The moan of an ambulance will sound outside, then only thunder and wind. The man will get up to make sure the kitchen window is fastened properly. He will return carrying a tray with two glasses of lemon tea and a plate of peeled oranges. A small wall light will cast a reddish-brown domestic glow on the two of them.

In the dark Fima felt a pang. These images not only aroused

nostalgia for Yael, but also gave him a strange feeling of longing for himself. As though one of these lighted windows concealed another Fima, the real Fima, not overweight, not a nuisance, not losing his hair, not in yellowing long underwear, but a hard-working, straightforward Fima, living his life in a rational way without shame or falsehood. A calm, punctilious Fima. Even though he had understood for a long time that the truth was not within his reach, he still felt a longing, deep inside, to get away from the falsehood that seeped through like fine dust into every corner of his life, even the most intimate parts.

The other, the real Fima was sitting at this moment in a cosy study, surrounded by bookcases punctuated by prints of Jerusalem as seen by travellers and pilgrims of earlier centuries. His head floated in a pool of light from a desk lamp. His left hand rested on the knee of his wife, who sat close to him on the edge of his desk, her legs dangling, as they exchanged ideas on some new theory about the immune system or quantum physics. Not that Fima had the slightest understanding of the immune system or quantum physics, but he imagined to himself that the real Fima and his wife, there in the warm, cosy study, were both experts in one or other of these subjects, working together on developing some new idea that would reduce the amount of suffering in the world. Was this study what Chili, or his mother, meant in the dream when she called him to come over to the Aryan side?

On the corner of Smolenskin Street near Prime Minister Shamir's official residence, Fima noticed a little girl on top of a bundle of blankets by the dustbins. Was she on a hunger strike? Had she fainted? Had she been killed? Had some grieving mother from Bethlehem deposited here the corpse of her daughter, killed by us? Alarmed, he bent over the tot, but it turned out to be nothing more than a damp heap of garden clippings wrapped in a sack. Fima lingered beside it. The idea of lying down here and mounting his own hunger strike suddenly appealed to him: it seemed both attractive and relevant. Looking up, he saw a single yellow light behind a drawn curtain in the last room on the upper floor. He imagined Yitzhak Shamir pacing up and down between the window and the door, with his hands behind his back, worrying over a telegram that lay before him on the windowsill, not knowing what to reply, perhaps feeling the winter pains of old age in his shoulders and back. After all, he was not a young man. He too had had his revolutionary years in the underground. It might be a good thing to set aside animosity for a while, go in there and cheer him up, ease his loneliness, talk to him all night, man to man, not with petty contentiousness or sermonising or accusations, but as one good friend to another gently trying to open the eyes of one who has been involved by bad people in a rotten business from which apparently there is no way out, but which actually has a rational and indeed straightforward and affordable solution that can be driven home even to the most stubborn mind with a few hours of talking, of calm, soothing conversation. Provided the friend who is in trouble does not shut himself up and take refuge behind a barricade of lies and rhetoric, but opens his mind, listens to you with humility, and contemplates a range of possibilities that he has so far ruled out, not from arrogance but because of prejudices, ossified habits of thought, and deeply rooted fears. And what is so wrong with compromise, Mr Shamir? Each side receives only a part of what it believes it deserves, but the nightmare is ended. The wounds begin to heal. And didn't you yourself achieve your present position as a sort of compromise candidate? Surely you must have compromised now and again with your colleagues? Or with your wife? Haven't you?

And, indeed, why not knock on the door? He would be received with a glass of hot tea; he would take off his coat and explain once and for all what reason dictates and which way history is pointing. Or, on the contrary, he would persuade the prime minister to put his own coat on and join him in a night stroll and a prolonged heart-to-heart discussion in the empty rain-swept streets lit here and there by a wet streetlight wrapped in mist and gloom. A stern, ascetic city, Jerusalem, on a winter's night. But nothing is lost yet, sir. There is still hope of opening a new chapter. The bloodstained introduction has occupied a hundred years here, and now let's make a compromise and move on to the main story. Let the Jewish people start living as a nation that has found rest in its own land and reveals at long last the innate powers of creativity and renewal that have been buried under murky layers of fear and resentment, pogroms, persecutions, annihilation. Shall we give it a try, sir? Cautiously? By small, well-thought-out steps?

The policeman sitting in the sentry box in front of the residence poked his head out and asked:

'Hey, you: are you looking for something?'

Fima replied:

'Yes. I'm looking for tomorrow.'

The policeman politely suggested:

'Well, go and look for it somewhere else, sir. Move along please. You can't wait here.'

Fima decided to take this advice. To move along. Keep going. Not give up. Go on struggling as long as he had the strength to fit one word to another and to discriminate between ideas. The question was, where could he move along to? What should he be doing? Wasn't the truth that he hadn't even begun? But begun what? And where? And how? At that moment he heard a calm, reasonable, prosaic voice somewhere nearby calling his name: 'Fima, where are you?'

He stopped and replied at once, with devotion:

'Yes. Here I am. I'm listening.'

But the only sound was of cats on heat behind the damp stone walls. Followed, like a sponge that wipes everything clean, by the soughing of the wind in the pines in the dark deserted gardens.

Sitra de-itkasia: the concealed side.

He continued walking slowly. The Terra Sancta Building stood in total darkness. In Paris Square he stood for a few minutes waiting for the traffic lights to change, then shuffled down King George Street towards the centre of town. He paid no attention to the cold that pierced him through his overcoat, nor to the waterlogged old cap on his head, nor to the few passersby, all walking fast, some perhaps eyeing askance this strange, muffled figure plodding wearily and apparently absorbed in a violent argument with himself, accompanied by gesticulations and mouthings. It was very bad that he had forgotten to take precautions that morning. What if he got Annette Tadmor pregnant? He'd have to jump aboard a tramp steamer again and run away. To Greece. To Nineveh. To Alaska. Or the Galapagos Islands. In the dimness of Annette's womb, in a dark labyrinth of moist tunnels, his blind seed was now forcing its way with ridiculous tail-movements, jerking hither and thither in the warm liquid, a sort of round, bald Fima-head, possibly wearing a microscopic wet cloth cap, ageless, brainless, sightless, and yearning out of the depths for the hidden source of warmth, nothing but a head and a tail and the urge to thrust and nestle, to ram the crust of the ovum, in every respect resembling its father, who longed only to cocoon himself once and for all deep in the feminine slime and there snuggle up cosily and fall asleep. Fima was filled with worry but also a strange jealousy of his own seed. Under a yellow streetlight in front of the Yeshurun Synagogue he stopped and peered at his watch. He could still catch the second showing at the Orion. Jean Gabin certainly wouldn't let him down. But where exactly was he supposed to pick Annette up? Or was it Nina? Or where were they supposed to pick him up? It looked as if this evening he was doomed to let Jean Gabin down. A boy and girl, young and noisy, passed him as he shuffled slowly past Beit Hama'alot, near the old parliament building. The boy said:

'All right, so let's both give in.'

And the girl:

'It's too late now. It won't make any difference.'

Fima quickened his pace, hoping to steal some more snatches of their conversation. For some reason he felt a compulsion to know what sort of concessions they were talking about and what it was that would make no difference now. Had they also forgotten to take precautions this evening? But suddenly the boy wheeled round furiously, leaped to the kerb, and waved his arm. At once a taxi stopped, and the boy bent over and started to get in without so much as a glance at his partner. Fima realised immediately that in another moment or two this girl would be left abandoned in the middle of the wet street, and he already had some opening words ready on the tip of his tongue, cautiously encouraging words that would not alarm her, a sad, wise sentence that would make her smile through her tears. But he did not get the chance.

The girl called out:

'Come back, Yoav. I give in.'

And the boy, not even troubling to close the door of the taxi behind him, rushed back and threw his arms around her waist, whispering something that made them both laugh. The driver hurled an oath after him, and Fima, without asking himself why, decided on the spot that his duty was to set matters to rights for the driver. So he got into the taxi, closed the door, and said:

'Sorry about the mix-up. Kiryat Yovel, please.'

The driver, a thickset man with greasy silver hair, small eyes, and a trim Latin moustache, grumbled irritably:

'What's going on here? First you hail a cab, then you remember to have a think about where you're going. Don't you people know what you want?'

Fima realised that the driver took him to be with the couple. He muttered apologetically:

'What's the problem. It took us half a minute to decide. We had a difference of opinion. There's nothing for you to get excited about.'

He resolved to initiate another political discussion, only this time he would not put up in silence with bloodthirsty savagery, but employ clear, straightforward arguments and irresistible logic. He was all ready to resume the sermon he had begun to deliver earlier to the prime minister, at the point where he had stopped in his thoughts. But when he began to feel his way cautiously, like a dentist probing to find the source of a pain, to find out what the driver felt about the question of the Territories and peace, the man interrupted amicably:

'Just drop it, will you, sir? Me, my views just get people worked up. They start listening to me and they head straight for a breakdown. That's the reason why I stopped having discussions long ago. So hang onto your temper. If I was in charge of this country, I'd have it back on its feet in three months. But Israeli people have given up thinking with their brains. They only think with their bellies. And their balls. So why should I waste my health for nothing? Every time I get in a discussion, it just burns up the nerves. It's hopeless. It's mob rule here. Worse than the Arabs.'

Fima said:

'What if I promise not to get worked up, and not to get you worked up? We can always agree to differ.'

'OK then,' said the driver, 'only just remember you asked for it. Well, for me it's like this: For a real peace, so called, with assurances and guarantees and comprehensive safeguards, for a peace like that I'd personally give them all the Territories except the Western Wall, and I'd even say thank you to them for taking Ramallah and Gaza off my arse. Ever since that shit landed on us in '67, the state's been going to the dogs. They've made a right mess of us. Well, how about it? Am I getting on your nerves? Are you going to start farting the Bible at me?'

Fima had difficulty containing his feelings:

'And how, may I ask, did you arrive at this conclusion?'

'In the end,' said the driver wearily, 'everybody will. Maybe only after we lose another few thousand dead. There's no other way, sir. The Arab is not going to evaporate, and neither are we, and we're about as capable of living together as a cat and a mouse. That's real life, and it's also just. It's written in the Torah: if two customers are holding onto a *tallit* and they're both shouting that it's theirs, then you take a pair of scissors and you cut it in half. That's what Moses himself decided, and you can take it from me he was no idiot. Better to cut the *tallit* than to keep cutting babies. Which street did you say?'

Fima said:

'Well done!'

And the driver:

'What do you mean, well done? What do you mean by that? What do you take me for, a cat that's learned to fly? If you happened to be of the same opinion, I wouldn't say well done to you just for that. What I will say to you, and listen hard, is there's only one man in this country who's strong enough to cut the *tallit* in half without getting cut in half himself, and that's Arik Sharon. Nobody else can do it. They'll take it from him.'

'Despite the fact that he's got blood on his hands?'

'Not despite: because. First of all, he's not the one with the bloody hands; it's the whole state. You and me too. Don't go

pinning it all on him. Besides which, I don't have a weeping conscience over the bloodshed. Sorrow, yes, but not shame. That's
for the Arabs, not us. It's not as if we wanted to shed blood. The
Arabs forced us to. Right from the word go. On our side we never
wanted to start the violence. Even Menahem Begin, a proud pat-
riot if ever there was one, the moment Sadat came along to the
Knesset to say sorry, he gave him what he wanted, just so long as
the bloodshed stopped. If Arafat came along to the Knesset to say
sorry, he'd get something too. So? Let Arik go and strike a deal,
gangster to gangster. What do you think, that some bleeding
heart Yossi Sarid or other is going to do business with that scum
Arafat? Yossi Sarid, the Arabs would make mincemeat out of
him, and then someone from our side would give him a bellyful of
lead, and that would be the end of that. Best let Arik do the cutting. Any time you've got to do business with a ravishing beast,
hire a hunter to do the job, not a belly dancer. Is this your block?'

When Fima realised that he didn't have enough money on him
to pay the fare, he offered to hand over his identity card or to
borrow a few shekels from a neighbour, if the driver didn't mind
waiting a few minutes. But the other said:

'Forget it. It's not the end of the world. Tomorrow or the day
after come and leave eight shekels at Eliyahu Taxis. Just say it's
for Tsiyon. You're not from the Bible League, by any chance, are
you? Or something like that?'

'No,' said Fima. 'Why?'

'I had a feeling I've seen you on TV. Must be someone who
looks like you. Spoke nice, too. Just a minute, mate: you've left
your hat behind. Where did you win that thing? What is it, a
leftover from the holocaust?'

Fima walked past his letter box without stopping, even though
he could see there was something in it. He made a detour around
the rolled-up mattress. When he reached the light of the staircase
and pulled out his key, a ten-shekel note folded into a small
square fell out too. He lumbered back hurriedly, hoping to catch
the taxi driver before he finished turning round at the bottom of
the road. The driver grinned in the dark.

'So what's the hurry? Afraid I'm leaving the country? That I'll be gone tomorrow morning? Let the scum leave; I'm staying to the end of the show. I want to see how it finishes. Good night, sir. Don't eat your heart out.'

Fima decided to have the man in his cabinet. He would relieve Tsvi of the Information portfolio and give it to the driver. And because the driver had talked about 'the end of the show', he suddenly remembered that Annette was probably waiting for him to ring her at home. Unless she was waiting outside the cinema. Unless it was actually Nina. Hadn't he promised Nina he'd pick her up at the office? Was it possible he'd inadvertently made a date with both of them? Or was it with Tamar? Fima was disgusted at the thought that he was going to have to get bogged down in lies and excuses yet again. He ought to ring and explain. Tactfully untie the knot. Apologise to Nina and hurry out to meet Annette. Or vice versa.

But what if it turned out he had only made a date with one of them after all, and when he started to lie his way out of it on the phone, he got deeper and deeper in the mud, and only succeeded in making a fool of himself? And what if at this very moment they were both standing in the foyer of the cinema waiting for him, not recognising each other, never imagining for a moment that it was the same idiot who had let them both down?

To hell with lies. From now on he would start a new chapter. From now on he would live his life in the open, rationally and honestly. How had the taxi driver put it: no 'weeping conscience'. There was no reason whatever to hide his lovers from one another. If they're both fond of me, why shouldn't they be fond of each other? They'll almost certainly make friends at once, they can cheer each other up. They have so many things in common, after all. They are both compassionate, good-hearted, generous human beings. They both seem to relish my helplessness. By coincidence, if it really is a coincidence, both their husbands are living it up in Italy at this moment. Who knows? Perhaps the husbands have met. Perhaps at this very minute Yeri Tadmor and Uri Gefen are sitting in a lively group of Israelis and foreigners in that café in Rome, swapping juicy stories about love and despair. Or discussing the future of the Middle East, with

Uri using arguments he's borrowed from me. Whereas my role in this situational farce that comes straight out of Stefan Zweig or Somerset Maugham is to bring together the two abandoned wives, who are about to come together this evening in friendship, solidarity, even a measure of intimacy, because they both wish me well.

In his mind's eye he saw himself sitting in the darkness of the cinema, with Jean Gabin becoming embroiled with a gang of ruthless killers while he himself had his left arm around Annette and slid the fingers of his right hand down over Nina's breasts. Giving a plausible imitation of a downmarket Uri Gefen. After the film he would invite them both to the little restaurant behind Zion Square. Sparkling and relaxed, he would regale them with spicy anecdotes and intellectual fireworks, shedding dazzling new light on old questions. When he excused himself for a moment to go to the lavatory, the two women would converse together in animated whispers. Comparing notes about his condition. Dividing up the tasks, establishing a kind of work rota for the Fimacare service.

These fantasies caressed him deliciously. Ever since his childhood he had loved to feel that there were grown-ups, responsible people, who discussed in his absence how to do the best for him, waiting till he was asleep before talking about the arrangements for his birthday, switching to Russian to discuss what present to surprise him with. If he summoned up the courage at the end of the evening at the restaurant to suggest to Annette and Nina that they come round to his place and spend the night together, there might be some momentary embarrassment but in the end he would not be refused. He had learned from Uri that such combinations hypnotised the female imagination too. And so at last he could look forward to an exciting Greek night. He would be rejuvenated. A new billy-goat year would begin.

For a few moments he mulled over the details in his mind, casting the characters and directing the scenes. Then he grabbed the receiver and dialled Nina's office. When the telephone made no sound, he tried Annette. Once again the response was total silence. He called both numbers alternatively five or six times, to no avail. All the systems in this country are breaking down. The lines of communication are congested, the hospitals are paralysed, the electricity supply is unreliable, the universities are going bankrupt, factories are closing down one after another, education and research are sinking to the level of India's, public services are collapsing, and all because of this obsession with the Territories, which is gradually ruining us. How did the taxi driver put it: 'Ever since that shit landed on us in '67, the state's been going to the dogs.' Fima waved the telephone in the air, banged it on the table, shook it, rattled it, pleaded with it, swore at it, bashed it, and thumped it, but nothing helped. Then it occurred to him that he had only himself to blame. How many times had he ignored the printed notices he had found in his letter box about the nonpayment of his bill. Now they had got their own back. They had cut him off from the world. Like a cantor on a desert island.

Cunningly he tried to dial again, very slowly and gently, like a burglar, like a lover. He could not remember if the emergency number for such eventualities was one four, one eight, or simply one hundred. He was ready and willing to settle his debt this very minute, to apologise in person or in writing, to give a lecture to the telephone workers on Christian mysticism, to pay a fine or a bribe, anything so long as they came round at once to bring his telephone back to life. First thing in the morning he would go straight to the bank. Or was it the post office? He would pay his bill and be rescued from the desert island. But tomorrow, Fima remembered, was Friday, and all public offices were closed. Perhaps he should ring his father and ask him to use his connections. Next week his father was turning his painters and plasterers loose on him. Maybe he should run away to Cyprus? Or the Galapagos Islands? Or at least to that guest house in Magdiel?

Suddenly he changed his mind. He saw the situation in a fresh light. Immediately he felt better. Fate must have intervened to save him from Jean Gabin and the orgy. The words 'desert island' filled him with joy. It would be wonderful to spend a quiet evening at home. Outside, the storm could rattle the windows to its heart's content: he would light the paraffin heater, sit down in the armchair, and try to get a little closer to the other Fima, the real one, instead of wearing himself out with diplomatic efforts to mollify two offended women and then exhausting himself all night to satisfy their appetites. He was particularly delighted that he was relieved, as though by the wave of a magic wand, of the obligation to put his coat and cap on again and go out into the empty, freezing, rain-lashed city. Had he really decided to act like Uri Gefen? To step into his father's shoes? To start leaping around like a billy-goat again, a shabby, mangy old bear like him? First let's see you piss once without stuttering.

Instead of playing the fool, better to sit down now at the desk, switch on the lamp, and compose a devastating reply to Günter Grass's speech. Or a letter to Yitzhak Rabin. Or write that article on the heart of Christendom. And for once he'd be able to watch the nine o'clock news without interruptions. Or fall asleep in front of the television in the middle of a brainless melodrama. Or, better still, curl up in bed with the book he had borrowed from Ted's, study the life of the whalers in Alaska, imagine the simplicity of primitive nomads, enjoy the strange sexual habits of the Eskimos. The custom of handing over a ripe widow to the adolescent boys as part of their initiation rites suddenly caused a delicious pulsing in his loins. And tomorrow morning he would explain everything to his lovers, who would surely forgive him: after all, it was more or less a case of force majeure. Besides the sense of relief and the message in his loins, he also felt hungry. He had eaten nothing all evening. So he went to the kitchen, and without even sitting gulped down five thick slices of bread and jam, devoured two tomatoes whole without bothering to slice them, ate a pot of yogurt, swallowed two glasses of tea with honey, and rounded the whole off with a heartburn tablet. To encourage his hesitant bladder he flushed the lavatory in the middle, lost the race, and had to wait for the cistern to refill. But he got bored waiting, and went around the flat turning the lights off, then stood at the window to examine what was new in the empty fields stretching away to Bethlehem: perhaps there was already some sign of a distant radiance. He took pleasure in the rattling of the windowpanes under the onslaught of the sharp black wind.

Here and there on the dark slopes a pale gleam shimmered: Arab stone cottages scattered among orchards and boulders. The shadows of the hills deluded him, as though they were exchanging elusive caresses that were not of this world. Once upon a time kings and prophets, saviours, world reformers, madmen who heard voices, zealots, ascetics, and dreamers walked around Jerusalem. And one day in the future, in a hundred years or more, new men, totally different from us, would be living here. Earnest, self-contained people. No doubt they would find all our troubles weird, unintelligible, perplexing. Meanwhile, and for the time being, between the past and the future, we have been sent to inhabit Jerusalem. The city has been entrusted to our stewardship. And we fill it with oppression, foolishness, and injustice. We inflict humiliation, frustration, torture on each other, not out of arrogance but merely from laziness and fear. We pursue good and cause evil. We seek to comfort and instead we wound. We aim to increase knowledge, and instead we increase pain.

'Don't you judge me,' Fima grumbled aloud to Yoezer. 'Just be quiet. Anyway, what can a wishy-washy individual like you understand? Who's talking to you anyway?'

Large sharp stars glowed before his tired eyes. Fima did not know their names, and he did not care which was Mars or Jupiter or Saturn. But he longed to understand where the vague feeling came from, that this was not the first time. That he had been here before, in days of yore. That he had already seen these glimmering stars on a cold deserted winter's night. Not from the window of this flat, but maybe from the doorway of one of the low stone cottages among the dark boulders opposite. And he had asked himself then what the stars in the sky wanted from us and what the shadow of the hills in the darkness was saying. Only then there was a simple answer. Which had been forgotten. Wiped away. Although for a moment he had the feeling that that answer was struggling on the threshold of his memory, so close he could reach out and touch it. He hit his forehead against the glass, and shivered with cold. Bialik, for one, claims that the stars have cheated him. They have not kept their promise. They have not kept their appointment, as it were. But surely it is really the other way round: they have not cheated us, we have cheated them. We are the ones who have not kept our promises. They called us, and we forgot to go. They spoke, and we refused to hear. Cranes wheeled – and were gone.

Say a word. Give me just a little pointer, a hint, a clue, a wink, and I'll get up and go at once. I won't even stop to change my shirt. Get up and go. Or prostrate myself at your feet. Falling in a trance with wide-open eyes.

Outside, the wind blew stronger. Sheets of water broke against his forehead through the windowpane. The hole in the clouds over the Bethlehem hills, through which the stars had been glimmering, was also dark now. He suddenly fancied he heard a shrill crying far away, as though a baby had been abandoned in a wet blanket on the slope of the wadi. As though he must run immediately and help his mother to find her lost child. But he said to himself that it was probably nothing but a creaking shutter. Or one of the neighbours' children. Or a cat freezing in the yard. However hard he stared, all he could see was darkness. No sign appeared, either in the hills or in the faint gleams of light in the cottages scattered on the slope, or in the dark sky. Isn't it unjust, wicked, to call me to go without giving me so much as a tiny clue where? Where the meeting place is. Whether there is or isn't to be a meeting. Whether I am the one who is being called or if it is actually one of my neighbours. Whether there is or isn't something inside this darkness.

And indeed, at that moment Fima sensed the full weight of the darkness lying over Jerusalem. Darkness on steeples and domes, darkness on walls and towers, darkness on stone-walled yards and on the groves of ancient pines, on convents and olive trees, on mosques and caves and sepulchres, on tombs of kings and of true and false prophets, darkness on winding alleys, darkness on government buildings and on ruins and gates and on stony fields and thistle-strewn waste plots, darkness on schemes and desires and lunatic visions, darkness on the hills and on the desert.

To the south-west, above the heights surrounding the village of Ein Karem, clouds began to move, as though an unseen hand were drawing a curtain. Just as his mother used to go around the flat drawing all the curtains on winter evenings. One night, when he was three or four, she forgot to draw the curtains in his bedroom. He woke and saw a dim shape outside staring motionlessly at him. A long, thin shape surrounded by a circle of pale light. Then it went out. It materialised again, like moon-touched mist, at the other window. Then it went out again. He remembered how he woke in a panic and sat up in bed crying. His mother came in and leaned over him in a nightdress that had an exquisite scent. She looked long and white and moon-touched too. She held him in her arms and promised him that there was nothing there, that the shape was just a dream. Then she drew both the curtains carefully, rearranged his bedclothes, and kissed him on the forehead. Even though he eventually stopped crying and burrowed under his blanket, even though she stayed on his bed until he fell asleep again, Fima knew, even now, with utter and absolute certainty, that it was not a dream, and that his mother knew it too and had lied to him. Even now, half a century later, he was still convinced that there really had been a stranger out there. Not in a dream but outside, on the other side of the windowpanes. And that his mother had seen him too. And he knew that that lie was the worst lie he had ever been told. It was that lie that snatched away his infant brother and doomed his mother to disappear in her prime, and himself to be here and yet not here all these years, seeking in vain for something he had not really lost, without the faintest idea what it was or what it looked like, or where to look or how.

Even if someday he found it, how would he know?

Maybe he had found it already, and dropped it and moved on, still searching like a blind man?

Cranes wheel and whirl and are gone.

The wind subsided in the panes. A frozen quiet reigned. At a quarter to eleven Fima changed his mind, put his cap and coat on, went into the empty street, where the cold was sharp and biting. He went to the public call box in the shopping centre at the other end of the housing estate. But when he lifted the receiver, the public telephone too gave only a deathly silence.

Maybe there was a problem in the whole district. Had the public telephone been vandalised? Or was the whole of Jerusalem cut off from itself and from the outside world again? He gave up and gently replaced the receiver. Shrugging his shoulders he said, 'Well done, pal,' as he remembered that in any case he did not have a token.

Tomorrow he would get up early and explain everything to his two lovers.

Or he would get out of here and go away.

The whispering of the soggy pines, the biting cold, the emptiness of the streets, all of these suited Fima well. And he carried on wandering towards the slope and the fields. His mother had a strange habit of blowing on her food, even if it had already cooled off, or if it was cold food, such as a salad or fruit compote. When she blew, her lips pursed into a kiss. His heart ached because at that moment, forty-four years after her death, he wanted to kiss her back. He wanted to turn the world upside down to find the blue baby bonnet with the loose pompom and give it back to her.

When he reached the end of the street, which was also the end of the housing development and the end of the city, Fima became aware of something transparent filling the world. As if thousands of soft silken footsteps were whispering on every side. As if his face were being touched by fingers that were no fingers. When his wonderment passed, he identified tiny snowflakes. Very fine snow was beginning to fall on Jerusalem. Though it melted as soon as it touched anything. It did not have the power to whiten the grey city.

Fima returned home and began searching in the wastepaper basket under his desk for the telephone bill he had screwed up and thrown away yesterday or the day before. He did not find the bill, but he did pick out a crumpled page of *Ha'arets*. He smoothed it out and took it to bed with him, and read about present-day false messiahs until his eyes closed and he fell asleep with the newspaper over his face. At two o'clock the light snow stopped. Jerusalem stood frozen and empty in the dark, as though the catastrophe had happened and all the people had been exiled again.

26

Chili

I N his dream Gad Eitan arrived in a military jeep with a machine gun mounted on the bonnet to summon Fima to a meeting with the president. The president's office turned out to be in
a small basement synagogue at the edge of the Russian Com-
pound behind the main police station. A foppish British officer
sat behind the desk, with a leather belt aslant his black uniform.
He urged Fima to sign a voluntary confession to the murder of
the dog, who had been transformed in the dream to a woman
whose corpse was lying, wrapped in a sheet soiled with black
blood, at the foot of the Holy Ark. Fima requested permission to
see the dead woman's face. The interrogator replied with a smile,
What for? Isn't it a pity to wake her? It's Chili again; she risked
her life for you, she brought you over to the Aryan side, she
saved your life repeatedly, and you betrayed her. When Fima
plucked up the courage to ask what punishment was in store for
him, the defence minister said, Look what a dummy you are. The
crime *is* the punishment.

27

Fima refuses to give in

A T half past six in the morning he woke with a start because
a heavy object fell in the flat above, followed by a woman
shouting, not for long or particularly loudly, but terribly, desperately, as though she had seen her own death. Fima leaped out of
bed and into his trousers, then hurried to the kitchen balcony to
hear better. No sound came from the upstairs flat. Only an invisible bird, which kept repeating three gentle syllables, as if it
had come to the conclusion that Fima was so slow on the uptake
that he would surely not understand. Shouldn't he go upstairs
quickly to find out what had happened? To offer help? Rescue?
To call the police or an ambulance? But he remembered that his
telephone had been cut off, so he was relieved of the obligation
to intervene. Besides which, it was possible that the crash and the
scream had happened in his sleep, and his inquiry would cause
nothing but embarrassment and derision.

Instead of going back to bed, he continued standing on the kitchen balcony in his long-sleeved vest, amid the vestiges of cages,
jars, and boxes where he and Dimi had once kept their can of
worms. Now these exuded the rank smell of decay, of wet saw-
dust mixed with blackened droppings and remains of rotting
food: carrots and cucumber peel and cabbage leaves and lettuce.
At the beginning of the winter Dimi had decided to free the tortoises, insects, and snails they had collected in the wadi.

And where was the snow of last night?

It was as if it had never been.

It had gone without trace.

Meanwhile the barren hills to the south of Jerusalem stood
purged, flooded in blue radiance, so that it was almost possible
to make out silvery flashes on the underside of the leaves of distant

olive trees along the ridge of Beit Jalla. It was a cold, sharp light, crystal clear, sent to us perhaps as an advance against the distant days when suffering would end, when Jerusalem would be freed from its torments, and the people who took our place would live their lives calmly, considerately, rationally, and with good taste: then the light of the sky would be like this forever.

It was bitterly cold, but Fima, in his yellowing winter vest, did not feel it. He stood leaning on the railing, filling his lungs with the winelike air, marvelling at the possibility of suffering in the midst of such beauty. A minor miracle occurred this morning below him in the back yard. An eccentric, impatient almond tree had decided suddenly to flower, as though it had got its dates wrong. It was covered with tiny glow-worms that had forgotten to switch themselves off at the arrival of dawn. Myriad raindrops sparkled on the pink blossoms. The glittering almond tree reminded Fima of a slim, pretty woman who has cried all night and not wiped away her tears. This image caused him childlike joy, and love, and a vague longing for Yael, for all women indiscriminately, with the bold resolve to open a new chapter in his life, starting this morning: to be from now on a rational, straightforward man, a good man, freed from falsehood and all pretence. So he put on a clean shirt and Yael's sweater. With a determination that surprised him he climbed the stairs and firmly pressed the upstairs neighbours' bell. After a few moments Mrs Pizanti opened the door in a dressing gown half unbuttoned over her nightdress. Her wide, childlike face struck Fima as distorted, or even somewhat battered. But perhaps that was more or less what anyone woken from sleep looked like. Behind her, in the pale neon light of the entrance hall, her husband's eyes were glittering. He was a hirsute, athletic-looking individual, much taller than his wife. She asked anxiously if something had happened. Fima said:

'On the contrary. Sorry. Nothing. I thought maybe something fell down in your flat? Or broke? I just thought, I imagined, I heard . . . something like that? I must have been mistaken. Perhaps it was just an explosion somewhere a long way away. Perhaps the Messianic Faithful have dynamited the Temple Mount and turned it into a Vale of Tears.'

'Sorry?' said Mrs Pizanti, staring at Fima with bewilderment and some apprehension.

Her husband, an x-ray technician, replied from behind her back in a tone that struck Fima as not entirely honest:

'Everything's a hundred per cent in here, Dr Nisan. When you ring the bell, I think maybe you got some kinda problem. No? You are shorta something? Outa coffee again? Blown a fuse? I come and change it for you?'

'Thank you,' Fima said, 'that's very kind of you. I've got plenty of coffee and the electricity is working fine. It so happens my telephone is out of order, but I'm quite pleased, actually; it means I can have some peace and quiet at last. Sorry to bother you so early in the morning. I just thought . . . Never mind. Sorry. Thank you.'

'No problem,' said Pizanti expansively. 'We always get up at six-fifteen anyway. If you need to make some phone call, just feel free. On the house. If you like, I come down and check your contacts. Maybe something come loose.'

'I was thinking,' Fima said, appalled at the words he heard coming out of his own mouth, 'of calling a lady friend of mine who may have been waiting for me since last night. Two lady friends, actually. But right now I think it wouldn't be such a bad thing to let them wait. It's not urgent. I'm sorry I disturbed you.'

As he was on the point of leaving, Mrs Pizanti said hesitantly:

'Could be maybe something fell down outside from the wind. Some washtub or something. But with us everything is fine.'

These words convinced Fima that once again he was being lied to. But he forgave the neighbours, because in fact he had no reason to expect them to tell him about the row they must have been having, and also because he himself had not told the truth about ringing his girlfriends. When he was back in his flat he said:

'What a fool you are.'

But he forgave himself too, because he had meant well.

He did his exercises in front of the mirror for ten minutes or so, shaved, dressed, combed his hair vaguely, boiled some water in the new electric kettle, made his bed, and for once managed all these activities without mishap. He hit her, he thought, he may

223

even have banged her head against the wall; he might have killed her; who knows, he might well do it one of these days, perhaps this very morning. What Hitler did to us didn't finish in 1945; it still goes on, it seems it always will. Murky things go on behind every door. Acts of cruelty and desperation. Underneath this whole state, a hidden insanity is simmering. Three times a week our long arm catches the murderers in their dens. We can't get to sleep before we have inflicted a little pogrom on the Cossacks. Every morning we kidnap Eichmann and every evening we nip Hitler in the bud. In the basketball we defeat Chmielnicki and in the Eurovision we avenge Kishinev. But what right do I have to interfere? I'd be happy to gallop up on a white charger and rescue that Pizanti woman, or the pair of them, or the whole state, if only I knew how. If only I had some idea where to start. There's Baruch with his Trotsky goatee and his carved walking stick; he does his bit to put the world straight by handing out donations and grants, whereas all I ever do is sign petitions. Maybe after all I should have persuaded that policeman last night to let me in to see Shamir? For a heart-to-heart chat. Or introduced Shamir to my taxi driver?

It occurred to him that he ought to sit down and compose a short but heartfelt appeal to the hawkish right. To suggest to them, in *Ha'arets*, the broad outline of a partial national consensus. A sort of new deal between the moderates and the non-messianic hawkish element, which might still be willing to swallow a return of some territories were it not for what it sees as the left's tendency to uncontrolled appeasement. The taxi driver was right: Our worst mistake over the past twenty years has been not to take seriously the sensibilities of Pizanti and his wife and hundreds of thousands of other Israelis like them, in whom the Arabs stir genuine feelings of anger, fear, and suspicion. Such feelings surely deserve not contempt but a gradual, rational effort to allay them by means of intelligent argument. Instead of reasoning with them, we emptied a chamberpot full of patronising ridicule on them. It would make sense therefore to try to draw up an agreement that would define the precise limits of our, the moderates', willingness to make concessions to the

Arabs. So that they don't imagine, like Baruch, that we are, so to speak, advertising a closing-down sale. So that they know what we, the left, are even prepared to go to war for again, if it turns out that the Arab side is reneging or taking us for a ride. In that way, we may be able to mollify some of the hawks and bring about a thaw.

The word 'thaw' reminded him that he had forgotten to light the heater. Bending down, he was relieved to discover that there was enough paraffin left. After lighting the heater, he felt the need to consult Tsvi Kropotkin before he sat down to compose his appeal. In his enthusiasm he did not care if he disturbed Tsvi in the middle of shaving again, because he felt his new idea was potentially fruitful and beneficial and indeed very urgent. But once again the telephone was silent. Fima thought the silence was, if anything, less deep than last night. A sort of intermittent rumbling sound, like the grinding of teeth, was almost audible. A groaning from the depths. Fima diagnosed faint signs of life, a first indication of recovery. He felt sure the instrument was not dead but merely in a very deep coma, and that now, even if it had not recovered consciousness, it was beginning to make a feeble response, a faint groan of pain, a slight pulse giving grounds for some hope. Even taking account of the fact that the fridge had just started rumbling in the kitchen. It was therefore possible that the hope was premature.

Even the expression 'hawkish element' suddenly struck him as repugnant: it was wrong to characterise human beings as 'elements'. Besides which, he thought it was ridiculous to put the right-wing thinkers on the psychiatrist's couch: it was not as if our camp was the embodiment of sanity. We too are troubled by despair, frustration, and rage. We too are caught in an emotional tangle, no less than our opponents. No less than the Arabs. But the expression 'our camp' is utterly ridiculous. What does 'our camp' mean? The whole country is a front line, the whole nation an army. Everything is divided into camps. The forces of peace. The battalion of moderation. The strike force of coexistence. The lookouts of disarmament. The commando of the brotherhood of nations. The spearhead of reconciliation.

Instead of writing the appeal Fima went and stood at the window to set his ideas in order. Meanwhile he watched the winter light spreading like a noble material over the hilltops and slopes. Fima knew and loved the idea of 'noble metals', although he had no idea which they were. Once, in his father's flat in Rehavia, Baruch and Dimi tried to pin him down and inflict an elementary chemistry lesson on him. Fima, like a stubborn child, defended himself with wisecracks and wordplay until Dimi said, 'Forget it, Granpa; it's not for him.' And the two of them embarked without him for the realms of acid and alkali which Fima loathed on account of his heartburn.

The light kissed the ridges, overflowed into the valleys, awakening in each tree and rock its dormant radiant quality that had been buried all these days under layers of grey, inanimate routine. As if here in Jerusalem thousands of years ago the earth lost its power to renew itself from within. As if only the gracious touch of this enchanted light could restore to things, however briefly, the primordiality that had been eclipsed of the days of yore. Will Your Worship condescend to favour me with a slight nod of the head if I go down on my knees and offer my humble prayers of gratitude? Is there something that Your Worship wishes me to do? Is Your Worship interested in us at all? Why did you put us here? Why did you choose us? Why did you choose Jerusalem? Is Your Worship still listening? Is Your Worship smiling?

The ancient Aramaic phrases, such as 'days of yore', 'not of this world', 'the concealed side', filled Fima with a sense of mystery and awe. For a moment he asked himself if it was not possible after all that the light and the mud, the glow-worms in the almond tree and the radiant sky, the arid land extending eastwards from here to Mesopotamia and southwards to Bab el-Mandeb at the tip of the Arabian Peninsula, and indeed his shabby flat and his ageing body and even his broken telephone, were all nothing but different expressions of the same being, condemned to be dissolved into countless flawed, perishable embodiments, even though in itself it is whole and eternal and one. Only on a winter morning like this, under the nuptial veil of limpid light, which is perhaps what is meant by the ancient Aramaic phrase 'supernal radiance', does the earth along with your watching eyes recover the thrill of that primordial touch. And everything returns to its state of original innocence. As on the day of its creation. For an instant the constant murky cloak of dreariness and lying is removed.

And so Fima's thoughts arrived at the hackneyed concept of 'the heavenly Jerusalem', to which he gave his private interpretation, valid solely for what he felt at that particular moment. He mused that there were times when sleeping seemed less tainted with falsehood than waking, and times when it was the other way round, and that ultimate wakefulness becomes the most longed-for ideal. He now reached the thought that it might be a matter of three states, not two: sleeping, waking, and this light that had been flooding him both from without and within ever since the start of this morning. For want of a fitting name he described this light to himself as the Third State. And he felt that it was not only a matter of the pure light on the hills but of the light truly flowing out of the hills and out of himself too, and that it was in the commingling of these rays of light that the Third State came into being, equidistant from complete waking and deepest slumber, and yet distinct from both of them.

There is no more tragic loss, he thought, in the whole world than missing the Third State. It happens because of the news on the radio, because of business, because of hollow desires and the pursuit of vanities and trivia. All suffering, Fima said to himself, everything that is ridiculous or obscene, is purely the consequence of missing the Third State, or of that vague nagging feeling that reminds us from time to time that there is, outside and inside, almost within reach, something fundamental that you always seem on the way to yet you always lose your way. You are called, and you forget to go. You are spoken to, and you don't hear. A door is opened, and you leave too late because you choose to satisfy some craving or other. *The sea of silence casts up secrets*, but you were preoccupied with trivial arrangements. You preferred to try to make an impression on someone, who himself missed it because he wanted to make an impression on someone else, who also . . . and so on, and so forth. Unto dust. Again and again you rejected what exists in favour of what does not, never did, and cannot exist. Gad Eitan was right when he said mockingly that wastefulness runs riot here. His wife was right to get away while she could. The order of priorities, Fima said to himself sadly and half aloud, is all wrong. What a pity, for instance, that Tsvi Kropotkin, such a hard-working man, should have spent three years chasing after the details of the Catholic church's attitude to the voyages of Magellan and Columbus, like someone sorting out the buttons of clothes that have long since become rags. Or Uri Gefen, running from one affair to the next, wide awake but with his heart asleep.

With that, Fima decided to stop standing idly at the window and to start getting the place ready for the decorators, who were coming after the weekend. The pictures would have to come down off the walls. Also the map of Israel on which he had once pencilled reasonable compromise borders. All the furniture would have to be moved into the middle of the room and covered with plastic sheeting. The books would have to be put away. So would all the crockery and the pots and pans. Why not take advantage of the opportunity to get rid of the piles of old newspapers, magazines, pamphlets, and newsletters? The bookcases will have to be dismantled, and that means enlisting Uri's help. Is it tonight he's coming back? Or tomorrow? Or the day after? And then Nina can deliver her detailed report of how she tried not once but twice to give me my regular service and how she found the tap blocked. Perhaps Shula Kropotkin can be brought in as reinforcements to help with putting all the kitchen things away. Possibly Annette Tadmor would be glad to lend a hand. And the Pizantis also expressed a readiness to help, provided they don't murder each other first. And Teddy will willingly come round to take down the curtains and the wall lights. Maybe he'll bring Dimi with him. The old man was quite right: it's well over twenty years since this old den was last spruced up. The ceiling's filthy, it's all grubby from the paraffin heater. There are cobwebs in the corners. There's damp in the bathroom. The ceramic tiles are cracked. The plaster is peeling. There are patches of mildew. There's a mouldy, sweaty smell here the whole year round, an old bachelor's stench. It's not only the old can of worms on the balcony that smells bad. You've grown so used to it that you don't even care.

Surely habit is the root of all evil. It's precisely what Pascal was thinking of when he wrote about the death of the soul.

In a corner of his desk Fima found a green advertisement announcing huge discounts at the local supermarket. On a corner of this notice he scribbled the words:

Habit is the beginning of death. Habits are a fifth column.

And underneath:

Routine = lies.

Habituation – deterioration – dilapidation.

His intention was to remind himself to improve and develop these thoughts over the weekend. And since he had remembered that tomorrow was Saturday, he deduced that today was Friday, from which he inferred that he ought to do some shopping. But Friday was his free day, the clinic was closed, so why should he hurry? Why start pushing furniture around at seven in the morning? Best wait for the reinforcements to arrive. There was no urgency. Even though when he glanced at his watch, he discovered that it was not seven o'clock but twenty past eight. Time to have a word or two with Tsvika, who would have finished his shaving ritual by now.

Had there been any further improvement in the condition of the telephone? Fima tried again. He could almost hear a faint sound, but it had not yet rallied to the point of being a dialling tone. Despite which, he dialled Yael's number. And concluded that he ought to wait for the patient to make a full recovery, because his impatient attempts might delay the process. Or was Yael's phone also out of order? Was the whole city cut off? Could it be a strike? Sabotage? Sanctions? Had the exchange been blown up in the night? Had a right-wing terrorist group seized all the means of communication and the other centres of power? Had there been a Syrian missile attack? Unless Ted Tobias was leaning on the phone again and preventing Yael from picking it up. Fima felt disgusted, not with Ted but with his own word games. He screwed up the supermarket advertisement and threw it at the wastepaper basket. He missed, but could not be bothered to crawl under the desk to look for it. No point. The whole place was going to be turned upside down soon to prepare for the decorators.

He made himself another coffee, ate a few slices of black bread and jam to quell the hunger pangs, then took a couple of tablets to quell the pangs of heartburn. Then he went to have a piss. He felt furious with his body, always bothering him with its endless needs, and preventing him from carrying through a single thought or observation. He stood for a few moments without moving, his head to one side, his mouth half open, as though deep in thought, with his penis in his hand. Despite the pressure in his bladder he was unable to release a single drop. He resorted to his usual subterfuge, pulling the handle in the hope that the sound of rushing water would remind his sluggish organ of its duty. But it refused to be impressed by such an old, well-worn stratagem. It seemed to be saying: It's high time you thought up a new game for me. Grudgingly it released a brief, thin trickle, as a special favour. As soon as the cistern stopped, this pathetic trickle ceased too. His bladder remained urgently full. Fima shook the offending member gently, then more violently, but nothing happened. Finally he pulled the handle again, but the cistern had not had time to fill, and instead of a roaring cascade it gave a sort of hollow, contemptuous grunt, as though it was mocking Fima in his misfortune. As though it was showing solidarity with the telephone in its gesture of defiance.

Nevertheless he persisted. He did not retreat. He would wage a war of attrition against this recalcitrant organ. We'll see who cracks first. The limp, shellfish-like flesh between his fingers suddenly put him in mind of a lizard, some kind of grotesque creature that had emerged from the depths of the evolutionary process and now clung irritatingly to his body. In another century or two people would probably be able to replace this troublesome appendage with a neat mechanical device that would drain the body's superfluous fluids at a touch. The whole absurd association between the processes of urination and copulation in a single organ struck him as a crude expression of vulgar adolescent humour, in poor taste: it would be no more distasteful if humans reproduced by spitting into each other's mouths or by blowing their noses into each other's ears.

Meanwhile the cistern had refilled. Fima pulled the handle again, and succeeded in releasing another intermittent jet, which once again ceased the moment the water stopped pouring. He was furious: to think of all the massive effort he had invested over the past thirty years in gratifying every whim and appetite of this pampered, selfish, corrupt, insatiable reptile, which turned you into a mere vehicle created for the sole purpose of conveying it comfortably from female to female, and after all that it repaid you with such ingratitude.

As though addressing a naughty child, Fima said:

'Right. You've got exactly one minute to make your mind up. In another fifty-five seconds by my watch I'm zipping up and going, and after that you can burst for all I care.'

These threats only seemed to reinforce the reptile's recalcitrance: it seemed to shrivel between his fingers. Fima was determined not to yield henceforth. Furiously he zipped up his fly and banged down the lid of the lavatory. He slammed the bathroom door behind him. Five minutes later he slammed the door of the flat, strode past the letter box without succumbing to the temptation to take out the newspaper, and marched resolutely towards the shopping centre. He had made up his mind to go to the bank to see to four transactions, which he recited to himself as he walked along, so as not to forget. First, draw some cash. He had had enough of going around without a penny in his pocket. Second, pay all his bills: telephone, water, paraffin, sewage, gas, electricity. Third, find out at last the state of his account. By the time he reached the newsagents and stationers on the corner, he had forgotten what the fourth thing was. He strained his mind, but it was no good. On the other hand he noticed a new issue of *Politics* displayed on the inside of the closed door of the shop. He went in and perused it for a quarter of an hour, shocked to read Tsvi Kropotkin's article, which maintained that the chances of peace were nil, at least for the foreseeable future. He must go round and see Tsvika this very morning, Fima decided, and read the riot act to him about the defeatism of the intelligentsia: not the kind of defeatism that our opponents on the hawkish right so stridently accuse us of, but something else, something deeper and in the long term more serious.

His upsurge of fury yielded some benefit: as soon as he left the shop, he cut across a waste plot, entered an unfinished building, and barely had time to unzip his fly before his bladder emptied itself with a rush. He felt so triumphant that he did not even mind getting his shoes and trouser bottoms muddy. Proceeding northwards, he walked past the bank without noticing it, but observed with excitement that the almond tree in his back garden was not the only one that had blossomed without waiting for the Trees' New Year. Although on second thoughts he was not sure about this, because he did not know the date according to the Jewish religious calendar. In fact he could not even remember the secular date. At any rate, there was no doubt that it was only February and already spring was raising its head. Fima felt that there was a simple symbolism here: he did not ask himself what it symbolised, but he felt happy about it. As though he had been given responsibility for the entire city, unasked, and to his surprise it turned out that he had not entirely failed in the discharge of his duties. The pale blue of the early morning had turned to a deep azure, as though the sea were suspended upside down over the city and were showering it with nursery-school cheerfulness. Geraniums and bougainvilleas blazed in front gardens. The low stone walls gleamed as though they were being caressed. 'Not bad, eh?' Fima said mentally to an invisible guest or tourist.

At the turning to Bayit Vagan stood a young man in an army windcheater, with a submachine gun over his shoulder and surrounded by buckets of flowers. He suggested that Fima take a bunch of chrysanthemums for the weekend. Fima asked himself if this wasn't a settler from the Territories, who grew his flowers on other men's land. He immediately decided that someone who was prepared to make peace with Arafat should not excommunicate his own domestic opponents. Although he could see arguments on both sides. But he could find neither hatred nor anger in his heart, perhaps because of the radiant light. Jerusalem this morning seemed to be a place where all should respect the different opinions of others, and so he put his hand in his pocket and easily found three one-shekel coins, no doubt the change he had been given last night by his new minister of information. He pressed the flowers to his chest as though to protect them from the cold.

'Pardon?' said Fima. 'Did you say something? I'm sorry, I didn't catch what you said.'

The boy selling the flowers said with a broad smile:

'All I said was have a good weekend. Good Sabbath.'

'Absolutely,' Fima agreed, laying the foundations for a new national consensus. 'Thank you. And a good weekend to you too.'

The air was cold and vitreous, even though there was no wind. As though the light itself contained a dazzlingly clear arctic ingredient. The words 'dazzlingly clear' afforded Fima a strange, secretive thrill. One must avoid malice, he thought, even when it disguises itself as principle. He ought to repeat to himself over and over again that the real enemy was despair. It was vital not to compromise with despair, not to submit to it. Young Yoezer and his contemporaries, the moderate, reasonable people who will lead their carefully modulated lives here in Jerusalem after us, will be astonished at the suffering we brought on ourselves. But at least they won't be able to remember us with contempt. We didn't give in without a struggle. We held on in Jerusalem as long as we could, against incomparably superior odds and stronger forces. We did not go under lightly. And even if we were overcome in the end, we still have the advantage of Pascal's 'thinking reed'.

So it was that, excited, unkempt and mud-spattered, at a quarter past ten in the morning, clutching a bunch of chrysanthemums and shivering with cold, Fima rang Ted and Yael's doorbell. When Yael came to the door, wearing grey corduroy trousers and a burgundy sweater, he said to her without any embarrassment:

'I happened to be walking past and I decided to look in just for a minute, to wish you a good Sabbath. I hope I'm not disturbing you? Shall I come back tomorrow? I've got the decorators in next week. Never mind. I've brought you some flowers for the Sabbath. Can I come inside for a minute or two?'

233

28

In Ithaca, on the water's edge

'ALL right,' said Yael, 'come in. Just bear in mind that I've got to go out shortly. Hang on, let me button your shirt properly. Tell me, when did you change it last?'

Fima said:

'You and I have got to talk.'

Yael said:

'Not again.'

He followed her into the kitchen. On the way he peeped into the bedroom. He was vaguely hoping to see himself still sleeping in the bed since the night before last. But the bed had been made and spread with a dark blue woollen counterpane. On either side of it were twin lamps on matching bedside cupboards on each of which was a solitary book and, as in a hotel, a glass of water and a note pad and pencil. There were even two identical alarm clocks.

Fima said:

'Dimi isn't well. We can't go on pretending there's nothing the matter with him. You'd better put the flowers in water; they're for you, for the Sabbath. I bought them from a settler. Besides which, it's your birthday around the end of February. You wouldn't make me a cup of coffee, would you? I've walked all the way from Kiryat Yovel and I'm half frozen to death. My upstairs neighbour tried to murder his wife at five o'clock this morning: I rushed upstairs to help and only made a fool of myself. Never mind. I've come to talk to you about Dimi. The other night, when you went out and I looked after him . . .'

'Look here, Efraim,' Yael cut in, 'why do you have to meddle in everybody's lives? I know Dimi isn't doing well. Or that we're not doing well with him. You're not telling me anything I don't know already. You're not doing too well yourself, if it comes to that.'

Fima understood from this that he ought to say good-bye and go. But he sat down on a low kitchen bench, looked up at Yael with doglike devotion, blinked his brown eyes, and started to explain that Dimi was an unhappy and dangerously lonely child. Something had come out the other evening while he was looking after the child, no point in going into details, but he had formed the impression that the boy might be, how to put it, in need of some help.

Yael plugged the kettle in. She put some instant coffee powder into two glasses. Fima had the feeling she was opening and slamming shut more cupboard doors and drawers than was strictly necessary. She said:

'Fine. Great. So you came round to give me a lecture on childhood and its problems. Teddy's got this friend, a child psychologist from South Africa, and we consult him occasionally. So just stop looking for disasters and things to worry about. Stop pestering everybody.'

When Yael mentioned South Africa, Fima had difficulty fighting back a sudden urge to explain his scenario about what was going to happen there in the near future, when the apartheid regime was toppled. He was convinced there would be a bloodbath, not just between whites and blacks, but also between whites and whites and blacks and blacks. Who could tell if a similar danger did not exist in Israel, too? But the word 'bloodbath' struck him as a tired cliché. Even the idea of a tired cliché struck him as rather trite at the moment.

Next to him on the kitchen table was an open packet of butter biscuits. Unconsciously his fingers reached for it, and he started eating the biscuits one by one. While Yael passed him his white coffee, he described to her in a somewhat oblique way what had taken place two nights previously, and how he had come to fall asleep in her bed while Dimi was still awake at one in the morning. It wasn't very fair of you two, either, having a night out in Tel Aviv and not even bothering to leave an emergency phone number. Suppose the child had had a bilions attack? Or electrocuted himself? Or poisoned himself? Fima got into a muddle because he did not want to give away, even indirectly, the business about the dog sacrifice. Nevertheless, he muttered something about the way the neighbours' children apparently made Dimi's life a misery. 'You know, Yael, he's not like the rest of them, he wears glasses, he's so serious, he's an albino, he's shortsighted, you could almost say he's half-blind, he's very small for his age, maybe on account of some hormonal disturbance that you ought to be doing something about, he's hypersensitive, he's an internal – no, that's not right – an introverted child – even that isn't exactly the right word – perhaps it's soulful or spiritual; it's hard to define. He's creative. Or, more accurately, he's an original, interesting, you might even say a deep child.'

From that Fima moved on to the difficulties of growing up in a time of universal cruelty and violence: every evening Dimi watches the TV news with us, every evening murder is trivialised on the screen. He also talked about himself when he was Dimi's age: he too had been an introverted child, he too had had no mother, and his father had systematically tried to drive him insane. And he said that apparently the only affective bond that this child had formed was with him of all people, even though Yael knew perfectly well that he had never seen himself as the fatherly type, fatherhood had always scared him to death, nevertheless he sometimes had the feeling that this had been a tragic mistake, that things could have been totally different, if only . . .

Yael cut him short again. She said frostily:

'Finish your coffee, Efraim. I have to go.'

Fima asked where she had to go. He'd be happy to go with her. Anywhere at all. He had nothing to do this morning. They could continue their conversation. He believed it was vital and quite urgent. Or would it be better if he stayed behind and waited for her to come back, and then they could carry on? He didn't mind waiting. It was Friday, his day off, the clinic was closed, and on Sunday he had the decorators coming in, so the only prospect facing him at home was the depressing task of dismantling and packing. What did she think? Could she spare him Teddy for an hour or two on Saturday morning, to help take down the . . . Never mind. He knew this was all ridiculous and irrelevant. Could he do some ironing till she came back? Or fold the clean washing? One day, some other time, he'd like to tell her about a thought that had been preoccupying him rather a lot recently, an idea that he called the Third State. No, it wasn't a political idea. It was more of an existential idea, if one could still say 'existential' without sounding corny. 'Remind me sometime. Just say "the Third State" and I'll remember at once and explain it to you. Though it may be just plain stupid. It's not important right now. After all, here in Jerusalem almost every other character you see is half prophet and half prime minister. Including Tsvika Kropotkin, including Shamir himself, that Brezhnev of ours. It's less like a city than a lunatic asylum. But I didn't come here to talk to you about Shamir and Brezhnev. I came here to talk about Dimi. Dimi says you and Teddy call me a clown behind my back. It may surprise you to learn that your son has taken to calling himself a little clown too. Doesn't that shake you rather? I don't mind being called a clown. It quite suits somebody whose own father sees him as a *shlemiel* and a *shlemazel*. Although he's ridiculous too. The old man, I mean. Baruch. In some ways he's even more ridiculous than me or Dimi. He's another Jerusalem prophet with his own personal formula for salvation in three easy stages. He's got some story about a cantor who gets stuck alone on a desert island for the High Holy Days. It doesn't matter. By the way, recently he's taken to whistling a bit. I mean wheezing. I'm rather worried. I may just be imagining things. What do you think, Yael? Maybe you could have a chat with him sometime, get him to go into hospital for some tests? He's always had a soft spot for you. You might be the only person who can curb his Revisionist obstinacy. Which is a good illustration of what I meant about every other Jerusalemite wanting to be the Messiah. But so what? All of us must look pretty ridiculous to an impartial outside observer. Even you, Yael, with your jet engines. Who needs jet engines around here when the only thing we are really short of is a bit of compassion and common sense? And all of us, including the impartial observer, are ridiculous when viewed by the mountains. Or the desert. Wouldn't you say that Teddy is ridiculous? That walking crate. Or Tsvika? Only this morning I was reading a hysterical article of his, which tries to

237

prove scientifically that the government is cut off from reality. As if reality lives in Tsvika's little pocket. Though there's no denying the government is full of people who are pretty dense, and some of them are quite unbalanced. But how did we get onto the government? That's what always happens to us: for once, we decide to have a serious chat about ourselves, about the child, about things that really matter, and somehow the government comes barging in. Where do you have to go in such a hurry? You don't have to go anywhere. It's a lie. Friday is your day off too. You're lying to me to get rid of me. You want me to leave. You're afraid, Yael. But what are you afraid of? Of facing up to thinking about why Dimi has started calling himself a little clown?'

With her back to him, folding teatowels and putting them away one by one in a drawer, Yael replied quietly:

'Effy, once and for all: You're not Dimi's father. Now drink up and go. I've got an appointment at the hairdresser's. The child you could have had twenty-five years ago I killed because you didn't want it. So don't start now. I sometimes feel as if I've never quite woken up from that anaesthetic. And now you come here to torment me. I'm telling you, if Teddy wasn't such a tolerant man, such a walking crate as you call him, you'd have been thrown out of this flat a long time ago. There's nothing for you here. Especially after what you did the other night. It's hard enough here even without you. You're a difficult man, Efraim. Difficult and also boring. And I'm still not convinced you're not one of the main causes of Dimi's confusion. Slowly but surely you're driving that child mad.'

After a moment she added:

'And it's hard to know if it's some sort of ruse of yours or just idle chatter. You keep talking, talking all the time: maybe you talk so much, you've really convinced yourself that you've got feelings. That you're in love. That you're partly Dimi's father. All sorts of half-baked delusions like that. Why am I talking to you about feelings, about love? You don't even know what the words mean. Once, when you still read books instead of just newspapers, you must have read something about love and unhappiness, and ever since then you've been all around Jerusalem preaching on the subject. I nearly said just now that you only love yourself, but even that isn't true. You don't even love yourself. You don't love anything. Except maybe winning arguments. Never mind. Get your coat on. I'm late because of you.'

'Will you let me wait for you here? I'll wait patiently. Till this evening if necessary.'

'Hoping that Teddy will get back before me? And find you asleep on our bed again, under my blanket?'

'I promise,' Fima whispered, 'that this time I'll behave myself.'

And as though to prove it, he jumped up and poured his coffee into the sink. He had not touched it, although he had absent-mindedly eaten all the butter biscuits. Noticing that the sink was full of dirty dishes and pans, he rolled up one of his sleeves and turned on the tap. Eagerly he waited for the water to run hot. Even when Yael said, 'You're crazy, Efraim, leave it, we'll put it all in the machine after lunch,' he took no notice but started washing up enthusiastically and laying the soapy dishes out on the marble draining board. 'It relaxes me,' he said. 'I'll be fin-ished in a few minutes, once the water finally makes up its mind to get hot. I'll be glad to spare you the need to run the dish-washer; and the dishes will come out much cleaner; and mean-while we can carry on talking a little longer. Which is the cold tap and which is the hot one? Where are we supposed to be, America? Everything's topsy-turvy here. But if you've really got to go, that's fine by me. You just go, Yael, and come back later. I'll promise to restrict myself to the kitchen. I won't wander around the flat, I won't even use the lavatory. Shall I polish the silver for you? Or clean out the fridge? I'll stay right here and wait, no matter how long you're gone. Like a male Solveig. I've got this book about whale hunters in Alaska, and it talks about this custom . . . Never mind. Don't worry about me, Yael, I don't mind waiting all day. Instead of worrying about me, you ought to worry about Dimi. To use Ted's amusing expression, you could say that Dimi is down. To my mind, the first thing we ought to do is find a totally different social setting for him. Maybe a boarding school for gifted children? Or the other way around, tame one or two of the neighbours' kids . . .'

Suddenly, as though translating her revulsion into fury, Yael snatched the soapy sponge and the frying pan he was holding.

'That's it. I've had enough of this farce. I'm fed up with the lot of you. Coming in here, washing the dishes, trying to make me feel sorry for you all the time. I can't feel sorry for you. I don't want to be a mother to you all. That child, he's always scheming for something, though I really don't know what he's missing in life, what we haven't bought him, a video, an Atari, a compact disc player, a trip to America every year, and next week he's even getting his own private TV in his room. You'd think we're bringing up a prince here. And then you come round all the time, driving him crazy and making me feel guilty, asking what sort of parents we are, and filling Dimi's head with the same sick birds that are fluttering around inside yours. I've had it up to here. Don't come here any more, Fima. You pretend you're living alone, but you're always clinging to other people. And I'm just the opposite; everybody clings to me, when the only thing I want really is to be alone at last. Go away now, Efraim. I've got nothing to give to you or to anyone. And I wouldn't even if I did. Why should I? I don't feel I owe anyone anything. And I've got no claims on anyone. Teddy is always a hundred per cent OK. Never just ninety-nine. He's like a year-planner that tells you what you've got to do, and when you've done it, you wipe it out and write more things to do. This morning he offered to rewire the flat to a three-phase system as a birthday present for me. Have you ever heard of a husband giving his wife a three-phase system for her birthday? And Dimi waters the houseplants morning and evening, morning and evening till they die, and Teddy buys new ones, and they get drowned too. Dimi can even handle the vacuum cleaner, once Teddy showed him how. He sucks at everything, even the pictures and mirrors. Even our feet. There's no stopping him. You remember my father, dear devoted comrade Naftali Tsvi Levin, founding member of the historic settlement of Yavne'el? He's an old pioneer now, he's eighty-three and completely gaga. He sits in his old people's home in Afula staring at the wall all day, and if ever you ask him a question, like how are you feeling, what's new, what do you need, who are you, who am I, where does it hurt, he invariably replies with the same three-word question: "In what sense?" He says it with a Yiddish lilt. Those three words are all he has left from the Bible, the Talmud, the Midrash, the Hasidic tales, the Haskalah, Bialik, and Buber, and all the other Jewish sources he knew by heart once. I'm telling you, Efraim, soon I'll only have three words left too. Not "In what sense?" but "Leave me alone." Leave me alone, Efraim. I'm not your mother. I've got a project that's been dragging on for years now because a whole bunch of toddlers have been tugging at my sleeves to wipe their noses. Once, when I was little, my father the pioneer told me to remember that men are really the weaker sex. It was a joke of his. Well, shall I tell you something, now that I've missed my hairdresser's appointment because of you? If I'd realised then what I know now, I'd have joined a nunnery. Or married a jet engine. I'd have given the weaker sex a miss, with great pleasure. Give them a finger, they want your whole hand. Give them your whole hand, they don't even want the finger any more. Just sit quietly over there, make the coffee, and don't interrupt. Don't draw attention to yourself. Do the washing and the ironing, get laid, and shut up. Give them a rest from you, and within a fortnight they're crawling back on all fours. What exactly did you want from me today, Efraim? A little early-morning screw in memory of the good old days? The fact is you don't even want *that*, any of you. Ten per cent lust and ninety per cent playacting. You turn up here when you imagine Teddy's out, loaded with flowers and fine phrases, an expert at comforting orphans and widows, hoping that this time I'll finally take pity on you and go to bed with you for a quarter of an hour. As a bribe to make you go away. I slept with you for five years, and all you ever wanted, ninety per cent of the time, was to get it over with, empty yourself, wipe up, turn on the light, and carry on reading your newspaper. Go now, Efraim. I'm a woman of forty-nine, and you're no spring chicken yourself. That story's over. There's no resit. I got a child by you and you didn't want it. So, like a good girl, I murdered it so as not to mess up your poetic destiny. Why do you keep coming back to mess me up, and everyone else too? What more do you want from me? Is it my

241

fault you squandered everything you had, and everything you might have had, and what you found in Greece? Is it my fault that life goes by and time gnaws at everything? Is it my fault that we all die a little every day? What more do you want from me?'

Fima stood up, chastened and humble, muttered an apology, started to look for his coat, and suddenly said shyly:

'It's February, Yael: it'll be your birthday soon. I've forgotten. Perhaps you've already had it? I don't remember the date. I haven't even got a three-phase system to give you.'

'It's Friday, February 16th, 1989. The time is 11:10 a.m. So what?'

'You said we all want something from you and you've got nothing more to give.'

'Surprise, surprise: so you've managed to take in half a sentence after all.'

'But the fact is, I don't want anything from you, Yael. On the contrary, I want to find something that will give you a little pleasure.'

'You've got nothing to give. Your hands are empty. In any case, don't you worry about my pleasure. It so happens I have a real feast every day, or nearly every day. At work, at my drawing board, or in the wind tunnel. That's my life. That's the only place where I really exist a little. Maybe you ought to start doing something, Efraim. That's the whole of your problem: you don't do anything. You just read the papers and get worked up. Why don't you give private lessons, volunteer for civil defence, do some translating, give lectures to soldiers about the meaning of Jewish ethics.'

'Somebody, I think it was Schopenhauer, wrote that the intellect divides everything up, whereas the intuition unites and restores the lost wholeness. But I'm telling you, Yael, that our farce doesn't divide into two but, as Rabin always says, into three. Schopenhauer and the rest of them ignore the Third State. Wait, don't interrupt. Just give me two minutes to explain it to you.'

But then he fell silent, even though this time Yael had not interrupted him.

At last he said:

'I'll give you everything I've got. I know it's not much.'

'You've got nothing, Effy. Just the scraps you shnorr from the rest of us.'

'Will you come back to me? You and Dimi? We can go to Greece.'

'And live on nectar and ambrosia?'

'I'll get a job. I'll work as a salesman for my father's firm. A night watchman. A waiter even.'

'Sure, a waiter. You'll drop everything.'

'Or else we could go and live in Yavne'el, the three of us. On your parents' old farm. We can grow flowers in hothouses, like your sister and her husband. And we'll get the fruit orchard going again. Baruch will give us some money, and little by little we'll bring the ruins back to life. We'll have a model farm. During the day Dimi and I will look after the livestock. We'll build a study for you with computers, a drawing board. And a wind tunnel, if you'll explain what that is. In the evening, towards sunset, we'll go and see the orchard together. The three of us. As it begins to get dark, we'll collect honey from the beehives. If you really want to take Teddy with you, I won't object. We'll have a little commune. We'll live without lies, and without the faintest shadow of spite. You'll see: Dimi will develop and really start to flourish. And you and I . . .'

'Yes, and of course you'll get up at half past four every morning, with your boots and your mattock and your hoe, a song in your heart and a plant in your hand, to drain the swamps and conquer the wasteland single-handed.'

'Don't poke fun, Yael. I admit I have to learn from scratch how to love you. So OK, little by little I'll learn. You'll see.'

'Of course you will. You'll take a correspondence course. Or study at the Open University.'

'You'll teach me.'

With a sudden outburst of timid courage he added:

'You know very well that what you said earlier isn't the whole truth. You didn't want the baby either. You didn't even want Dimi. I'm sorry I said that. I didn't mean it. It just slipped out. But I want Dimi. I love him more than my own life.'

She stood over Fima as he huddled on his bench, in her worn

243

corduroy trousers and slightly threadbare red sweater, as though she were straining with all her might not to hit his plump face. Her eyes were dry and flashing, and her face was wrinkled and old, as if it were not Yael but her elderly mother who was bending over him, smelling of black bread and olives and plain toilet soap. And she said with wonderment, with a strange taut smile, speaking not to him and not to herself but into space:

'It was also in the winter. It was February then too. Two days after my birthday. In 1963. When you and Uri were completely absorbed in the Lavon affair. The almond tree behind our kitchen in Kiryat Yovel had started to flower. And the sky was just like today, perfectly clear and blue. That morning there was a programme of Shoshana Damari songs on the radio. And I went in a rattling old taxi to that Russian gynaecologist in the Street of the Prophets, who said I reminded him of Giulietta Masina. Two and a half hours later I went home, as fate would have it in the same taxi with the little photograph of Princess Grace of Monaco over the driver's head, and it was all over. I remember I closed the shutters and drew the curtains and lay down in bed listening to a Schubert impromptu on the radio, followed by a lecture about Tibet and the Dalai Lama, and I didn't get up till evening, and by then it had started raining again. You had gone off early in the morning with Tsvi to a one-day history conference at Tel Aviv University. It's true you offered to skip it and come with me. And it's true I said, For Heaven's sake, it's no worse than having a wisdom tooth out. And in the evening you came home all glowing with excitement, because you had managed to catch Professor Talmon out in some minor contradiction. We murdered it, and we shut up. To this day I don't want to know what they do with them. Tinier than a day-old chick. Do they flush them down the lavatory? We both murdered it. Only you didn't want to hear when or where or how. All you wanted to hear from me was that it was all over and done with. What you really wanted to tell me was about how you'd made the great Talmon stand there on the daïs in confusion like a first-year student flunking an oral. And that same evening you rushed round to Tsvika's, because the two of you hadn't had time on the bus back to Jerusalem to finish your argument about the implications of the Lavon affair. He could have been a boy of twenty-six by now. He could be a father himself, with a child or two of his own. The eldest might be about Dimi's age. And you and I would go into town to buy an aquarium and some tropical fish for the grandchildren. Where do you think the drains of Jerusalem empty out? Into the Mediterranean, via Nahal Shorek? And the sea joins up with Greece, and there the king of Ithaca's daughter might have picked him up out of the waves. Now he's a curly-haired youth sitting playing the lyre in the moonlight on the water's edge in Ithaca. I believe Talmon died a few years ago. Or was that Prawer? And didn't Giulietta Masina also die some time ago? I'll make some more coffee. I've missed the hairdresser now. It wouldn't do you any harm to have a haircut. Not that it would do you much good either. Do you still remember Shoshana Damari, at least? *A star shines in the sky, / And in the wadi jackals cry?* She's completely forgotten now, too.'

Fima had closed his eyes. He tensed himself, not like someone who is afraid of being hit but like someone who is hoping for it to the very tips of his nerves. As though it were not Yael, not even Yael's mother, but his own mother bending over him and demanding that he give back at once the blue bonnet that he had hidden. But what makes her think that he hid it? And why does Yael assume it was a boy? What if it was actually a girl? A little Yael with long soft hair and a face like Giulietta Masina? He laid his arms on the table and without opening his eyes hid his weary head on them. He could almost hear Professor Talmon's scholarly nasal voice declaring that Karl Marx's understanding of human nature was naïve and dogmatic, not to say primitive, and in any case one-dimensional. Fima responded mentally with Yael's old father's perpetual question:

In what sense?

The more he thought about this, the less he could find an answer. Yet on the other side of the wall, in the next flat, a young woman was singing a forgotten song which had been on everyone's lips years ago, about a man called Johnny: *There was never a man like my Johnny, / Like the man they called Johnny*

Guitar. The melody was feeble, childish, almost laughable, and the woman on the other side of the kitchen wall was no singer. Fima suddenly recalled making love to Yael, half his lifetime ago, one afternoon in a small boarding-house on Mount Carmel, when he was accompanying her to a conference at the Technion. She conceived the fantasy that he should pretend to be a stranger and she a young girl who had never been touched before, inno-cent, shy, nervous. His task was to seduce her, taking his time. And he managed to give her pleasure that was close to pain. He drew forth cries for help, pleas, tender exclamations of surprise. The more he played the stranger, the more the pleasure intensi-fied and deepened, until a mysterious sense of hearing developed in his fingertips, in every cell of his body, enabling him to know precisely what would feel good to her, as if he had planted a spy inside the dark network of nerves of her spinal column. Or as if he had become one flesh with her. Until they ceased to touch and be touched like a man and woman, and became a single being quenching its thirst. That afternoon he felt not like a man having intercourse with a young woman but as if he had always lived inside her womb, that her womb was now not hers but theirs, his penis not his but theirs, his skin enveloping not his body but theirs.

In the early evening they dressed and went for a walk in one of the verdant valleys on the side of Mount Carmel. They strolled until nightfall among the luxuriant vegetation without talking or touching, until a night bird repeated to them a short, poignant phrase which Fima imitated to perfection, and Yael, with a warm low laugh, said, Do you have any plausible explanation, good sir, why it should be that I suddenly love you, even though we're not blood relations or anything like that?

He opened his eyes and saw his ex-wife, shrunken, almost shrivelled, an ageing Giulietta Masina, in grey cords and a dark red sweater, still standing with her back to him folding teatowels. It's not possible, he thought, that she's got so many teatowels that she can go on folding them forever. Unless she's refolding them because she wasn't satisfied with the way she did it the first time. So he stood up like a man who knows exactly what to do, and embraced her from behind, putting one hand over her mouth and the other over her eyes, and kissed the nape of her neck, the roots of her hair, her back. An odour of plain toilet soap mixed with a hint of tobacco from Ted's pipe reached his nostrils, dizzying him with a vague desire, along with a sadness that snuffed it out. He picked up her thin little girl's body in his arms, and just as he had carried her son two nights before, he carried Yael now and laid her on the same bed in her bedroom, and just as he had stroked Dimi, he now stroked her cheek. But he did not attempt to remove the counterpane, nor did he try to take off his clothes or hers, but he pressed himself against her along the whole length of their bodies and buried her head in the hollow of his shoulder. Instead of saying I've missed you, he was so tired that he whispered I've messed you. They lay side by side, close but not embracing, motionless, speechless, his body's warmth radiating into hers and hers into his. Until she whispered to him: Right. Now be good and go.

Fima silently obeyed. He got up and found his coat, drank the remains of his second coffee, which had gone cold like its predecessor. She told me to go into town and buy an aquarium and some tropical fish for Dimi, he thought to himself, so that's what I'll do. On his way out he managed to close the door behind him so carefully that it did not make the slightest sound. Then, as he walked northwards, the same silence continued in the street and in his thoughts. He walked slowly the whole length of Hehalutz Street, to his own surprise trying to whistle the tune of the old song about the man they called Johnny Guitar. There, he said to himself, you could say that everything's lost or you could say that nothing's lost, and the two things are definitely not mutually exclusive. The situation seemed strange yet wonderful: he had not slept with his wife, yet he felt no lack in his body but rather the opposite, an exhilaration, an elation, a fulfilment, as though in some mysterious way there really had been a deep and accurate intercourse between them. And as if in that intercourse with her he had finally begotten his son, his only son.

But in what sense?

The question seemed meaningless. In a senseless sense. So what.

When he reached Herzl Street, the fine rain reminded him that he had left his cap behind at Yael's, on the edge of the kitchen table. But he was not anxious, because he knew he would return. He still had to explain to her and to Dimi, and why not to Ted too, the secret of the Third State. But not now. Not today. There was no hurry. Even when he thought of Yoezer and the other reasonable, sane people who would live in Jerusalem instead of us a hundred years from now, he felt no anguish, but, on the contrary, a sort of shy inner smile. What's the matter? What's the hurry? Let them wait. Let them wait quietly for their turn. We definitely haven't concluded our business here yet. It's a slow business, a rotten business, there's no denying it, but one way or another we still haven't said our last word.

A few moments later he boarded the first bus that stopped, without bothering to check its number or its destination. He sat down behind the driver still humming to himself, shamelessly out of tune, the song about Johnny Guitar. He saw no reason to get off before the terminus, which happened to be Prophet Samuel Street. Despite the cold and the wind, Fima was in very good form.

29

Before the Sabbath

H E was so happy that he did not feel hungry, despite having eaten nothing since the early morning, apart from the biscuits he nibbled in Yael's kitchen. When he got off the bus, the rain had stopped. Among the wisps of dirty cloud, islands of blue were shining. For some reason it seemed that the clouds were standing still and the blue islands were floating westwards. And he felt that this blueness was aimed at him and was calling him to follow.

Fima began walking up Ezekiel Street. The first two lines of the song about Johnny Guitar were still resounding in his chest. But how did the song go on? Where in the world did Johnny end up? Where is he playing now?

There was a Sabbath eve smell in the Bukharian Quarter, even though it was still only half past twelve. Fima vaguely attempted to identify the components of this thick smell which reminded him of his childhood and of that fine excitement that used to course through him and through Jerusalem as the Sabbath approached. The smell sometimes began to fill the world even on Thursday afternoon, with the washing and the scrubbing and the cooking. The maid used to cook stuffed chicken's necks sewn up with a needle and thread. His mother would make a plum compote that was as sweet and sticky as glue. And sweet stewed carrots, and gefilte fish, and pies, or a strudel, or pastries filled with raisins. And all kinds of jams and marmalades, one of which was called *varyennye* in Russian. Vividly there came back to Fima, as he walked, the smell and appearance of the wine-coloured borscht, a semi-solid soup with blobs of fat floating on the surface like gold rings, which he used to fish for with a spoon when he was little.

And every Friday his mother would wait for him precisely at midday at the gate of his school, with her blond plait framing her head like a wreath and a brown tortoiseshell comb planted at her golden nape. They would go together to do the last-minute shopping in Mahane Yehuda Market, he with his satchel on his back and she clutching her wicker shopping basket, a sapphire ring gleaming on her finger. The smells of the market, sharp, savoury Oriental smells, filled them both with childish glee. As though they were conspiring secretly against the heavy Ashkenazic sweetness of the pies at home and the cloying carrot and the strudel and the compote and the sticky jams. And indeed, his father disliked these Friday raids on the market. He grumbled sardonically that the child ought to be doing his homework or improving his body with exercises, and in any case they paid a fortune to have a maid, whose job it was to do the shopping, and surely one could buy everything nearby in Rehavia, so there was no need to drag the child among those filthy stalls with foul liquids swilling on the pavement. The Levant was swarming with germs, and all those pungent spices with their clamorous smells were nothing but a camouflage for filth. He made a joke of his wife's attraction to the enchantments of the Thousands and One Nights, and what he termed her weekly quest for Ali Baba. Fima trembled inwardly at the recollection of the illicit thrill of helping his mother to choose from among various kinds of black olives, with their almost indecent smell and their sharp, dizzying taste. Sometimes he vaguely noticed the smouldering look one of the stallholders fixed on his mother, and although he was too young to know its meaning, he could faintly feel, as in a dream, an echo of a tremor that ran through his mother's body and seemed to overflow into his own. He could hear her voice now, in the distance. Look what they've done to you, stupid. But this time he answered cheerfully, Never mind, you'll see that I still haven't said my last word.

On their way home after the market he always insisted on carrying the basket. His other arm he linked in hers. They always had lunch on Fridays in a little vegetarian restaurant in King George Street, a red-curtained establishment that made him think of abroad as he knew it from the cinema. It was run by a refugee couple, Mr and Mrs Danzig, a charming pair who looked so alike they might have been brother and sister. As indeed, Fima thought, perhaps they were. Who could tell? Their gentle manners brought a smile to his mother's face like a beam of light. Fima felt a pang of longing as he recalled it. At the end of their meal, Mrs Danzig always placed two exact squares of almond chocolate in front of Fima. And she would say with a smile:

'That is for gutt-boy who didn't leave anything on his plate.'

She pronounced 'gutt-boy' without an article, as though it were his name. As for Mr Danzig, he was a round man with one cheek that was like raw butcher's meat: Fima did not know if he had a chronic skin disease or a strange birthmark, or if it was a mysterious trace of an extensive burn. Mr Danzig would intone a verse, like a ritual, at the end of those Friday lunches:

'Efraim iss a lovely child,
He finish all his dinner;
So now he vill be strong and vild,
And in our town the vinner –

Vot town?'

Fima's role in this ceremony was to reply:

'Jerusalem!'

But once, he rebelled and perversely answered: 'Danzig!' which he knew from his father's stamp collection and also from the heavy German atlas that he used to browse in for hours on end, spread-eagled on the carpet in a corner of the salon, especially on winter evenings. This reply made Mr Danzig smile wistfully and say something that ended with *mein Kind*. Meanwhile his mother's eyes for some reason filled with tears, and she suddenly squeezed Fima's head to her bosom and covered his face with a volley of quick kisses.

What became of the Danzigs? They must have died ages ago. A branch of a bank had stood for years on the site of that little restaurant that gleamed with a cleanness which even now, a thousand years later, Fima could feel in his nostrils, and which for some reason smelled to him like fresh snow. On each table, on the spotless white tablecloth, there was always an upright rose in a glass vase. The walls were adorned with calm landscapes of lakes and forests. Sometimes at a table in the far corner near the potted palms a slim British officer would be lunching on his own. He would sit stiffly, with his peaked cap parked at the foot of the rose. Where have those pictures of lakes and forests ended up? Where in the world is that lonely English officer eating now? A city of longings and madness. A refugee camp, not a city.

But you could still get away from it. You could take Dimi and Yael away from here and join a kibbutz in the desert. You could propose to Tamar or to Annette Tadmor, settle down with her in Magdiel, and get a job as a clerk in a bank, in the health service, or in national insurance, and start writing poetry again in the evenings. Start a new chapter. Get a little closer to the Third State.

His feet led him of their own accord into the maze of narrow streets which is the Bukharian Quarter. Slowly he shuffled underneath gaudily bedecked washing lines stretched across the grey street. On balconies with rusting wrought-iron balustrades he could see dried skeletons of palm booths left over from the festival of Sukkoth, heaps of scrap iron and junk, suspended washing coppers, mouldering packing cases, jerry cans, all the refuse of the run-down flats. Almost every window here was curtained in garish colours. On the windowsills stood glass jars inside which cucumbers were slowly pickling in a broth of garlic, dill and parsley. Fima suddenly felt that these guttural places, built around courtyards with ancient stone wells, smelling of grilled meat, onions, baking pastry, spiced dishes, and smoke, offered him a simple, straightforward answer to a question he had totally failed to frame. But he felt something hammering urgently at his chest both outside and within, gently plucking and gnawing, like the long-forgotten music of Johnny Guitar, like the lakes and forests on the walls of the little restaurant that his mother used to take him to after shopping in the market on Fridays. And he said to himself:

'That's enough. Drop it.'

Like someone scratching at a sore, unable to stop even though he knew he should.

In Rabbenu Gershom Street he passed three short, plump women who looked so alike that Fima supposed they were sisters, or perhaps a mother with her daughters. He eyed them with an intrigued gaze. They were lush, generously fleshed women, as curvaceous as slave girls in a painting of an Oriental seraglio. His imagination pictured their expansive, abundant nakedness, then their submissive, obedient surrender, like waitresses dishing out warm helpings to a queue of starving men without taking the trouble to distinguish the recipients or their handouts, bestowing the gift of their bodies indifferently, out of habit, and with a hint of boredom. The boredom and indifference seemed far more sexual and provocative to Fima at that moment than any sensuous excitement in the world. A moment later came a wave of shame that extinguished his desire. Why had he forgone Yael's body that morning? If he had only invested a little more cunning and patience, if he had only persevered, surely she would have given in. Without desire, but so what? Was it a question of desire?

But then, what was it a question of?

The three women disappeared round the corner, but Fima stayed rooted to the spot, staring blankly, excited and ashamed. Surely the truth was that this morning he had not craved Yael's emaciated body. Rather, he had longed vaguely for a different kind of union, not a carnal union, nor the union of child and mother, perhaps no union at all, something that Fima could not even name, but nevertheless he felt that this thing, elusive as it was and too fine to be defined, if he could only be blessed with it once, just once might change his life for the better.

On second thoughts he changed his mind. The words 'change his life for the better' seemed to suit a muddled, acne-ridden adolescent rather than a man who was capable of leading a nation out of crisis and onto the road to peace.

Later, Fima lingered outside a tiny shoeshop which was also a cobbler's, to inhale the smell of caoutchouc, the intoxicating cobbler's glue. And meanwhile he caught a snatch of conversation between a middle-aged religious man, who looked like the bursar of a charitable foundation or a minor synagogue functionary, and an overweight, shabby, unshaven reservist in ill-fitting fatigues.

The soldier said:

'The thing with them is, the boy always looks after the granny. He doesn't budge from her side all day long. Every thirty seconds he checks to make sure she hasn't got away again, Heaven forbid! Her head's gone to pieces but she's still got the use of her legs, and take it from me, she's as quick as a cat on them.'

The older man, the bursar, remarked sadly:

'The mind inside the head looks like a piece of cheese. Sort of yellowy-white, with wrinkles. They showed it on the TV. And when your memory goes, the scientists have discovered that it comes from the dirt. It's little worms that get inside and nibble at the cheese. Till it's all rotten. You can even get a whiff of it sometimes.'

The soldier corrected him knowledgeably:

'It's not worms, its bactaria. The size of a grain of sand. You can hardly see them even with a magnifying glass, and there are hundreds of them born every hour.'

Fima went on his way, thinking over what he had heard. For a moment his nostrils could almost catch the smell of rotting cheese. Then he lingered in the doorway of a greengrocer's. Crates of aubergines, onions, lettuces, tangerines and oranges were laid out on the pavement. Around them hovered flies and one or two wasps. It would be good to go for a walk down these lanes with Dimi someday. He could feel the warmth of the boy's fingers in his empty hand. And he tried to imagine what sort of intelligent remarks he would hear from the pensive Challenger when they strolled here together, in what new light he would be made to see all these sights. Dimi would certainly notice aspects that were hidden from him, because he lacked the boy's powers of observation. Who did Dimi get them from? Teddy and Yael were always concentrating on the tasks in front of them, whereas Baruch was absorbed in his anecdotes and morals. Maybe the best plan of action would be to move in with them. He could begin, for instance, with a temporary invasion, a bridgehead, using the decorators as an excuse, assuring the family at first that it was only for a day or two, a week at the most, he wouldn't be a nuisance, he'd gladly sleep on a mattress in the utility room off the kitchen balcony. As soon as he arrived, he'd start cooking for them, washing up, ironing, looking after Dimi while they were out, helping him with his homework, washing Yael's underwear, cleaning Teddy's pipe for him; after all, they were out a good deal, whereas he was a man of leisure. After a few days they'd get used to the arrangement. They would appreciate its advantages. They would come to be dependent on Fima's domestic services. They wouldn't be able to manage without him. It might well be Ted, a broad-minded, unprejudiced individual, a clear-thinking scientist, who would see the all-round benefits. Dimi would no longer be left to roam around alone outside all day, relying on the kindness of the neighbours, at the mercy of their bullying children, or condemned to solitary confinement in front of the computer screen. Ted himself would be relieved of the burden of living constantly tête-à-tête with Yael, and so he too would be liberated a bit. As for Yael, it was hard to predict: she might accept the new arrangement with an indifferent shrug of the shoulders, she might just give one of her occasional silent laughs, or she might walk out and go back to Pasadena, leaving Dimi to Ted and me. This last possibility bathed Fima's mind in a supernal glow of light. It seemed really exciting: a commune, an urban kibbutz, three male friends, devoted to one another, full of consideration, tied to each other by bonds of affection and mutual attentiveness.

The whole neighbourhood was pullulating with feverish preparations for the Sabbath. Housewives carried overflowing shopping baskets, traders hoarsely cried their wares, a battered pick-up with one rear light shattered like a black eye manoeuvred backwards and forwards four or five times until miraculously it managed to squeeze into a parking spot on the pavement between two equally battered trucks. Fima rejoiced at this success, as though it held a hint of an opportunity that lay in store for him too.

A pale East European with sloping shoulders and protruding

eyes, who looked as though he suffered from ulcers if not a malignant illness, panted heavily as he pushed a squeaking pram laden with provisions in paper or plastic bags and a whole platoon of soft drinks up the hill. On top of the pile was an evening paper whose pages fluttered in the breeze. Fima squinted at the headlines as he reached out and carefully tucked the paper in among the bottles, so it wouldn't blow away.

The old man merely said in Yiddish:

'*Nu. Shoin.*'

A tawny dog sidled up obsequiously with its tail between its legs, timidly sniffed an apprehensive Fima's trouser-bottoms, found nothing special, and moved away with lowered snout. Was it possible, Fima mused, that this dog was a son of a son of a daughter of a daughter of the notorious Balak, that went mad here eighty years ago and terrorised these very streets before dying in agony?

In a front yard he saw the remains of a castle built by children out of crates and broken packing cases. Then, on the wall of a synagogue named Redemption of Zion, Lesser Sanctuary of the Meshed Community were several graffiti that Fima stopped to inspect. 'Remember the Sabbath day to keep it holy.' Fima thought he detected a minor mistake in the Hebrew, although he was alarmed to find he was not entirely certain. 'Kahana's the master – Labur's a disaster.' 'For slanderers be there no hope.' Be there? May there be? Let there be? Again, he was not certain, and decided to check later, when he got home. 'Shulamit Allony scrues with Arafat.' 'Remember thou art but dust.' Fima agreed with this last motto and even nodded his head. 'Rachel Babaioff is a scruber.' To the left of this inscription Fima was pained to read: 'Peace Now – pay later.' But, then, he had always known that it was essential to plough deep. And then: 'An eye for an eye for an', which made Fima smile and wonder what the poet had meant. A different hand had written: 'Traitor Malmilian – souled his mother!' Fima, while realising that the author had meant to write 'sold', nonetheless found the error rather charming. As though a poetic inspiration had guided the writer's hand to produce something he could not have been aware of.

Across the street from the Redemption of Zion stood a small shop, hardly more than a hole in the wall, selling stationery. The shop window was dotted with dead flies and still marked with the traces of crisscrossed tape put up against explosions, a souvenir of one of our vainly won wars. In the small window were displayed various types of dusty notebooks, exercise books whose covers were curling with age, a faded photograph of Moshe Dayan in lieutenant general's uniform in front of the Wailing Wall which had also not been spared by the flies, plus compasses, rulers, and cheap plastic pencil cases, some of which bore pictures of wrinkled Ashkenazi rabbis or Sephardi Torah sages in ornate robes. In the midst of all this Fima's eye tracked down a thick exercise book in a grey cardboard binding, containing several hundred pages, the sort that writers and thinkers of earlier generations must have used. He felt a sudden longing for his own desk, and a profound resentment towards the painters who were threatening his routine.

In three or four hours from now the siren would be wailing here to herald the advent of the Sabbath. The bustle of the streets would subside. A beautiful, gentle stillness, the silence of pines and stones and iron shutters, would spill down from the slopes of the hills surrounding the city and settle on the whole of Jerusalem. Men and boys in seemly festive attire, carrying embroidered *tallit* bags, would walk calmly to evening prayers at the innumerable little synagogues dotted around these narrow streets. The housewives would light candles, and fathers would chant the blessings in a pleasant Oriental tune. Families would gather together around the dinner table: poor, hard-worked people who placed their trust in the observance of the commandments and did not delve into things too deep for them, people who hoped for the best, who knew what they must do, and who were ever-confident that the powers that be also knew what to do for the best and acted wisely. Greengrocers, shopkeepers, hawkers and peddlers, apprentices, lowly clerks in the municipality and the civil service, petty traders, post office workers, salesmen, craftsmen. Fima tried to picture the weekday routine of a district like this and the enchantment of Sabbaths and festivals. Even though he did not forget that the residents here no doubt earned their meagre crusts with the sweat of their brow and were burdened with debts, worries about making ends meet, and mortgages, nevertheless he felt that they lived decent, truthful, restful lives, with a quiet joy that he had never known and never would, to his dying day. He suddenly longed to be sitting in his own room, or perhaps in the elegant salon in his father's flat in Rehavia, surrounded by the lacquered furniture, the oriental rugs, the Central European candelabra, and books and fine china and glass, concentrating at last on what really mattered. But what was it that really mattered? In God's name, what was it?

Perhaps it was this: to sweep away at a single stroke, starting today, from the onset of this Sabbath, the empty talk, the wastefulness, the lies that buried his life. He was ready to accept his misery humbly, to reconcile himself finally to the solitude he had brought on himself, to the very end, with no right of appeal. From now on he would live in silence, he would cut himself off, he would sever his repugnant links with all the do-gooding women who flocked around him in his flat and his life, he would stop pestering Tsvi and Uri and the rest of the gang with casuistic sophistry. He would love Yael from a distance, without being a nuisance. He might not even bother to have his telephone repaired: from now on it too could be silent. It could stop boasting and lying.

And what about Dimi?

He would dedicate his book to him. Because, starting next week, he would spend five or six hours before work in the reading room of the National Library. He would systematically recheck all the extant sources, including the most obscure and esoteric ones, and in a few years' time he would be in a position to write an objective and dispassionate history of the Rise and Fall of the Zionist Dream. Or perhaps he would write instead a sort of whimsical, half-crazy novel about the life, death, and resurrection of Judas Iscariot, based on himself.

In fact better not to write. Better to say good-bye now and forevermore to the papers, the radio, the television. At most he would listen to classical music programmes. Every morning,

summer and winter alike, he would get up at daybreak and walk
for an hour in the olive grove in the wadi below his flat. Then he
would have a leisurely breakfast: vegetables, fruit and a single
slice of black bread with no jam. He would shave – no, why
should he shave; he'd grow a shaggy beard – and sit and read and
think. After work every evening he would devote another hour
or two to strolling around the city. He would get to know Jerusalem systematically. He would gradually uncover its hidden
treasures. He would explore every alley, every back yard, every
recess; he would find out what was hiding behind every stone wall.
He would not accept another penny from his demented father. And
in the evening he would stand alone at the window listening to
his inner voice which up to now he had always tried to silence
with inanities and buffoonery. He would learn a lesson from
Yael's senile father, the veteran pioneer Naftali Tsvi Levin, who
sat staring at the wall for whole days, answering every remark
with the question 'In what sense?' Not a bad question, in fact.
Although on second thoughts even this question could be dispensed with, the term 'sense' being itself apparently devoid of
meaning.

Snows of yesteryear.

Azoy.

Fima remembered with disgust how the previous Friday, exactly a week ago, at Shula and Tsvi Kropotkin's the conversation
had turned after midnight to the Russian component which had
had such a strong influence on various strands of Zionism. Tsvika made ironic fun of the naïve Tolstoyism of A. D. Gordon and
his disciples, and Uri Gefen recalled how once the country had
been full of fans of Stalin and songs about Budyonny's cavalry.
Whereupon Fima stood up, stooped slightly, and had the whole
room doubled up with laughter when he began declaiming in
liquid, orotund tones a typical passage from an early translation
of Russian literature:

'Dost thou here also dwell, my good man? Beside Spasov I
dwell, close by the V— Monastery, in the service of Marfa Sergeyevna, who is the sister of Avdotya Sergeyevna, if Your Honour might condescend to recall, her leg she broke as from the

carriage she leaped, when to the ball then she was going. Now beside the monastery she dwells, and I – in her house.'

Uri had said:

'You could go around the country giving public performances.'

And Teddy said:

'It's straight out of the wedding scene in *The Deerhunter* – what was it called in Hebrew?'

Whereas Yael remarked drily, almost to herself:

'Why do you all encourage him? Just look at what he's doing to himself.'

Fima now accepted those words of hers like a slap in the face that brought tears of gratitude to his eyes. And he resolved that he would never again make a fool of himself in her presence. Or in front of the others. From now on he would concentrate.

While he was standing there preparing his new life, staring at the names of the residents inscribed on a row of tatty letter boxes in the hallway of a grey stone building, startled to see that there was a Pizani family here too and half surprised not to find his own name underneath it, a smooth-talking Sephardi rabbinical student, a thin, bespectacled youth clad in the costume of an Ashkenazi Hasid, addressed him politely. Warily, as if fearing a violent reaction, he urged Fima to fulfil the commandment of putting on *tefillin*, here, on the spot. Fima said:

'So, will that hasten the coming of the Messiah, in your opinion?'

The youth replied at once, eagerly, as though he had prepared himself for this very question, in a North African accent with a Yiddish lilt:

'It will do your soul good. You will feel relief and joy instantly, something amazing.'

'In what sense?' asked Fima.

'It's a well-known fact, sir. Tried and tested. The arm *tefillin* cleanses the defilement of the body and the head *tefillin* washes all the dirt out of the soul.'

'And how do you know that I have a defiled body and a dirty soul?'

'Heaven forfend that I should say such a wicked thing. Lest I sin with my lips. Every Jew, be he even a sinner – may it not happen to us – his soul was present at Mount Sinai. This is a well-known fact. That is why every Jewish soul shines forth like the heavenly radiance. Nevertheless, sometimes it happens, sadly, on account of all our troubles, on account of all the rubbish that life in this lower world is always heaping on us, that the heavenly radiance inside the soul becomes dirty, so to speak. What does a man do if he gets dirt inside the engine of his car? Why, he takes it to be cleaned out. That is an allegory of the dirt in the soul. The commandment of putting on *tefillin* cleanses that dirt out of you instantly. In a moment you will feel like new.'

'And what good will it do you if a non-believer puts on *tefillin* once and then goes on sinning?'

'Well, you see, it's like this, sir. First, even once helps. It improves the maintenance. One commandment leads to another. It's also like a car: after so many kilometres you service it, clean out the carburettor, change the oil, and all that. Naturally, once you've invested a little something in maintenance, you start to take better care of your car. So it keeps its value. Gradually you get into a daily maintenance routine, as we call it. I give you this example only as an illustration, to help you grasp the idea.'

'I don't have a car,' Fima said.

'No, really? You see, it's true what they say: everything comes from Heaven. I've got something for you. A bargain like you've never seen. A once-in-a-lifetime chance. But first let's mark the difference between sacred and profane.'

'I can't drive,' said Fima.

'We'll get you through the test for three hundred dollars all in. Unlimited lessons. Or we'll find a way to include it in the price of the car. Something special. Just for you. But first put on *tefillin*: you'll see, you'll feel like a lion.'

Fima laughed:

'Anyhow, God's forgotten me.'

'And secondly,' the young man continued, oblivious, with ever-mounting enthusiasm, 'you should never say "nonbeliever". There's no such thing as a non-believer. No Jew in the world can be a nonbeliever. The very expression is tantamount to slander, or even – Heaven forfend! – to blasphemy. As it is written, a man should not reckon himself as wicked.'

'I happen,' Fima insisted, 'to be a one-hundred-per cent non-believer. I don't observe a single commandment. Only the six hundred and thirteen transgressions.'

'You are mistaken,' the young man said, politely but firmly, 'totally mistaken, sir. There is no such thing in the whole world as a Jew who does not keep some commandments. There never has been. One does more, another does less. As the Rebbe says, it is a matter of quantity, not quality. Just as there is no such thing as a righteous man who never sins, so there is no such thing as a sinner who does not perform some righteous acts. Just a few. Even you, sir, with all due respect, every day you observe a few commandments, at least. Even if a person considers himself a total *apikoros*, he still observes a few commandments each day. For example, the fact that you're alive, you're already keeping the commandment "Thou shalt choose life". Every hour or two, every time you cross the road, you choose life, even though you could have chosen the opposite, Heaven forfend! Am I right? And then the fact that you've got kids – they should be healthy! – you have observed the commandment "Be fruitful and multiply". And the fact that you're living in the Land of Israel – that's another half-dozen commandments. Then if you feel happy sometimes, you've got another one. Every one's a winner! Sometimes you may have an overdraft up in heaven, but they never cut off your credit. Unlimited credit, that's what you get. And meanwhile, for the few commandments that you do keep, you've got your own private savings plan up there, and every day you invest a bit more and a bit more, and every day they credit you with interest and they add it to your capital. You'd be amazed, sir, how rich you are without even knowing it. As it is written, the ledger lies open and the hand writes. Five minutes to put on *tefillin*, less than five minutes even – believe me, it doesn't hurt – and you accumulate an extra bonus for Sabbath. Whatever your line of business in the lower world, believe me there's no other five-minute investment that will give you a higher yield. It's a tried and tested fact. No? So it's not so terrible. Maybe it's just that your time hasn't come yet to put on *tefillin*. When it comes, you'll know. You'll receive a signal there's no mistaking. The main thing, sir, don't forget: The gates of repentance stand ever open. Around the clock, as they say. They never close. Sabbaths and festivals included. Now, about the business of the car and the driving test, here, take these two phone numbers.'

Fima said:

'Right now I haven't even got a phone.'

The missionary shot him a pensive sideways glance, as though he was making some kind of mental assessment, and hesitantly, in a voice that was close to a whisper, he said:

'You're not in some kind of trouble, are you, sir? Shall we send someone round to see what we can do to help? Don't be embarrassed to say. Or maybe the best thing would be, why don't you come and make Sabbath with us? Feel what it's like to be among brothers, just for once?'

Fima said:

'No, thank you.' This time there was something in his voice that made the young man timidly wish him a good Sabbath and move away. He turned twice and looked back towards Fima, as though he was afraid he was being pursued.

For a moment Fima was sorry he had not given this peddler of pious deeds and used cars a vitriolic answer, a theological knockout blow that he would not forget in a hurry. He could have asked him, for example, whether you got five credit points up there for killing a five-year-old Arab girl. Or whether to bring a child into the world that neither you nor the mother wanted was a virtuous act or a transgression. After a moment, to his surprise, he felt some regret that he had not said yes, if only to afford a small pleasure to this North African youth in the Volhynian or Galician costume, who, despite his transparent guile, seemed to Fima to be innocent and goodhearted. No doubt in his own way he too was trying to put right what cannot be put right.

Meanwhile he shuffled past a carpenter's workshop, a grocer's that smelled strongly of salt fish, a butcher's shop that struck him as murderously bloodstained, and a dingy shop selling snoods and wigs, and he stopped at a nearby newsstand to buy the weekend editions of *Yediot*, *Hadashot*, and *Ma'ariv*. And so, laden with newspapers (for once he also bought the ultra-pious paper *Yated Ne'eman*, out of vague curiosity), Fima entered a small café on the corner of Zephaniah Street. It was a sort of family restaurant, with three tables covered with peeling pink Formica, and lit by a single feeble bulb that cast a tacky yellow light. Lazy flies wandered everywhere. A bearlike man was dozing behind the counter, with his beard between his teeth, and Fima wondered for a moment at the possibility that this was actually himself behind the reception desk at the clinic transported here by magic. He dropped onto a plastic chair that seemed none too clean, and tried to recall what his mother used to order for him on those Fridays a thousand years ago at the Danzigs' restaurant. Eventually he asked for chicken soup, beef stew, a mixed salad, pitta and pickles, and a bottle of mineral water. As he ate he rummaged in his pile of papers until he fingers were black and the pages were grease-stained.

In *Ma'ariv*, on the second page, there was a report about an Arab youth in Jenin who had been burned to death while trying to set fire to a military jeep that was parked in the main street of the town. Investigations had shown, the newspaper reported, that the Arab mob which gathered round the burning youth had prevented the military orderly from offering him first aid and did not allow the soldiers to get close enough to douse the flames, apparently in the belief that the young man burning to death in front of them was an Israeli soldier. He roasted for about ten minutes in the fire that he himself had lit, uttering 'fearful screams', before finally expiring. In the town of Or Akiva, on the other hand, a minor miracle had occurred. A five-year-old boy who had fallen from an upper storey, receiving serious head injuries, had been lying unconscious since the Day of Atonement. The doctors had written him off and placed him in a home, where he was expected to live out the rest of his days as a vegetable. But the mother, a simple woman who could neither read nor write, refused to give up hope. When the doctors told her the child did not have a chance and that only a miracle could save him, she prostrated herself at the feet of a famous rabbi in Bnei

Brak, who told her to employ a certain rabbinical student who was known to be brain-damaged himself to repeat a page of the Zohar about Abraham and Isaac day and night into the ear of the unresponsive child (whose name was Yitzhak or Isaac). And indeed, after four days and nights the boy began to show signs of life, and he was now fully recovered, running around and singing hymns and attending a religious boarding school, where he had a special scholarship and was gaining a reputation as a budding genius. Why not try reading the same passage of the Zohar into the ears of Yitzhak Rabin and Yitzhak Shamir, Fima chuckled to himself, and then muttered when he spilled some sauce on his trousers.

In the religious paper, *Yated Ne'eman*, he skimmed through various malicious rumblings about desertions from the kibbutzim. According to the paper, the younger generation of kibbutzniks were all wandering around the Far East and the Indian mountains, attaching themselves to all sorts of terrible pagan sects. And again in *Ma'ariv* a veteran columnist argued that the government should not be in a hurry to rush off to all sorts of dubious peace conferences. We should wait until the Israeli deterrent was renewed. We must not go to the negotiating table from an inferior position, with the sword of the intifada, as it were, at our throats. Discussions about peace might be desirable, but only when the Arabs finally realised that they had no chance politically or militarily, indeed no chance at all, and came pleading for peace with their tails between their legs.

In *Hadashot* he came across a satirical piece more or less suggesting that instead of hanging Eichmann we should have had the foresight to spare him, so we could make use of his experience and his organisational skills at the present juncture. Eichmann would be well received among the torturers of Arabs and those who wanted to deport them to the east en masse, an area in which he was known to have particular expertise. Then in the weekend magazine of *Yediot Aharonot* he came across an article, illustrated with colour photographs, about the ordeals of a once well-known singer who had got hooked on hard drugs, and now, just when she was fighting the addiction, a heartless judge had deprived her of custody of her baby daughter by a famous soccer star who refused to acknowledge his paternity. The judge ruled that the baby should be handed over to a foster family, despite the singer's protest that the foster father was actually a Yugoslav who had not been properly converted and might not even be circumcised. When Fima had searched all the pockets of his trousers, his shirt, and his overcoat and almost given up hope, he eventually fished out of the inside pocket of the coat, of all places, a folded twenty-shekel note which Baruch had managed to plant there without his noticing. He paid and took his leave with a muttered apology. He left all his newspapers on the table.

Outside the restaurant the cold had intensified. There was a hint of evening in the air, even though it was still only midafternoon. The cracked asphalt, the rusty wrought-iron gates, some of which had the word 'Zion' worked into them, the signboards of the shops, workshops, Torah schools, estate agencies, and charities, the row of dustbins parked along the pavement, the distant view of the hills glimpsed beyond neglected gardens – everything was becoming clothed in shades of grey. Occasionally alien sounds penetrated the regular hubbub of the streets: church bells, high and slow, punctuated by silence, or low or shrill or heavy and elegiac, and also a distant loudspeaker, and pneumatic drills, and the faint blaring of a siren. All these sounds could not subdue the silence of Jerusalem, that permanent underlying silence, which you can always discover if you look for it underneath any noise in Jerusalem. An old man and a boy walked slowly past, grandfather and grandson perhaps. The boy asked:

'But you said that the inside of the world is fire, so why isn't the ground hot?'

And the grandfather:

'First you must study, Yossel. The more you learn, the more you'll understand that the best thing for us is we shouldn't ask questions.'

Fima remembered that when he was a child, there was an old huckster who went round the streets of Jerusalem wheeling a squeaky, broken-down handcart, with a sack on his back, buying and selling secondhand furniture and clothes. Fima remembered in his bones the old man's voice, which sounded like a cry of despair. At first you would hear it a few blocks away, indistinct and ominous, ghostlike. Slowly, as though the man were crawling on his belly from street to street, the shout grew closer, raucous and terrifying – *al-te za-chen* – and there was something desolate and piercing about it, like a desperate cry for help, as if someone were being murdered. Somehow this cry was associated in Fima's mind with the autumn, with overcast skies, with thunder and the first dusty drops of rain, with the secretive rustling of pine trees, with dull grey light, with empty pavements and gardens abandoned to the wind. Fear would seize him, and it sometimes invaded his dreams at night. Like a final warning of a disaster that had already begun. For a long time he did not understand the meaning of the words *al-te za-chen*, thinking that the terrifying broken voice was addressing him, saying in Hebrew, *Al tezaken*, 'Do not grow old.' Even after his mother explained to him that *alte zachen* was Yiddish and meant 'old things', Fima remained under the spell of the bloodcurdling prophecy that advanced through the streets one by one, getting closer and closer, knocking at the garden gates, warning him from afar of the approach of old age and death, the cry of someone who has already fallen victim to the terrible thing and is warning others that their time will also come.

Now, as he remembered that ghost, he smiled and comforted himself with the words of the sacked clerk from Mrs Scheinfeld's café, the man whom God had forgotten: 'Never mind, we all dies.'

Going up Strauss Street, Fima passed the garish window of an ultra-pious travel agency named Eagles' Wings. He stood for a while contemplating a brightly coloured poster picturing the Eiffel Tower set between Big Ben and the Empire State Building. Nearby, the Tower of Pisa leaned towards the other towers, and next to it was a Dutch windmill, with a pair of plump cows grazing blankly below. The wording on the poster read: 'With G-d's help: COME ON BOARD – TRAVEL LIKE A LORD!' Underneath, in the characters normally reserved for holy books: 'Pay in six easy instalments, interest free.' There was also an aerial photograph of snow-covered mountains, across which was printed in blue letters: 'OUR WAY'S POSHER – STRICTLY KOSHER.'

Fima decided to go inside and ask the price of a bargain ticket to Rome. His father would surely not refuse to lend him the fare, and in a few days' time he would be sitting with Uri Gefen and Annette's husband in a delightful café on the Via Veneto, in the company of bold, permissive women and pleasure-loving men, sipping a cappuccino, discoursing wittily about Salman Rushdie and Islam and feasting his eyes on the shapely girls walking past. Or else he would sit alone by a window in a little *albergo* with old-fashioned green wooden shutters, staring at the old walls, with a notepad in front of him, and occasionally jot down aperçus and pithy musings. Maybe a crack would open in the blocked-up spring, and some new poems gush forth. Some light, easy encounters might take place, lightheartedly, with no strings attached, weightless relationships of the sort that are impossible here in this Jerusalem teeming with dribbling prophets. He had read recently in a newspaper that religious travel agents knew how to fiddle things so that they could sell flights for next to nothing. Over there in Rome, amid impeccable palazzos and stone-paved piazzas, life was carefree and gay, full of fun and free from guilt and shame, and even if acts of cruelty or injustice occurred there, the injustice was not your responsibility and the suffering did not weigh on your conscience.

An overweight, bespectacled young man, with clean-shaven pink cheeks but with a broad black skullcap, raised his childlike eyes from a book that he hastily hid behind a copy of *Hamodia*' and greeted Fima with a smug Ashkenazic accent:

'And a very good day to you, sir.'

He was only about twenty-five, but he looked prosperous, supercilious, and eager to please.

'And what might we do for you, sir?'

Fima discovered that in addition to foreign travel the shop also sold tickets for the national lottery and various other draws. He leafed through a brochure offering 'holiday packages' in splendid religious hotels in Safed and Tiberias, combining treatment for the body under the care of qualified medical staff, with purification of the soul by means of devotions 'at the Holy Tombs of Lions of Torah and Eagles of Wisdom'. At that moment, perhaps because he noticed that the young travel agent's starched white shirt was rather grubby at the collar and cuffs, just like his own, Fima changed his mind and decided to postpone his trip to Rome. At least until he had had a chance to talk to his father about it and consult Uri Gefen, who was coming back today or tomorrow. Or was it Sunday? Nevertheless he took his time, leafed through another brochure with pictures of kosher hotels in 'splendiferous Switzerland', hesitated between the national lottery and the football pools, and decided to buy a ticket for the Magen David Adom draw so as not to disappoint the agent, who was waiting patiently and politely for him to finish making up his mind. But he had to make do without even this, because all he could find in his pocket, apart from Annette's earring, was six shekels, the change from his meal in the flyblown cafeteria in Zephaniah Street. He therefore accepted with thanks some illustrated leaflets containing the itineraries and minutest details about organised tours for groups of Torah-True Jews. In one of them, written in Hebrew, English, and Yiddish, he found that by the grace of Almighty G-d it was now once again possible to make one's devotions at the tombs of 'aweful saints' in Poland and Hungary, to visit 'Holy Places destroyed by the persecutors, may their name be blotted out!' and to enjoy 'the mind-broadening beauties of Japheth – and all in an atmosphere of real *yiddishkeit*, strictly kosher under the auspices of qualified, pious, and seemly guides, and all with the blessing and recommendation of Leading Giants of Torah.' The travel agent said:

'Maybe you will change your mind and come and see us again when you have had a chance to think it over, sir?'

Fima said:

'Maybe. We'll see. Thank you anyway, and I'm sorry.'

'Don't mention it, sir. Our honour and pleasure. And a very good Sabbath to you.'

As he walked on up towards the Histadrut building, it occurred to him that this obsequious, overfed young man with the sausagelike fingers and starched shirt that had a grimy collar and cuffs was more or less the same age as the son that Yael had got rid of two minutes away from here at some clinic in the Street of the Prophets. And he smiled sadly to himself because, apart from the skullcap and cantorial tenor voice, it was possible that an impartial observer might find a certain resemblance between you and that podgy, grubby, smooth-talking young travel agent who was so eager to please. And in fact it was hard to be certain about the cantorial tenor voice. Could Yael feel any maternal affection for that bloated creature, with his murky blue eyes behind thick glasses and his porky-pink cheeks? Could she have sat and knitted him a blue woollen bonnet with a pompom bobbing on top? Could she have linked arms with him and let him choose spicy black olives for her in Mahane Yehuda Market? And how about you? Would you really feel the need occasionally to tuck a folded banknote in his pocket? Or get the decorators in for him? Which goes to prove that Yael was right. As always. She was born being right.

However, Fima thought wryly, it might have been a girl. A miniature Giulietta Masina with soft bright hair. She could have been named after his mother: Liza, or, in its Hebrew mutation, Elisheva. Although it is fairly certain Yael would have vetoed this.

A cold, bitter woman, he said to himself with surprise.

Was it really only your fault? Just because of what you did to her? Just because of the Greek promise that you didn't keep and could not have kept and that no one could have kept? Once, next to Nina Gefen's bed he saw an old translated novel, in a shabby paperback edition, called *A Woman Without Love*. Was it by François Mauriac? Or André Maurois? Or was it Alberto Moravia? He must ask Nina sometime if it was about a woman who did not find love or a woman who was incapable of loving. The title could be taken either way. Though at that moment the difference struck him as all but insignificant. Only very rarely had he and Yael used the word 'love'. With the possible exception of the period of the Greek trip, but at that time neither he nor the three girls had been particular about their choice of words.

Wains curled. And vanished.

As he crossed the road, there was a squeal of brakes. The van driver cursed Fima and shouted:

'You there, are you crazy?'

Fima considered, shuddered belatedly, and muttered sheepishly:

'I'm sorry. Really. Very sorry.'

The driver screamed:

'Bloody half-wit: you've got more luck than sense.'

Fima considered this too, and by the time he reached the other kerb he agreed with the driver. And with Yael, who had decided not to have his son. And also with the possibility of being run over here in the street this Sabbath eve instead of running away to Rome. Like the Arab child we killed two days ago in Gaza. Be switched off. Turned to stone. Reincarnated. As a lizard perhaps. Leaving Jerusalem to Yoezer. And he decided that this evening he would call his father and tell him firmly that the decorating was off. In any case he would be getting out of here soon. This time he would not give in or compromise; he would see it through, and get Baruch's fingers out of his pockets and out of his life once and for all.

Near the Medical Centre at the corner of Strauss Street and the Street of the Prophets a small crowd had gathered. Fima approached and asked what had happened. A small man with a birdlike nose and a thick Bulgarian accent informed him that a suspicious object had been found, and they were waiting for the police explosives experts to arrive. A girl with glasses said, What do you mean? It wasn't like that at all. A pregnant woman fainted on the steps, and the ambulance is on its way. Fima burrowed towards the centre of the crowd, because he was curious to know which of these two versions was closer to the truth. Although he bore in mind that they might both be mistaken. Or indeed they might both be right. Imagine if it was the pregnant woman who had discovered the suspicious object and fainted from the shock?

From the police patrol car which drew up with flashing lights and siren blaring, someone with a megaphone told the crowd to disperse. Fima, with a good citizen's reflex, obeyed at once, but even so he was pushed roughly by a sweaty middle-aged police-man whose peaked cap was tilted back at a comical angle.

Fima was furious.

'All right, all right, no need to push, I've dispersed already.'

The policeman roared at him with a rolling Romanian accent: 'You better stop being clever, quick, or you'll get it.'

Fima restrained himself and moved off towards the Bikur Holim Hospital. He asked himself whether he would go on dis-persing until one day he too collapsed in the street, or expired at home like a cockroach, on the kitchen floor, and was only dis-covered a week later, when the smell wafted out onto the land-ing, and the upstairs neighbours, the Pizantis, called the police and his father. His father would no doubt be reminded of some Hasidic tale about instant, painless death, often called 'death by a kiss'. Or he would make his usual remark about man being a paradox, laughing when he ought to cry and crying when he ought to laugh, living without sense and dying without desire, frail man, his days are like the grass. Was there still a chance to halt this dispersal? To concentrate at long last on what really mattered? But if so, how to start? And what in God's name was it that really mattered?

When he reached the Ma'ayan Shtub department store on the corner of the Jaffa Road, he absent-mindedly turned right and walked towards Davidka Square. And because his feet hurt, he boarded the last bus to Kiryat Yovel. He did not forget to wish the driver a good Sabbath.

It was a quarter to four, close to the beginning of the Sabbath, when he got off at the stop in the street next to his. He remem-bered to say thank you and good-bye to the driver. The early evening twilight had begun to gild the light clouds over the Beth-lehem hills. And suddenly Fima realised sharply, with a vague pain, that another day was gone forever. There was not a living soul to be seen in his street apart from a swarthy ten-year-old child who pointed a wooden submachine gun at him and made him raise his arms in surrender.

Thinking about his own room filled him with disgust: that arid expanse of time stretching from now till tonight, and in fact till

Saturday night, when the gang might be getting together at Shula and Tsvi's. Everything he'd meant to do today and hadn't, and now it was too late: shopping, the post office, the telephone, cash from the bank, Annette. And something else that was urgent but he couldn't remember what it was. Added to which, he still had to get ready for the decorators. Shift the furniture and cover it. Pack away the books and kitchen things. Take the pictures down, and the map of the country with the compromise borders pencilled in. Ask Mr Pisanti to dismantle the bookcases for him. But first of all, he decided, he must call Tsvi Kropotkin right away. Explain to him tactfully, without offending him this time, without being sarcastic, how his article in the latest issue of *Politics* was based on a false and simplistic assumption.

Provided the telephone had recovered in the meantime.

Right in front of the entrance to his building, inside a white car with the windows closed, Fima noticed a large man sitting bent over, his arms resting on the steering wheel and his head buried in his arms, apparently dozing. What if it was really a heart attack? Murder? A terrorist attack? Suicide? Gathering his courage, Fima tapped lightly on the windowscreen. Uri Gefen straightened up at once, lowered his window, and said:

'So there you are. At last.'

Startled, Fima tried to respond with something witty, but Uri cut him short. He said softly:

'Let's go upstairs. We have to talk.'

Nina has told him everything. That I had it off with her. That I didn't. That I humiliated her. But what's he doing here anyway? Isn't he supposed to be in Rome? Or has he got a secret double?

'Look here, Uri,' he said, the blood leaving his face and draining into his liver, 'I don't know what Nina's told you, but the fact is that for some time now . . .'

'Hold it. We'll talk when we get upstairs.'

'The fact is, I've been meaning for some time . . .'

'We'll talk inside, Fima.'

'But when did you get back?'

'This morning. Half past ten. And your phone's not working.'

'How long have you been waiting for me out here?'

'Three-quarters of an hour or so.'

'Has something happened?'

'Just a minute. We'll talk when we get upstairs.'

When they were in the flat, Fima offered to make some coffee. Although the milk seemed to have gone off. Uri looked so tired and thoughtful that Fima was ashamed to bring up the question of dismantling the bookcases. He said:

'I'll put the water on first.'

Uri said:

'Just a moment. Sit down. Listen carefully. I've got some bad news.' And with these words he laid his big, warm peasant hand, which was rough like the bark of an olive tree, on the back of Fima's neck. As always, the touch of this hand on his flesh made Fima shudder pleasurably. He closed his eyes like a stroked cat. And Uri said:

'We've been looking for you since lunchtime. Tsvi's been here twice and left a note on your door. Because your clinic's closed on Fridays, Teddy and Shula have been rushing around for two hours trying to locate your doctors. We didn't know where you'd got to after you left Yael's. And I just dropped my luggage off and came straight here to catch you as soon as you got back.'

Fima opened his eyes. He looked up at Uri's towering form with an anxious, pleading, childlike expression. He did not feel surprised, because he had always expected it would be something like this. With his lips only, without any voice, he asked:

'Dimi?'

'Dimi's fine.'

'Yael?'

'It's your father.'

'He's not well. I know. For several days now . . .'

Uri said:

'Yes. No. Worse.'

In a strange and wonderful way Fima was infected with Uri's habitual self-possession. Softly he asked:

'When exactly did it happen?'

'At midday. Four hours ago.'

'Where?'

'At home. He was sitting in his armchair drinking Russian tea with a couple of old ladies who had come to ask him for a donation to some charity or other. The Blind Society or something. They said he was just starting to tell a joke or a story, when he suddenly groaned and passed away. Just like that. Sitting in his armchair. He didn't have time to feel anything. And since then we've all been searching for you.'

'I see,' said Fima, putting his coat back on. It was strangely sweet to feel his heart filling not with grief or pain but with a surge of adrenalin, of sober, practical energy.

'Where is he now?'

'Still at home. In the armchair. The police have been. There's some sort of a delay about moving him – it doesn't matter right now. The woman downstairs, who's a doctor, was there within a couple of minutes, and she checked that it was all over. Apparently she was a close friend of his too. Tsvi and Teddy and Shula are supposed to be waiting for you there. Nina is going straight from her office as soon as she's finished making all the arrangements and dealing with the formalities.'

'Good,' said Fima. 'Thank you. Let's go there.'

After a moment he added:

'What about you, Uri? Straight from the plane? You just dropped your luggage off and came looking for me?'

'We didn't know where you'd got to.'

Fima said:

'I ought to make you a cup of coffee at least.'

Uri said:

'Forget it. Just concentrate for a moment and think carefully if there's anything you need to take with you.'

'Nothing,' Fima replied at once in a military tone, with uncharacteristic firmness. 'No time to waste. Let's get moving. We'll talk on the way.'

30

At least as far as possible

I T was a quarter past five when Uri parked his car on Ben Maimon Avenue. The sun had sunk behind pines and cypresses, but a strange greyish light full of vague flickers still hovered in the sky, a light that was neither day nor night. Upon the avenue and the stone buildings lay a fine, heart-gnawing Sabbath eve melancholy. As if Jerusalem had stopped being a city and returned to being a bad dream.

The rain had not resumed. The air was saturated, and Fima's nostrils picked up the tang of rotting leaves. He recalled how once when he was a child, at such a time as this, at the onset of the Sabbath, he was riding his bicycle up and down the dead street. Looking up at this building, he saw his mother and father standing on the balcony. They were stiffly erect, of similar height, both dressed in dark clothes, standing very close to each other but not touching. Like a pair of waxworks. And he had the impression that they were both in mourning for a visitor whose arrival they had long since despaired of and yet whom they continued to expect. For the first time in his life he sensed then, vaguely, the depth of the shame concealed in the silence that stretched between them, all through his childhood. Without any quarrels or complaints or disagreements. A polite silence. He got off his bicycle and asked shyly if it was time for him to come in.

Baruch said:

'As you wish.'

His mother said nothing.

This memory awoke in Fima a pressing need to clarify something, to ask Uri, to make inquiries. He had the feeling that he had forgotten to check the thing that mattered most. But what it was that mattered most he did not know. Although he sensed that at that moment his ignorance was thinner than usual, like a lace curtain behind which dim shadows moved. Or a threadbare garment that covers the body but no longer warms it. While he knew in his bones how much he longed to continue not knowing.

As they climbed the stairs to the second floor, Fima put his hand on Uri's shoulder. Uri seemed tired and gloomy. Fima felt a need to encourage with this touch his large friend, who had once been a well-known combat pilot and still went around with his head thrust aggressively forward, a sophisticated airman's watch on his wrist, and his eyes sometimes giving the impression that he saw everything from above.

And yet he was a warm-hearted, honest, devoted friend.

On the door was fixed a brass plate inscribed, in black letters on grey: FAMILY NOMBERG. Underneath it, on a square piece of card, Baruch had written in his firm handwriting: 'Kindly refrain from ringing the bell between the hours of one and five p.m.' Unconsciously Fima shot a glance at his watch. But there was no need to ring anyway, as the door was ajar.

Tsvi Kropotkin intercepted them in the hall, like a conscientious staff officer who has been detailed to brief newcomers before admitting them to the operations room. Despite the ambulance drivers' strike, he said, and the approach of the Sabbath, the tireless Nina had managed to arrange on the phone from her office for him to be moved to the mortuary at Hadassah Hospital. Fima felt a renewed affection for Tsvi's shy embarrassment: he looked less like a famous historian and head of department than a sort of external youth leader whose shoulders have begun to stoop, or a village schoolmaster. Fima also liked the way Tsvi's eyes blinked behind his thick lenses, as though the light was suddenly too bright, and his habit of absentmindedly fingering everything he came in contact with, dishes, furniture, books, people, as though he always had to wrestle with secret doubts about the solidity of everything. If it had not been for the Jerusalem mania, and Hitler, and his obsession with Jewish responsibility, this modest scholar might have settled down in Cambridge or Oxford and lived quietly to be a hundred, dividing his time between the golf course and the Crusades, or between tennis and Tennyson.

Fima said:

'You were right to move him. What would he have done here all weekend?'

In the salon he was surrounded by his friends, who reached out from every side and touched him gently on his shoulder, his cheek, his hair, as though through his father's death he had inherited the role of invalid. As though it was their duty to check carefully to see if he was too hot or too cold or shivering, or planning secretly to leave them without warning. Shula thrust a cup of lemon tea with honey into his hand. And Teddy sat him down gently at one end of the brocade-covered sofa on which embroidered cushions were scattered. They all seemed to be waiting expectantly for him to say something. Fima responded:

'You're all wonderful. I'm sorry to spoil your Friday night like this.'

His father's armchair was standing exactly facing him: deep, wide, upholstered in red leather and with a red leather headrest, looking as though it were made of raw flesh. The footstool seemed to have been pushed slightly to one side. Like a royal sceptre, the cane with its silver band rested against the right-hand side of the chair.

Shula said:

'At any rate, one thing's certain: he didn't suffer at all. It was over in a moment. It's what they used to call death by a kiss: only the righteous are granted it, so they used to say.'

Fima smiled:

'Righteous or not, kisses were always an important part of his repertoire.' As he said this, he observed something that he had never noticed before: Shula, whom he dated more than thirty years ago, before the billy-goat year, and who at that time had a fragile girlish beauty, had aged and gone quite grey. In fact her thighs had grown so fat that she looked like an ultra-pious woman worn out by childbearing but who accepts her decrepitude with total resignation.

A dense, close smell of thick-pile carpets and antique furniture that have been breathing their own air for many years hung in the room, and Fima had to remind himself that it had always been here and was not the smell of Frau Professor Kropotkin's advancing age. At the same time his nostrils caught a whiff of smoke. Looking around, he saw a cigarette on the edge of an ashtray; it had been stubbed out almost as soon as it was lit. He asked who had been smoking here. It turned out that one of the two old ladies, his father's friends, who had been here on a fund-raising mission at the time, had put out her cigarette soon after lighting it. Had she done this when she noticed that Baruch was wheezing? Or when it was all over? Or at the very moment he groaned and expired? Fima asked for the ashtray to be removed. And he was delighted to see how Teddy jumped to carry out his order. Tsvi asked, feeling the central heating pipes with his long fingers, if he wanted to be taken there. Fima did not understand the question. Tsvi, hardly able to control his embarrassment, explained:

'There. To Hadassah. To see him. Perhaps . . .'

Fima shrugged.

'What is there to see? I expect he's as dapper as usual. Why bother him?' And he instructed Shula to make some strong black coffee for Uri, because he had been on the go ever since he got off the plane in the morning. 'In fact, you ought to give him something to eat too: he must be starving. I figure he must have left his hotel in Rome at about three this morning, so he really has had a long, hard day of it. Come to think of it, you look pretty tired yourself, Shula; in fact, you look worn out. And where are Yael and Dimi? I want Yael here. And Dimi too.'

'They're at home,' said Ted apologetically. 'The boy took it quite hard. You might say he had a special attachment to your father.' He went on to say that Dimi had locked himself in the utility room, and they had had to ring a friend of theirs, the child psychologist from South Africa, to ask what to do. He told them just to leave the child alone. And, sure enough, after a while Dimi had come out, and then he'd glued himself to the computer. The South African friend had advised them . . .

Fima said:

'Balls.'

And then, quietly and firmly:

'I want them both here.'

As he spoke, he was surprised himself at this new assertiveness he had acquired since his father's death. As if it had given him an unexpected promotion, entitling him henceforward to issue orders at will and to command instant obedience.

Ted said:

'Sure. We could go and fetch them. But from what the psychologist said, I think it might be better if . . .'

Fima nipped this appeal in the bud:

'If you wouldn't mind.'

Ted hesitated, held a whispered consultation with Tsvi, glanced at his watch, and said: 'Okay, Fima, whatever you like. That's fine. I'll pop round and collect Dimi. If Uri wouldn't mind lending me his keys; Yael's got our car.'

'Yael too, please.'

'Right. Shall I call her? See if she can make it?'

'Of course she can make it. Tell her I insist.'

Ted went out, and at that moment Nina arrived. Small and thin, practical, razor-sharp in her movements, her thin vulpine face projecting common sense and a survivor's shrewdness, brimming with energy, as though she'd spent the day rescuing casualties under fire rather than making arrangements for a funeral. She wore a light grey trouser-suit, her glasses were shining, and she was clutching a stiff black attaché case that she did not put down even when she gave Fima a quick angular hug and a kiss on the forehead. But she found no words.

Shula said:

'I'm going to the kitchen to get you all something to drink. Who wants what? Would anyone like an omelette? Or a slice of bread with something?'

Tsvi remarked hesitantly:

'And he was such a robust man too. So full of energy. With that twinkle in his eyes. And such a zest for life, good food, business, women, politics, the lot. Not long ago he turned up at my office on Mount Scopus and gave me a furious lecture about how Yeshayahu Leibowitz is making demagogic capital out of Maimonides. Neither more nor less. When I tried to disagree, to defend Leibowitz, he launched into some story about a rabbi from Drohovitz who saw Maimonides in a dream. I would say, a deep lust for life. I always thought he'd live to a ripe old age.'

Fima, as though delivering the final verdict on a dispute that was not of his making, declared:

'And so he did. He wasn't exactly cut off in his prime, after all.'

Nina said:

'It was a sheer miracle that we managed to complete the arrangements. Everything's fixed for Sunday. Believe me, it was a mad race against the clock, to get it all done before the Sabbath. This Jerusalem of ours is getting worse than Teheran. You're not angry we didn't wait for you, Fima? You'd simply vanished; that's why I took the liberty of dealing with the formalities. To spare you the headache. I've put announcements in Sunday's *Ha'arets* and *Ma'ariv*. Maybe I should have put it in some other papers, but there simply wasn't time. We've arranged the funeral for the day after tomorrow, Sunday, at three o'clock in the afternoon. It turns out that he'd fixed himself up with a plot, not in Sanhedriya, next to your mother, but on the Mount of Olives. Incidentally, he purchased an adjacent plot for you. Right next to him. And he left detailed and precise instructions in his will about the funeral arrangements. He even chose the cantor, a *landsman* of his. It was a sheer miracle I managed to locate him and catch him on the phone a minute and a half before the Sabbath came in. He even left his own wording for the tombstone. Something with a rhyme. But that can wait till the end of the first month, if not till the anniversary. If a quarter of the people who benefited from his philanthropy come to the funeral, we'll have to allow for at least half a million. Including the mayor and all sorts of rabbis and politicians, not to mention all the broken-hearted widows and divorcees.'

Fima waited until she had finished. Only then did he ask quietly:

'You opened the will by yourself?'

'At the office. In the presence of witnesses. We simply thought . . .'

'Who gave you permission to do that?'

'Quite frankly . . .'

'Where is it, the will?'

'Here, in my attaché case.'

'Give it to me.'

'Right now?'

Fima stood up and took the black attaché case out of her hand. He opened it and drew out a brown envelope. Silently he went out and stood alone on the balcony, at the very spot where his parents had stood that Friday evening a thousand years before, looking like a pair of shipwrecked survivors on a desert island. The last light had long since faded. Stillness wafted up from the avenue. The streetlights flickered with an oscillating yellow radiance mixed with drifting patches of mist. The stone buildings stood silent, all shuttered. No sound came from them. As if the present moment had been transformed into a distant memory. A passing gust of wind brought the sound of barking from the Valley of the Cross. The Third State is a grace that can only be achieved by renouncing all desires, by standing under the night sky sans age, sans sex, sans time, sans race, sans everything.

But who is capable of standing thus?

Once, in his childhood, there lived here in Rehavia tiny, exquisitely mannered scholars, like porcelain figurines, puzzled and gentle. It was their custom to greet one another in the street by raising their hats. As though to erase Hitler. As though to conjure up a Germany that had never existed. And since they would rather be thought absent-minded or ridiculous than impolite, they raised their hats even when they were not certain if the person coming towards them was really a friend or acquaintance or merely looked like one.

One day, when Fima was nine, a short time before his mother's death, he was walking down Alfasi Street with his father. Baruch stopped and engaged in a lengthy conversation, in German or perhaps in Czech, with a portly, dapper old man in an old-fashioned suit and a dark bow tie. Eventually the child's patience ran out and he stamped his foot and started tugging at his father's arm. His father hit him round the head and bellowed '*Ty durak, ty smarkatch*.' Later he explained to Fima that the other man was a professor, a world-famous scholar. He explained what 'world fame' meant and how it was acquired. Fima never forgot that explanation. The expression still afforded him a mixture of awe and contempt. And once, seven or eight years later, at half past six in the morning, he was walking with his father again, in Rashbam Street, when they saw coming towards them, with short, vigorous strides, the prime minister, Ben Gurion, who lived at that time on the corner of Ben Maimon and Ussishkin and liked to start his day with a brisk early-morning walk. Baruch Nomberg raised his hat and said:

'Would you be good enough to spare me a moment of your time, sir?'

Ben Gurion stopped and exclaimed:

'Lupatin! What are you doing in Jerusalem? Who is guarding Galilee?'

Baruch replied calmly:

'I am not Lupatin, and you, sir, are not the Messiah. Despite what your purblind disciples no doubt whisper in your ear. I advise you not to believe them.'

The prime minister said:

'What, you're not Grisha Lupatin? Are you sure you're not mistaken? You look very like him. So, a case of mistaken identity. In that case, who are you?'

Baruch said:

'I happen to belong to the opposite camp.'

'To Lupatin?'

'No, sir, to you. And if I may allow myself the liberty of saying so . . .'

But Ben Gurion had already begun to stride ahead, and all he said as he went was:

'So, oppose, oppose. But don't be so busy opposing that you fail to raise this charming boy to be a faithful lover of Israel and a defender of his people and his land. All the rest is irrelevant.' And so saying, he marched on, followed by the good-looking man whose function was apparently to protect him from being pestered.

Baruch said:

'Genghis Khan!'

And he added:

'See for yourself, Efraim, whom Providence has selected to save Israel: the bramble from the parable of Jotham.'

Fima, who had been sixteen at the time, smiled in the dark as he recalled how astonished he had been to discover that Ben Gurion was shorter than himself and potbellied, with a huge red face and a dwarf's legs, and a voice as loud and raucous as a fishwife's. What had his father been trying to say to the prime minister? What would he himself say to him now, with hindsight? And who was that Lupatin or Lupatkin who neglected the defence of Galilee?

Was it not possible that the child Yael had not wanted might have grown up to be world famous?

And what about Dimi?

Suddenly Fima had a brainwave: he realised that it was actually Yael, with her research on jet-propelled vehicles, who was likelier than any of us to achieve what Baruch had never given up dreaming of for him. And he asked himself if he was not himself the bramble from the parable of Jotham. Tsvika, Uri, Teddy, Nina, Yael – they are all fruiting trees, and only you, Mr Eugene Onegin of Kiryat Yovel, go through life generating foolishness and falsehood. Drivelling on and pestering everybody. Arguing with cockroaches and lizards.

Why should he not decide to devote the remainder of his days, starting today, or tomorrow, to smoothing their paths for them? He would shoulder the burden of bringing up the child. He would learn how to cook and do the washing. Every morning he would sharpen all the coloured pencils on the drawing board. Every so often he would change the ribbon on the computer. If computers have ribbons. And so, humbly, as the unknown soldier, he would make his own modest contribution to the development of jet propulsion and the acquisition of world fame.

In his childhood, on warm summer evenings here in Rehavia,

solitary sounds of a piano could be heard through barred shutters. Even the stifling air seemed to mock these sounds. Now they were gone and forgotten. Ben Gurion and Lupatin were dead. The refugee scholars with their homburgs and bow ties were dead. And between them and Yoezer, we lie and fornicate and murder. What is there left? Pine trees and silence. And some battered German tomes with the gold lettering on their spines already fading.

Suddenly Fima had to fight back tears of longing. Not longing for the dead, or for what once existed here and no longer did, but for what might have been and was not, and never would be. There came into his head the words 'his place does not know him'. But however hard he tried, he could not remember whom he had heard pronounce this terrifying phrase within the past two or three days.

It struck him now as precise and penetrating.

The minarets on the hilltops surrounding Jerusalem, the ruins and the stone walls enclosing secretive convents, topped with sharp broken glass, the heavy iron gates, the wrought-iron grilles, the cellars, the gloomy basements, a brooding, resentful Jerusalem, sunk up to its neck in nightmares of prophets stoned and saviours crucified and redeemers hacked to pieces, surrounded by a string of barren rock-strewn hills, the emptiness of slopes pockmarked with caves and gullies, apostate olive trees that had almost ceased to be trees and joined the realm of the inanimate, solitary stone cottages in the folds of incised valleys, and beyond them the great deserts extending southwards to Bab el-Mandeb and eastwards to Mesopotamia and northwards to Hama and Palmyra, the lands of asp and viper, expanses of chalk and salt, haunt of nomads with herds of black goats and with vengeful knives in the folds of their robes, dark desert tents, and encircled in the midst of all this, Rehavia with its melancholy piano music in tiny rooms at evening, its frail old scholars, its shelves of German tomes, its good manners, its raised homburgs, silence between the hours of one and five, crystal chandeliers, exiled lacquered furniture, brocade and leather upholstery, china dinner services, sideboards, the Russian excitability of his father, and Ben Gurion and Lupatin, the monkish halo of light around the desks of dour scholars gathering footnotes on their way to acquiring world fame, and we, following in their footsteps with helpless, hopeless perplexity, Tsvika with Columbus and the church, Ted and Yael and their jet-propelled vehicles, Nina orchestrating the liquidation of her ultra-pious sex boutique, Wahrhaftig struggling to defend a civilised enclave in his abortion inferno, Uri Gefen roaming the world conquering women and mocking his conquests with his wry humour, Annette and Tamar, the unwanted, and you yourself with your Heart of Christendom and your lizards and your late-night letters to Yitzhak Rabin and the price of violence in a time of moral decline. And Dimi with his slaughtered dog. Where was it all leading? Where did that Chili get lost on her way to the Aryan side?

As though this were not a district of a city but a remote camp of whale hunters who had settled at the world's end, on a godforsaken coast in Alaska, throwing up a few shaky structures and a rickety fence in the boundless waste, among bloodthirsty nomadic tribes, and then they all set off together far out on the grey water in search of a nonexistent whale. And God has forgotten them, as the proprietress of the café across the road said yesterday.

Fima had a vivid image of himself standing guard, alone in the dark, over the abandoned whalers' camp. A faint lantern sways in the wind at the top of a pole, flickering, guttering in the black expanse, and there is no other light in all the length and breadth of the Pacific wastes extending northwards to the Pole and southwards to the tip of Tierra del Fuego. A solitary glow-worm. Absurd. Its place does not know it. And yet, this precious radiance. Which it is your duty to keep alive as long as possible. It must not stop glimmering in the depth of the frozen expanse at the foot of the snow-covered glaciers. It is your responsibility to prevent it from being blown out by the wind. At least as long as you are here and until Yoezer arrives. Never mind who you are and what you are and what you have to do with whalers who never existed, you with your myopia, your flabby muscles, your floppy breasts, your ridiculous, clumsy body. The responsibility is yours.

But in what sense?

He put his hand in his pocket to look for a heartburn tablet, but instead of the little tin his fingers dredged up the silver earring, which sparkled for an instant as though bewitched in the light that came from the room behind him. As he hurled it into the heart of darkness, he seemed to hear Yael's sardonic voice:

'Your problem, pal.'

And with his face to the night, in a low, decisive voice, he answered:

'Correct. It *is* my problem. And I am going to solve it.'

And he smiled to himself again. But this time it was not his habitual, sad smile of self-deprecation, but the astonished curled lip of a man who for a long time has been seeking a complex answer to a complex question and suddenly discovers a simple one.

With that he turned and went inside. At once he noticed Yael, who was deep in conversation with Uri Gefen on the sofa, their knees touching. Fima had the impression that laughter had frozen on their lips as he entered. But he felt no envy. On the contrary, a secret joy welled up inside him at the thought that he had slept with every woman in this room, Shula, Nina, and Yael. And yesterday with Annette Tadmor. And tomorrow was another day.

At that moment he caught sight of Dimi kneeling on the carpet in a corner, an elderly, philosophical child, slowly revolving with his finger Baruch's huge terrestrial globe, which was illuminated from within. The electric light painted the oceans blue and the land masses gold. The child seemed absorbed, detached, concentrating entirely on what he was doing. And Fima remarked to himself, like a man making a mental note of the whereabouts of a suitcase or an electric switch, that he loved this child more than he had ever loved any living soul. Including women. Including the boy's mother. Including his own mother.

Yael got up and approached him, as though uncertain whether to shake his hand or just rest a hand on his sleeve. Fima did not wait for her to make up her mind, but hugged her hard and pressed her head to his shoulder, as though it were she, not he, who needed and deserved consolation. As though he were making her a present of his new orphanhood. Yael mumbled into his chest something that Fima did not catch and did not even want to hear, because he was enjoying the discovery that Yael, like Prime Minister Ben Gurion, was shorter then he by almost a head. Even though he was not a tall man himself.

Then Yael broke away from his clasp and hurried, or escaped, to the kitchen, to help Shula and Teddy, who were making open sandwiches for everybody. It occurred to Fima to ask Uri or Tsvi to call the two gynaecologists on his behalf, and also Tamar, and why not Annette Tadmor too? He had a sudden urge to gather together all the people who had some bearing on his new life. As though something inside him was planning, without his knowledge, to have some kind of a ceremony. To preach to them. To try to tell them something new. To announce that henceforth . . . But perhaps he was confusing mourning with a farewell party. Farewell to what? What sort of sermon could he preach? What news did a man like him have to give? Be holy and pure, all of you, in preparation for the Third State?

He changed his mind, and abandoned the idea of a gathering.

However, he suddenly chose not to sit in the place vacated by Yael next to Uri on the sofa, but in his father's armchair. He stretched his legs comfortably on the upholstered footstool. He relished the soft seat that took his body as though it had been made to measure for him. Without thinking, he banged twice on the floor with the silver-headed cane. But when they all stopped talking and looked at him attentively, ready to do his bidding, to offer him affection and condolence, Fima smiled benignly and exclaimed:

'Why this silence? Carry on.'

Tsvi, Nina, and Uri tried to draw him into a conversation to distract him, a light exchange about subjects dear to his heart, the situation in the Territories, the way it was presented on Italian television, which Uri had been watching in Rome, the significance of the American overtures. Fima refused to be drawn. He contented himself with not removing the absent-minded smile from his face. For a moment he thought of Baruch lying in a refrigerated compartment in the basement of Hadassah Hospital, in a sort of honeycomb of freezer drawers, populated, in part or in whole, by the fresh Jerusalem dead. He tried to feel in his own bones the frost, the darkness of the drawer, the dark northern ocean bed below the whaling station. But he could find no pain in his heart. Or fear. No. His heart was light, and he almost began to see a funny side to the metallic mortuary honeycomb with its drawers of corpses. He recalled his father's anecdote about the argument between the Israeli and the American railway boss, and the story of the famous rabbi and the highwayman who exchanged their cloaks. He realised he would have to say something. But he had no idea what he could tell his friends. However, his ignorance was growing thinner and thinner. Like a veil that only half hides the face. He got up and went to the lavatory and rediscovered that here at his father's the bowl was flushed by a tap that could be turned on or off at will, with no race, no defeat, no constant humiliation. So that was one less thing to worry about.

Returning, he joined Dimi on the carpet, got down on his knees, and asked:

'Do you know the legend of Atlantis?'

Dimi said:

'Sure I do. There was a programme about it once on educational TV. It's not exactly a legend.'

'What is it then? Fact?'

'Of course not.'

'So, if it's not a legend and it's not fact?'

'It's a myth. A myth is not the same thing as a legend. It's more like a nucleus.'

'Where was this Atlantis, roughly?'

Dimi turned the illuminated globe a little and gently placed a pale hand on the ocean that glowed from the depths in the radiance of the electric light between Africa and South America, and the boy's fingers were also illuminated with a ghostly glow.

'Roughly here. But it makes no difference. It's more in the mind.'

'Tell me something, Dimi. Do you think there's anything after we die?'

'Why not?'

'Do you believe Granpa can hear us right now?'

'There isn't that much to hear.'

'But can he?'

'Why not?'

'And can we hear him?'

'In our minds, yes.'

'Are you sad?'

'Yes. Both of us. But it's not good-bye. You can go on loving.'

'So – we shouldn't be afraid of dying?'

'No, that isn't possible.'

'Tell me something, Dimi. Have you had any supper tonight?'

'I'm not hungry.'

'Then give me your hand.'

'What for?'

'Nothing. Just to feel.'

'Feel what?'

'Nothing special.'

'Stop it, Fima. Go back to your friends.'

At this point their conversation was interrupted, because Dr Wahrhaftig burst into the room, red-faced, panting, and ranting, as if he had come to put a stop to some scandal rather than offer his condolences. Fima was unable to conceal his smile when he suddenly noticed a superficial resemblance between Wahrhaftig and the Ben Gurion who bellowed at his father in Rashbam Street forty years before. Tamar Greenwich arrived with the doctor, nervous, rather weepy, full of good intentions. Fima turned towards them, patiently accepted the handshake and the hug, but did not grasp what they were saying to him. For some reason his lips muttered vacantly:

'Never mind. No harm done. These things happen.'

Apparently they too failed to catch what was said. They were quickly given a glass of tea.

At half past eight, seated again in his father's armchair, with his legs comfortably crossed, Fima pushed away the yogurt and the roll with pickled herring that Teddy had placed in front of him. He removed the arm that Uri put round his shoulder. And he declined Shula's offer of a blanket for his lap. He suddenly handed back to Nina the brown envelope he had removed from her attaché case earlier and told her to start reading the will aloud.

'Now?'

'Now.'

'Even though usually . . .'

'Even though usually.'

'But Fima . . .'

'Now, please.'

After a hesitation and an exchange of rapid glances with Tsvi and Yael and Uri, Nina decided to comply. She drew two closely typed sheets of paper from the envelope. In the silence that had fallen she started to read, at first with some embarrassment and then in her professional voice, which was calm and detached.

First came detailed, punctilious instructions concerning the conduct of the funeral and the memorial service and the tombstone. Then came the substance. Boris Baruch Nomberg bequeathed two hundred and forty thousand United States dollars to be divided in unequal parts among the sixteen foundations, organisations, associations and committees that were listed in alphabetical order, each name accompanied by the relevant sum of money. At the head of the list came the Association for the Promotion of Religious Pluralism and at the bottom the Zeal for Torah Orthodox School. After this last item and the signatures of the deceased, the notary, and the witnesses, came the following lines:

'With the exception of the property in Reines Street, Tel Aviv, mentioned in the annexe, I hereby bequeath and leave all my belongings to my only son, Efraim Nomberg Nisan, who is adept at distinguishing good from evil, with the hope that henceforth he will not be content merely to distinguish but will devote his strength and excellent talents to doing what is good and refraining so far as possible from evil.'

Above the signatures came another line in a bold hand: 'Signed, sealed, and delivered, the testator being of sound mind, here in Jerusalem capital of Israel, in the month of Marheshvan 5749 corresponding to 1988 of the civil era, the fortieth year of the uncompleted renewal of the sovereignty of Israel.'

From the annexe it emerged that the property in Reines Street, Tel Aviv, which Fima had never heard of before, was a modest block of flats. The old man left it 'to my beloved grandchild, the delight of my soul, Israel Dimitri, son of Theodore and Yael Tobias, to be held in trust for him until he reaches his eighteenth birthday by my dear daughter-in-law Mrs Yael Nomberg Nisan Tobias née Levin, who shall enjoy the usufruct thereof, the capital to be reserved for my grandson.'

It further transpired from the annexe that henceforward Fima would be the sole proprietor of a medium-sized but solid and profitable cosmetics factory. He would also own the flat in which he had been born and brought up and in which both his parents had passed away at an interval of more than forty years. It was a large second-floor flat with five spacious rooms and deep-silled windows, in a quiet, prosperous neighbourhood, lavishly furnished in a solid, old-fashioned Central European style. He also received various stocks and shares, a building plot in Talpiyot, declared and concealed bank accounts in several banks in Israel and Belgium, a safe-deposit box containing cash and valuables, including his mother's jewellery of gold and silver set with precious stones. He also inherited a library of several thousand volumes, including a set of the Talmud and other sacred texts bound in morocco, a collection of Midrashic works, some of which were rare, besides hundreds of novels in Russian, Czech, German, and Hebrew, and two shelves of chemistry books in the same languages, and the poems of Uri Zvi Greenberg, including some very rare editions, biblical studies by Dr Israel Eldad, the works of Graetz, Dubnow, Klausner, Kaufman, and Urbach, and a cabinet of old erotica in German and Czech which Fima could not read. Furthermore he was henceforth the owner of collections of stamps and old coins, nine winter suits and six summer ones, some twenty-five ties of a conservative, rather old-fashioned style, and an attractive walking stick with a silver band.

Fima did not ask himself what he would do with all these things, but he pondered on what someone like himself understood of the manufacture and sale of cosmetics. And since the Hebrew language does not tolerate such constructions, he corrected himself mentally: the manufacture of cosmetics and their sale.

And suddenly he said to himself:

'It doesn't tolerate? So let it not tolerate!'

At ten o'clock, after he had conducted Dimi to a bedroom and told him a short adventure story about the Argonauts and the Golden Fleece, he sent all his friends home. He dismissed all their entreaties and protests. No, thank you very much, there was no need for anyone to stay the night. No, thank you very much, he did not want to be driven to his flat in Kiryat Yovel either. Nor did he have any desire to stay with any of them. He would spend the night here. He wanted to be alone. Yes. Absolutely. Thank you. No. Absolutely. No need. Kind of you to offer anyway. You're all wonderful people.

When he was left alone, he was tempted to open a window to let in some fresh air. On second thoughts he decided not to, but instead to close his eyes for a while and try to discover the precise composition of the strange smell of this flat. A smell of doom. Although there was no apparent connection between the smell and the sad event that had taken place here earlier in the day. The flat had always been kept spotlessly clean and tidy. At least outwardly. Both before and after his mother's death. Twice a week a home help came to polish everything, even the candlesticks, the brass lamps, the silver goblets that were used for religious rituals. His father had taken a cold shower every morning, summer and winter. And the flat had been redecorated regularly every five years.

So what was the source of the smell?

Since he had stopped living here after his military service, his nostrils had recoiled from it every time he came back to visit the old man. It was a faint whiff of something malodorous, half hidden always behind other scents. Was it a dustbin that needed emptying? Dirty linen lingering too long in the basket in the bathroom? Some defect of the drainage system? Mothballs in the wardrobes? Faint cooking odours of thick, oversweet Eastern

European food? Fruit that had sat too long in the fruit bowl? Stagnant water in vases that had not been changed although the flowers were changed regularly twice a week? Behind the elegance and tidiness there was always a sourness hovering, minimal and latent admittedly, but deep and persistent, like damp. Was it an ineradicable relic of the opaque, glassy politeness that had spread and frozen here between his father and his mother, and not ceased even with her death? Was there any chance that now it would evaporate?

One would think, Fima mused ironically, that in your own flat in Kiryat Yovel the air is perfumed with myrrh and frankincense, you with your Trotskyite kitchen and your can of worms on the balcony and your decrepit lavatory.

He stood up and opened a window. After a moment he closed it again. Not because of the cold but because he felt sorry to lose this doom-laden smell, which he would probably never be able to recall once he allowed it to disperse. Let it stay a few more days. The future was just beginning. Yet it would have been nice to sit in the kitchen now, over a glass of steaming Russian tea, and argue with the old man late into the night. Without mockery or levity. Like a pair of intimate adversaries. Far from Hasidic tales and all the casuistry, the witticisms, the anecdotes, the clever wordplay. Not provoking the old man, not annoying him with impieties perverse, but with real affection. Like a pair of surveyors representing two countries in a dispute but themselves working together with amicable professionalism on the precise demarcation of the border. As one man to another. Sorting out at last what has been, what is, what is over and done with, and what might still be possible here if we only devote ourselves to it with our remaining strength.

But what is it that he must sort out with his father? What is the border that needs demarcation? What does he need to prove to the old man? Or to Yael? Or to Dimi? What does he need to say that is not a quotation, or a paradox, or a refutation, or a clever wisecrack?

The inheritance neither weighed him down nor lifted him up. True, he knew nothing about cosmetics, but the fact was he had no real understanding of anything. There might even be a certain advantage in that, although Fima could not be bothered at this moment to try to define what it was. Moreover, he had no needs. Apart from the most simple, basic needs: food, warmth, and shelter. He had no desires, either, except perhaps a vague desire to appease everybody, to heal disputes, to sow some peace here and there. How could he do that? How does one bring about a change of heart? Soon he would have to meet the employees of the business, find out about their working conditions, see what could be improved.

The upshot was that he needed to learn. And learning was one thing he did know about. So he would learn. Gradually.

He would make a start tomorrow. Although in fact tomorrow was already here: it was past midnight.

For a moment he pondered whether to get into his father's bed and sleep there, fully dressed. After a moment he decided that it was a pity to waste this unique night. He ought to explore the flat. Discover its secrets. Start to acquire a preliminary orientation in the ways of the new realm.

Fima prowled around until three o'clock in the morning, opening wardrobes, exploring the recesses of the heavy black tallboy, peering into every drawer, prying under mattresses and among pillows and in the heap of his father's white shirts waiting to be ironed. Stroking the brocade upholstery. Fingering and weighing the silver candlesticks and goblets. Running his hand over the lacquered surface of the old-fashioned furniture. Comparing tea trays. Discovering under a muslin cover the silent Singer sewing machine and extracting a single hollow note from the gleaming Bechstein piano. Selecting a cut-glass goblet and pouring himself some French cognac, raising his glass towards the six vases of tall gladioli. Undressing with a rustle of cellophane a magnificent box of Swiss chocolates and tasting the exquisite contents. Tickling the crystal chandeliers with a peacock's feather he found on the desk. Very cautiously extracting delicate little ringing sounds from the fine Rosenthal china. Riffling through the piles of embroidered napkins, faintly scented handkerchiefs, lace and woollen shawls, the array of kid gloves, and the selection of umbrellas, among which he discovered an ancient blue silk parasol, and combing through the records of Italian opera that his father had enjoyed playing to himself at full volume on the old gramophone, joining the singers with his own cantorial tenor, sometimes in the company of one or two of his lady friends, who all threw him rapturous glances while sipping their tea with the little finger crooked. He drew snowy table napkins out of their gilded rings engraved with stars of David and the word 'Zion' in Hebrew and Roman characters. He examined the paintings on the walls of the salon, one of which featured a handsome gypsy with a dancing bear that seemed to be smiling. He patted the bronze busts of Herzl and Vladimir Jabotinsky and asked them politely how they were feeling this evening, then poured himself another cognac and helped himself to another chocolate and discovered in an out-of-the-way drawer a collection of silver snuffboxes studded with pearls and semiprecious stones, and among them he caught sight of the tortoiseshell comb that his mother used to put in her blonde hair at the nape of her neck. But the blue knitted baby's bonnet with the woolly bobble was nowhere to be found. The bathtub stood on brass lion's paws, and on the ledge behind it he discovered foreign packets of bath salts and oils, beauty creams, medicines, and mysterious ointments. He was surprised to find, hanging up, a pair of antiquated silk stockings with a seam at the back, the sight of which stirred a faint pulse in his loins. Going through to the kitchen he made a mental note of the contents of the refrigerator and the bread bin. Then he returned to the bedroom, where he sniffed at the silk underwear meticulously folded away on the shelves. Fima saw himself for a moment as a relentlessly systematic detective studying the scene of the crime inch by inch in search of the one and only clue, which was minute but crucial. But what clue? What crime? He did not bother to ponder this, because his spirits were rising by the minute. All these years he had ached to find a place where he could feel at home and he had never managed to, either in his own flat, at the gynaecology clinic, at his friends', in his city, his country, or his time. Maybe because it was a self-defeating wish from the start. Beyond his reach. Beyond everybody's reach.

Tonight too, among all those exciting objects that insisted on concealing from him the thing that really mattered, this wish still seemed beyond his reach, and he said to himself:

'Right. Exile.'

And he added:

'So what?'

Shakespeare's King Richard vainly offered his kingdom for a horse. Whereas Efraim Nisan, close to three in the morning, was ready to exchange the whole of his legacy for one day, one hour of total inner freedom and of feeling at home. Although he had a suspicion that there was a tension and perhaps even a contradiction between the two, which could not be resolved even by Yoezer and his happy friends who would be living here in our place in a hundred years' time.

At five in the morning he fell asleep fully dressed, and he slept till eleven. Even then he did not wake of his own accord: his friends had returned to sit with him and cushion his grief. The women had brought pots of stew, and they and the men tried their best to surround the orphaned Fima with love and kindness, warmth and affection. Again and again they tried to draw him into political discussions which Fima did not wish to join, but he condescended to contribute an occasional smile or a nod of the head. On the other hand, he called Dimi and was delighted to learn that Dimi was interested in the collections of stamps and coins, provided he could be partners with Fima. Fima said nothing about the hundreds of tin soldiers from his childhood, which he had found in a drawer. They would be a surprise for his Challenger.

On Saturday evening, at the end of the Sabbath, Fima suddenly put on his father's winter overcoat and, leaving his friends to keep up the mourning, went out to get some air, promising to be back in a quarter of an hour.

Next morning at eight he intended to visit the offices of the cosmetics factory in the Romema Industrial Zone. The funeral was set for three p.m., and in this way he could put himself in the picture beforehand. But this evening he could surely be allowed to take one last aimless stroll.

The sky was dark and clear, and the stars went out of their way to attract his attention. As if the Third State was obvious and self-evident. Intoxicated by the Jerusalem night air, Fima forgot his promise. Instead of returning to his friends after his stroll, he chose to ignore the protocol of mourning and take a short break. Why not go, at long last, alone, to see the early showing of that comedy film with Jean Gabin, about which he had heard only good reports? He queued patiently for twenty minutes, bought a ticket, and, entering the cinema shortly after the beginning of the film, sat down in one of the back rows, which were almost empty. But after a few moments' confusion he realised that the Jean Gabin film had ended its run and a new film was showing from this evening. So he decided to leave the cinema and check what was new in the pretty, old lanes of Nahalat Shiva, which he had loved since he was a child and which he had walked with Chili a few nights previously. Because he was tired, and perhaps also because his heart was light and clear, he stayed sitting in the cinema, huddled in his father's overcoat, staring at the screen and asking himself why on earth the characters in the film kept inflicting all sorts of agonies and indignities on one another. What was it that kept them from taking pity on each other occasionally? It would not be difficult for him to explain to the heroes, if they would only listen for a moment, that if they wanted to feel at home, they ought to leave each other alone, and themselves too. And try to be good. At least as far as possible. At least as long as eyes can see and ears can hear, even in the face of mounting tiredness.

Be good, but in what sense?

The question seemed like sophistry. Because everything was really so simple. Effortlessly he followed the story. Until his eyes closed and he fell asleep in his seat.